SHADOWS AT STONEWYLDE

Also by Kit Berry from Gollancz:

Magus of Stonewylde
Moondance of Stonewylde
Solstice at Stonewylde
Shadows at Stonewylde

SHADOWS
at
STONEWYLDE

The Fourth Novel of Stonewylde

KIT BERRY

Copyright © Kit Berry 2011

The right of Kit Berry to be identified as the author of
this work has been asserted by her in accordance with
the Copyright, Designs and Patents Act 1988.

First published in Great Britain in 2011 by Gollancz
An imprint of the Orion Publishing Group
Orion House, 5 Upper St Martin's Lane,
London WC2H 9EA

An Hachette UK Company

This edition published in Great Britain in 2012
by Gollancz

A CIP catalogue record for this book
is available from the British Library

ISBN 978 0 575 09891 6

1 3 5 7 9 10 8 6 4 2

Typeset by Input Data Services Ltd,
Bridgwater, Somerset

Printed in Great Britain by Clays Ltd, St Ives plc

The Orion Publishing Group's policy is to use papers
that are natural, renewable and recyclable products and
made from wood grown in sustainable forests. The logging
and manufacturing processes are expected to conform to
the environmental regulations of the country of origin.

www.stonewylde.com
www.orionbooks.co.uk

Slowly, silently, the moon rose over Stonewylde, flooding the land with ethereal light. Velvet shadows deepened as the hills and valleys welcomed the Bright Lady's quicksilver kiss. Moonlight tiptoed down ancient paths, danced in fields and on hilltops, shimmered over rivers and pools. She was everywhere, bestowing her cold caress on the waiting landscape.

She sent a path of rippling silver across the sea and onto the white disc of stone at Mooncliffe. The eerie cliff-top was deserted; no moongazy maiden stood on the circle feeding her magic to the hungry snakes. At Quarrycleave, the Lady glanced over the carved pillar and peered into the canyons of stone. Her beams rustled through the ivy but her magic failed to banish the greedy shadows that lay below.

On silver feet she swept across the curves of the land and brushed the entrance to the Dolmen. The ancient gateway stood as it always had, a portal to the world of myths and dreams. A small fire smouldered at the entrance and a lone figure sat sentinel, entranced by the moon's magic.

The Stone Circle embraced her, gathering her into the arena where the great stones stood guard around the heart of Stonewylde. She pirouetted on the soft earth floor and stroked the Altar Stone with silver fingertips, tingling as she encountered the Green Magic that eddied here.

The great megalith on top of the hill stood in lonely glory. Hares, their tawny coats bleached to dull pewter and their eyes gleaming in the moonlight, danced the sacred spirals around the single stone. Bats flickered against the starry skies and a silver-feathered barn owl glided from the woods to perch on the stone that marked the spiral's vortex. These creatures knew the ancient power here; they instinctively understood the magical patterns of the land and this mysterious monthly alchemy. For millennia the moon-dance of Stonewylde had been honoured at this special place on the hill. Here the Bright Lady kissed her sister the Earth Goddess, enchanting her with quicksilver magic.

1

The girl slipped down the path, her cloak flaring behind her as she hurried on light feet. She clutched the wicker basket containing the precious fruits she'd gathered. Her eyes still shone with the moonlight and she wished she'd had longer in the woods under the Hunter's Moon. She loved the Moon Fullness, the magic that thrilled all around in the crisp October night. It was so bright that even in the depths of the woods she'd had no need of her lantern. Carefully she opened the cottage back door; it was late and she should've been home long ago. A faint light glowed through the curtains but hopefully her mother would be asleep by now.

Golden candlelight from the lamp on the dresser dazzled her as she tiptoed into the kitchen. In the sitting room, Maizie looked up from her papers and removed her reading glasses to glare through the kitchen doorway at her daughter, still oblivious of her presence. The girl blinked in the golden brightness and quietly shut the heavy wooden back door behind her. She placed her basket on the scrubbed kitchen dresser, and shrugged off her cloak, hanging it on the peg. So far, so good.

'Leveret! Come in here this minute!'

The sharp voice made her jump and her heart sank.

'Where have you been, my girl? 'Tis almost midnight! What've you been doing?'

Maizie's face was pinched with anger as she glared at her daughter. This girl, her seventh child, was more trouble than the other six put together. Even in his wildest days Yul had been more obedient than she was. Although, Maizie thought ruefully, Alwyn's reign of terror had probably been responsible for that. This girl was different – unruly, wilful and a law unto herself, and she had no father to keep her in check.

Maizie took a deep breath and gathered the papers into a tidy pile, not wanting to think of the man she'd been forced to wed all those years ago. He'd ruled his family's lives with brutality and she wouldn't wish that on anyone, not even this wayward daughter of hers. Alwyn had collapsed in this very room, choking and spluttering on a piece of cake whilst the petrified children gaped at their father foaming at the mouth. She remembered the terrible silence so clearly and could still picture their shocked faces, eyes round with terror – Rosie, Geoffrey, Gregory, Gefrin, Sweyn, even Yul – all frozen at the awful spectacle. Only Leveret had watched without fear and then broken the spell with her gurgle of laughter. Little Leveret – Maizie's lastborn, Maizie's moment of madness. And now, at fourteen, she was a nightmare.

'Answer me, Leveret! Where have you been?'

The girl sighed and shook her dark curls further over her eyes, frowning at her mother from beneath them. Should she tell the truth? Would her mother understand or would it be better to lie?

'It's the Moon Fullness tonight, Mother, the Hunter's Moon.'

'Yes I know, Leveret. That's all the more reason for you to be safely indoors by the hearth and not out cavorting. I know exactly what goes on at Moon Fullness and a girl shouldn't be out and about with all that moon lust flying around. You're far too young for such things.'

Maizie of all people knew the trouble a girl could get into on the night of the full moon, when the body was ripe and aching with want, and the boys bursting with passion and energy. She understood only too well the forbidden joy of casting aside everything sensible and everyday for that brief crescendo of bliss. But that was not for Leveret to hear of, not yet.

'Where have you been? You still haven't answered me.'

4

Leveret scowled, knowing that whatever she said would be the wrong thing.

'I was in the woods. I had to—'

'*The woods?*' screeched Maizie. 'You stupid girl! That's the worst place to be at the Moon Fullness, especially at the Hunter's Moon. You should know that! Who were you with?'

'Only Magpie.'

'*Magpie?* Oh for goddess' sake, Leveret, when will you learn? When will you start behaving responsibly? I've told you time and time again to stop spending time with Magpie, especially not at night, especially not in the woods, and *especially* not at the Moon Fullness. You're in such trouble, my girl! And if I have the slightest reason to think you and Magpie have been up to no good . . .'

She stopped for breath, quivering with anger at her daughter's foolishness. Sixteen-year-old Magpie was most definitely not an appropriate companion. Maizie had plans for her youngest child, important plans, and they didn't include the mute, half-witted boy. Magpie was a constant irritant and, hard as she'd tried, Maizie couldn't stop her daughter's friendship with him. It had always been like this from their early childhood; in the Village Nursery the clumsy, strange boy with vacant eyes had latched onto tiny, quick-witted Leveret, and the pair had been inseparable ever since. Over the years in her role as Village Welfare Councillor Maizie had endured regular dealings with Magpie and his nasty mother. The little boy had been neglected and the unpleasant task of reminding his awful family of their duty had fallen to Maizie. She'd had little success and received much hostility and abuse from the lot of them, but luckily Magpie had survived his deprived upbringing and was now an adult. Although Maizie felt pity for the poor boy, she didn't want her daughter anywhere near him. Yet, try as she might to keep the pair apart, they remained bound together with an inexplicable closeness.

'Can I go to bed now?' asked Leveret wearily, keeping her eyes down.

'No you can *not*! I told you to stay in tonight and I trusted you to do as I said. That was a mistake, wasn't it? You're only fourteen, but the minute my back's turned you're out cavorting with boys, and—'

'No Mother, I had to pick some special mushrooms tonight! It was important to pick them at the Moon Fullness, but that's all I was doing, honest.'

'Why? Why was it so important you had to disobey me? How do you know these things, Leveret? I know you're not learning that at school, about mushrooms and when you should pick them, so who's been teaching you? Where's all this coming from?'

Leveret shrugged. It was her very special secret and she'd never divulge it to her mother. She'd face any punishment and let her mother imagine the very worst, which she was always so quick to do, rather than tell her of the secret. The only one who knew was Magpie and he wasn't capable of speaking to anyone but her. So she merely glared at her mother from behind her curls and remained silent.

Maizie was at a loss as to how to punish her daughter; nothing seemed to make much difference to Leveret. It didn't help that she was so busy herself with constant meetings to attend and work to do, with Leveret left to her own devices for long periods of time. That had been the problem all along. Since that fated Winter Solstice when the community had risen up to overthrow their magus, Maizie had played a leading role. She and Miranda had been the ones who guided their pair of star-blessed children through those difficult years, helping to run Stonewylde. Together with Clip, the two women had set up the Council of Elders; Maizie had worked incredibly hard ever since and her children had been forced to fend for themselves.

There'd been so much to do in the early days. The loss of Magus had been deeply felt by everyone and the future of Stonewylde had seemed very shaky. Sheer determination on the part of Clip, Maizie and Miranda, along with others appointed to the Council, had eventually averted the crisis. Together they'd re-organised the great estate in a way that Magus would've hated.

The longer she did the job, the more grudging respect Maizie felt for him; Magus had single-handedly done what it now took a whole group of people to do. And in her heart she sometimes wondered if the people of Stonewylde were any happier today, with their education and freedom, than they'd been under his rule. Not that she'd ever voice such thoughts, and especially not to her son, who was in his own way as hard and single-minded as his father had been. Such treachery from his own mother would infuriate him.

'Sit down, Leveret,' said Maizie tersely, struggling to remain calm and in control. The girl groaned loudly and flung herself down onto one of the wooden chairs. She slumped across the table and gazed moodily at her mother. She knew exactly what was coming now: the lecture about her place in the society of Stonewylde, how as the magus' sister she must set a good example to other young people, how she let Maizie down with her behaviour, how different she was from her perfect sister Rosie, and finally how, if she didn't change her ways, Yul would be informed and there'd be a severe punishment.

She rolled her green eyes in boredom as the familiar tirade began, and started to make a mental list of the fungi still to be harvested before the Dark Moon at the end of the month. The fact that the Dark Moon fell on the night of Samhain itself was very exciting indeed. She was planning to try a spell that night, for if ever a spell were to work it'd be at the moment when the Dark Moon coincided with Samhain. She shivered with anticipation and a small smile spread across her mouth.

'... and Rosie would never have— *Leveret, you're not even listening!*'

To their mutual astonishment her mother jerked forward and slapped her sharply round the face. Leveret gasped and stared at her in shock, placing a hand on the stinging imprint on her cheek. Maizie gaped in horror too and sank back into her seat, covering her mouth with her hand. She'd broken one of the most fundamental laws of Stonewylde; the first one passed by Yul and the one he cared most passionately about.

Nobody shall ever strike a child.

'That was your fault!' whispered Maizie shakily. 'I'm sorry I did it, but you are the rudest child I've ever met and I've had enough of it.'

'You hit me!' squeaked Leveret in disbelief, tears springing to her eyes. 'I can't believe you hit me.'

'Oh for goddess' sake, girl, I hardly touched you. 'Twas just a little slap.'

'No it wasn't – it hurt and I bet there's a mark on my face.'

'Not really. And besides, that just shows how you've pushed me to the end o' my rope! Six children I've raised before you, five of 'em unruly lads, and I've never lifted a hand to any of them. But you ...'

'You *hit* me, Mother.'

Maizie tried to laugh.

'Rubbish! You've no idea what being hit means. Believe me, Leveret, that were nothing. If you could've seen what went on in this very cottage in the old days to your poor brother ... the beatings that boy took right here in this room. Don't make a fuss about a silly little thing like that. You know I didn't mean it.'

Leveret stood up angrily, the tears forgotten and her nostrils flaring as she blazed her fury at her mother.

'Nothing I say or do or feel ever matters one bit, does it, Mother? Because it's *nothing* compared to what happened to Yul or Rosie or any of the boys. Whatever it is, however big or small, it's never anything compared to what *they* did!'

'Now Leveret, I'm—'

'No! Let me finish for once! Nobody ever listens to me! I'm sick to death of hearing about Yul all the time. I hate my brother being the magus and I wish he'd never become magus. I wish we had the old magus back because he can't have been as bad as you all say, and even if he was it'd be better than having my perfect brother held up as some kind of god all the time! I hate you and Yul and Rosie – all of you – and as soon as I'm old enough I'll leave this stupid Village and go and live by myself somewhere! And if you ever touch me again I'll tell Yul! We'll see if he'll

8

banish his own perfect mother or if he'd bend the rules for you!'

Her tirade finished on a crescendo and she stopped for breath, chest heaving. Maizie had stood up too and faced her daughter across the table.

'Keep your voice down!' she hissed. 'The whole Village'll hear you!'

'I don't care!' shouted Leveret. 'I don't care if they hear me!'

'Well I do!'

'Oh yes, *you* do because we can't have the ordinary Villagers seeing that Yul's mother isn't the perfect woman she makes herself out to be! Oh no, *she* hits her daughter! What would they say to that?'

Leveret laughed triumphantly, green eyes still blazing, delighted to gain the upper hand for once. But Maizie was having none of it.

'Get to your bed, Leveret! I was wrong to slap you, but you've shown me no respect at all. Don't you *dare* speak to me like that!'

'Or what? What'll you do?'

'You'll see,' muttered Maizie darkly, feeling quite willing to inflict a deserved punishment on her. 'Go upstairs. We'll talk tomorrow when you've remembered how to behave towards your mother.'

Knowing the row had gone as far as it could, Leveret marched into the kitchen and snatched her wicker basket off the dresser. If it hadn't been so late she'd never have risked bringing it here tonight. Chin in the air, she stomped back into the sitting room and headed for the stairs.

'Leave that basket!' commanded Maizie.

'No!' yelled Leveret and raced up to her room, sliding the wooden bar across the door with a loud and final thump.

Sylvie sat in the window seat, forehead pressed against the cold, latticed glass. As the bright moon rose higher behind the trees, her fingertips tingled and her heart beat faster ... but only a little. She smiled wistfully at the memory of her frantic desperation as a young girl. As dear old Professor Siskin had

9

warned, moongaziness wasn't necessarily a blessing. Even though she'd been released from the bonds of the Stonewylde moon-dance that had claimed her every month, she still felt the pull on her soul. Part of her longed to be with the wild hares up on the hill, dancing like a moon angel in the starry night, singing her ethereal song and marking the magic spirals into the earth with her bare feet.

Curled into the cushions and bathed in silver light, Sylvie gazed up at the brilliant moon riding the shredded clouds. The Hunter's Moon held dark memories that she found impossible to lay to rest. Even now, thirteen years later, she felt the past close behind her. It was as if the dust had never settled properly but still swirled and danced in the air with a life of its own. The pool of moonlight around her failed to penetrate the shadows of the cavernous sitting-room, and Sylvie peered alone into the darkness.

She'd put up so much resistance when, after their hand-fasting, Yul had wanted to move into these apartments. This was where her final ordeal had taken place, the prison Magus had kept her in for the last weeks of his life. Today, the leather sofa where she'd slept in silk and diamonds was gone, as was the black marble bathroom and all the priceless fittings of his great bedroom. The only way she'd been persuaded to use these chambers was by altering them beyond recognition; by wiping out all traces of the man who'd been so obsessed by her moongaziness but had treated her so cruelly.

Yet still he haunted her as if he'd never truly gone. So red-blooded and commanding when alive, echoes of Magus rever-berated all around Stonewylde, particularly in the Hall and especially in these rooms. At moments like this, when the full moon blazed through the whorled glass, Sylvie felt Magus close by. She sensed the gleam of his silver hair and the flash of his black eyes just beyond the corner of her vision. She could almost – but not quite – hear his deep voice whispering her name, feel the brush of his fingers on her bare skin. It never happened when she was busy or surrounded by other people; it was always when she was alone. She'd mentioned it to others of course, but she knew from their reactions that they thought her ridiculous, or maybe even displaying something more alarming – a return to her illness. So Sylvie had learnt to keep quiet about her fears, hoping that as the years passed Magus' spectre would fade until eventually, one day, she'd be free of his presence altogether.

She rose and switched on a table lamp. The room sprang into existence, still luxurious but very different to Magus' rooms. This was her home and not a shrine. She shouldn't sit in the darkness like that. It was silly to give memories the chance to smother her, silly to let ghosts from the past find the opportunity to visit. She must be firm with herself and keep her wandering thoughts under control.

Sylvie went through the connecting door into the playroom, formerly Magus' dressing room, then into the bathroom. This was now decorated with pearly fittings and pale wood rather than dark marble and onyx. She moved on into the bedroom, an airy room with diaphanous drapes and soft turquoise walls, and a far cry from Magus' lair of scarlet damask and dark mahogany. The next room was a smaller bathroom and then there was the children's bedroom, tucked away in a room originally put aside for Sylvie and her clothes. Here, Cherry had hidden food for her under the bed and Magus had laced her tightly into a Tudor gown. The room was now bright and colourful, full of the pretty paraphernalia of young girls.

She stepped softly across the floor to stand between the beds and gaze down at her two daughters, Celandine and Bluebell. Two white-blond curly heads lay in tousled sleep, little bodies curled up against the October chill. If her girls were moongazy they didn't show it for both slept soundly, Bluebell with her thumb in her mouth. Sylvie felt the familiar heart-wrench of love as she watched them in the bright moonlight. They liked to sleep with the curtains open to the moon and the stars, and made up stories about a family of owls who had unlikely adventures, and a tribe of woodland elves who lived in a giant toadstool.

They were beautiful little girls and Sylvie knew Yul loved his daughters dearly, but she found it difficult not to feel a sense of failure in denying him the little boy he'd longed for. It wasn't so bad when Celandine was born, but with Bluebell's birth his hopes had been smashed. If Stonewylde were to survive the population explosion that Magus had encouraged, urging people to have enormous families, then there had to be a limit to reproduction now. The quota for every couple was a maximum of two children and neither of theirs was a son. Yul always went to great lengths to show how little it mattered, but Sylvie knew better.

She returned to the sitting-room and contemplated lighting the fire as it had turned very chilly this evening. It seemed a waste of good logs to heat this vast room just for her, so instead she found her woollen shawl and curled up on the sofa, picking up her book. There was a tap on the door and Miranda peered in.

'All alone? Can I come in for a minute?'

Sylvie was glad of the company and welcomed her mother. Miranda, now in her forties, was an attractive woman. Apart from a few silver threads, her hair still gleamed like newly-shelled conkers and her face showed serenity and purpose. She sat in an armchair and surveyed her daughter, bundled up in the thick shawl.

'It's freezing in here! Why don't you light the fire? Where's Yul?'

'In his office I suppose. You know how hard he works.'

'Yes, but it's late – he should be with you. I'll go as soon he comes up I promise.'

Sylvie nodded; she couldn't tell her mother that some nights he didn't come to bed at all.

'Are you alright, darling? You look tired.'

'I'm fine, thanks. Bluebell's been a bit disturbed lately at night-time – she wakes up with bad dreams. You know how it is.'

'You were just like that! Up and down all night when you were little. I've been very lucky with Rufus – he sleeps like a log.'

Miranda smiled and Sylvie recognised that same echo of

mother-love that burned so strongly in her own heart.

'I was watching him at lunch time,' she said. 'He's grown so much recently – he's going to be tall.'

'Like his father, no doubt,' said Miranda, without any bitterness. 'It's becoming more obvious now he's reaching puberty. I can't believe he'll be thirteen at Imbolc and not my little boy any longer. But he only takes after Magus in looks – he's such a sweet child and I've been really blessed with him.'

Sylvie nodded; despite the awful way Magus had treated Miranda and the fact that he'd been born posthumously, Rufus had grown up as a sunny and loving boy, if a little shy.

'That's actually what I wanted to ask, Sylvie. I know Yul's busy, but do you think he'd spend a little time with Rufus this winter? He could really do with a bit of male bonding now he's growing up. They're kind of double brothers, aren't they? The same father and being linked through us as well. Rufus really looks up to Yul, you know. There's a bit of hero-worship there I think.'

Sylvie grimaced; they'd all like to spend a little time with Yul, his daughters included.

'I'm sure he'd be happy to, Mum – I'll mention it. But he's so busy working and we hardly get to see him ourselves. Celandine was only asking this evening why he doesn't read their bedtime story any more, and I never seem to have him to myself nowadays.'

Miranda eyed her daughter carefully. Sylvie had always been pale and slim but her face looked drawn and there was a sadness about her eyes – very different to the sparkling girl who'd spent such happy teenage years growing into a woman with her handsome young man by her side. Even though Sylvie and Yul had been separated when they went off to different universities, their joy in each other on every return to Stonewylde was very evident. When had this sadness crept in?

'You're not feeling ill again, are you?' she asked, anxious as ever not to pry, but unable to completely let go. 'Hazel's keeping an eye on you?'

'Yes, Mum, I'm fine. You know that was just a hormonal thing after Bluebell was born and it won't come back again, especially not with the implant. No, I just feel ... a bit at a loose end, I suppose.'

She swallowed, annoyed at the catch in her throat. Her mother was not going to see her cry.

'I guess you have more time on your hands now that Bluebell's in the Nursery every day,' said Miranda gently. 'But there must be so much for you to do in the running of the estate, surely?'

Sylvie shook her head. This was the problem. She'd been the one to study estate management and agriculture, whilst Yul had been persuaded to broaden his world by studying the Arts. Yet as soon as she'd fallen pregnant with Celandine, not long after graduation and marriage, Yul had begun what she now saw as a careful process of protecting her from the exhausting demands of Stonewylde. And her dreadful illness after Bluebell's birth had sealed her fate – Yul was in charge and her role was simply to be wife and mother.

'Yul has it all under control, he says. It's hard to find something that I can organise without treading on anyone's toes.'

Miranda smiled and patted Sylvie's arm.

'You can always help in the schools,' she said. 'Either up here with the seniors or even down in the Village with Dawn. It's not so bad in the primary school, mind you, since Yul insisted on cutting back on the birth-rate – that's helped tremendously. But up here we're bursting with teenagers. You know I've had to employ two more teachers recently, and we could still do with an extra pair of hands if you wanted to help.'

'I'd be useless at teaching,' said Sylvie, 'and I find all those teenagers a bit terrifying, to be honest. You're better off with properly trained teachers. What are the new ones like?'

'They're lovely and so in sympathy with the Stonewylde ethos. Do you remember some of the disasters we had in the early days, trying to find suitable teachers?' Miranda chuckled, warming to her favourite subject. 'But recruiting from the Druid communities was such a good idea. They seem to be totally in tune with Stonewylde and how we live and there's no conflict of philosophy

14

at all. I like both our new recruits, especially David the art teacher. Merewen's far too busy with the Pottery to teach full time and she's delighted to hand over her teaching to him. He seems really good.'

'Do I detect a bit of a love interest there, Mum?' laughed Sylvie. 'I saw him the other day and he looks nice.'

'Not from me, I can assure you!' said Miranda. 'Once bitten, twice shy. I'm perfectly happy, thank you, with more than enough on my plate running our education system here. I love it, Sylvie, really love it, and there's Rufus to care for, and you, and my little grand-daughters. Oh no, the last thing I'd want is some man to mess it all up again. But I wouldn't be surprised if we see Dawn taking an interest. They were having a good old chat yesterday and she seemed very animated.'

'Really? That's brilliant! It's about time she found herself a man and settled down. She must be thirty now, or maybe thirty-one? I'm sure she wants children of her own.'

'Yes but I don't want to lose her from the primary school. She's a great head-teacher. I'll have to warn her off David if I think she'll abandon us.'

'She'd never do that, Mum – she's as passionate a teacher as you are. I think it'd be wonderful. She's a lovely woman and she deserves to find her soul-mate.'

'Not everyone's as lucky as you, Sylvie,' said Miranda. 'What you and Yul have is quite extraordinary. Most people never find that complete harmony.'

'I know, but remember – Yul has a mistress too.'

Miranda's mouth dropped open.

'No, Mum, don't be silly! I meant Stonewylde – I must share my husband with her! Stonewylde is his life, just as much as I or the girls are. I can't compete with her and she's far more demanding than all of us put together. I get what's left of Yul when she's had her fill of his time and energy.'

'Well maybe you should be more demanding, Sylvie. Where is he? I'll go now as I'm sure he'll be up any minute, won't he? Try and get him to ease off a bit and spend more time with his family.

And Rufus too please, if possible. He's never had a father and he thinks the world of Yul.' She stood up and bent to kiss her daughter. 'You tell him, Sylvie. Not just for Rufus but for you and the girls too. He's neglecting you and it's just not necessary – there are plenty of others around to help run the community and he doesn't have to take it on single-handed. I don't like to see you all alone up here in the evening.'

When Miranda had gone, Sylvie left the lamp on just in case Yul did come up, and made her way to bed. It was chilly, and as she slid between the fine linen sheets she shivered with longing. She imagined him yawning, stretching his long limbs, running his hands through his dark curls and giving her that special smile that made her melt inside. He'd hold her in his arms, warming her with his vitality and passion, kissing her hard, brushing her hair from her face, murmuring his love for her . . . Sylvie sighed. It wasn't going to happen. He'd have made the bed up in the office, as he often did when he worked late. She wouldn't see him until he joined them for breakfast, with the girls jumping all over him and the day's demands already jostling for his attention.

She turned the bedside light off and lay there alone, gazing out at the moon. It was just visible through the latticed panes, at its zenith now, a small shiny disc. Sylvie suddenly felt unutterably sad. She shut her eyes against the silver reminder of youthful passion and the hot tears that had welled up behind her lids.

In the study downstairs Yul looked up from the papers spread about him on the old leather-topped desk and rubbed the back of his aching neck. He hadn't experienced Sylvie's qualms about using his father's things at all; in fact he took delight in doing so. He tapped some figures into the computer and printed out a couple more sheets. The illiterate Village boy had gone forever, all traces of him obliterated in this confident, articulate man of the world. At almost twenty-nine, Yul was in his prime and had exceeded his earlier promise. He was as tall and well-muscled as his father had been, fit and powerful. His chiselled face had lost all boyishness and was a study of fine, classical bones and strong planes. Yet the slanted, deep grey eyes still smouldered beneath a tousle of wild black curls.

Yul nodded as he scanned the sheets of paper; Harold had come up with yet another idea for the company and Yul was sure he was onto something promising. Stonewylde toiletries – rosemary soap, lilac bath oil, watercress face wash – a range of pure and organic products attractively presented in tiny hand-woven wicker baskets. It wasn't an original idea, but, as ever, Harold had done his research and found there was a huge market for luxury, home-grown toiletries. Harold had such a talent for sniffing out opportunities and Yul had learned that going with his ideas invariably paid off.

Harold had even located an under-used barn near the Village which could be easily converted into a cottage-style factory to produce the soaps and oils. All Yul needed to do was give him the go-ahead and Harold would set the wheels in motion, organising prototypes and preparing finely-adjusted costings. Best of all, it was women's work – not taking any labour away from food production or maintenance and building work, which at trad-itional Stonewylde still tended to be done by the burlier men. Even the children and old ones could help make the little baskets as everyone was expected to make some contribution to the community's economy. This was just the right sort of money-making scheme to add to the ever-growing portfolio, and Yul was delighted.

Yawning, he switched off the computer and stood up, stret-ching hugely and feeling his spine realign with a crack. His body ached from sitting still too long. He'd have liked to ride Skydancer now, galloping along Dragon's Back in the moonlight with the cold air on his face. But if he went to the stables now he'd wake people and then they'd wait for him to come back. He'd have to make do with a long, hard early morning ride instead.

Yul strode across to the French windows and flung them wide, welcoming the crisp October night air. He stepped out onto the terrace overlooking the sunken garden where Sylvie had sat and talked with Professor Siskin all those years before. He breathed deeply, drawing in lungfuls of air. The brilliant moon was visible as it hung on high, just clearing the edge of the vast building and all its turrets, roofs and chimney stacks.

Yul stood absolutely still then, his breath clouding around him as he looked up at the moon. He felt a stirring deep inside, a primeval need that Stonewylde had bred into him. Tonight the women were ripe, and as the dominant male it was his duty to ensure the survival of the tribe. He smiled slightly in acknowledgement of the instinctive urge and quelled it with an intellectual denial. He had two children and the community couldn't survive any more population increase or in-breeding. He wouldn't be out and about indulging his moon lust as generations before him had done, but would instead do the civilised thing and quietly go to bed.

Yul turned his back on the moon and the night and stepped into his study, leaving the French windows slightly ajar for the fresh air. He used the adjoining small bathroom and then quickly made up his bed on a sofa. He stretched out his long limbs and closed his eyes, thinking longingly of his beautiful wife upstairs alone in their bed. He was sure Sylvie would've gone to sleep ages ago and he didn't want to disturb her. He found it impossible to sleep in the same bed and not make love to her, but it wasn't fair to wake her up so late. By staying down in the study he'd contain himself and let her sleep in peace.

Yul was careful not to impose himself on Sylvie, not to be selfish or demanding. She'd retained that air of fragility and delicacy that had clung to her as a girl; as a woman she still seemed to command a gentle touch. Yul knew how important it was to keep his wildness and constant desire for her curbed and under tight control. He wanted her no less now than he had as a young lad, when such a thing had been an impossibility. Yet now, he thought wryly, when he could have her company whenever he chose, he seemed to have less time with her than ever before. Real life got in the way of their relationship to an extent he'd never envisaged. But it couldn't be helped and there was no point dwelling on what couldn't be. Stonewylde must come first; they both understood that.

All around him, the Hall sank into slumber. The huge building, a many-storeyed labyrinth of wings, rooms, corridors and staircases, settled down for the night like a great beast. So many people, so much stone, glass and wood, all under his control and his guardianship. As Yul drifted off to sleep the moon moved round further, to begin its descent in the night sky. It shone on his closed eyelids and he dreamed of hares and an owl and a great standing stone on the hill. He dreamed of a magical dancing girl with long silver hair and the moon in her eyes, a girl who'd set him on fire with longing and who'd turned his life on its head. In his sleep, with moonbeams patterning his face, Yul was pierced suddenly with a sharp sense of loss.

2

Leveret was up long before dawn and out of the cottage before Maizie awoke; she needed to get the mushrooms safely stored before her mother could interfere. The October morning was cool and damp and there was no light whatsoever; the changes at Stonewylde had not included street lights. All Villagers knew the streets blindfolded and Leveret could've stood under any of the massive trees on the Green and said exactly where she was just by the feel of the bark. So finding her way to Mother Heggy's home in complete darkness was no problem at all.

Thirteen years had taken their toll on the ancient cottage. After his sad discovery on the morning of that Winter Solstice, Yul had removed a few keepsakes and closed it up. Occasionally he'd brought his little sister up to the cottage, unbeknown to Maizie. He'd told the little girl of the wise old crone who'd lived there with her crow, the same bird that now lived with them. Leveret had been enthralled, sitting in the battered rocking chair with her little leather boots barely reaching the edge of the seat and gazing around the hovel in wonderment. She'd confided to him, when she was about six, that one day she'd be the Wise Woman of Stonewylde. Yul had laughed and said it was a brave ambition.

Yul never visited the old cottage now, having no time for such nostalgia. He never gazed, as he'd first done, at the empty wooden rocking chair, or the battered table, or the filthy old range and fireplace where no cauldron would ever bubble again. The place had been left to the elements and stood forlorn and deserted.

But Leveret had continued to visit, coming here alone as soon as she was old enough to slip away unnoticed. This was her place of refuge, and where she longed to live one day.

Leveret opened the door silently and slipped in. She found the matches and candle on the shelf and soon the tiny cottage flickered to life. Leveret sighed with relief – she felt safe now. She opened the dresser cupboards and found the things she needed, then began to carefully thread her basketful of mushrooms onto twine. When she'd finished she hung them from a rafter along with the many other strings of fungi, all in various stages of desiccation. She made a small label and attached it to the end of the new string, then sat back in the chair and closed her eyes, rocking gently. She longed for a creature to join her, remembering Mother Heggy's old crow. Leveret had grown up with that crow, which had lived a further eight cantankerous years before finally succumbing to old age and a cold winter. This cottage needed an animal or bird, but Leveret knew that whatever belonged here would find the place when it was ready.

She considered lighting a fire and brewing some tea but she didn't really have time. The most important thing was to record these latest mushrooms. As with all the fungi she collected, and many of the herbs and plants too, she wasn't completely sure she had the right ones. There was nobody apart from Old Violet who really knew all the species, and Leveret certainly wasn't going to ask that wicked crone for advice. So she had to rely on the Book and that wasn't easy. The drawings and writing had been done many years before and were faded and in places almost illegible. Much of her harvesting was therefore guesswork.

Leveret took the school exercise book entitled 'Mushrooms' from its secret hiding place and found a pencil in the dresser drawer. She then wrote about the fungus in careful detail, describing not only the mushrooms themselves but also their exact location in the woods and the date they'd been picked. She'd leave the illustration for Magpie as his drawing skills were so much better than hers. When she'd finished, she leafed back through the book reading some of the entries. It was almost full now and she longed for the day when she could get hold of a big, beautiful book bound in soft black leather and filled with thick sheets of parchment. She wanted to write her descriptions in proper ink that she'd made herself, and Magpie to paint the illustrations in soft watercolours. Leveret sighed again. She knew it would happen one day. Her own Book was what she wanted most in the world.

Her green eyes flew open from their drowsing as the door swung open and the candle guttered, but of course it was only Magpie. Nobody else ever bothered with the place. She noticed, before he shut the door, that the sky was lightening outside and she knew she must get home very soon. But Magpie put paid to that. He lurched across the tiny room and placed a hand on her hair, stroking the silky curls. His lips curled in his twisted smile and his beautiful eyes, usually blank and devoid of any focus, shone at her.

'Blessings, Magpie,' she laughed. 'What a lovely surprise. I've just recorded the mushrooms. Do you want to draw them now before they start to dry up?'

He shook his head and fished in the voluminous pockets of his large and disgusting coat. Magpie's coat was infamous; he wore it in all weathers, clinging to it even in the heat of the summer. It was ancient and filthy but he refused to part with it. From the pocket he drew a hunk of loaf and a handful of roasted chestnuts, and then a small metal can on a handle. He fetched two mugs from the dresser and clumsily poured milk for them both and shared out the food. She smiled gratefully and sank her sharp teeth into the stale bread as Magpie sat down on the floor to eat his breakfast. Magpie always sat on the floor to eat. Leveret finished quickly and brushed the crumbs from her lap.

'I must get back now, Magpie,' she said. 'Mother was furious last night. I'm in such trouble so if you don't see me around for a few days you know why. But look for me at school and hopefully we can walk home to the Village together each day.'

She started to get up but Magpie, still on the floor, shook his head and laid it on her knee, holding her calves tight.

'What is it, Mag?' she asked softly, knowing she must get home quickly. Even now it was probably too late. Magpie started to sob, the horrible guttering noise that she knew so well. Poor Magpie had a lot to cry about and it was one of the few ways he could express himself. Leveret stroked the hair, matted and lank, away from his face. He was always dirty unless Maizie or someone else involved in Welfare intervened and insisted that he have a bath. Maybe she should start helping him herself, taking him to the Bath House every week and ensuring that he went in and cleaned himself up. It'd never really bothered her before, as she'd grown up with a filthy Magpie by her side, but lately he'd started to smell horrible. She realised that even someone as different and backward as Magpie had finally reached adolescence.

He must have sensed her thoughts for he looked up at her with sad eyes. Magpie's eyes were his best feature – large, clear and a beautiful turquoise. When he washed his long hair it was lovely too, a rich butterscotch colour, but usually it was several shades darker and duller with dirt.

'*Magpie hurts.*'

'Where does it hurt?' she asked.

He pulled back the hair from his temple and she saw a small blue lump. Then he rolled up a dirty trouser leg and she saw another blue lump, much bigger, on his shin. He looked like a kicked puppy and her heart went out to him as always. He led such a miserable life, neglected by his mother, grandmother and great aunt, and badly bullied by his cousin Jay and anyone else who could be roped in to have a go.

'Who did it, Magpie?' she whispered, gently touching the bruise on his temple. 'Was it Jay?'

He nodded and tears trickled down his dirty cheeks. His cousin Jay was the torment of his life. The abuse had started at an early age in the strange household where they grew up together, little Magpie neglected whilst young Jay ruled the roost. Eventually it had become clear that Magpie wasn't developing normally but despite Hazel's tests, the cause was never really clear. Old Violet had delivered the baby herself and Hazel suspected there'd been oxygen starvation; whatever the cause of his slowness, Magpie never spoke but remained silent and unfocused, living in his own private world. Leveret had always been his only friend and she hated Jay who was a few years older than her and went around in a gang with her brothers Sweyn and Gefrin. All three were bullies, unchecked by fathers.

Leveret found a bottle on the dresser and tipped some of the astringent contents onto a piece of rag, holding it against the blue swelling on Magpie's leg.

'Witch-hazel, Magpie,' she said. 'It'll help the bruising. He didn't hurt you for taking the milk and bread, did he?'

Magpie shook his head and started the complex communication he'd developed with Leveret to explain the train of events. She sensed images of Jay returning at night, with the full moon shining, and kicking Magpie. She felt the boy's pain and bewilderment and clearly saw Jay's face contorted with sadistic glee.

'He's horrible, isn't he? I expect he'd been turned down by a girl – not surprising really. Next Moon Fullness you must stay out of his way. Thank you for the breakfast, Magpie. It was lovely but now I must get home. You can draw the mushrooms next time but don't leave it too long or they'll dry up completely. I think they're the right ones but so many of them look the same. Don't touch the Book of Shadows when I'm not here, will you Magpie? You're never, ever to do that.'

He shook his head solemnly. She'd tried to impress this on him so many times, for the Book was the most precious thing in her life. She knew she'd have to find a new hiding place for it soon, one which Magpie knew nothing about. He just couldn't be trusted not to touch it or give its presence away if forced. She smiled at him and bent to kiss his cheek. He stood up quickly and engulfed her in a hug. He really did need a bath.

A thin-lipped Maizie was waiting back at the cottage. Leveret could think of no good reason for her early morning absence so remained obstinately silent, which made her mother even angrier.

'I'm now late for my meeting at the Hall! Yul will wonder where on earth I am and you're late for school. If we hurry now 'twon't be so bad but there's no time for breakfast so don't even think about it.'

Leveret wasn't. She was plotting how to get hold of some more empty bottles for her potions; there were ways, but she had to be careful. Everything at Stonewylde was used thoughtfully and bottles were a precious commodity.

'Leveret! Come on! You're day-dreaming again and I haven't finished with you yet. We'll talk about it on the way.'

They left the house and the girl trudged along beside her mother, their two dark curly heads so alike. Maizie's, greying around the temples now, bobbed and shook as she launched into another tirade about last night's lateness. Leveret's remained bowed as the words washed over her. She was grateful that all the younger children were safely tucked up at the Village School, whilst the older ones would already be in assembly in the Galleried Hall, so nobody would see her mother working herself up to a fine lather. A few women at the water pump greeted them as they walked briskly through the cobbled streets of the Village. Mother and daughter hurried on past the Green with its blanket of fallen autumn leaves, past the Jack in the Green pub and the Great Barn and towards the track out of the Village.

They heard singing coming across from the Village School and Leveret recognised the Samhain songs she'd sung when she was younger. She knew the children would be busy making their papier-mâché crows and skulls ready to hang in the Great Barn in two weeks' time, and practising their dances and drama to perform to the magus and the rest of the community. Soon each Stonewylder would go down to the beach and choose their handful of white stones ready to mark out the labyrinth on the Green. Leveret loved Samhain and this one should be really special, with the Dark Moon falling as it did on the night of the festival. She was ready to cast her first spell. She smiled to herself at the thought and let Maizie's scolding pour over her unheeded.

They continued out of the Village and onto the paved track that led to the Hall. The sun had risen higher and now gilded the trees all around them in soft October hues. The air was fresh and pure and Leveret sniffed appreciatively, not hearing any of Maizie's words. Instead she heard the bright music of blackbirds and the mew of a buzzard overhead, and in the distance the drone of a tractor as the sound of children's singing receded.

Leveret walked where the fallen leaves were thickest, delighting in the noisy scrunching her feet made amongst the brown, curled leaves, kicking them up to make even more noise. All around her more leaves fell gently from the branches in the slight breeze. She watched in wonder as many of the golden flakes were carried upwards, defying gravity to whirl about overhead. She noticed a jay flying fast through the trees, the distinctive flash of black and white on its rump a contrast to the pink-brown body. A group of magpies screamed and squabbled in the branches, and she thought how inappropriate it was that Magpie was named after such an aggressive and noisy bird. The shy jay would've been far more fitting.

'Stop shuffling in the leaves, Leveret!' said Maizie sharply. 'You'll scuff your boots.'

'Mother, why don't you do something to help Magpie?'

'What? Have you been listening to anything I've said? You and Magpie are to stop seeing each other, and—'

'Jay's been hurting him again and I can't bear it.'

She stopped, remembering she mustn't let on that she'd seen Magpie earlier that morning. Maizie might start wondering where they'd met and it was vital that her visits to Mother Heggy's cottage remain secret.

'I'm sorry to hear it, and goddess knows how many times I've tried to get them all to show the boy a little more care. But you know as well as I do, Leveret – that family are a law unto themselves.'

'But they shouldn't be! Jay shouldn't get away with hurting poor Magpie and you could stop it.'

'No I couldn't. Do you think Old Violet would listen to me?'

'It's not his grandmother, it's Jay. He makes Magpie's life a misery.'

'I can't just march in there and tell Jay off. That's up to Magpie's awful mother, Starling. And Magpie's an adult now, even though he's so soft in the head. 'Tis not my place to interfere with what goes on there.'

'Yes it is, Mother! You're in charge of Village Welfare, aren't you? You could say something to the women, even if you don't want to speak to Jay. Or are you too scared of them?'

'Don't be so cheeky! O' course I'm not scared. 'Tis just that ... well, they do as they wish in that cottage and me going barging in now and telling them how to run their lives would do no good. 'Twould most likely make things worse, getting 'em all riled up again as it's done many a time in the past when I've tried to put things straight there. You know they've never liked me and besides, Magpie's alright – or as alright as he ever is, being so dirty and simple. The boy is strange and he's no fit company for you, my girl, as I've been telling you for years.'

Leveret kicked angrily at the drifts of leaves, disappointed that as always her mother, the one person in the Village who should intervene, failed to understand what went on in Magpie's home. She knew her mother was scared of the three women but would never admit it, preferring to turn a blind eye to Magpie's suffering. She was very good at turning a blind eye to what went on right under her nose, as Leveret knew only too well. She'd respect her mother far more if she did something about Magpie's awful situation, which had been going on for far too long.

'Besides, Jay lives up at the Hall now,' said Maizie. 'You'd do well to concentrate on your own behaviour rather than telling tales about his. You've always been too fond of moaning on about others' wrongdoings. Your brothers, for instance. The number of times you've come to me complaining about a whole cloud of nothing! 'Tis one of your shortcomings, Leveret, being a little tell-tale-tit, and I'm sick of it. I always— Oh look, there's Sylvie!'

Up ahead where the paved track turned into the gravel drive

to the Hall they saw a tall, slim figure walking in the same direction. Leveret's heart sank.

'Blessings!' called Maizie, quickening her step. Sylvie stopped and turned, her pale face slipping into a smile as she waited for them to catch up. Leveret watched her, noting the droop of her shoulders and the shadows under her eyes. The morning after the Moon Fullness was often an anti-climax, a first step towards the waning of the moon and the Dark Moon two weeks later. But she sensed that there was something more than that bothering her sister-in-law.

She was as beautiful as ever, her hair like polished silk and her skin as flawless as alabaster. Her eyes were like a wolf's, silver with darker edges to the irises. Every feature was exquisitely perfect and refined. Two children hadn't spoiled her slim body; she moved with the grace and elegance of a dancer. Yet something was not right. Leveret stared from beneath her dark curls, knowing that as ever Sylvie would barely notice her. It was one of several reasons why she disliked her brother's wife.

'Good morning, Mother Maizie. Leveret. You're late today!' she said brightly as they all fell into step together. 'I've just taken Celandine and Bluebell to the Nursery and they're all off to the woods in a minute to search for cobnuts and squirrels and giant puffballs. I wish I'd joined them. They were so happy and excited.'

'Bless them! Just like Yul at their age, always wanting to play in the woods. How's my son today?'

A shadow passed over Sylvie's face.

'I haven't seen him yet. He went for an early morning ride I think, and wasn't back in time for breakfast with us. The girls weren't impressed but he often misses joining us for breakfast. It's just the wrong time to fit in with his day, and the girls can take so long in the mornings. But I'm hoping to see him when I get back.'

'You know there's a meeting this morning? I'm late,' said Maizie, 'and I hope he won't be annoyed. We've a visitor from the Outside World today, coming to talk to us about the Nursery.

28

Put us right, I suppose! Hasn't Yul asked you to come? I know Miranda'll be there.'

Sylvie looked a little non-plussed but smiled anyway. Leveret noticed the small lines around her mouth.

'Oh, I expect he mentioned it but you know how forgetful I am. Why are you so late this morning? It's not like you to oversleep.'

Maizie jerked her head angrily at her daughter.

'This young maid's fault! Not only was she out gallivanting in the woods till close on midnight last night, but then she disappeared this morning as well. She's out of hand and I'm going to ask Yul to deal with her.'

Sylvie flicked a glance at her young sister-in-law but quickly looked away. The sullen girl with dark curls and fathomless green eyes disturbed her. She'd always felt uncomfortable with Leveret who'd openly disliked her from a very young age.

'Oh no – is that really necessary, Maizie?' she said quickly. 'He's exhausted as usual although he won't admit it, and he's so very busy at the moment.'

'Well, I'll see, but something must be done. This girl shows no respect for me at all and I can't trust her alone for a second. I don't know what to do with her.'

'Couldn't she go to Rosie when you're busy?'

'Aye, but Rosie's got her own family to think about and Robin won't want this darkling sitting under his nose every night upsetting his little ones, will he?'

'What about your younger boys? Maybe they could babysit for you?'

The look Leveret gave her was pure venom.

'That's not such a bad idea,' said Maizie slowly. ''Tis only since Sweyn and Gefrin've started boarding at the Hall that she's got so bad. They always did keep her in check. Yes, I'll speak to them today. Thank you, Sylvie.'

They left the canopy of golden beech trees overhanging the gravel drive and approached the great turning circle in front of the Hall. The vast building sat as it had done for so many hundreds of years, an imposing edifice of pale stone all quarried at Stonewylde. It seemed to grow out of the land, its thousands of diamond-shaped panes of glass glinting and reflecting light. The Hall was irregular and almost organic in design, as if parts of it had sprouted from the enormous main block of their own accord; as if the very stone itself had grown and developed extra limbs and dimensions to accommodate those who lived there. Every period of history was represented, from the early mediaeval era when the present structure was first begun, to Edwardian. Inside, meanwhile, the technological effects and improvements of the twentieth and twenty-first centuries were evident.

It was a true stately home, but it was also a working one, a place used daily by the people of Stonewylde as a home, a school and an office. No longer the luxurious preserve of a privileged few, it had become the property of everyone at Stonewylde. The Hall was used by all and lived in by many. Maizie and Leveret approached it with as much confidence as Sylvie, entering the enormous porch and going through into the stone-flagged entrance hall. The place exuded an atmosphere of busyness, with voices audible from many directions and people moving about purposefully.

'Go to your lessons right now,' said Maizie to Leveret. 'You've missed assembly but make sure you say sorry for being so late. What've you got first?'

'Geography,' mumbled Leveret from behind her curls.

'You need a haircut, my girl,' said her mother sharply. 'I'll do it tonight. Wait for me here after school and we'll walk home together. Do you understand, Leveret?'

'Yes. And I don't want my hair cut. I like it how it is.'

'You'll do as I say, Leveret – it's a mess. Do you understand? This wildness and disrespect is going to stop right now. Sylvie's right – your brothers will help me. Maybe you'll toe the line for them if you won't for me, and if that don't work, I'll speak to Yul.'

'I wouldn't mind speaking to Yul either,' said Leveret softly. 'There's something I could tell him, isn't there, Mother?'

Sylvie looked at the girl, surprised at her tone and Maizie's reaction. She didn't envy Maizie her role and hoped that her own daughters would be easier to handle when they were fourteen. At least they had a father around, unlike Leveret whose father had died thirteen years ago this Samhain. Maybe that was why the girl was being so difficult; perhaps the anniversary of her father's death upset her. She must suggest it discreetly to Maizie in case it was a factor in Leveret's behaviour.

'Don't you dare threaten me, Leveret! I'll be telling Yul myself. Now get yourself off to your lessons.'

The girl swung around and stormed off down one of the many corridors. Sylvie grimaced in sympathy and Maizie shook her head.

'She's awful! What did I ever do to deserve her – and when life should be so much easier and calmer now? You raise six children and think you know it all, and then the seventh turns out to be worse than all o' the brood put together.'

'What's she threatening you with?' asked Sylvie. 'What happened?'

Maizie's face darkened.

'For goddess' sake don't you tell Yul, will you? I lost my temper last night and I slapped her.'

Sylvie gasped.

'Maizie! You must be feeling awful about that! Will she tell Yul?'

'So she says. I'm calling her bluff, saying I'll tell him myself, but I hope it don't come to that. He'd never understand, would he?'

'I doubt it. You know how he's so adamantly against any sort of violence towards children. Though it's understandable after what he went through, isn't it?'

'Oh yes,' nodded Maizie, images flashing through her mind of a bruised and bloody boy lying crumpled on the floor at his stepfather's feet. 'Yul has good reason to feel that way. But honestly, this were only a little slap, nothing like he suffered, and nothing meant by it. Well, I must get to this meeting, Sylvie. Are you coming?'

Sylvie shook her head. She hadn't even known about the meeting and was sure she hadn't been invited. The Nursery wasn't her domain, although both Celandine and Bluebell went there every day. She'd thought about helping but it was well run by others, with Rowan in charge, and she thought her presence might hinder some of the women there. Although there were no social distinctions at Stonewylde anymore, nevertheless as Clip's daughter and Yul's wife, Sylvie occupied a position of authority. People watched what they said in front of her. She belonged to Stonewylde, would one day be the owner of the estate, and yet at times she still felt like an Outsider. Unlike Miranda, who'd devoted herself to remodelling the education system since her son was born, and now ran the Senior School at the Hall along with much of the adult education in the Great Barn. Miranda was completely integrated into Stonewylde and had become a key figure, while Sylvie still seemed to be on the outside looking in.

She sighed and bent to kiss Maizie's plump cheek and give her a hug. She was very fond of her mother-in-law and had often considered confiding in her. But although Maizie was the first to point out Yul's shortcomings, her loyalty towards her first-born was intense and Sylvie wasn't sure she'd be the best person to hear about their problems. And now she knew that Maizie had such a difficult time with the wayward Leveret, she couldn't burden her any further.

So, with a small smile, Sylvie left the hall and slowly climbed the great wide-stepped staircase, gazing up at the glorious stained-glass window on the half-landing ahead. She remembered Magus bounding up these stairs in his riding clothes, the red and purple light from the glass shining onto his handsome face and transforming him into a royal deity. She remembered the scent of him with a sharp thrill, the energy that blazed from him. Her hand caressed the ancient polished wood of the banister rail as she climbed the stairs, and she thought of how many times over the course of his life that Magus' hand must have run along the smooth oak. She stopped and closed her eyes.

'Are you alright?'

Her eyes flew open and she saw a figure coming down the stairs, silhouetted against the bright wall of coloured light. The body was tall and well-built, the hair pale.

'I'm fine thanks, Martin,' she smiled. 'Just besieged by memories.'

She drew level with him at the landing halfway up, under the stained glass. Martin looked down at her, concern in his eyes.

'Memories? Yes, I feel them too, all the time,' he said quietly. 'Some things just don't go away, do they?'

Sylvie looked at him more carefully. Martin definitely had Hallfolk blood and she was sure he was closely related to Clip. She'd heard rumours that they shared the same father, Basil, and it didn't surprise her; the two of them were very alike. Over the years, since the events of that terrible Winter Solstice, she'd tried hard to accept Martin. It had been difficult in the early days as he'd been hostile towards her when Magus was alive and had made no secret of where his loyalties really lay. But Clip had insisted that Martin remain as major-domo. In a period of complete chaos, Stonewylde needed all the stability it could muster and Martin had always done an excellent job of running the Hall.

Clip and Martin had apparently buried their differences, although every time Sylvie saw the horrible scar on Martin's temple and eyebrow she was reminded of Clip in his swirling crow-feather cloak with that lethal staff in his hands. And sometimes she caught Martin looking at her in such a strange way that made her feel quite spooked. But past troubles had to be put firmly aside and she always tried hard to get on with him. Nobody else seemed to have any trouble doing so. She smiled at him ruefully as they stood on the half-landing.

'I sometimes feel the past sitting on my shoulder, peering over and breathing in my ear. It's hard to shake off.'

Martin looked gravely into her eyes; they reminded him so strongly of the wild woman Raven, whom he remembered from his childhood. His mother and aunt had hated her with a vengeance and he knew that Sylvie aroused similar emotions in them. But Martin must work diligently and treat the present magus and his wife with deference and respect, whatever history had gone before. He had a major role to play and personal issues would never jeopardise that.

'You see the past as a crow on your shoulder, but to me the past is a cloak to be worn,' he said, still gazing into her strange eyes and noticing how the light shining through the coloured glass was staining her silver hair and white skin a deep blood red. 'If you discard it completely you'll reveal the nakedness of your future.'

She frowned at him.

'That's very deep, Martin. Where does it come from? I don't think I've heard it before.'

He tapped the side of his head and smiled faintly.

'Must get on, Miss Sylvie – there's lots of work to be done and I can't stand chatting all day. The girls should've finished cleaning your chambers by now if you need to go and sit down.'

'Thank you, Martin. I've got lots to do too.'

She carried on up the stairs knowing Martin was well aware how untrue that was – she had absolutely nothing to do. Stonewylde was running like clockwork, thanks to the efforts of Yul, Clip and the Council of Elders. Everyone worked really hard but she herself had no responsibilities. She opened the heavy door to their apartments and sniffed appreciatively at the smell of beeswax polish. A great vase of bronze chrys-anthemums now stood on the table and everything was clean and very tidy. Cherry, in charge of organising the work duties for all the older teenagers who boarded at the Hall, always checked their chambers herself and ensured they'd been cleaned to perfection.

Sylvie wandered down through the rooms but there was nothing that needed doing. The beds were made and someone had lined up all the girls' little knitted animals on the windowsill. They'd like that. She thought of them now, running and playing in the autumn woods with all the other under-eights. No chanting of times-tables for little Stonewylders, she thought gladly. Maybe she should've stayed and helped with the Nursery children this morning, especially if Rowan was up here at a meeting. She frowned, imagining Miranda, Maizie, Rowan and probably Dawn all at this meeting with her husband discussing the nursery education at Stonewylde, whilst she was twiddling her thumbs. Why hadn't he told her about it?

She sat down on Celandine's bed, with its pretty patchwork quilt and embroidered pillow-cases. She hadn't even made these herself, still finding fine sewing a challenge after all these years. She preferred working at the loom, although they didn't have one up here in their private rooms. Yul had said no to that, trying as ever to shield her from the simple duties every other woman at Stonewylde performed. She should've insisted as she enjoyed weaving, and remembered the hours she'd spent with Rosie in the early days learning the ancient skill.

Sylvie gazed at her reflection in the dressing-table mirror and realised just how pale and shadow-eyed she looked. No wonder Yul thought her fragile and in need of protection . . . but it simply wasn't true. She had been ill – really very ill – when Bluebell was born four years ago. She'd suffered from severe post-natal depression, which was common enough, but this had turned into something more serious. Sylvie had developed puerperal psychosis, and she knew it was why Yul had become so ridiculously over-protective.

But the spell in the private nursing home, well away from Stonewylde and her babies, Yul and all the triggers, had sorted her out. Now she couldn't bear to think about that period of her life, and the horrible treatment she'd undergone, without a shudder. It had been a very dark phase, but one that she'd firmly put behind her. It was just a shame that Yul seemed unable to do the same, treating her as if she were made of glass. Like every woman at Stonewylde of child-bearing age who'd either had her children or didn't yet want any, Sylvie was fitted with a contraceptive implant. Hazel said it had the added bonus of keeping her hormones steady. She was in good health physically and there was no reason at all why she shouldn't be working as hard as everyone else at Stonewylde.

Pulling on her cloak and determined to enjoy a brisk walk to clear these dusty old cobwebs away, Sylvie resolved to confront Yul and start the process of improving things between them. Miranda had been right last night – Yul was neglecting her whilst he worked too hard, refusing to allow her to share the burden in any way. They needed to return to a relationship based on equality. For they were the darkness and the brightness of Stonewylde, the balance that held everything together in harmony. Together, they were the very heart of Stonewylde.

3

The thin, white-haired man gazed out unseeing across the landscape from the Solar at the top of the mediaeval tower. His pale grey eyes were vacant as his thoughts rambled unchecked, like a dragonfly dancing on water. He'd been standing at the pointed window, lost in reverie, for over an hour. His hollow-cheeked face was deeply lined and Clip looked far older than his fifty-three years. His stomach growled with emptiness, which he ignored as he was fasting in preparation for a journey at Samhain. This year he'd decided not to join the community at all for the celebrations. Yul could manage it all, he was sure. Clip would be in the Dolmen alone, in body at least, whilst his spirit journeyed to other realms. He sensed a major change ahead, a shift of events that would affect everyone at Stonewylde. At present he had no idea what was to happen but he hoped to find out at Samhain. He was, after all, the shaman of Stonewylde.

The thirteen years since his brother's death at Quarrycleave had been tortuous for Clip. He'd only ever wanted to be a shaman, never the leader of such a complex community, and despite being the legal owner of Stonewylde he'd always taken a back seat in the running of the estate. But the death of Magus had been a huge and shocking blow to the community, even to those who'd wanted him gone. In the aftermath, Clip had had to step into the void and assume the role he'd always been happy to leave to his brother. Tough as they were, Yul and Sylvie had been far too young to take charge. But perhaps now, thirteen years on . . .

There was a knock on the door two floors below which Clip, deep in his dreaming, failed to hear. Cherry bustled in from the corridor connecting this tower to the oldest part of the Hall, the Galleried Hall, and stood at the bottom of the stone spiral staircase looking up.

'Master Clip!' she called. 'May I come up?'

Although the whole tower was private and used exclusively by Clip, he rarely used the circular room on the ground floor where it joined the Hall. The middle floor was his bedroom with a small bathroom enclosed within it, and the top floor – the Solar – was where he spent most of his time surrounded by his books, gongs and collection of sacred objects.

Cherry huffed her way up the staircase carrying a tray and Clip started with surprise as her grey head appeared.

'You've had no food for days now,' she gasped, her large bosom heaving. She set the tray down with a crash on an old chest, covering the papers and drawings that lay scattered across it. 'Oh my stars, that don't get any easier!'

'Here, sit down and catch your breath, Cherry,' said Clip quickly, clearing a space for her on the battered sofa. 'You shouldn't be carrying heavy trays upstairs, though it's very kind of you I must say.'

'Well, a body must eat,' she wheezed, looking around the circular room with a frown. 'Oh Master Clip, do let me send someone in to give this place a dusting.'

'No, Cherry. We've discussed this before and you know I don't like the thought of some youth poking about amongst all my precious things,' he replied.

'Then I'll do it for you!' she said, shaking her grey head in disapproval. ''Tis a mess and all that dust can't do you no good. I've heard your cough many a time, and—'

'That's nothing to do with dust,' he chuckled. 'That's too many nights spent out in the cold taking their toll, I'm afraid. No, really, Cherry, please don't fuss about my tower – you know this is how I like it.'

'Mmn,' she muttered. ''Tis not fitting for the Master o' Stonewylde to be living in such a muddle, but there's naught I can do if you won't let me clean it. But please do eat some o' this food. Marigold prepared it specially for you – look, there's a lovely piece o' beef pie and some jam sponge pudding too. We don't like seeing your bones poking out the way they do.'

'Thank you, Cherry, and please convey my thanks to your sister too. It's very kind of you both and I'll eat a little later on. Now, if you've got your breath back . . .'

'Aye,' she grunted, heaving herself to her feet, 'I best be getting along.'

She eyed the collection of African masks suspiciously and tutted at the layer of dust on the desiccated frogs that lined one of the many window-sills.

'Oh – some books arrived for you,' she said. 'They were in the entrance hall but I couldn't manage them. One o' the lads'll bring 'em up later.'

'Please, Cherry, don't send people up here,' said Clip. 'You know I really don't like being disturbed.'

'Aye, well – 'tis done now. It were Swift in fact and I didn't ask him – he offered. Now, make sure you eat that and don't forget to bring the tray back down, will you? Else I'll have to send someone up for it. I'm not having dirty plates mouldering away in here.'

Clip smiled good-naturedly at her, wishing her gone so he could return to his solitude. She clumped down the stairs and eventually he heard the door on the ground floor shut. He sighed, eyeing the tray of unwanted food with distaste. It was vital to fast before a major journey – the odd apple and handful of hazelnuts were all he'd permit himself – and now he'd have to somehow dispose of this without Cherry noticing. He appreciated her and Marigold's concern, but it was wearing to be fussed over.

He turned back to the window and then gasped in agony as, without warning, excruciating pain sliced through his abdomen.

His eyes darkened with shock and he tried to ride above it, but it gripped him with vicious coils. Clip's thin body bent double and a long groan escaped. He fell to his knees, clutching his stomach, whimpering as the pain bit deeper and deeper into his guts.

Then it was gone as suddenly as it had come. Clip straightened and took a deep, ragged breath. Was it some sort of omen of things to come? Shakily he stood up, grasping hold of the window ledge to steady himself. He went to a cupboard recessed in the ancient stone walls and selected a bottle of murky liquid. He'd prepared this remedy to ward off the emptiness that gnawed at him before a journey – maybe a draught would ease the cramp. He could cope with hunger but not pain like that. He'd no idea where it had come from and fervently hoped never to encounter it again.

He groaned again as there was another knock at the door downstairs, which this time he heard clearly. The trouble was anyone standing in the corridor on the other side of the heavy oak door couldn't hear his reply. He'd have to start bolting the door, he decided, as he really hated all these disturbances. The door opened below and a lad's voice carried up the stairs.

'Just leave the books down there please!' called Clip, leaning over the head of the spiral stairs and trying to see where the boy was. Swift – Martin's son, he thought, always a little hazy on the names and identities of that huge generation. Clip recalled the small pale-haired boy, much younger than Martin's other children.

'Oh for goddess' sake!' he muttered as he saw a blond head circling up the staircase. 'Why can't everyone just leave me alone?'

Swift surprised Clip by being a young man, and he realised with a jolt just how out of touch he was becoming. The youth was slightly built, not tall like Martin, and handsome with straight silvery blond hair that fell into his eyes. He smiled disarmingly at Clip, not in the slightest bit out of breath. He carried a large brown package that looked heavy.

'Your books!' he said cheerfully, looking around with interest.

'Very kind of you,' said Clip. 'Just put them down on that chair. Thanks for bringing them up for me, Swift.'

'My pleasure,' said the lad charmingly. 'And you remember who I am!'

'Well, I—'

'It's a beautiful place, your tower. I love all your collections.'

To Clip's dismay, the lad put the books down and sank onto the sofa with another grin.

'I'd love to hear about your travels one day,' he said. 'Father says you've travelled all over the world and I know your Story Webs are full of tales from different cultures, but you never talk about where you've been.'

'No, I suppose not. Though my travels in recent years have been negligible.'

'You must miss it,' said Swift sympathetically.

'Yes, I do. It's all I ever really wanted to do, but somehow ...' Clip spread his hands and shrugged in a gesture of acceptance at his fate.

'Father says that life doesn't always work out as we expect,' nodded Swift. 'But surely you can take time out now and go travelling again?'

'Yes, I'm hoping that next year, when—' Clip stopped abruptly, realising he shouldn't confide his plans to this boy before telling anyone else.

'Next year you'll go travelling again? That's great! Where were you thinking of going?'

Swift smiled encouragingly but Clip shook his head, frowning down at his thick felt slippers.

'Nowhere. I didn't mean that. Now, Swift, if you don't mind ...'

'I wanted to ask you something,' said the boy quickly, flicking the long straight hair out of his eyes. 'It's a bit of a strange request, but I wondered if I might call you "uncle"?'

'*Uncle?*' Clip stared at him.

'Yes, because according to my grandmother that's what you are – my uncle.'

41

Clip was completely dumbfounded at this and continued to stare at the lad. Swift looked up candidly at the tall, careworn man with his lined face and faraway pale-grey wolf's eyes.

'I was visiting Granny Violet yesterday,' he said. 'Father sends me round there with things for her, and she was talking about you – her and my Great-Aunt Vetchling and Aunt Starling. Granny said you used to like her cakes.'

Clip nodded ruefully at this.

'Granny's annoyed that Marigold makes the ceremony cakes nowadays – she said in Magus' time it was her job?'

'That's right – it's one of the things Yul changed when he became magus.'

'She's still upset about losing the job even though it was so long ago – she felt honoured to do it in the past. Anyway, she was talking about the old days which she does a lot, and she wanted to know how you were doing.'

'Really?'

Clip shuddered involuntarily at the thought of the crone. He hadn't had many dealings with her over the years, still remembering clearly how she'd spoken to him that terrible Winter Solstice Eve up at Hare Stone. Clip recalled how she'd frozen him to the spot and frightened him with her dabbling in Dark Magic. He recognised the malignant power Old Violet held and wanted nothing to do with her or the other women in her household.

'She was talking,' continued Swift blithely, 'about how you and Father were half-brothers.'

'Oh.'

Clip had no idea how to respond to this. There'd always been talk and speculation, and knowing that perhaps Martin was his half-brother had certainly coloured Clip's judgement about keeping him on at Stonewylde to run the Hall; he felt he owed the man some familial loyalty. But Violet had never made it public knowledge before that he and Martin shared the same father. He wondered vaguely why she would do so now?

'Yes, so I reckon that makes me your nephew and you my

uncle, and I wanted to be allowed to call you Uncle Clip. Is that okay then? You don't mind?'

Clip shook his head helplessly, unable to think of a good reason to object, but still sensing something not quite right about the situation. What was Old Violet up to?

'I suppose if your grandmother chooses to make it known that your father and I are half-brothers . . .'

'Thanks!' said Swift, standing up. 'I'll leave you in peace then, Uncle Clip. Hope you enjoy your new books, and maybe I could come and see you again sometime? I'm really interested to hear about your travels and look at all the stuff you've got up here.'

Clip smiled briefly, and then his eyes fell upon the unwanted tray.

'Can you get rid of that for me please, Swift? Discreetly though – don't let Marigold or Cherry see.'

As soon as the boy had gone Clip decided to escape his tower before anyone else could come barging in. He slipped a cloak over his thin robe, having abandoned ordinary clothes completely several years before, and changed his green felt slippers for the traditional brown leather Stonewylde boots. Taking his ash staff and a small flaxen bag, for Mother Earth was ever bountiful and sometimes offered the most unexpected treasures, he opened the door leading to the flat roof of his tower. From this vantage point, gazing out across the vast expanse of roofs and chimneys of the Hall, he soaked up the golden October sunshine of late afternoon and let his vision roam across Stonewylde.

The trees that massed around the Hall were every shade and hue of gold, daily shedding their final fruits, seeds and leaves onto the waiting soil. All the crops were safely gathered and the autumn sowing completed. Clip turned about slowly on the crenellated roof of the tower, which offered views over the Hall and parkland, but also the woods and farmland too. With one hand shading his eyes he looked across at the hazy fields, in soft gold focus, and reflected on the success of Stonewylde as a self-sufficient community. The cows had been brought down into the close pastures for over-wintering, the lambs were well-grown to face the cold months ahead and the geese were fattening for Yule. The slaughter of the pigs had begun in earnest now for some mediaeval methods were still interwoven with modern farming techniques, although the pork was no longer laid into salt barrels for preservation. Instead it was cured as bacon and ham or frozen in the vast freezer houses – powered by the wind-turbines – that stored so much of Stonewylde's produce.

He liked this phase of the Wheel of the Year, with the old year drawing to a close at Samhain. Even the frugal Clip appreciated the security of knowing all the produce and foods were now safely harvested and stored for the winter months ahead. He knew this was a very busy time for everyone. The tanners were working flat out to cope with the influx of animal skins waiting to be processed into leather. The flax, harvested in the summer and put to one side after retting, was now being dyed and woven on the hand looms that graced almost every cottage. Wool sheared in the late spring had been cleaned and dyed, and then either put aside for felting or to be spun into yarn. Every evening the click of wooden knitting needles could be heard throughout the Village and the Hall as new garments were made.

Diligence was still a virtue at Stonewylde and self-sufficiency from the Outside World still held sway. The people took pride in feeding and clothing themselves well and, despite the many changes since Magus' demise, consumerism had not taken a hold and traditional values had been maintained. The biggest difference was that the Hallfolk no longer lived off the backs of the Villagers; all had an equal share in the work and in the bounty of the community, and Clip's sense of moral justice was delighted at this. In the old days he'd often felt rather uncomfortable about the polarity of Stonewylde's society.

Clip descended carefully down the other stone stairway that helter-skeltered around the outside of the tower, the ancient steps worn and shiny. He slipped away from the Hall, nestling like a great golden creature amongst the trees and lawns, and made his way up into the hills behind it. The sun felt good on his face and

44

he forgot the earlier slash of pain that had so taken him by surprise. Long legs stretching, he quickly covered the distance and began to climb. After a while, with no thought to where he was heading, Clip found himself walking along the path that led to the Hare Stone.

He came here every so often, for since the Winter Solstice Eve thirteen years ago it had become a magical place for him. He'd seen his daughter moon-dance here for the first time, in her scarlet cloak within a ring of Woodsmen guarding her from danger. Here she'd honoured the rising of the Frost Moon whilst Magus had fought the final battle with his son up at Quarrycleave. Clip had never forgotten the thrill of seeing Sylvie stretch her moon-wings, stand on tiptoe and launch herself into the spiral dance, singing her ethereal song that had no words, with the silver moon reflected in her strange eyes. The sight of the hares leaping around her, the barn owl swooping low, and her hair swirling in a silver halo was something he'd carry to his grave.

Now Clip wandered up the hill past the outcrops of rocks and boulders that lay strewn below the summit and remembered the other event of that night, when Sylvie had sensed danger on the hill. He recalled the terror he'd felt as the three women had risen up from nowhere in a flurry of darkness and wickedness, and petrified him where he stood. The sight of Starling and Vetchling crushing his daughter whilst Violet capered about with a knife ready to cut her had been dreadful, and even today Clip felt uneasy about what had taken place there. The three hags had kept their heads down over the years, but Swift's remarks today had shaken Clip. Why was Violet acknowledging Martin's paternity after all this time?

Clip reached the great standing stone at the top of the hill and leant back against the rock, feeling the peculiar comfort that such sacred stones bring. He was alive to the energy of the place, receiving it and yet not diminishing it. As he stood gazing across at the sea in the distance, mist began to swirl in from the fields below. It came slowly at first, soft tendrils extending cool fingers across the warm land but gathering in mass as more cold air poured in from the sea shore. Being right on the coast and backed by hills, Stonewylde had its own microclimate which could change with remarkable speed.

His thoughts were still of Sylvie, not as she'd been all those years ago but as she was today. He loved her dearly although found this difficult to express. He and his younger brother had led a cold and unloved childhood and Clip was well aware of his stunted emotional nature, though he hoped Sylvie knew how deeply he cared for her. He'd been worried about her lately. Wrapped up though he was in his world of dreams and shadows, and bogged down in reality by the responsibility of leading Stonewylde, even he'd noticed the aura of sadness about her. She was such a gentle soul, very like him in many ways, although not cursed with the weaknesses he so despised in himself. He'd tried to shield her from the relentless duty that ownership of such a vast place entailed.

He knew that Yul, now almost twenty-nine years old and experienced and well educated, was ready and desperately keen to officially don the mantle of full leadership. Yul was a strong and intelligent man and Clip knew he could pass on the responsibility with complete confidence. Yul had the same talent for leadership as his father, but without the vices. And yet ... something wasn't quite right. Sylvie was unhappy and until he'd unravelled the problem, maybe he should hold on just a little longer. He didn't doubt Yul's love and passion for his beautiful wife, but if she was sad there must be a good reason.

His decision made, Clip closed his eyes, enjoying the warmth of the stone at his back and the coolness of the autumn mist below. Reality began to spiral away. He embraced the familiar trance sensations so easily conjured after a lifetime of journeying into other realms. With so much hallucinogen residue in his system, it was often difficult to distinguish between what was real and what was not – and even more difficult to care. For after all – what was reality other than just another layer of meaning?

He saw a beautiful golden hare, her eyes amber and her fur flecked with all shades of autumn, sitting in a pool of sunlight. Her great ears stood upright with the dark tips slightly bent outward and she looked him straight in the eye.

He glanced up above the clearing in the woods at a circling bird of prey. The buzzard mewed and called as it floated on the thermals, white wing markings clearly visible. Many corvids perched up in the branches watching the hare intently, then the great hawk let out a piercing cry and all the birds flew up out of the trees.

Now it was night time but still the hare waited, ears and whiskers twitching. She watched as the Green Man appeared from the dusky shadows, his wild hair wreathed with leaves. Together the hare and the man gazed up at the darkening sky as the full moon rose and the Goddess as Mother walked silently in the fields of the starry heavens.

But the air became cold with a terrible, black iciness, and then it was coming – an unmentionable evil that lurched and dragged itself from the Wildwood and out into the open, making all hope and beauty wilt. Slowly it slithered across the silver moon, eclipsing the brightness till all was dark and crimson. The woodland shrivelled and everything began to wither; the Green Man bowed his head in sorrow at the decay all around him. Only the hare remained undaunted, and then suddenly she leapt, her golden eyes gleaming with star fire and magic, as she flew up into the dark night sky straight into the deep blood-red eye of the moon ...

With a jolt Clip came back to the misty autumn afternoon and found himself surrounded by a sea of fog. It lapped around the island of Hare Stone where he stood with his back against the stone. The sun blazed brightly above him, failing to penetrate the cold mist that crept up from the lower ground. Clip felt his heart race from the vision he'd seen, cloaked as it was in symbolism and mystery. He'd never unravel its meaning directly – it must be approached obliquely and deciphered piece by piece – but he still felt the prickle of terror roused by the evil thing lumbering from its lair.

He blinked in the glare reflected off the white blanket below, and then a strange sight caught his eye. Was he was still dreaming? Further down the hill he saw a head, seemingly disembodied in the thick mist; a head that bobbed about as it climbed slowly towards him. It was Yul, but Yul as a boy, when his hair was wild and full of curls and bits of leaves. Then the head looked up and he saw the face, small and elfin, with pointed features and slanted green eyes that widened as they recognised him. The mouth parted to reveal sharp white teeth stretched into a gasp of shock. Not Yul at all but Yul's youngest sister – who looked as if she were about to turn and flee.

'Stop! Come up here!' called Clip, raising his staff.

She hesitated, obviously wanting to disobey, but then slowly approached him and emerged from the mist. She kept her head down and stood before him, tiny next to his lanky height.

'Blessings,' he said, trying desperately to remember her name. He was terrible with names and Yul had such a large family with all those brothers whom he always muddled up. But this girl he really ought to remember, Maizie's last one . . . there was the older sister Rosie and this girl . . . Leveret!

'Blessings,' she mumbled, fidgeting nervously.

'A very thick and sudden mist, Leveret,' he said conversationally, wishing now that he hadn't called her up here. Too late he remembered she was a strange girl, not like her mother or sister who were sociable and chatty. He doubted he'd ever spoken to her much and he felt uncomfortable being alone with her now, especially as she wouldn't meet his eye. He noticed she wore a very coarse flaxen tunic and leggings, with sandals on her feet and a bag like his own in her hand. Dressed so simply, she looked like the Stonewylde children of old. The young people had become more fashion conscious as they began to visit the Outside World regularly after the age of fifteen, but Leveret was pure Stonewylde right down to her dirty hands and the smears of lichen on her cheeks.

'What've you got in your bag?' he asked gently. 'Have you been collecting cob nuts?'

'Nothing!' she said quickly, gripping the bag tighter.

'Don't be shy – let me see,' he insisted and reached to take the flax bag. As his fingers brushed her hand she cried out and he felt a jolt like an electric shock. She moaned and then, to his dismay, she crumpled. He caught her and stood awkwardly holding her limp body upright, before deciding to set her down on the grass. He had no idea what was wrong with her; her breathing was deep and rasping and her eyes had rolled up in their sockets with only the whites showing. Clip was extremely ill at ease and smoothed the tousled dark curls away from her face, which was now sheened with perspiration. She was trembling quite severely.

'Leveret! Leveret, it's alright,' he said softly, at a loss for what to do. He racked his brain, trying to remember if Maizie or Yul had ever mentioned fainting fits. He looked down at her carefully and was struck again by her strong likeness to Yul as a boy.

Then, as suddenly as she'd collapsed, the fit was over and her eyes rolled back to normal. She gazed up at him blankly.

'The serpent in your belly will poison you,' she whispered. 'You have one year, Son of Raven.'

'*What?*' he gasped. 'What do you mean?'

She shook her head in confusion.

'Did you see the evil?' she asked, her voice barely audible. 'Did you feel it? It's coming – it'll eclipse everything good at Stonewylde and it's coming for us now.'

She shuddered, and he saw tears well in the corners of her clear green eyes.

'Sit up now, Leveret,' he said firmly, trying to pull her upright. 'Sit up and snap out of this.'

A few minutes later she was back to normal and looking embarrassed.

'Do you do this often, go into a trance?' Clip asked as they made their way together down the hill. She shrugged.

'I used to pass out quite a lot, I think, although I could never remember it. Mother called it my blanknesses and Hazel calls it absences, but I thought it was getting better. Please don't tell

Mother or she'll make a fuss and keep me cooped up even more.'

He nodded – she hadn't come to any harm, after all.

'You never did show me what you'd collected,' he said.

She grimaced, still reluctant, but passed her bag to him.

'Fly Agaric!' he exclaimed, looking inside the bag at the large, brilliant red toadstool with its white spots. 'What a beauty! But you know that's not allowed, Leveret. What are you going to do with it?'

She looked up at him solemnly and he was struck by the strange beauty of her green eyes framed with dark, glossy curls.

'You know what I'm going to do with it – why does anyone gather such a thing? It's for Samhain. But please, please don't tell on me. I'd get into such trouble and I do know what I'm doing, I promise. Please?"

He smiled down at her, liking her all of a sudden. She was very different and it must be hard for her living in her brother's shadow. Yet she had a quiet confidence that implied she did indeed know what she was doing, so he nodded.

'Alright, I won't say a word. But be very careful, Leveret – we both know how powerful Fly can be. You know how to prepare it? Only take a very tiny amount. And one more thing – in return for my silence.'

'Yes?' she asked, looking up into his kindly face.

'Show me where you found it. It's the best specimen I've seen this year.'

4

'Remember I'm going out this evening, Leveret,' said Maizie as she wiped down the scrubbed table in the kitchen to remove all traces of their meal. 'We're meeting in the Barn to sort out the food for Samhain. It'll be a really good feast this year with the harvest we've had. I want you to carry on with the weaving tonight while I'm gone.'

'But Mother, you know how useless I am at weaving,' groaned Leveret. She'd planned a pleasant evening in the scullery decanting elderberry wine ready to smuggle some up to Mother Heggy's cottage at a later date. She intended to add it to another tincture she was preparing.

''Tis about time you knuckled down to learning these sorts o' things,' said Maizie firmly, wringing out the piece of cloth with a grip of steel. 'You're always saying that you want to stay at Stonewylde when you're an adult, after you've finished your education, of course. So you'll need to make cloth for your family like every woman does.'

'But I'll have different skills, Mother, which I can trade for cloth that other women have made. Like Hazel – she doesn't weave.'

Maizie's eyes gleamed.

'Like Hazel? Are you saying that you want to be a doctor, Leveret?'

She stopped fussing over the kitchen surfaces and grasped her

51

daughter by the shoulders, peering into her eyes. Leveret tried to look away, uncomfortable under the scrutiny.

'No, I meant . . .'

'Because Leveret, I've said nothing until now, but 'tis my dearest, dearest wish that you become a doctor like Hazel. Another proper doctor for Stonewylde.'

Leveret started to protest and tried to move away but Maizie gripped her harder and carried on relentlessly.

'I've seen you messing about with potions and herbs, don't think I haven't noticed. I know you've a natural gift for healing. Remember when little Snowdrop had those awful stomach cramps and it was you that cured her? And when the chickens got that mange? And all the wild creatures you've healed? Oh Leveret, you're a natural born doctor! I've talked to Yul about it and we thought—'

'No, Mother!' said Leveret firmly, pulling away. 'I don't want to be a doctor. I know what it means, all the years at university and in hospitals. I've told you: I'm not leaving Stonewylde. This is where I belong and where I want to be, not in some horrible place in the Outside World.'

'But Leveret, 'tis only a few years of learning and you'd be back in the holidays like all the others, helping with the harvest and suchlike. And it'd be worth it! Just think—'

'No! I don't want to go Outside at all.'

'But you have to leave after your exams to go on to college for your higher exams. And if—'

'No, Mother! You don't understand – I'm not leaving at all. Not ever. I'll do my exams here because you said I had to, though I'd rather have done the practical course like my brothers and Rosie. I only agreed to the exams because you said it'd make you proud, but I'm not doing any more after my last year at school here. I know exactly what I want to do and it's not studying in the Outside World.'

Maizie stared at her youngest child in dismay, two bright spots of anger burning on her plump cheeks.

'Oh, so you do know what you want to be, then? And what is

that, Leveret? A farm labourer like Gefrin? Or a tanner like Sweyn? Or in the orchards with Geoffrey? Maybe thatching like Gregory? Or in the dairy with your sister?'

'No, I—'

'You're the only one with a bright star inside you, Leveret! The only one who could go on to university and study and—'

'Except for Yul.'

'Well yes. Yul did it and you could be like him too! You're a very clever girl – don't throw it all away.'

'I won't throw it all away. I want to be a healer, a herbalist, and—'

'Then be a proper doctor!'

'NO!! I won't go away and study to be a doctor! I want to be a Wise Woman, Mother, like there used to be at Stonewylde.'

'*A Wise Woman?*' Maizie's voice cracked in disbelief. 'You mean like that nasty old biddy Violet? And her crazed sister Vetchling? Is that what you mean?'

'No! I mean like old Mother Heggy.'

There was a silence, then Maizie let out a harsh laugh and banged the iron skillet she was drying onto the table. She shook her head, the spots on her cheeks grown now to large flushes.

'What would you know about that old crone? 'Twas because of *her* and her mad prophecies that your poor brother suffered all those years. 'Twas because of *her* that Magus turned against me and became such a wicked man. If she'd only kept her wild rantings to herself! She were raving mad and she's a lot to answer for!'

'But I thought you all honoured her? Yul and Sylvie honoured her and I heard she was gifted and magical.'

'Oh yes she was, and Yul and Sylvie did honour her right enough because 'twas she as brought 'em together. But Old Heggy caused so much misery too, with her crazy caperings up at the Stone Circle when your brother were born, summoning the Dark Angel, blighting the boy's childhood. And you want to be like her? Hah! If you want to end up a filthy old hag on a hill with no friends nor family, my girl, then good luck to you!'

Leveret looked sadly at her mother, who'd worked herself up into a spitting rage. She knew just how upset Maizie was but there was nothing she could do.

'I'm really sorry, Mother. I don't want to disappoint you, but it's better you know now, isn't it?'

'Oh don't you worry about how I feel!' snapped Maizie, snatching her cloak from the peg. 'Next year you'll be living up at the Hall along with all the other fifteen-year-olds. Then I can wash my hands o' the lot of you. Nearly twenty-nine years I've spent raising children and I'll be glad to be done with it. 'Tis a thankless task, I can tell you. You go ahead, Leveret, and become a "Wise Woman". But don't expect any customers. Folk at Stonewylde want a proper doctor nowadays, not some old biddy with dandelion tea and love potions, and Yul won't let you do it for long. Everyone here has to earn their living and he'll find you something fitting, I'm sure. Maybe he'll let you grow vegetables up at the Hall. And in the meantime, my girl, I want this cloth woven tonight. Do you understand?'

'Yes, Mother.'

'Sweyn should be here any minute and—'

'No! Oh Mother, please don't get him round! You know I'm behaving myself and I promise I'll stay in and do the weaving. *Please!*'

But Maizie smiled tightly.

'You let me down once too often and now I don't trust you, Leveret. Sweyn's coming to keep an eye on you and from now on him or Gefrin'll make sure you behave yourself. I'm very glad Sylvie thought of it.'

'Please, Mother, I *beg* you! You don't know what he's like when he gets me alone.'

'You're wasting your breath, Leveret, and talking rubbish too. I told you all this before, many a time – I won't listen to your lies about your brothers. Sweyn's a fine young man and I'm proud o' him. That sounds like him now.'

The front door crashed open and Sweyn barged in. It was as if Alwyn had been reincarnated for his youngest son was the image of him, right down to the gingery bristles on his sausage fingers and the brutish under-bite of his pugnacious lower jaw. He even wore an enormous brown leather coat as his father had done, and he looked older than sixteen. The stink of the tannery came with him into the cottage.

'Sweyn! Just in time!'

Maizie went over to peck his ruddy cheek and he hugged her gruffly.

'Alright, Mother?'

'I am now. I've left you cake and some nice cheese in the pantry, and there's cider too if you fancy it. Take what you want, son.'

'I will, Mother – you know how I miss my home comforts. Gefrin said he might come by too.'

'Good. Thank you, Sweyn – I'm grateful for this. She shouldn't need looking after at her age but there you are – she's let me down once again.'

'Has she upset you tonight? You're looking like a rosy apple.'

Maizie bobbed her head, curls shaking, and patted his arm as he hung up his coat.

'I should be used to it by now. But never mind that – I don't want to think about it. She's been told to weave tonight so you make sure she does. No sloping off to her room in a sulk – she's got work to do.

Sweyn smiled and nodded.

'Don't you worry, Mother, I'll sort her out.'

As soon as Maizie had gone, Leveret sat on the stool before the loom and started to organise the shuttles. She kept her head down so her hair hung over her face, hoping Sweyn would be distracted by the thought of food and drink in the pantry. He was as greedy as their father had been – not that Leveret remembered him, for she'd only been a year old when he'd collapsed in his chair. But she'd heard about him from Rosie, Geoffrey and Gregory, who remembered Alwyn with fear and loathing. Yet even now Maizie rarely spoke out against him. He was their father, after all. Yul never, ever mentioned him.

Sweyn had sat down comfortably in the great armchair by the fire; the late October nights were getting chilly. He relaxed into the old, soft leather and surveyed his younger sister. Far from resenting his mother's request, he was delighted. He'd moved up to the Hall last year along with the others in their final year at school, and had been missing his favourite pastime – tormenting Leveret. Over the years he and his older brother Gefrin had developed it into a fine art. Although neither of them was very bright, they were inventive in their torture and clever at avoiding detection.

Leveret had never known anything but their constant bullying, and if something were ever noticed, it was always put down to the rough and tumble of growing up in a large family. A small girl with older brothers, so Maizie had always said airily, should expect some teasing and Leveret was the youngest of seven. Since they'd left home she'd generally been able to avoid them and was no longer bruised by their casual violence or intimidated by their constant tormenting. But by asking them to keep an eye on her, Maizie had given them the perfect opportunity to resume their cruelty.

'Go and get me the food she's left,' commanded Sweyn, watching Leveret fiddling with the loom. She decided not to protest and went into the pantry to fetch the cake and cheese. She was sure he'd already have eaten a good meal in the great Dining Hall tonight, but Sweyn could always find room for more. He took the plate from her without a word and began to eat. The moment she sat down he spoke again, through a mouthful of food.

'Get me some cider too.'

She stood up once more and poured him a tankard of cider from the small barrel in the pantry. She hoped he wouldn't drink too much because he never held his drink well. But he downed it in one long, noisy draught and demanded another. It was when she sat down again and was commanded once more to get up and stoke the fire that Leveret realised he didn't plan to let her do any weaving at all.

The door opened and Gefrin stood at the threshold grinning. At seventeen he was a year older than Sweyn but seemed the younger of the two. He was lankier and more scrawnily built, although the two years spent farm labouring had developed his strength and stamina. He had an inane grin that rarely left his face and took his lead from Sweyn, who was marginally brighter than him. They were close as brothers, paired by their position in a large family and united in their enjoyment of teasing Leveret, whom they both deeply resented.

'Alright? Mother gone already?'

'Yeah. Get Gefrin a tankard too, Hare-brain.'

When she returned with it they both sat and looked at her.

'Don't improve with age, does she?' laughed Sweyn.

'Still ugly and skinny. I pity the man who ends up with her.'

'Doubt anyone'd have her – nobody'd be that desperate.'

Leveret ignored them. They'd been mocking her looks since she was a small child and by now she thoroughly believed what they said.

'Is there anything else or can I get on with the weaving now?' she asked evenly.

'Are you getting uppity?'

'No.'

'Is she meant to be weaving then?' asked Gefrin, gulping at his cider.

'Yeah, and she's upset Mother good and proper tonight. Her cheeks were bright red – you know how they go when she's rattled.'

'Can't have that, can we?' giggled Gefrin, shaking the lank hair from his face.

'No we can't,' agreed Sweyn. 'Poor old Mother. Things have

slipped since we left, haven't they? I think Leveret needs to be taught a lesson tonight.'

'Yes, a good lesson. What did you have in mind?'

'Let's have a little think. More cider, Lev! More cider, and then you can wait out in the scullery. Shut the door behind you.'

They wouldn't let her take a cloak or shawl and made her stand in the chilly scullery for a good half hour. When she was summoned back inside she was shivering and pinched with cold.

'Don't stand next to the fire!' said Sweyn sharply. 'No point trying to warm up, not where you're going.'

'No, not where you're going!'

They both laughed and Leveret took a deep breath, keeping her eyes down. She contemplated running, but there was little point – Gefrin's long legs were faster than hers and having to chase and catch her always made them worse.

'Mother'll be really angry if I don't do any weaving,' she said neutrally.

'Too right she will,' agreed Gefrin.

'I expect she'll punish you for it. Poor Lev.'

Sweyn heaved himself up from the chair and burped loudly. He gripped her arm and swung her round so she stumbled into him. Then he pushed her away into Gefrin who also shoved her hard, making her fall into the table and bang her hip. They laughed again; this had been a favourite childhood game they called 'Pass the hare'.

'Come on then, up you go,' said Sweyn, pushing her towards the stairs.

'Where?' she whispered, her heart sinking.

'You know where,' said Gefrin. 'Have a guess.'

'Your favourite place!' chuckled Sweyn. 'Somewhere you haven't been for a long time.'

'Far too long, seeing as how you used to love it when you were little. Good job you're still little.'

Leveret stopped at the foot of the staircase, panic rising within her.

'Please!' she said quietly, her mouth dry. 'Please don't put me in there. I didn't fit inside last time and that was over a year ago.'

Gefrin giggled and poked her in the back sharply.

'Upstairs, Lev. You're going in the cupboard and we'll make you fit.'

'Please! Sweyn, please, I—'

'Shut up, Leveret – you should've thought before you upset our Mother. Good job we came round tonight to put you straight. UPSTAIRS!'

They dragged and pushed her up the staircase to the first floor and then up the wide ladder to the attic above, where Rosie and Yul had slept all those years ago in the tiny bedrooms under the eaves. In one of the rooms, tucked in a nook between the roof and a wall, was a small cupboard built into the recess and extending back under the eaves. It was here that, as a small child, they'd locked Leveret in the darkness for hours on end.

They'd filled her head with frightening tales which they elaborated on each time, of how a child had once died in the tiny space and how, if she were very quiet, she'd hear his ghostly heart-beat and soft breathing. It was in here that her trances had begun, for they'd made her so frightened that she always lost consciousness. Not that the boys knew this – once the door was bolted, they assumed her silence was down to terror and when they dragged her back out they put her paleness and trembling down to fear.

It was their favourite torture and the one they generally reserved for occasions when they had plenty of time and were bored with everything else. The fun lay in getting her up the stairs and stuffing her into the cupboard; once she was actually in there they lost interest and sometimes they went off and forgot about her. They'd warned her once, long ago, of the folly of calling out. That was what had happened to the other child, they said – he'd tried to call out and a rat had leapt at his throat in the darkness and he'd bled slowly to death. She'd learnt to keep quiet early on; the sound of her strangled voice in the darkness just frightened her more.

'Didn't think we'd be doing this again,' laughed Gefrin as they crowded into the cramped room that had once been Yul's. Sweyn leant over and pulled back the bolt of the cupboard door. It was low and had never been high enough for her to stand in, even as a child; now she couldn't even sit up in it.

'It's her own fault for being such a naughty girl,' he grunted, shoving Leveret towards it. 'Get in there – you're wasting time. Move!'

'No!' she cried, wriggling and trying to get away from the dark, gaping mouth of the tiny cupboard. 'I'm not going in there! *No!*'

Gefrin crushed her down, twisting her flailing arms, and Sweyn kicked her hard. Together they manhandled her onto her knees and forced her to crawl into the small space. She had to crouch sideways with her knees bent up to her chin and her head wedged down. Her shoulder and arm still poked outside but Sweyn started to shut the old wooden door, pushing and squeezing her in.

'No, no, please Sweyn! I beg you – don't!'

He stopped and looked at her, with her face squashed up and twisted sideways against her knees.

'What?'

'Please don't do this,' she whimpered, her voice high with terror. 'I can't breathe – it's too tight and I might die in here. Please don't shut me in.'

'Well, I'm not sure. What do you think, Gef?'

'Ooh, I don't know. Shall we let her out? It's so hard to decide, isn't it?'

'Let her out or lock her in? Choices, choices. I think . . . LOCK HER IN!'

With a yell he shoved violently on the door and her arm and shoulder were crammed inside. He pushed and pushed on the thick wooden door, harder and harder. Gradually the breath was forced out of her and somehow her body squeezed and squashed into the tiny space. The crack of light gradually disappeared and the bolt was finally driven into its socket. The darkness was complete and the smell made her heart almost stop – the smell that haunted her nightmares, of old wood and damp thatch with something decaying too. If she'd been rational she'd have realised it was only a mouse or bird, but the tale of the dead child still lingered in her subconscious.

Leveret would've been trembling violently with absolute terror, but she was so tightly squashed and contorted that no movement was possible. Very quickly she felt her feet and hands go numb and she couldn't take a proper breath for her lungs were so compressed. She had to take small, shallow breaths that hurt and made her feel dizzy. She heard muffled laughter on the other side of the door and then footsteps receded as her brothers left her trapped in there. Leveret took a constricted breath and her eyes rolled up in their sockets.

In the office, Yul and Clip sat on the leather sofas facing each other in silence. Yul sipped his coffee and regarded his uncle steadily. Lamplight fell onto Clip's lined face and Yul thought how he'd aged lately, becoming more other-worldly than ever before. He seemed never to change his threadbare blue robe and his long white-blond hair was stringy and matted. Only his eyes blazed as brightly as before, pale grey in his thin, whiskery face.

Clip was thinking that he'd stepped back in time. Were it not for the glossy dark curls and deep grey eyes, the handsome man opposite him, as taut and controlled as a coiled spring, could've been his brother. They were virtually identical; that chiselled face, the powerful body – Yul even tapped his thigh impatiently in the same way that Magus had done and spoke in the same deep, softly resonant voice.

'I want to abandon the Death Dance altogether this year,' said Yul without preamble. 'It's a disgusting custom and has far outlived its original purpose.'

'It'd be a mistake to just abandon it,' said Clip quietly. 'I agree it's outmoded and unnecessary, but to simply forbid them to do it this year at such short notice would be cruel. You know how the older folk value it. Let it be known that next year the labyrinth will no longer be built in the Stone Circle. People could continue the custom up in the clearing by the Yew of Death if they wanted, which would still be appropriate with the pyre built there. But you need to give the people some notice rather than announce it now.'

'I don't want it to take place this year,' said Yul, almost as if Clip hadn't spoken. 'I said so last year and the year before that I wanted it stopped once and for all.'

'You did, and I advised against it,' replied Clip evenly. Yul could be as dominating and even as arrogant as his father, but Clip wasn't scared of him as he'd been of his brother. If Yul possessed a similar cruel streak then he had it firmly under control, for Clip had never seen any evidence of it. Nor was he manipulative or devious, as Magus had been. If Yul had an opinion he expressed it directly, although sometimes this forthrightness had its own difficulties.

'I don't want it taking place this year,' Yul repeated. 'I intend to tell the Elders at the Council Meeting tomorrow.'

'No,' said Clip quietly. 'You have—'

'Yes!' said Yul. 'I won't allow it! As the magus I think I have the right to decide on anything to do with ceremonies and rituals. It's my decision to make, not yours.'

'You have to give people notice,' insisted Clip. 'You can't act so suddenly like this. Wait until next year, Yul – by Samhain next year . . . things will be different.'

Yul put his coffee cup down onto the table and looked hard at Clip.

'What do you mean by that?'

Clip also set down his cup and gazed back at Yul. His likeness to Magus really was uncanny. He recalled sitting here all those years ago with a cake tin in his lap whilst his brother over-rode his feeble objections and disquiet. He hated being in this position; all he wanted was peace and harmony, not power struggles.

'Well?'

Yul was as still as a panther about to spring. Clip sighed and turned his gaze to the framed photo of Sylvie on a side table, hoping that he was taking the right course of action. There was a sense of inevitability about it all.

'I'm prepared to step down this coming year. By next Samhain I'll be gone and then you can do what you like.'

Yul jerked and his eyes widened. His sharp intake of breath told Clip just what a surprise this was, but he quickly regained his composure.

'Excellent news!' he said slowly. 'What's brought this on? It's thirteen years since my father died and I was beginning to think you intended to lead the community for ever.'

'That was never my intention. You know I've never wanted leadership of Stonewylde.'

'Precisely! You promised that as soon as everything was on an even keel you'd leave me in charge, but it's been so many years that I wondered if you'd ever hand over. Why the change of heart?'

'Because you're ready now.'

'Clip, I've been ready for years! Of course I was too young when Magus died, but when I came back after University you should've retired then.'

'You weren't ready then – you thought you were but you weren't, and neither was Sylvie. But now . . . I'm longing to leave Stonewylde and travel the world, to follow my star. I want no more responsibilities or ties, just freedom.'

'I take it you've told no one else this news yet? Not Sylvie?'

'No, you're the first. I've been thinking about it very carefully. I want to do what's right and not shirk my duties, but I think I've paid my dues now, done everything I can to redress my past laziness and wrong-doing. The slate is clean and I feel the time has come where I can leave Stonewylde with a clear conscience, knowing I've done my best for everyone. So during the year ahead I'll shift all the responsibility to the pair of you and I'll legally sign everything over as well.'

Yul nodded but then frowned.

'You said to the pair of us. I realise that on paper it'll be shared, of course. But I'll be running Stonewylde, not Sylvie. I don't want her put under any sort of pressure or stress – you know how delicate she is. She can take part in some of the ceremonies if she wants, but all decision making and actual leadership of the estate will come to me.'

Clip looked into Yul's eyes. They met his unwaveringly.

'How does Sylvie feel about that?' he asked. 'I thought she believed it would be an equal partnership. Does *she* want you to do everything and not make any contribution herself?'

'I expect so. She'll agree if I say so.'

Clip raised his eyebrows at this.

'I think you're being a little high-handed, Yul. Surely Sylvie has some say in this? She seems—'

'This is one area where I won't compromise. I won't do anything to risk her becoming ill again. Hazel said it was due to too much pressure, too many demands on her. So there'll be no pressure and no demands. All she has to worry about are the girls and they're at Nursery anyway.'

'It wasn't pressure that caused Sylvie's breakdown, surely? We all know it was a hormone imbalance after Bluebell was born – puerperal psychosis. She's long over that, Yul, and she's perfectly healthy now.'

'Yes, because I've made sure she leads a stress-free life. She has no worries or burdens at all and she's completely carefree.'

'That's as may be, but she's not happy.'

'Of course she's happy!' he snapped, stung by Clip's observation.

'I really don't think she is. Why not talk to her and find out what's wrong. But don't assume she'll do everything you say – my daughter has a mind of her own and she's much tougher than you give her credit for. I'm not prepared to hand anything over to you alone if Sylvie isn't in complete agreement.'

Yul glared at him.

'I'll thank you to keep your views on our marriage to yourself. I think I know whether or not my own wife is happy, and her happiness has no bearing on running Stonewylde anyway. Sylvie wouldn't have a clue where to begin. It's such a complex venture with so many difficult issues and problems – she doesn't have the knowledge or skills to deal with any of it. '

'I recall she studied agricultural management and business studies at university especially so that she could one day run the estate,' said Clip mildly. 'I'd say Sylvie was far better trained in the skills needed to run Stonewylde than you'd appear to be. You chose to study the Arts.'

'On yours and Miranda's advice,' muttered Yul, scowling. 'You said I should broaden my intellect and understanding of the world.'

'Quite so. You couldn't even read until the age of sixteen and had no knowledge of – or interest in – anything outside Stonewylde. You needed to expand your horizons and I'm sure you don't regret it.'

'Of course not. But since then, I've also studied estate management, agriculture, sustainability, alternative power, ecological issues ... you know I never stopped studying. There's so much I still don't know and I want to learn it all. But I think I know a great deal more than Sylvie about the best way to run Stonewylde, whatever she may've learnt years ago at university.'

'Just talk to her – see what she has to say on the subject.'

'I know what she has to say about it. Sylvie and I talk all the time. You've got the wrong idea about her and what she feels – she's perfectly happy and she'll willingly do whatever I advise her.'

Yul stood up and stretched, seeming to fill the room. Looking down at Clip he indicated subtly, but leaving no doubt, that the conversation was now over.

'If this really is your final year then I'm prepared to allow the labyrinth to be built one last time up at the Stone Circle. But I shall let it be known at the meeting tomorrow that this will be the final one. Thank you for your time, Clip – and your wonderful news.'

As Clip left the office he felt like a servant who'd been dismissed.

5

Sylvie sat alone in the circle of chairs laid out on the stone-flagged floor of the Galleried Hall. The huge carved wooden chair with boars' heads on its arms dominated the circle; this was where Clip sat, as leader of the community. Sylvie was the first to arrive for the Council of Elders meeting, looking forward to hearing the annual reports that were always presented at this special meeting the day before Samhain. Earlier Yul had told her that there was really no need to bother herself with what promised to be a long and probably tedious day. But she'd been determined not to miss this meeting.

She gazed up at the Green Man motifs carved on the ceiling bosses of the ancient roof, remembering Professor Siskin and all he'd told her about the history of Stonewylde. He'd been convinced that Yul was the Green Man of Stonewylde, returning to take his rightful place at the heart of the community. Yul – her beloved husband. He'd awoken her early that morning with kisses, before the children could disturb them. She recalled the feel of his skin under her fingertips, how she melted when his mouth found hers. She loved the way his eyes darkened with longing and urgency, and how clear and bright they were afterwards when he lay propped on an elbow gazing down at her.

The years had not caused their hunger for each other to abate, although she wished that they still made love up in the hills or amongst the bracken in the woods as they'd done in the early days. He was always so gentle and careful now, and they never indulged their passion outside the comfort of the bedroom. This morning had been perfect and Yul had seemed so happy, much more like his old self. He'd watched her as she lay drowsy and smiling, his hand tenderly stroking the hair back from her face. He'd told her how much he loved her, that she was his whole world, and how lucky he was to have such a beautiful, loving wife. All her recent feelings of neglect vanished in the warmth of his attention. He'd then made tea for them both and sat talking with her until the girls woke up and came bundling in for their morning cuddle.

Sylvie sighed happily, her body still languid and satiated from love-making despite a brisk shower and the walk down to the Village Nursery with her daughters. She was pleased with herself for getting to this meeting and being the first one here as she felt that Stonewylde was slipping away from her. She needed to get back in touch and today would be her first step in doing so. She'd listen very carefully to everyone's reports and try to find herself a niche in the running of Stonewylde.

Gradually the members of the Council arrived, greeting one another and taking their places in the circle. There were representatives from every field: Miranda, Dawn and Rowan from the three schools, Martin and Cherry from the Hall, Edward, Hart and Robin from the farms, orchards and dairy, Greenbough from the woods, Tom and Maizie from the Village, Harold from Stonewylde.com, Hazel the doctor, and of course, Clip as the owner, with Sylvie as his heir, and Yul as the magus.

They filed in, taking a seat until all were present except Clip. The great carved chair stood empty at the head of the circle and Yul looked impatiently at his watch. Surely Clip wouldn't forget the most important meeting of the year, where every member presented the report they'd prepared on their area of the community. Clip had insisted on running the estate as a committee, not wanting a return to the autocracy of Magus' rule, although he'd long-since delegated the organisation of the meetings to his son-in-law.

Stonewylde did need a leader, someone with the vision and ability to hold the whole thing together. Clip knew that but had been openly worried that, given the freedom, Yul would abuse his power and gradually take over altogether until Stonewylde was run just as it had been in Magus' day. Yul often became exasperated when the discussions went round in circles with people arguing endlessly over a minor point. He made decisions quickly and intuitively and had no patience with debate and woolliness. It was mainly for this reason – his concerns about Yul's over-confidence – that Clip had held on for so long.

The fifteen people already present sat chatting easily together as they waited, sipping the coffee and herbal teas served by youngsters on work detail that week. Cherry eyed the three teenagers critically, for they were under her jurisdiction.

'I still don't like them silly skirts,' she muttered, glaring at one of the girls.

'Oh Cherry!' laughed Miranda. 'It's what everyone's wearing in the Outside World. You need to take a trip yourself and see what's in fashion, or at least watch the television occasionally. That skirt is nothing, really.'

''Taint decent,' grumbled Cherry. 'They'll catch their death o' cold when the weather turns.'

'We all will if something's not done soon about the boilers,' agreed Martin. 'My report will be depressing for some. There's a lot of work needs doing at the Hall in the year ahead.'

'Same in the Village,' said Tom. 'A whole load o' work to keep the cottages in repair, and we have to do something soon about the young 'uns wanting their own places. We've no room and that's a fact.'

He shook his grizzled head and slurped at his tea.

'I've got some ideas about that issue,' said Hazel. 'But I'll wait till we give our reports. How's your arthritis now, Greenbough?'

'Still playing me up when 'tis damp, but mustn't grumble. I think after this year ahead I'll put myself out to pasture though.

'Tis all a bit much for me in the woods nowadays and my goodwife keeps on as how I should be biding at home with her in my old age.'

'You and me both,' said Hart, who'd taken over from Old Stag in the orchards a few years ago but was advanced in years himself. 'Reckon I'm about ready to do my last harvest.'

'And how are the schools getting on with the Samhain preparations?' Sylvie asked. Yul and Harold were quietly discussing something, excluding themselves from the general chat.

'Very well,' smiled Dawn. 'The crows are all painted now and they look lovely.'

'The Seniors are finishing carving the Jack o' Lanterns today,' said Miranda. 'They'll put them up in the Barn tonight.'

'Celandine and Bluebell were very excited about their Samhain masks,' Sylvie said to Rowan, trying to draw her into the conversation. At twenty-nine, Rowan was a beauty, tall and statuesque with rich brown hair and skin like cream. As a result of her stint as May Queen all those years ago, she'd given birth to a pretty little girl called Faun, and had then taken advantage of the changes at Stonewylde and continued her education. Rowan was a determined and patient young woman and several years later, having worked in the Nursery as Faun grew up, she eventually took over the running of the place as the older women retired.

Rowan continued the excellent traditions, where the children roamed out of doors for much of the day and played freely. She combined this Stonewylde philosophy with what she'd learnt at college about child development, and did an excellent job as head of the Nursery. She was quiet and reserved, raising her daughter with the help of her family and never looking to be hand-fasted; she made no secret of the fact that Magus was the only man she'd ever loved. Sylvie found her difficult to engage in conversation even though she saw Rowan every day at the Nursery. Rowan nodded, agreeing that the masks had been particularly artistic this year.

'And they're really looking forward to the Samhain dance,'

continued Sylvie, determined to get her talking. 'Celandine told me how pleased you were with it.'

'It's hard not to be pleased with Celandine,' said Rowan. 'Her dancing is better than anyone else's. I think she has a rare gift.'

'Thank you,' said Sylvie, glowing with pride. 'And how's Faun getting on at school? I noticed her in the library the other day. She's so tall and such a beauty, isn't she?'

Rowan glanced at Sylvie and looked away quickly. She shuffled her report and replied a little stiffly that Faun seemed to be doing well in her first year at Senior School. Sylvie gave up and spoke to Dawn instead, recalling her recent conversation with Miranda.

'What do you think of our latest arrivals at the Hall School?' she asked innocently. She liked Dawn and had been so pleased when the Council of Elders had agreed to her return, after graduating as a teacher. Very few Hallfolk had stayed after Yul took over as magus, but Dawn had always been kind to Sylvie when all the others had ostracised her and Sylvie knew she had a good soul. Dawn, like Rowan, had worked her way up and was now head teacher at the Village School which all children aged seven to twelve attended. Everyone was taught to read and write of course, and Dawn blended sound pedagogy with the Stonewylde way of life.

She noticed Dawn blush slightly and smiled to herself, thinking it was high time that Dawn found herself a partner.

'They both seem very nice indeed,' she replied. 'The art teacher, David, already has some ideas about an art project involving the older students coming into the Village and working with our little ones.'

'That sounds interesting,' said Sylvie. 'Let me know, won't you Dawn, if there's anything I can do in the school. I'd love to help out now that the girls are in Nursery full time.'

Just then Clip arrived, apologising for his tardiness. He still wore his cloak and his boots were slightly muddy; he'd obviously been outside and forgotten the time. Yul scowled at him and glanced pointedly at his watch, but nobody else seemed to mind

71

and finally the meeting commenced. It had been a good year for harvest and many of the reports were very positive. The three women who ran the schools spoke first and everyone was pleased to hear that the children were thriving. However Miranda expressed concerns again about the lack of space and facilities for so many teenagers.

'But we're coming to the end of the bulge, aren't we?' said Yul. 'This latest year group at Senior School is the last one born in my father's time. All the younger year groups are much smaller and now we've firmly established the two children per family rule, this will be a diminishing issue.'

'True,' Miranda agreed, 'but there's still the problem of how to cope now. We're bursting at the seams. And looking ahead, all these present teenagers will be growing up in the next few years and producing their own children, so we'll have another bulge in a few years' time.'

'Aye,' growled Tom, clearing his throat, 'I wanted to say something on that matter. 'Tis sort of part o' this problem. A whole load of these youngsters are adults now and they're wanting their own cottages. Wanting to settle down and be handfasted and raise their own families. Me and Maizie been talking about this and we're worried there ain't no spare cottages. What's to be done about that?'

''Tis a problem right enough,' said Edward. 'My eldest, Iris, is hoping to be handfasted next year but seems they'll have to live at home with the rest of us.'

'If I may speak about this?' asked Hazel. 'The shortage of cottages may not seem related to my field, but I've been thinking about it for a while now. We haven't yet heard from Harold, but the way the business is going, more and more women are working almost full-time hours. This is having an impact on the elderly living in the Village. Whereas in the past, the women would be about in their homes for most of the day and able to care for their parents, that's not always the case nowadays. And if, as I suspect, Harold's report is going to tell us that more female labour is needed in future, this problem will only get worse.'

She looked around the circle and saw that several people were nodding. All were thinking of a recent incident where a very old woman had fallen and not been found till too late, when her family returned home and visited her in the evening.

'So although it goes against what's traditionally been seen as the Stonewylde way, living and dying in your own home, I was wondering if we could move the more frail and less mobile folk up into a separate part of the Hall, into a sort of geriatric wing if you like. We have rooms near the hospital wing which are no good as classrooms for the youngsters, but with a bit of adapting could be made into comfortable accommodation for the elderly. And our medical staff would be close at hand too.'

There was a buzz of comment which Yul cut through.

'Thanks for coming up with that solution, Hazel. Maybe at our next meeting when I've ... when we've had a chance to think about it, we can talk some more. It could certainly help create some space in the Village. Some of the elderly live alone in cottages which could accommodate a couple or family. It does seem like a good idea.'

'Just to return to the issue of my Seniors,' said Miranda, 'Although they all have a choice to continue their education in an Outside college or remain in Stonewylde and apprentice to a trade, the majority of those who choose to study finish their two years' further education and then return here. Very few are choosing to move permanently to the Outside World, preferring to live and work at Stonewylde.'

Yul nodded; this had been one of the earlier decisions made. Every person growing up at Stonewylde would have access to further education, even university if they wished, and would then have to choose to either live and work permanently in the Outside World, or return home.

'So my point is this,' continued Miranda, 'I'd like more guidance for them earlier as to what work will be available at Stonewylde. What choices of trade or jobs they'll have and what opportunities there'll be if they stay here – particularly for the girls. The traditional roles are quite restrictive and now they're thinking about their vocations, but there isn't a proper system in place to give them advice about their options.'

'That's largely because Stonewylde.com is still so new and we haven't really established a careers guidance system,' said Yul. 'But I think after Harold's report in a minute we'll be clearer on that. Certainly we need to co-ordinate better between the labour available and the jobs to be filled.'

'I could do that!' cried Sylvie. Everyone turned to look at her, startled at her excited outburst, and she blushed. 'I mean, I could liaise with Yul and Harold about what opportunities there are, and which trades are likely to need more apprentices. And I could have a little office where I meet regularly with every teenager to talk about their interests and ambitions, what they're best at, and—'

'Very nice idea, Sylvie,' said Yul, 'and we'll talk about it later, though we'll probably find that sort of role is better suited to one of the teachers.'

'But—'

'We'll discuss it privately,' he said smoothly. 'And now I think we need to break for lunch.'

Tables were brought in by students and lunch was served, as it was so noisy and busy in the Dining Hall. Maizie ate her food pensively, recalling what had just been said about further education and vocational training for the youngsters. She thought sadly of the recent row with Leveret. She'd hoped for so long that her youngest child would become a doctor. All the signs had been promising; Leveret was a natural healer and was certainly bright enough for the long years of study involved. But on the night of their fight she'd been so adamantly against it that Maizie now despaired of it ever happening. And Yul would've been so proud of his little sister.

Maizie was still angry with her wilful daughter, despite her apparent contrition. Leveret had been very quiet and subdued since that night. When Maizie had returned she'd found the girl sitting on the rug by the fire in a trembling huddle, whilst Sweyn and Gefrin played cards at the table and finished off the barrel of cider. It was lovely to see such a cosy domestic scene – all three of her youngest children together and getting on well. Although Maizie had been furious that Leveret hadn't done any weaving, Sweyn explained that she'd had one of her funny turns and so they'd let her off. Apparently she'd fallen and was quite shaken up. The boys had wrapped a blanket round her and Maizie was pleased to see them being so considerate towards their sister.

She knew that in the past they'd been like most big brothers and Leveret had put up with quite a bit of teasing. Maizie sympathised for she herself had older brothers and remembered the tricks they'd played on her as a girl. But she hated tale-telling and Leveret had a real tendency to whinge on about Sweyn and Gefrin. Maizie had made it clear from an early age that she wasn't interested in hearing any tales and Leveret would just have to ignore them until they lost interest. She thought her two youngest boys had grown up lately and it was good to see them acting responsibly and kindly. Sweyn had said they both enjoyed coming home and pointed out what a good thing they'd been there when Leveret came over funny.

Leveret hadn't said a word, merely sat shivering in the blanket and staring into the flames, her face pinched and white. She'd been peaky ever since and Maizie hadn't broached the subject of her future again. Leveret had another year at school after this one and hopefully during that time she'd come to her senses and agree to study medicine in the Outside World.

Old Greenbough was thoughtful too during lunch. He still found it difficult to be in Hallfolk territory and he couldn't relax and enjoy the delicious food. He chuckled to himself as Dawn and Hazel made conversation with him during the meal. Who'd have thought it'd turn out like this? Old Greenbough the Woodsman hob-nobbing with Hallfolk! He remembered waiting here for an audience with Magus, when he was worried about Yul. Magus had dismissed his concerns about Alwyn's cruelty, blaming the boy for making his brutal father angry – at which point Greenbough had begun to turn against his master.

Looking at the dark young man now, it was impossible to believe that this was the same lad who'd once worked for him in the woods; the boy he used to cuff if there was any slacking or cheek, the one who could shin up trees and the bonfires like a squirrel. He recalled the boy's dirty face, often sporting a black eye or split lip, and the matted hair that always hung in his eyes. Hard to believe he'd grown up into this determined, powerful man. Hard to believe the wild boy was now the magus, keeper of the magic.

'Shall we get started again?' said Yul impatiently, signalling to the waiting students to clear lunch away. 'We've still got a lot to get through.'

Sylvie watched him as the afternoon progressed and he became increasingly restless. Yul found it difficult to sit still for such a long period and his quick mind raced ahead of some of the slower, older ones there. She sympathised with Greenbough and Tom, who stumbled through their reports. They, along with everyone else, had been obliged to attend the adult education classes held every evening in the Great Barn and Village School. Miranda had enjoyed organising them in the early days and prided herself that now nearly every Stonewylder was more or less literate. The two old men preferred to talk from memory than from notes though, and Sylvie felt for them as they groped for words in front of an audience. This must be quite an ordeal and Yul's barely hidden exasperation was almost tangible, for all the two men were dear to his heart.

Whilst Martin droned on interminably about the boilers, the roofs and chimneys and the state of the floors at the Hall, Yul drummed his long fingers and gazed up at the roof carvings and stained-glass windows with glazed eyes. Sylvie longed to stand behind him and massage his tense shoulders, or sit on his lap and kiss his annoyance away. She understood him so well; the battles he fought with himself, knowing how important it was that the people had their say, but also knowing that he'd run the estate far better without their interference.

'Alright, Martin, thank you. I think we are now fully aware of the dilapidated state of the Hall. And yes, Tom, of the Village too. I'll study your reports in detail later. The point is that whilst we do have materials and labour here, we also need hard cash for some of the repairs and renovations needed. The cost for a new heating system in the Hall is astronomical and it's one of the things we simply cannot do ourselves.'

Yul looked around at the circle of faces, annoyed to see that Clip seemed to have gone off into a trance. Not that he could blame him, really. Sylvie smiled at him encouragingly and he understood her message.

Don't be hard on them and don't get angry – they're all doing their best.

He grimaced at her and raised his eyebrows. These Samhain annual report meetings felt like stirring set honey and it only seemed to get worse each year. He was just grateful that Clip allowed him to chair the meetings, or it'd be even more rambling and tedious.

'So, we're going to hear the final report now, which comes from Harold. Before he begins, I want to stress how important it is that everyone—'

'Oh, Yul – sorry to interrupt, but could I just say something?' said Dawn. 'It may be relevant, about the money problem. It's just that . . . I had an e-mail the other day from Rainbow. Do you all remember her? She—'

'I didn't realise you were in touch with the old Hallfolk,' said Yul slowly. Sylvie noticed the tightening of his mouth.

'I'm not, not really. But I think she knows David, the new art teacher, and she got my e-mail address from him. It's not difficult to work out, is it? Once you know that we're all to be found at Stonewylde.com. Anyway, she was very nice and it turns out she's doing really well in the art world. She's quite a successful painter and she asked if she could come and stay at Stonewylde next summer as a paying guest. She has wonderful memories of the place, she said. She wants to take a sabbatical and spend the summer here relaxing and painting, and she really wants to see Merewen too.'

Sylvie swallowed. Rainbow? At Stonewylde?

'We'll have to think about it,' said Yul. 'I'm not sure ... we always said that we'd never have any of the exiled Hallfolk back. Present company excepted, of course.'

'I suppose she was only a child,' said Miranda. 'What was she ... thirteen when Magus died? Not much more than that. She can hardly be tarred with the same brush as everyone else. And if she's a successful artist, she may be able to do something to help us financially.'

'But if you let one in, you'll be letting 'em all in. 'Specially if she pays,' said Greenbough, his old face furrowed with concern. 'Like ants – this girl's the scout and the others'll follow on. We'd be overrun with 'em afore we know it.'

'What do you think, Sylvie?' asked Dawn, thinking that she'd find an ally. Nobody had a kinder heart than Sylvie.

'I don't know. My initial reaction is no, never. As Greenbough says, she could be the thin end of the wedge. But ... I remember Rainbow's art and it was wonderful. She was a talented girl and if she's become a proper artist now ...'

She trailed off, hating the thought of Rainbow breaching the Boundary Walls but despising her meanness of spirit.

'Clip? Any thoughts on this?' asked Yul, thinking to catch him out in his day-dreaming.

'Stonewylde is a magical place,' Clip replied gently. 'Impossible for those banished not to dream of it. If her heart is right, we should allow the girl a visit. But let's find out more about her before we make a decision.'

Everyone nodded at this.

'Sorry to bring it up now,' said Dawn, a little flushed. 'I just thought ... what you were saying, Yul, about Stonewylde needing money. I thought maybe Rainbow could help or something.'

'That's fine, and we will consider it. So, back to Harold's report. I was talking about our difficult financial situation. You all know my father subsidised the estate with his own personal wealth earned through his London business. I don't have access to that and nor would I want to – the only way we can raise any cash is through our efforts at Stonewylde. You all know how well Harold has done in setting up Stonewylde.com to sell our excess produce. He's also begun certain new ventures, looking into ways to raise money, and he has some exciting ideas for the future. So first let's hear what we've achieved this year, Harold.'

All eyes turned to the thin young man sitting beside Yul. He coughed nervously and pushed his glasses back up his nose. Shuffling his pages of figures, he launched into a rapid recount of the success achieved by the company. He'd worked diligently and was a natural project manager, but he wasn't a natural speaker and much of what he said went straight over the Council of Elders' heads.

Although Yul knew the contents of the report, he listened with a smile as Harold spoke of Stonewylde.com. The Internet business had been set up to sell the surpluses produced at Stonewylde; it was the ideal way to make money without having to leave the estate. Their business had evolved from very humble beginnings, when a few jars of honey and bottles of cider had been advertised on a very basic website, to the huge enterprise that it was today. Customers could now browse through many categories and buy all sorts of lovely things: beautiful white nightdresses of finest Stonewylde linen, craftsman-built oak furniture, beeswax candles, handcrafted felt slippers and hats, wines and meads of every flavour, leather goods, patchwork quilts ... the list was extensive.

Harold, the young lad who'd got Yul a copy of the key to Sylvie's room all those years ago, and who'd secretly taught himself to read, write and use the Hallfolks' computers, had a remarkable gift for retail and marketing. A large barn near the Gatehouse had been converted into a storage warehouse and it was from here that many of the goods were now packaged and despatched. Harold had commissioned a corporate logo and all Stonewylde products were branded; every item sold was of highest quality and aimed at the luxury market. Many people worked in the warehouse, both packaging the products and fulfilling the orders ready for despatch.

Harold gabbled to a finish, his ears burning. There was a silence.

'Excellent, Harold! I'm sure everyone agrees that Stonewylde.com is a credit to your hard work and business prowess; you've demonstrated superb profits. I know you've prepared detailed plans for next year and some new lines you'd like to try out. Would you prefer me to tell the Council about this?'

Harold nodded gratefully and looked a little shyly at the circle of faces around him. He'd grown up a Villager, just like Yul, and was immensely proud of his work for Stonewylde. He glowed with pride at Yul's praise and relaxed a little now his ordeal was over.

'Harold's been researching various different markets, to determine what we could sell and what profit we would make. So firstly, we're going to launch a Stonewylde range of luxury organic toiletries using wild herbs and flowers, and that's work women can do. We need our men for the heavier farming and production work, so enterprises that'll employ women are especially welcome. Even the children can get involved, gathering flowers and herbs, and older members of the community can weave the tiny baskets we'll need. There's a lot of money in the cosmetic and toiletry market.'

There was a buzz of interest at this. Stonewylde had always made its own soaps and lotions, so this seemed a logical progression. Yul held his hand up for silence and continued.

'We're also looking into selling venison on a large scale to one of the quality supermarket chains who're very keen to take our meat, thanks to Harold's negotiations. We're overrun with deer in the Wildwoods, and it'd be the perfect solution to that problem. Wild venison fetches a very good price. The same with our geese, ducks and game birds – we have a guaranteed market for all these. We heard earlier from Robin how well the dairies are doing, with a great demand for Stonewylde cheese. We sell a lot of it and we need to increase milk production to cope with demand. Rosie's goat herd is doing splendidly as we know, and she'll be expanding goats' milk, yoghurt and cheese outputs this coming year when she increases the herd. We're looking also at breeding a herd of llama for their wool. There are plenty of other excellent ideas, and I'll make the list available for everyone here. Stonewylde.com is really becoming a—'

Clip sighed loudly and Yul stopped abruptly.

'Did you want to add anything, Clip?'

'No, not really,' the older man replied wearily. 'I know Harold has worked very hard and is doing his job well. It's just that . . . I wonder about the ethics of the whole enterprise.'

'The *ethics*? There's nothing unethical about Stonewylde.com! Our quality control is second to none and customers return again and again—'

'I meant the ethics of selling Stonewylde produce in this way for such profits. And the ethics of using our people to work in what amounts to a factory warehouse. Surely it goes against all the principles that Stonewylde stands for.'

Yul's face darkened and he sat up very straight. Sylvie watched with a sinking heart as his eyes flashed; she knew the signs of Yul's anger and wished that Clip had kept quiet. And yet she also knew that her father was right.

'You stick to chanting and trances, Clip, and we'll deal with harsh reality,' Yul said coldly. 'We might seem self-sufficient but we most certainly are *not*. You've heard about the extensive repairs needed to maintain the Hall and the Village, and the acute shortage of housing for all our young people. We *have* to make money somehow and there's nothing unethical about using our abundant resources.'

Yul continued to glare at the older man, who bowed his head and shrugged. Many of the Council members looked uncomfortable.

'I realise that,' said Clip. 'I only meant—'

'What my father meant,' said Sylvie coolly, surprising even herself, 'is that whilst it's fine to sell off our surplus produce and use the money for those things we can't grow or make ourselves, Stonewylde.com has gone beyond that. We're now actually looking for money-making ideas rather than selling what we don't need. You're suggesting that we grow and manufacture things specifically for the Outside market and not for Stonewylde at all, like this llama herd and toiletries all packaged up prettily. Do we really want to slaughter our wild deer and put them on supermarket shelves? Do we really want the folk to become what amounts to factory workers, sitting all day at production lines to churn out stuff for rich Outsiders?'

'Sylvie, we weren't—'

'Hear me out, Yul. Stonewylde.com is great and the profits are very welcome. But we mustn't forget the principles of Stonewylde itself, our values and our whole philosophy. Mother Earth provides for us, but she's not there to be exploited and neither are our people.'

There was a stunned silence and then Miranda clapped slowly.

'Bravo, Sylvie – well put. I agree with you.'

Maizie nodded vigorously.

'Sylvie's right! The business is taking over. It comes before us Stonewylders. Just last week I went to get a new pair o' boots for winter, and Larch the cobbler told me I'd have to wait till after Yule because they were all busy making boots and shoes for the warehouse orders! I can't wait seven weeks with holes in my boots. I did wonder what were going on.'

'Aye,' said Edward. 'My wife was told we couldn't replace our old bedstead till Spring Equinox at the earliest as they're rushed off their feet in the furniture workshop making four-poster beds for the Outside World. I've mended our bed as best I can but it's done for, and we've never had to wait so long before when something's broke. So I agree too – Stonewylde first, then Stonewylde.com. Not the other way round.'

Yul glared at them all, a flush staining his cheeks. Sylvie watched detachedly as he calmed himself down and smiled coldly.

'I'm sorry to hear about your problems, Mother and Edward. If anything like that ever happens to anyone, let me know and I'll deal with it personally. Of course our folks' needs will always come first. Thank you, Sylvie, for so eloquently explaining the point that Clip was attempting to make. In fact this leads me on to the final thing I wished to say. I'm sure we've all had enough today and need to conclude this meeting. What I'm about to tell you is of great significance to all of us in the community.'

Everyone sat up and focused on Yul, the ethics of Stone-wylde.com now completely forgotten. He smiled again, scanning the faces until he had everyone's total attention.

'Yesterday Clip told me that after this Samhain, in the new year, he intends to stand down from leading the community. He'll be signing everything over to me – and to Sylvie of course – as he feels the need for rest after all these long years.'

There was an instant babble of noise. Sylvie stared across at Clip, a sharp prickle of hurt in her throat. Why hadn't he told her first instead of letting Yul announce it to the Council? But then she saw Clip's expression and it was clear this wasn't what he'd intended. As she wondered what'd been said before, Yul continued.

'When Clip retires he'll be leaving Stonewylde for good so he can extend his travels. He told me that he has full confidence that I'm ready to lead the community. With the help of my wife, of course.'

He smiled across at Sylvie, who was surprised by how annoyed she felt.

'This is not confidential so please feel free to spread the word throughout the community. It is, after all, what Mother Heggy predicted.'

There was a buzz of approval at this.

'Oh – and one more thing. This'll be the last time that we build the labyrinth in the Stone Circle. You all know how much I despise the custom, and why. In future any Stonewylders who wish to meet the Dark Angel at Samhain may hold a private ceremony at the Yew of Death. It's a more appropriate place than the sacred Circle, which is a place of life and energy. Please explain this to the folk.'

'That'll be difficult,' muttered Martin, shaking his silver-grey head. 'Many of the old ones feel very strongly about the Dance of Death. They hold on for months to die at that special time.'

'They can still die at that special time,' replied Yul. 'Just not in the Stone Circle. That's all – the meeting is now closed. Bright blessings to you all for Samhain. These are exciting times for Stonewylde and I know it'll be a very good year ahead.'

6

Leveret sat rocking in Mother Heggy's ancient chair, her woollen cloak wrapped tightly around her against the cold. She'd been looking forward to this special day for so long, ever since she realised that the Dark Moon would fall at Samhain. She'd always felt drawn to the magic of the Dark Moon, always felt a thrill of power shiver through her when the stars glittered in a moonless sky. She didn't know that she shared this affinity with Yul, as he had always been secretive about it too.

The day had started auspiciously when she'd been woken by a crow cawing in the trees outside her bedroom. She'd smiled as she dragged herself from the world of sleep and dreams and had greeted the spirit of Mother Heggy. Leveret was convinced that the old Wise Woman was watching over her and that tonight, when the veil was at its thinnest, the crone would make contact with her from the Otherworld.

She planned to journey for the first time after she'd walked the labyrinth in the Village Green. The Fly Agaric, harvested the week before, would take her on this journey. She knew what to do and had secretly prepared the mushroom's scarlet cap as instructed in the Book. Even without the hallucinogenic effects of the mushroom Leveret was already a little light-headed as she'd been fasting for three days. It had taken some doing with Maizie breathing down her neck, and she'd had to feign an upset stomach to avoid her mother's hearty meals.

Not everyone was so delighted that the Dark Moon fell on the day of the festival. The Great Barn was needed for the children's drama this afternoon and the dancing that would continue for most of the night. If the weather turned wet, the feast would be eaten in there too. But this was also the day when most women of Stonewylde began menstruation. The first couple of days, at least, were spent in the Great Barn and usually the Dark Moon nearest to Samhain was spent knitting long woollen socks; a pair for each member of the community. These dark green stockings were for Yule and would be filled with small gifts for each person.

But today menstruation had to take second place; not such a hardship as it would have been since the compulsory contraceptive implant had been introduced, making women's periods lighter and less uncomfortable. The women were busy preparing food for the feast and putting the finishing touches to the decorations in the Great Barn. Leveret should have been in there now, helping to arrange the carved Jack o' Lanterns and attaching the papier-mâché crows and skulls and the elder twigs to the walls and rafters.

Instead she sat in the battered wooden chair, its back scarred from years of assault by the crow's scrabbling claws, clutching her stomach. She ached from the onset of her period, for she was too young for the implant, and she felt hollow from lack of food. Although everyone else was fasting today as part of the Samhain rituals, this was her third day and she was very hungry. But the Book was clear; fasting was important before Samhain and especially before a journey. She also knew that Fly could induce severe nausea, so a completely empty stomach was best. Leveret sighed and thought grimly that becoming the Wise Woman might be tougher than she'd imagined.

Yul stood under his special tree on the Village Green hidden beneath the dark green foliage. From this shelter he surveyed the people of Stonewylde – his people. He felt the familiar stirring inside, a heady cocktail of pride and power. He breathed deeply of the earthy scent and threw back his head, shutting his eyes. Swirls and eddies of magic threaded around the ancient bole and wreathed him in their enchantment. This yew tree held many memories for him and he visited it regularly, especially when he wanted to think about Sylvie.

They'd shared their first kiss here on the Summer Solstice of her fifteenth birthday, while Magus was at the Stone Circle performing his rituals. They'd snatched forbidden meetings here during the December Dark Moon, whilst Magus held her captive in his rooms at the Hall. And the most vivid, electrifying memory of all – here, on the soft earth where nothing else grew, he and Sylvie had first made love.

Yul could still recall the smell of the dew out on the Green and the old yew needles mixed in with the fine, dry soil. He vividly remembered the grainy softness of the earth under their bodies, the seclusion of the great dark dome of foliage, and the magical sight, smell and feel of the girl he loved as they finally came together after waiting for so long. The years had not dimmed the memory in the least. Yul recalled every tiny detail of that passionate consummation so strongly that he groaned aloud and quickly opened his eyes, wishing she were here right now. Then he shook his head impatiently; no, not here in the open with the weather so crisp. She deserved better – only finest linen sheets and goose down pillows for his Sylvie. Only the safe cocoon of softness, comfort and luxury; she must be treated with the utmost care, even though he was still angry with her.

Yul watched the black-robed figures, skull masks in place, slowly shuffling around the labyrinth on the Village Green towards the great wicker dome in the centre. He shuddered, hating everything about the Samhain rituals. He was still haunted by nightmares where he relived the lurching movement of the sledge being dragged inexorably towards the centre of the labyrinth in the grotesque Dance of Death. He still endured horrible flashes from that night of Jackdaw's leering face, Magus laughing with glee, the funeral pyre so high above him and pale bodies in their white tunics lying motionless beside him as that dark figure stalked the Circle. Yul shuddered again.

Next year it'd all be gone and he couldn't wait – nor could he wait for Clip to leave. Yul had never trusted him, not since he'd hypnotised Sylvie into submitting to Magus' torture on the rock at Mooncliffe every month. Yul had no patience with Clip's weaknesses and vacillations and little respect for him. He'd found it so difficult to hold his tongue while Clip dithered, growing older and vaguer by the year. He resented Clip's interference and his influence over Sylvie and longed for the day when he would take up the reins of power. Yul knew in his very marrow that this was his destiny, and Clip had blocked it for too long.

He stepped forward slightly from the shadows of the yew tree, absently watching the cloaked figures on the Village Green, fingers drumming against his thigh. He must go into the Great Barn soon to see the children's Samhain drama. Celandine and Bluebell were both in it, although at four years old, Bluebell's part was limited to that of an acorn. He smiled, remembering how excited the girls had been that morning. Celandine was part of the autumn wind dance and had been prancing around the Hall for weeks, practising her twirling and whooshing. As magus he must watch and applaud all the children but he wished there was time to return to the Hall first. He was waiting for something important and needed to check his e-mails. Yul tried to put it to the back of his mind; Harold would phone down to the Barn if it came through and Sylvie was right – he did need to sort out his priorities. This was what really mattered; celebrating the festival, not business deals going through.

They'd had the most awful argument on the night of the last Council Meeting. Yul had tried to hide his anger but they knew each other too well for deception and she'd been just as angry with him. They'd hurled accusations at each other and then taken their fight away from their sleeping children to his office downstairs, where it had continued to rage. Sylvie shouted that he was a control freak like his father and had forgotten what mattered at Stonewylde; he yelled that she was as woolly and soft as her father and had no idea how to run their community.

She'd stood, hands on hips, her hair wild about her flushed cheeks and eyes flashing sparks of rage and the row had ended abruptly. Overwhelmed by desire for her, he'd manoeuvred her onto the large sofa and made love to her as passionately as he'd argued with her only minutes before. Her furious protests had been quenched by his greedy mouth and in moments they both knew that her resistance was merely token, and soon abandoned. But afterwards, as their breathing returned to normal and their heated bodies cooled, she'd made it clear that she was still furious about his arrogance at the Council meeting.

'Remember, Yul,' she'd flung at him, 'that Clip could decide to sign it all over to me alone. Remember that before you attempt to shut me out altogether. You may channel the Earth Magic but I'm the heir to Stonewylde, not you. Stop trying to push me out!'

As she'd struggled out of his grasp and adjusted her twisted clothing, he'd been so tempted to fling back an equally nasty retort. At least he still received the Earth Magic, whereas she no longer moondanced and channelled the moon energy. He'd bitten back the cruel words and merely glared at her as she stormed out of the office and up to bed. But she wouldn't have the final word. Nobody, not even his beloved wife, ever got the better of Yul nowadays.

Unbeknownst to Yul, one of the masked figures now treading the labyrinth on the Village Green was his youngest sister. Flicking a glance at the nine robed teenagers following the white stones of the path, Yul strode round the edge towards the Great Barn where the children were almost ready for their dance and drama. Leveret didn't notice him either; her eyes were fixed on the narrow path marked by the pebbles and she was fighting waves of nausea that made her sway alarmingly. She'd decided to eat the mushroom before she walked the labyrinth, knowing it could take some hours for the effects of Fly Agaric to reach their peak.

Leveret wished that she could've asked somebody's advice. She knew the mushroom's effects had three distinct phases: the initial nausea and physical reactions, the dreamy, calm state, and finally the hallucinatory stage. It was during the final phase that she hoped to journey, as her spirit left her body and travelled into other realms, and she wanted this to happen during the afternoon. Then she'd be free to cast her first spell that night after sunset and make contact with Mother Heggy. She thought she'd eaten the dried mushroom early enough but was only guessing at the timings. As she lurched around the labyrinth, Leveret realised she'd made a mistake.

Inside the wicker dome the man in the crow mask chanted to the slow-beating drums, indicating the mats where the youngsters should sit. Leveret's legs had turned to jelly and she crumpled onto the hemp mat, swallowing the saliva that suddenly filled her mouth. Her stomach was clenching and bloating and the gulps of saliva threatened to boil over like a geyser any minute. Suddenly her face was on fire, burning as scarlet as the cap of Fly she'd consumed. She tore at the mask, desperate for air, but as she wrenched it off she noticed the other teenagers had done the same. Now the crow man was passing around the tiny skull cups of blood. Her mouth flooded again and she started to gag.

'Drink of the blood of death and rebirth,' the crow intoned, and everyone put the vessels to their lips. They sipped gingerly, knowing it was only elderberry wine laced with something stronger but still reluctant to swallow the dark, viscous liquid. Leveret gasped for air, unable to drink, but the tall, dark crow put one hand at the back of her head and the other under the cup and tipped it so she had no choice but to swallow. She felt the blood-red juice swirling into the void of her stomach, which started to heave. The others were now lying down whilst the drumming increased in intensity and aromatic smoke filled the tiny space. Leveret fell back and immediately the smoky dome started to spin. She heard far-away laughter and the raucous croak of a crow. The black emptiness spiralled and she was disappearing down into a great maw of nausea, flailing at the sides but falling down, down.

Strong hands jerked her to her feet and she recognised Martin's voice hissing at her.

'Behave yourself, Leveret! The others are outside already. Walk the path and think of what you want to achieve this year, and don't you *dare* spoil this sacred ceremony with any of your messing about!'

She staggered out into the cool, grey light clutching her mask, and walked unsteadily along the coiling path that led eventually out of the labyrinth. She hoped Martin wouldn't tell her mother or Yul that she'd acted strangely. The nausea had receded and she was relieved to find herself at the exit where another masked person handed her a slip of yew. She hoped to quietly steal away now and make her way to Mother Heggy's cottage, where she'd curl up on the wooden settle and maybe start the dreaming.

But she heard the cry of a familiar voice and her heart plummeted.

'Leveret! Come into the Barn with me and watch the Dance of Samhain! 'Tis just about to start.'

Her mother took her arm and led her firmly inside through the great wooden doors that were flung wide open. Inside, the vast area had been transformed for Samhain and was filled with grinning Jack o' Lanterns and realistic crows and skulls. The centre of the Barn was clear, with carved tree-trunks standing upright to mark a large circle for the drama.

'Please, Mother, I don't feel well,' groaned Leveret, her stomach beginning to tighten again in spasms.

Maizie peered into her face, noting the moist pallor of her skin and the glassiness of her eyes. She put an arm around her youngest child, tiny underneath her black cloak.

'You don't look good, my love. Stay here with me for the drama – Celandine and Bluebell are in it, and Snowdrop and little Edrun, and I promised them I'd watch. When 'tis over I'll take you home for a lie-down. You haven't eaten properly for days but we'll have to wait until the feast, for you can't break the fast early, not at Samhain. Just hold tight, Leveret. They are your nieces and nephew after all.'

Leveret closed her eyes and swayed on her feet. The last thing she needed now was to watch some silly little girls prancing around. She didn't mind Rosie's children so much but she couldn't stand Yul's daughters whom he doted on, exactly as he'd used to dote on her when she was a small girl. Nowadays they rarely spoke and he'd often stride past in the Hall and not even register who she was. Leveret didn't care; she didn't even like him anymore.

But now here he was, her big brother the magus, stepping into the centre of the Barn so tall and handsome. Dressed in splendid dark grey robes embroidered with silver cobwebs, a circlet of black feathers and ivy on his glossy curls, he raised his arms and there was silence.

'Folk of Stonewylde,' he said softly, so everyone must strain to hear, 'we're honoured to watch our children perform their celebration of Samhain. At this festival we say farewell to autumn and greet winter, we look back over the past year and peer into the mists of the new year. At this festival we remember those who've passed through the veil into the Other World and send them our blessings. The Samhain Dance!'

There was a roll of drums and he moved to stand beside his wife, dressed in the normal black Samhain robes. She'd change into her special ceremonial attire soon, before the evening's festivities started. Leveret noticed how Yul's hand automatically slipped into hers and how he raised it to his lips. The smile she gave him seemed a little tight but then their attention was taken by the arrival of the Autumn Wind, swirling in a golden eddy into the circle. Their eyes were locked onto one little girl amongst the many, her long hair a mass of white curls. She danced beautifully and with complete dedication, gracefully pointing her slim legs and leaping as if she were weightless. Leveret scowled and tried to edge away but Maizie gripped her firmly.

'Just look at our Celandine!' she whispered. 'Isn't she wonderful? The girl's a natural dancer. Yul must be so proud of her.'

Half an hour later Leveret could barely stand. She was bored stiff by the Samhain Dance and even the sight of Bluebell dressed as an acorn had only made her smile a little. The tiny, plump girl had looked almost as ridiculous as her soppy parents when she skipped on and sang her daft song with all the other acorns.

92

Leveret's sickness and flushing seemed to have passed and she now felt incredibly sleepy. All she wanted to do was sit down quietly.

'The crows are black,' she said, looking up at the papier-mâché birds that perched and hung everywhere, some moving gently in the warm air raised by the dancing. Maizie frowned, relieved to see the pallor had gone from her pointed face but puzzled by the girl's air of vacancy.

'Of course the crows are black!'

'Their feathers are night's fingers,' said Leveret in a sing-song voice.

'What's that? You're looking very strange,' said Maizie, peering into her daughter's green eyes and noting her dilated pupils. 'Go and sit down over by the door and I'll take you home in a minute.'

Leveret stumbled out of the throng of people and headed for the fresh air. Then she noticed Sweyn and Gefrin lounging near the doors talking to Jay. They were all laughing and she felt a chill ripple over her skin. Jay was as cruel as they were, although most of his aggression was directed at poor Magpie. Leveret imagined Jay pecking and pecking and her mind started to unravel so she turned and wandered in the opposite direction. She meandered through lots of black-robed people and then hit something solid. She looked slowly up the expanse of grey and silver and her eyes met the deep grey ones of her eldest brother, who frowned down at her.

'What are you up to?' he asked. 'Did you enjoy the Dance?'

'Like the snow enjoys the rain,' she mumbled.

'What? That's a strange thing to say. I've been meaning to speak to you, Leveret. I've been hearing things that I don't like.'

'I understand now about the caterpillar.'

'*What?* What on earth are you talking about?'

He gripped her arms and pulled her slightly towards him, trying to look into her eyes.

'The hookah-smoking caterpillar on the mushroom, and the

way the girl shrew and grank. Grew and shrank. You know, the door and the glass table.'

'Leveret, what are you on about?'

'Don't you remember it anymore? Alice in Wonderland. You read it to me long, long ago when you were still my lovely brother. I've read it many times since but I didn't really understand until now.'

Yul shook his head in exasperation.

'You're being ridiculous but I can't waste time on you now. I must watch all the children dance, not just my own. But I'm warning you, Leveret, I'm not happy with what I've been told and we're going to have a serious talk soon. Make sure you behave yourself tonight.'

He released her and she edged away, muttering darkly to herself. She noticed an empty corner and scuttled over, curling up on the floor and hiding herself under her cloak. At last she could just close her eyes and taste all the visions that crowded in. They were sweet and salty and their colours were noisy, except for the silver feathers that sounded like a harp and smelled of soft water. Leveret wanted to stroke those with her eyes, comb them with her breath. She swallowed that thought and it tasted like birdsong, blossoming into a shimmering rainbow inside her empty stomach that filled her with luminosity.

Sylvie had slipped into one of the small side-rooms attached to the Great Barn to change into her ceremony robes. Like Yul's they were soft and grey but hers were embroidered with black crows. Her headdress was a skullcap of blue-black feathers with long strings hanging down amongst her hair, trailing ivy leaves. There was also a mask which attached to the skullcap, made of moulded black silk with a beak that covered the upper part of her face and made her look like an Egyptian goddess. As she brushed out her flowing silver hair before donning the cap and mask, the door opened and Hazel came in.

'Hi, Sylvie. How are you doing?'

'Fine thanks – almost ready. Would you mind helping me with

this cap? It has to be pinned securely before I attach the mask and it's always awkward.'

'It's quite tricky, isn't it? Give me the pins and I'll do the back.'

Sylvie turned to face the mirror and watched Hazel in the reflection, frowning as she began pinning on the feathered skull-cap. Sylvie liked Hazel, which was just as well for the doctor knew everything there was to know about her. Hazel looked up, her soft brown eyes meeting Sylvie's strange grey ones in the mirror, and Sylvie grimaced.

'You know, Hazel, you're the one person who's seen me in my very darkest hour. You saw things that not even Yul saw.'

Hazel smiled gently.

'I'm a doctor, Sylvie, remember that. We're meant to be there at the darkest hour to pick up the pieces.'

'I even attacked you, didn't I?'

'Forget it, Sylvie. It was more than four years ago and you've made a complete recovery.'

'Hazel . . . I worry about it sometimes. Will it ever come back?'

'It was an extension of severe post-natal depression so unless you have another baby it won't come back – and even if you did, the odds are you wouldn't become psychotic again. It's extremely rare and you were very unlucky to be so acutely affected. Just put it behind you, Sylvie – I thought you had.'

'So did I. In fact I have – it's Yul who can't forget. He still treats me as if I may crack at any moment. He wraps me in cotton wool and smothers me with his carefulness and I can't stand it.'

'Do you want me to speak to him?'

'It might help, but I think I've got to prove to him that I'm completely well. He's so strong and it's such hard work standing up to him – it's so much easier just to let him have his way. But that's going to stop. Have you noticed how arrogant he's become lately? He's growing more and more like Magus.'

Hazel looked away and busied herself pinning the cap.

'I never had a problem with Magus, Sylvie. Not that I condone everything he did, of course, but . . .'

'Sorry, I forget sometimes that not everyone was against him. He was very charming, wasn't he?'

Hazel nodded, blushing slightly.

'I know it's stupid,' she said softly, 'because he was an evil man and I realise that now. But at the time I thought he was a god. I was as bad as Rowan and Wren and all the other girls under his spell.'

'Not to mention my mother and even me for a little while,' agreed Sylvie.

'He was so ... so ... well, I really can't put it into words. But when you were with him, when you had all his attention, it was the best thing in the whole world. The very best thing and nothing else mattered at all. And once you'd been with him that was all you thought about until the next time. It wasn't just sex, although that was incredible, it was much more than that – it was *him*, his very essence. The way he looked into your soul with those velvety black eyes, I just ...'

She stopped and guiltily looked up to meet Sylvie's gaze again in the mirror.

'Sorry, Sylvie. You must think I'm mad, still mooning about him after thirteen years like some love-sick teenager. You're one of the very few women here who didn't fall under his spell and yet he wanted you more than anyone else. You were so young, far too young for a man like him, but he was like someone possessed over you. It was horrible to watch – not simply out of jealousy but because it was so very wrong.'

'It wasn't really me he wanted. He was obsessed with my moongaziness and he wasn't used to being turned down either. He knew it was Yul I wanted and not him, which makes Yul becoming more and more like him so ironic. Sometimes Yul looks at me and it could be Magus.'

Hazel had secured the cap and Sylvie lifted the mask to her eyes, pressing the fasteners to attach it. Hazel reached across and took over.

'We need to put Magus firmly in the past where he belongs, along with your illness and anything else that's bothering us,' she said. 'I'll speak to Yul and I'll do it casually so he doesn't think you've primed me. Don't let him dominate you, Sylvie. Nip that in the bud and stand up to him – you two have always been equals. Everything else is alright between you, isn't it? I mean ...'

Sylvie grinned at her, the mask covering half her face but her pretty white teeth flashing her amusement.

'Yes, it couldn't be better. I'd always imagined our passion would wear off a little, after we got used to each other, but it hasn't – just looking at him makes me go weak at the knees. I only wish he wasn't constantly busy and distracted. Some nights he doesn't come to bed at all and I miss him so much.'

Hazel smiled wistfully.

'You're very lucky, Sylvie. Not many couples have that sort of relationship after thirteen years together. Enjoy it.'

'Oh I do!' she laughed.

The late October sun was sinking fast, gilding the woods all around the Stone Circle with a fiery glow. As the shadows lengthened inside the ancient arena, the sound of rooks from the treetops was deafening. The massive standing stones were painted with crows and skulls and in the centre sat the pyre, ready to receive the corpses. Elder branches, the tree of the crone, had been woven into a doorway that framed the entrance into the Stone Circle. This led to the white stones and red lanterns which patterned the soft earth and marked out the Labyrinth of Death. As the night of Samhain approached, the place felt dark and foreboding.

Old Violet and her sister Vetchling stood by the Altar Stone unpacking bottles from a battered leather bag, setting out cakes and wine. Both were old and whiskery and Violet especially was wizened and bent with arthritis. Their black robes were fusty and well-worn for they used them on many occasions other than Samhain. They both muttered bad-temperedly like a couple of growling cats spoiling for a fight.

'How many do we expect this year?' whined Vetchling, poking at the cakes with a filthy finger.

'I told you – five tonight for the Dance of Death. Five to meet the Dark Angel. 'Tis a good number.'

'Aye, five is a good number. Quick, sister, 'tis getting dark and the sun will soon be gone. We must be ready.'

'Aye, the others will be here shortly and there's much to be done afore the veil draws aside tonight. The invitation must be powerful.'

''Twill be very powerful, too powerful for him to resist. Are many coming to help in the summoning, sister?'

'Aye, a goodly number – thirteen of us for the summoning, and the five on the sledges also. It shall be enough. He cannot refuse the invitation, nor will he want to. I've felt him waiting, waiting to be let in, and tonight the veil will be thinner than it's been in many a year at Samhain for we have Dark Moon also. The Dark Magic will aid us, sister, and the Dark Angel hisself.'

Vetchling cackled at this.

'Well said, sister. There, all is prepared and we're ready now to cast.'

In the Great Barn Maizie paced up and down wringing her hands. Gefrin and Sweyn stood awkwardly nearby whilst Rosie tried to hold on to her two excited children and sympathise with her mother at the same time.

'Don't worry, Mother, she'll be safe enough.'

'I know, I know, but she looked so strange earlier. You know how pointed and peaky she is at the best o' times. She were much worse tonight, and her eyes! Oh, they were enormous with great black pupils like a cat's. I told her to sit down by the door and then she disappeared. Where on goddess's Earth can she be?'

'Mother, we've got to go outside – 'tis almost sunset, Yul's on the Green and everyone's in the labyrinth ready. We'll miss the ceremony if we don't go now.'

'Blast that girl! She'll really be in trouble when I find her. If she's with that Magpie again—'

'No, Mother, she ain't. I can see him out on the Green – he's the only person not wearing a black cloak,' said Gefrin. 'Come on, we got to be in the labyrinth or we won't get the Earth Magic tonight.'

They all began to troop out of the Barn and onto the Green, when Sweyn noticed the small black heap by the wall. He prodded it hard with his boot and let out a whoop of triumph.

'Hey, Mother, don't worry, I found her! She's been lying here under her cloak all the time, leading us a merry dance! Look – she's not ill at all, just asleep!'

'Ooh, just wait till the ceremony's over!' said Maizie through gritted teeth. 'She's really for it this time, making me worry like that. Come on, we'll leave her here. She'll be alright for a while.'

But as they left the Barn, Sweyn looked back and saw the heap stir, disturbed by the heaviness of his boot. He waved the others on and went back into the Barn. Slowly Leveret sat up, swaying and barely able to open her eyes. Sweyn watched as she pushed herself up and, holding onto the wall, managed to stand upright. Carefully she stepped away, one foot at a time, towards the doors.

'Not so fast!' said Sweyn, reaching out and grabbing the hood of her robe to yank her back. 'Not so fast, little sister. You've upset Mother again so it's time for another lesson.'

Yul stood on the roof of the wicker dome in the very centre of the Village Green, resplendent in his grey and silver robes. The green and purple glass lanterns flickered their eerie light around the labyrinth as the sun sank behind the trees. It was a beautiful clear night, the sky bright blue and gold with wisps of clouds lacing the heavens. Yul stood tall and straight with his arms raised and hands open, chanting the sacred words that he'd learnt from Clip. His heart was full of love for the wonders of the Earth and the sky, for his people of Stonewylde, for the magical dance of the year as the wheel turned. He felt the Earth Magic pulsing through his body, spiralling around the Village Green, snaking through the labyrinth. His deep voice chanted, interwoven with the beat of the soft drums inside the dome beneath his feet. The Stonewylders, spread throughout the twisted coils of the labyrinth swayed and hummed, enraptured by the magic they too could feel emanating from their magus and entering their very souls.

Sylvie stood at the foot of the dome gazing up at the hundreds of birds that clustered around the Green, perching blackly on the boughs of all the great trees that surrounded the area. She thought of her dear Professor Siskin who'd loved this place more than any other. She remembered his words of wisdom; how he'd believed that the Green was the remnants of a place so ancient and magical that even now the energy lingered here. He'd believed the Green had originally been a woodland temple, a clearing in the wildwood that clothed the land in pre-history, a place where the Earth Energy had been channelled long before the Stone Circle or any of the other sacred sites at Stonewylde had been built. Sylvie could feel the old man's presence in the circle tonight, here where his small, curled body had been discovered the morning after that Winter Solstice, frosty and stiff but with a smile on his face. She greeted his spirit and felt a rush of sadness that he hadn't lived to see Yul become the magus, just as he'd predicted.

When the Green Man returns to Stonewylde, all will prosper.

The Green Man had returned and she supposed all was prospering. She turned her gaze to her husband, tall and erect, his face tipped back in rapture. He was so powerful and strong, so rooted here. Why did she feel this need to challenge him? Why couldn't she just accept his rule and bask in his adoration? She knew that he worshipped her; surely that was enough? Then he looked down at her and their eyes met. She saw the strange light glowing from within him, the green light sacred to this place, and she felt the love pouring from him, not just for her but for everything that was Stonewylde. She smiled at him, honoured that he loved her above all others. The air almost crackled with the power of their attraction and she felt herself literally drawn towards him, as if he were magnetised.

Yul reached down and beckoned, grasping her outstretched

hand and whisking her up so her feet climbed the domed wicker walls. She stood beside him on the roof of the shelter, feeling the radiance of his power throbbing from a hidden source. Her breath caught in her throat and her eyes filled with tears under the black silk mask. Yul was the true magus and she belonged by his side – this was as it should be. The drums increased in their intensity and he began to chant again, joined by the voices of the hundreds of people all around him.

Clip stood in the deepening shadows under an ash tree, its bunches of seed pods dark and shrivelled. He watched the scene on the Village Green and he too felt the power of the Earth Energy channelled by Yul. Like Sylvie, he knew that this was how it should be. Yul was ready, was already all-powerful, and Clip could safely leave the ceremonies to him. He was free to pass on the responsibility at last after all these years, and follow his own inner journey.

Clip smiled and let out a great sigh of relief. He'd be free to wander the whole earth, not just this tiny corner of it. He could travel again and commune with spiritual people from different cultures, join in their celebration of the Earth and the sky and the glorious deity that manifested itself through nature. He turned away from the spectacle as the light thickened to dusk, heading for the Dolmen where he planned to spend the Samhain night greeting the Otherworld that shimmered so close at this time of year. He'd awaken to the dawn of a new year, the year when he'd finally gain his freedom.

Clip slipped past the open doors of the Great Barn where the folk of Stonewylde would eventually finish their celebrations tonight. First they'd light the bonfire on the playing fields by the river and dance in huge concentric circles around the roaring fire to symbolise the turning wheel of the year. Then they'd break their fast with delicious food cooked outside on smaller fires, and later they'd crowd into the Barn for party games and dancing. The festivals were an important factor in bringing the community together, but it wasn't for Clip. He had another, less worldly, path to follow tonight.

But as he passed the Barn, Clip heard a sound that made him stop in his tracks. It was the sound of somebody choking, followed by a growl of laughter. Puzzled, he peered into the vast cavern of the building. The Jack o' Lanterns hadn't yet been lit but ordinary lanterns glowed around the walls. The games had been set out already and it was by the big half-barrel of water, filled with bobbing apples, that he saw them. Two figures in black cloaks – Clip gasped as the man forced the girl's head over the edge of the barrel and into the water filled with floating apples. Her head was held underwater and her arms flailed wildly about as she fought to escape while he laughed, keeping her in position almost effortlessly.

In horror Clip watched her struggles becoming weaker and her body limper as the man relentlessly held her head down. Shouting, Clip launched himself across the floor and the man looked up in surprise, releasing the girl as he did so. She staggered upright, coughing and choking and making a terrible rasping noise as she struggled to fill her lungs with air.

'What in the goddess' name are you doing?' yelled Clip, wrenching her from his grasp. The wet face turned to him and he saw it was Leveret, her eyes almost starting from her head, her lips blue. He realised that the man was very young, only just a man, and he recognised the porcine features of one of Leveret's brothers whose name he never remembered. The lad was scarlet with fury but backed away at the sight of Clip.

'Just teaching her a lesson, that's all,' he mumbled thickly. 'No harm done.'

'No harm done? You bloody idiot, you've practically drowned her! Get out of here! And I'll be talking to your mother about this!'

Clip took hold of Leveret's shoulders and made her breathe more slowly, pushing the wet hair away from her face and rubbing her back rhythmically to help her calm down and take steadier breaths. Gradually her lips lost their blue tinge and the whooping sounds stopped. She leaned into him and he put his arms around her, comforting her in her distress.

'It's alright, Leveret,' he said soothingly, 'it's alright. Your brother's gone and you're safe now.'

She began to sob and he held her tight, small and pathetic in his arms like a frightened wild creature. Clip felt a great rush of affection for her and thanked the goddess that he'd arrived when he did. He heard the chanting outside as darkness fell and knew he must get up to the Dolmen quickly before he became swept up in the celebrations. He held the girl away from him slightly for a better look, and was shocked at how very dilated and unfocused her eyes were.

'How are you feeling now?' he asked softly.

'The stars glitter but the night is dark,' she whispered in a strange, faraway voice. 'I need to fly in the blackness.'

'You took the Fly Agaric,' he said, nodding. 'Silly girl, you should never take it alone when you're inexperienced. You said you knew what you were doing and I thought you'd have friends with you to take care of you. When did you take it?'

'The blue is black and it's so speckled.'

'Leveret! When did you eat the mushroom?'

She gazed up at him with unseeing eyes. Her bedraggled curls were stuck to her face and her eyes were enormous, the pupils great black pools and only the bright green rim of her irises showing. She was a strange girl, he thought, feeling an affinity with her. He knew she was in another reality altogether and not aware of him or where she was.

'I can't leave you here alone in this state, not when you're so new to this. You'd better come to the Dolmen with me.'

There was no response so he took her arm and led her out of the Barn and up the track leading away from the Village. She followed docilely enough but darkness was deepening by the minute, so he scooped her up in his arms and carried her. It reminded him of the Moon Fullnesses when he and Magus had carried Sylvie to and from the great stone at Mooncliffe. He felt a stab of guilt at the awful memory, but this was different. He was helping this girl, rescuing her, and it was the Dark Moon not the Full Moon. He sensed Leveret was a girl of darkness and depth, not quicksilver and brightness like Sylvie. Clip realised there was a lot more to Leveret than met the eye. She was different and other-worldly, and maybe before he left Stonewylde he could help set her straight on her own journey.

7

A small fire burnt in the mouth of the cave keeping the darkness and cold at bay. The guardian owl sprinkled something onto the flames which crackled blue and green and the temple filled with aromatic smoke, heavenly in its sweetness. She breathed deeply and laid her head down again in the darkness, comforted by the fire and the owl. He wore a strange cloak of dark feathers but had a silver head, and he crouched by the entrance protecting her. Already he'd saved her from the waters, carrying her in his wings high into the hills to this temple cave where she was warm and safe. Curled up on a coarse old blanket and a bed of crispy bracken she smiled and let her mind roam free.

Some time later she became aware that her owl was completely still and silent, sitting sentry at the mouth of the Dolmen. She heard his deep, rhythmic breathing in the darkness and knew his mind was travelling, roaming, journeying. She hoped his wings were carrying him to great heights, soaring above the everyday and into the realms of dream. She'd been there herself tonight, to the place between the worlds where all is shadow and smoke. Despite the rush of terror the place induced she loved it, glimpsing things beyond her knowledge and experience, feeling the thrill of the mystery. But now there was a strange feeling – a pulling and tugging at her soul. There was something she should be doing now, something very important, but she'd forgotten what it was. Her eyelids grew heavy as she felt herself drift away again.

The black-robed figures dragged the heavy burdens around the labyrinth, lurching in the soft earth. On their sledges the five white-clad bodies lay motionless, already close to death from exposure to the crisp night air. In the centre stood the masked figure representing the Bird, who led the Death Dance. The Bird looked up and noted the hundreds of black birds perched on the standing stones and jostling in the trees around the Stone Circle. That was how it should be; raven, crow, rook, jackdaw, starling and blackbird. All were here to pay their respects to the Dark Angel, having left the labyrinth in the Village Green once the great bonfire had been lit for the wheel-turn dance.

The Bird nodded and continued chanting, calling upon the Dark Angel to visit tonight, to walk this labyrinth of death and take with him those souls ready to depart. Soon this part of the ceremony would be over as the people pulling the sledges reached the centre of the labyrinth and left their white burdens there, arranged around the funeral pyre ready for the cup which the Bird would offer them. Then came the long vigil through the dark hours of night until dawn.

Over by the Altar Stone the two crones were silently watching the sledges' inexorable progress. Tonight they'd performed a special ceremony; using the powerful magic of the Dark Moon, they'd cast a great circle within the Stone Circle itself and marked the five points of the pentangle. They'd summoned the elements, calling upon the powers of earth, air, fire, water and spirit. They'd raised the energy and even now it was spiralling deeper and stronger, strengthened by the sacred pattern within the labyrinth, by the chanting and the drumming, by the fear of those taking part in the Dance of Death. It was negative energy, a dark malignant energy, whose climax would be reached at midnight when the Wheel of the Year notched full circle and Samhain flowered fully into dreadful bloom. Then the gateway into the Otherworld would be wide open momentarily and the invitation could be made.

Already the veil was thin and gauzy, allowing tantalising

glimpses into the place where the dead walked. Already contact had been made with those who'd passed on, those who crowded at the door looking back. There were many waiting, layer upon layer of faces jostling for a glimpse of all they'd left behind, hoping their loved ones were also waiting on their side to greet them. A glimpse was all they could hope for because the portal was one way only, living to dead. Unless ... unless the magic could be raised by those who knew how, who knew the right words and the right rituals. And two such ones did know, the two who waited patiently by the Altar Stone watching the energy growing, waiting for midnight. Then the invitation would be made under the spell of the Dark Moon, and maybe it would be received and accepted by the one to whom it was made. Maybe he'd be able to cross back into the world of the living and walk once more upon the earth of the goddess. Maybe, if the ritual was perfect and the will was strong.

In the Village the celebrations were in full swing. The huge bonfire in the playing fields still blazed but the initial conflagration had died down to a white heat. Smaller cooking fires burned low all around, the forgotten fragments of food burning to a crisp. The air was rich with the smells of roasting meat, baked potatoes and toasted chestnuts. The damp grass had been trampled by many feet shuffling and dancing in great circles, faces scorched by the inferno and hearts leaping with excitement. Samhain was a wonderful festival enjoyed by most at Stonewylde.

Older children still raced around outside in their black cloaks. Some wore masks and others had paint daubed on their faces, scaring each other and chasing around like kittens in the wind. Everyone had feasted well and the majority were now inside the Great Barn dancing and drinking. The younger ones had been taken home or to the Nursery and put to bed, away from all the wild behaviour.

The doors of the Great Barn were flung open to the night for it was very hot inside. The Jack o' Lanterns flickered and grinned wickedly and the papier-mâché birds and skulls fluttered in the hot air. The musicians were playing frenziedly; the whole place shook with the vibrations of noise and thundering feet. Maizie sat in a quieter corner with Rosie and Robin, sipping miserably at her glass of elderberry wine.

'Mother, do stop fretting about her,' said Rosie, patting Maizie's hand. 'Remember what Sweyn said? She was all dozy and he splashed her to wake her up and then she went off with Clip. So we know she'll be safe.'

'But why did she leave the Barn? Where is she now?'

'She's probably up at the Hall. You said she looked strange – he's doubtless taken her somewhere quiet. We all know how stubborn and difficult Leveret can be, but I can't think of a safer pair of hands than Clip's – you know how gentle he is.'

'Dratted girl! She's completely ruined Samhain with her antics,' muttered Maizie. 'Tis a difficult time anyway, with all the memories . . .'

'Just forget it, Mother Maizie,' said Robin. 'She doesn't have to spoil it for you – for all of us – so forget Leveret and drink up.'

'Aye, come and have a dance, Mother, and cheer up,' said Rosie, knowing that Robin had just about had enough of Maizie's fretting. 'I'll talk to Leveret in the morning and we'll get Yul involved too. She's behaving terribly at the moment but we'll sort her out.'

Sweyn, Gefrin and Jay stood by the bar where the enormous oak barrels and smaller kegs were lined up, drinking cider by the tankard. They'd already had a great deal but this was Samhain and it was usual for the young men to drink themselves to the floor. They were flushed and over-excited; Sweyn in particular was sweating like a pig. Earlier on he'd told the others about his run-in with Clip and they'd sympathised with him. None of them liked Clip much, for he represented the old and traditional element of Stonewylde, the voice of reason and moderation. News of his intended departure during the coming year had spread like wildfire and the trio were drinking to celebrate this fortunate turn of events.

'Here's to the old fart leaving once and for all!' cried Gefrin, spilling as much cider as he swallowed and not caring one bit.

'I wish I could bob his head in the apple water right now!' roared Sweyn. He gulped at his tankard and wiped his mouth with the back of his hand. 'Bloody old fool, interfering like that. How dare he? She's my sister and I'll do what I like to keep her in line, as Mother asked. Who does he think he is interfering with family business? She was only getting a little wet, after all.'

'We'll get her another day,' said Gefrin, grinning with anticipation. 'She'll wish Clip had left well alone by the time we've finished with her.'

'Count me in too,' said Jay, swaying on his feet. 'I can't stand her. She looks at me all funny with those nasty green cat's eyes and it gives me the bloody creeps. There's something weird about her and she's always hanging about with that half-wit cousin of mine, which ain't natural. Magpie's crazy and so's she. If she needs sorting out I'll help.'

They raised their tankards to this and downed what was left. As they waited by the barrels for their turn to refill, they noticed Swift across the floor.

'Hey, Swift! Over here!'

The slim blond youth somehow heard them over the hubbub and made his way towards them. He was in his last year at school and was clever and quick, having grown up with the run of the Hall where his father worked, seeing and hearing a great deal. He was the mastermind behind many pranks and escapades and lads like Sweyn, Gefrin and Jay treated him with respect.

'Come and have another tankard with us!' Jay yelled over the noise. Swift looked at the flushed and bleary-eyed trio and smiled his acceptance, but whilst they downed their cider, he merely sipped.

'We were just drinking to Clip buggering off next year,' continued Jay, his bright blue eyes bulging just as his father's had done. Jay was remarkably like Jackdaw; tall and strongly built with well-developed muscles and a bullet-shaped head. He also

109

shared Jackdaw's brutish disposition and threw a heavy arm around the younger boy's shoulders.

'Come on, mate – drink up! We was thinking on how things'd change when Clip's gone and Yul's fully in charge.'

'If he is,' muttered Swift.

'What?' Jay could barely hear him over the noise.

'I said "if". Maybe Yul won't be in charge.'

The three others stared at Swift in confusion. He grinned enigmatically and beckoned them to move away from the bar and into a quieter spot where they sat down on log stools.

'What do you mean?' asked Sweyn. 'Who else'd be in charge?'

'I don't know,' replied Swift. 'It's just something I overheard. Not everyone here likes Yul as much as he thinks they do. Sorry, I know he's your brother.'

'Half-brother. Yeah, well, I'm not too keen on him myself, to be honest. He's never done me no favours.'

'Nor me,' agreed Gefrin. 'Too high and mighty and he treats us like fools. I don't like him at all but don't tell Mother that. He's always been her favourite.'

'What about you, Jay?'

Jay glared belligerently, his eyes dull with alcohol and a sense of injustice.

'Old Violet and my Aunt Starling and Granny Vetchling, they told me my father died thanks to Yul. Yul were protected by the old crone Mother Heggy and she helped him become magus. It was her crow as pecked my father's eyes out up on that bloody stone at Mooncliffe and killed him. My dad was only doing what the old Magus told him – he were Magus' right-hand man, Granny Vetchling said, and it ain't true what everyone says about him. So no, I don't like Yul.'

Swift nodded.

'Yes, I've heard that too. So none of you are for Yul then? If there was someone else ready to step in, you'd support him?'

'Too right! Why, who is it?'

'I don't know,' said Swift. 'It's just something I heard. But we're ready, aren't we, if the time comes? I don't like Yul myself –

arrogant bastard. Look at Martin, my father – he's worked hard all his life and he has to kow-tow to Yul and treat him like the master. My father remembers when Yul was just a Village woodsman. He remembers your father, Alwyn, beating the shit out of him, and the old magus too, both of them having a good go. They locked Yul up in a stable and practically killed him, Father said. Yul was nothing then, in fact he had to answer to my father and it's not right that my father has to take orders from him now.'

'Is that what Uncle Martin says? I didn't know he felt like that,' said Jay.

'No, he doesn't,' said Swift hurriedly. 'I mean, I've never heard him say that directly because he wouldn't speak out against the magus. He's very loyal – too bloody loyal. He should think of himself instead of serving others. He's just as much right to run Stonewylde as they have, after all. But don't say anything about this, will you? It's secret, confidential.'

The three nodded solemnly.

'We won't say a word,' said Gefrin.

'I'd like Yul out of the way,' said Sweyn slowly, the implications dawning on him. 'He's never liked me and I'd be free to do what I like. Sort out that ugly little bitch of a sister once and for all. Yeah, I'd like that.'

'What about Kestrel?' asked Jay, thinking of the ring-leader of their group. 'Does he know about this?'

'Oh yes,' said Swift. 'He knows and he feels the same.'

'Where is he anyway?'

Swift laughed and got up from the stool.

'Can't you guess? He was with Primrose at the feast so chances are they went to the hayloft. I'm sure he'll be done soon and then he'll come in for a drink.'

'Where are you off to?' asked Jay.

'Oh, just wandering about.'

But Swift knew exactly where he was going. Midnight wasn't far off and something was happening at the Stone Circle tonight. He didn't know what but he intended to find out.

Yul stood quietly in the shadows of a great stone buttress, breathing deeply of the night. It was so hot and noisy inside the Barn and he'd been dancing for hours, trying to spend time with everyone. The ceremony in the Village Green labyrinth had gone very well but as always he was drained afterwards. The feeling he experienced as the Earth Magic poured into him from its serpent source was exhilarating, flooding him until he felt he would burst. Then he must share the magic with everyone and this was the exhausting part. There were so many words of the ritual to remember, all to be chanted perfectly in harmony with the drums. By the end of the ceremony Yul always felt completely worn out, and then he must start socializing.

All he wanted to do now was go home to bed and sleep with Sylvie by his side. He closed his eyes with longing at the thought of it, imagining the silkiness of her skin and the smell of her silvery hair. She'd already left for the Hall, also worn out by the heat and noise. He'd seen her signalling that she was leaving whilst he was dancing with one of the teachers. He hadn't liked to cut the dance short but wished she'd stayed so they could be together. He hated Samhain night and Sylvie was the one person he could confide in. Over the years she'd helped him deal with his terrors until gradually they'd receded and become manageable. Nobody knew exactly what he'd gone through that fateful Samhain all those years ago, but she understood better than most. She knew he still had nightmares about it, and understood the fear that memories could arouse.

Yul knew it must be approaching midnight and then he could say his farewells and walk up the track to the Hall. He wandered away from the Barn and onto the Village Green, gazing up at the brilliant stars overhead. They were so much brighter in the black, moonless skies and he felt a shudder of excitement which overcame his Samhain fears. He'd always felt this when the Dark Magic was strongest but kept it hidden, for most people at Stonewylde only celebrated the Moon Fullness and were a little nervous of the Dark Moon. As he stepped into the labyrinth of white pebbles he felt a tug at his soul. Midnight was close and the magic was strong. He felt its power thrilling through his veins, re-energising him all over again.

Yul walked along the winding labyrinth path towards the wicker dome in the centre, deciding he should be in there at midnight. He wanted to talk to the dead and hopefully get a glimpse of old Mother Heggy. It'd happened a couple of times since her death almost thirteen years ago and he hoped that as it was the Dark Moon as well this year maybe he'd be lucky again. He still missed her wisdom and loyalty. He wished she'd lived long enough to see him as the new magus and to be proud of all he'd achieved since his sixteenth birthday.

He reached the dome and bent almost double to enter. Inside it was still rich with aromatic smoke. The black feathers hanging from the roof brushed his face as he sat down on the mats. He crossed his legs, straightened his back and closed his eyes, calling upon the power of Samhain and the Dark Moon to give him a glimpse of Mother Heggy, maybe even let him speak to her through the veil of death that separated his living world from the Otherworld. He shivered suddenly and felt the hairs on the back of his neck start to rise. Despite its emptiness, he knew suddenly that he wasn't alone in the wicker dome.

Sylvie had almost reached the beech-lined gravel drive leading up to the Hall. She knew she should've stayed by Yul's side until the end, but watching him dancing endlessly with every woman at Stonewylde or stand around drinking cider with all the men was difficult. She must wait patiently, smiling at everyone, dancing with the men, ignoring the looks many women gave her husband and pretending she didn't mind. She knew it was ridiculous, that he was only doing his duty as magus, but she still remembered Holly and how the girl had thrown herself at Yul. That was all so long ago now but Sylvie hated being reminded of her jealousy and negativity. So rather than hang around uselessly in the Barn watching people drinking, she'd decided to go to bed. It'd be peaceful and quiet as everyone was still down in the Village and hopefully Yul would come back soon too and leave the others to their revelry.

As she walked under the great beech trees, finally relinquishing their hold on their leaves, Sylvie breathed deeply of the cool night air. She remembered walking along this drive with Professor Siskin, and that funny way he had of skipping with excitement, babbling on about his theories and research. She wished so much that he were still alive. She often worried that her invitation to return to Stonewylde had hastened his death and wished she could see him and say sorry.

Sylvie felt his presence close as she walked along the crunchy gravel, almost sensed him by her side, a good head shorter than her and struggling to keep up with her long-legged strides. Her skin begin to prickle and she had the overwhelming feeling that he actually was walking beside her, his head cocked to one side like the little bird he was named for.

'Professor Siskin, I'm sorry,' she whispered. Tears choked her throat and her skin crawled with a strange emotion – almost dread. She stared straight ahead, terrified that if she did turn to look she'd see him there.

'No matter, my dear, no matter,' he would've said. Did he say it? Was she imagining the voice or was it really there? 'Be careful, Sylvie, and look to yourself. You must fight all over again, my dear girl. You must be so strong in the dark times ahead.'

In the dark cave Leveret stirred again on her bed of dried bracken. The fire had died low and Clip still sat near the entrance, motionless in the light of the glowing embers, his mind far away from his body. He was protecting her and yet she felt alone in the darkness. She struggled to remember something vital that she'd forgotten and then, in a moment of lucidity, she realised where she was – up in the Dolmen with Clip, with the red and white magic of Fly Agaric coursing through her. But it was so late. This should've happened in the afternoon, so that in the evening she could ...

It hit her like a punch to the stomach. It was Samhain! She'd prepared everything so she could cast a circle in the old hovel, try her very first spell, and contact Mother Heggy. Yet here she was miles away in a stone cave up in the hills with the owner of Stonewylde, her mind still spiralling out of control from the effects of the mushroom. Leveret cried out loud, a sound of utter despair. It was the Dark Moon and Samhain – goddess knew when the two would coincide again. She was in the wrong place with none of the things she needed for the spell, and she sensed with the inner Stonewylde knowledge that it was only minutes away from the magic hour of midnight. The veil would be drawn aside very soon and there was nothing she could do. She'd missed her chance to call upon Mother Heggy for help to become the new Wise Woman.

Leveret struggled to sit up in the darkness, just able to make out the motionless shape of Clip in his black-feathered cloak at the mouth of the cave. She hung her head in misery – how could she have been so stupid? How could she have misjudged it so badly? She buried her face in her hands, curls hanging down. Something brushed her shoulders in sympathy, a brief, light touch on her bent back. Leveret stiffened, too frightened to look up for fear of what she might see. She tasted words, words that danced towards her on dark wings.

'Little hare, I'm waiting for you. You're the dark one with the gift and you won't walk alone. I'm here, waiting and watching.'

She felt something brush her cheek and shrank in terror. Was she imagining all this? She must still be hallucinating. Slowly she lowered her hands from her face, and in her lap she found a black feather.

A wind had sprung up, starting as a slight breeze but increasing in intensity. The leaves on the Village Green stirred and then began to dance across the grass. Youngsters still fooling about outside felt the coolness on their overheated skin and began to think they'd had enough. They made their way back to the Barn where the Jack o' Lanterns flickered precariously in the steady draught. Out of the blue came a really sharp gust of wind and many of the guttering flames were extinguished in an instant. People gasped as it suddenly became much darker inside and the Samhain decorations took on a more sinister cast.

Inside the wicker dome Yul felt the wind pushing through the gaps. The hanging black feathers fluttered and spun around him. His dark curls lifted from his forehead in the gusts and he breathed deeply, feeling wild and free. He loved the elements and the touch of this wild wind made him want to leap on Skydancer and gallop hard along the Dragon's Back ridgeway. He felt the muscles in his legs tensing and laughed as the breeze suddenly tore through the wicker and snatched his breath away.

Sylvie sensed the leaves falling all around her as she walked under the beech trees, the breeze sighing mournfully in the branches, louder and louder and whipping her black cloak out behind her in a sudden gust. She was glad to reach the massive oak door in the porch and tug it open, holding it tightly so it didn't swing back in the strengthening wind. She crossed the vast entrance hall, unusually deserted, and started up the wide stairs, her fingers brushing the oak banister rail. Only a couple of dim night-lights burned and it was deathly quiet in the Hall. Everyone must still be down in the Village or already in their beds.

She felt the size of the building around her, so huge and silent. Turning at the top of the stairs into the dark corridor that ran the length of the huge front block, Sylvie opened the heavy door leading into the sitting room of their apartments. It was pitch black inside and she padded silently across the carpet towards a table lamp by the cold fireplace, craving the warmth and reassurance of light. Outside, the wind battered against the diamond window panes, moaning and rattling at the glass. Sylvie shivered in her grey and black robes and felt an inkling of why Yul disliked Samhain so much.

Up in the Stone Circle the flames in the red lanterns danced in the gusting wind. The five white figures, supine on the sledges, were motionless; only the material of their thin tunics moved in the breeze. The Bird and the crones, with the robed figures who'd dragged the sledges into the centre and a few chosen others, all stood within the circle of salt cast inside the Stone Circle. They'd been dancing for a while, weeks of preparation paying off as they cried their chant perfectly to the dark night, singing the words wildly and raising the energy to screaming pitch. The thirteen now stood breathing heavily after their frenzied cavorting, arms raised in supplication to the black skies. The wind howled around them and then there was a rumble of thunder, long and low, from beyond the hills.

'He comes, sister!' cried Violet, the words snatched from her mouth by the rising wind. Long grey straggles of hair whipped from under her hood across her face.

''Tis thunder,' said Vetchling. 'Only the thunder.'

'Nay, you fool! He is of the elements and he rides the storm, he *is* the storm. He's coming to our midst, sister, and we must be prepared to greet him. The Dark Magic has worked, as I knew it would.'

Vetchling shook her head, still unsure. She looked across at the Bird who stood with upturned face and raised hands, his mask in place. Slowly he started to turn on the spot, chanting as he did, creating a black vortex of movement. The thunder rumbled again, much louder this time, and Violet chuckled. There was a flicker of blue light behind the hills as the charged air sought to send its energy to the earth. This time Vetchling cackled with glee too.

'You speak true, sister – he is summoned and he comes. I feel it! I feel the elements coming together in a cauldron o' fury. When will we see him?'

Violet shook her head and the wind grabbed her hood clear. Her stringy hair flew out around her face like a halo of rats' tails.

'We cannot see what has no form. He's not of this world, sister, not of the living. He's of the elements – I told you so. But he'll be here, his spirit moving amongst us, his soul entering our dreams and our thoughts. He's ethereal and he's almost here!'

Again the dark clouds flashed with electricity and thunder rolled in a great peal, only a couple of seconds behind the lightning. Crouched behind one of the standing stones Swift watched the scene. He hugged his cloak close around him, cold in the violent wind that kept trying to tear it from him and more than a little scared. The dark figures, the Bird and the crones were silhouetted against the remaining red lanterns, scarcely visible. Then another brilliant slash of blue illuminated the hill top and their faces became shockingly clear down to every harsh detail.

Violet screamed an incantation and the air seemed to expand and crackle, pouring upwards in a spiral. Suddenly there came a great tongue of blinding blue-white light. It snaked down from the heavens overhead and plunged directly into the Circle, narrowly missing the people. At the same instant, thunder cracked above them so violently that even the crones jumped in terror, their ears ringing. Swift's heart leapt in his chest and he hid his face inside his cloak at the last moment, not wanting to see what appeared in the Circle.

In the Village, the Barn doors were pulled shut, the musicians had ceased playing and the dancing had stopped. There was a sense that the party was over. Cloaks were pulled on over party clothes just as heavy rain began to fall like iron nails to the ground.

Outside in the wicker dome, Yul felt the earth leap the moment the lightning blasted into the ground up at the Stone Circle. In his deepest core, the Earth Magic turned from green to blue for a few jagged instants. A stab of pain shot through him as the serpent writhed in shock, its back zigzagged with the discharge of elemental force. Yul cried out from the terrible intensity of it, clutching at the ground as he was shot through by the unearthly power. His skin tingled as if crawling with ants but the sensation inside him was worse. It was as if, at the moment the huge bolt of lightning had struck, the very polarity of his body had suddenly flipped from positive to negative. He felt like he'd been spun through a complete somersault and everything was now back to front and upside down inside him. As the rain fell, splashing down through the woven wicker, Yul found he was trembling from head to foot and tears coursed down his cheeks. He felt desperately in need of Sylvie's comfort.

Leveret heard the wind howling around the hill and felt the fine down on her arms rise in the charged air. The embers in the entrance were fanned to brightness but Clip sat like a stone, oblivious to everything. Leveret's mind was far from clear; she was still hallucinating freely. In the distance she saw the violent flashes and flickers of blue white light over the Circle and felt the thunder rolling around the hills. She hugged her arms around her, still curled in the dry bracken at the back of the cave, and wondered if she'd be safe in an electrical storm so high up. The wild elements usually touched a nerve of delight in her but tonight she was apprehensive. The chaotic energy crackled all around her and it was too much – too powerful in its fury. She saw the great forked tongue flicker and then stab violently into the earth. As Stonewylde writhed and screamed at the abuse, Leveret felt overwhelmed by the magnitude of the storm's power.

Sylvie laid her cloak over a chair and sank down onto the window seat in the darkness, looking out as sheets of heavy rain gusted against the glass. The dim table lamp had given a brief flash of light and then died, so the room was black all around her. She knew she should get up and light some candles but felt rooted to the spot. She could see little outside other than the nearest large tree bending madly in the gale. She thought of all the young people who lived in the Hall but were now stranded down in the Barn, and of her own children tucked up in the Nursery. She hoped they were sleeping through this terrible storm and not crying for her. She thought of Yul, also down in the Village. Sylvie wished he were here now with her, lying wrapped around her in their bed, whispering into her ear so she felt safe and loved. Instead she was totally alone, perhaps the only person in the Hall. Why hadn't she waited for him?

The climax of thunder cracked in the sky and the livid white-blue lit up the dark world outside. It reflected shockingly in the huge mirror over the empty fireplace, making the room suddenly stark and unreal. Everything was illuminated in that instant. Sylvie cried out in terror and hugged her arms around her, shrinking inside to a closed kernel of fear. Because, along with the noise and the ghastly flash, something else had come into the chamber. She hadn't smelt that aroma in many years and yet here it was silently wafting towards her, threading through and insinuating around the dark shadows of the room. She knew it well; it was heady, aromatic, and exotic. It was the scent of Magus.

8

In the Great Barn, folk shivered and glanced nervously at the dark shadowy corners. Everyone wanted nothing more than to be back home now, safe in their beds. Many of the teenagers who lived in the Hall decided to stay the night in the Village in their parents' cottages, and others were offered beds for the night to save them walking back in the violent wind and rain. There was also the fear of lightning strike, and nobody wanted to be caught exposed on the track leading up to the Hall.

As he stood inside the Barn amidst the turmoil, Yul realised with a jolt that Sylvie was all alone. He hoped desperately that she'd reached the shelter of the Hall before the storm really broke. Whilst people going back to the Hall milled around finding cloaks and lanterns and gathering to walk home together, Yul knew he must get back immediately. There was a phone-line in the Barn and he tried to ring the extension in their apartments but the tone sounded strange and there was no answer.

Pulling his cloak tightly around his Samhain robes, Yul hurried out into the wild night. His hood was blown back immediately and, lowering his head, he ran as fast as he could against the wind. He was hampered by his robes and cloak flapping around and tangling between his legs, becoming wetter and heavier by the minute. The trees danced frenziedly in the howling gale as Yul raced up the track, focusing on the thought of Sylvie alone and scared, trying not to think of the other fears that jostled him in the darkness. He felt hag-ridden – as if malignant forces were all around trying to stop him reaching the Hall. Several times he stumbled to his knees in the darkness and once fell headlong over a fallen branch, grazing his hands and jarring his wrists.

At last the huge blackness of the Hall loomed into sight. Almost crying with relief, his face awash with rain and hair plastered to his skull, Yul made a final surge towards the great wooden doors. He was exhausted by the struggle to get home and the events of Samhain, and frantic to find Sylvie – as much for his own comfort as hers. He skidded across the hall's polished parquet floor, his sodden cloak heavy around his legs, and raced up the dimly-lit stairs. All was gloomy as he crossed the landing and wrenched open the door to the grand apartments.

He was hit by a wall of darkness when he'd expected light. It was almost palpable and beneath his wet cloak and damp robes, Yul's flesh raised in goose-bumps.

'Sylvie?' he called, but his voice came out hoarsely. 'Sylvie, where are you? I've come back!'

His skin prickled with fear – where was she? Maybe she'd gone to bed? He tried to turn the lights on but nothing happened, so he stumbled through the grand sitting room, bumping into furniture in his haste, and made his way down to the bedroom.

'Sylvie?'

Still no response and his heart thudded with dread. He shivered violently, his head ringing with the heavy silence. He groped around on the dresser where he knew there were candles and matches. His cold hands fumbled with the box and he dropped it, the matchsticks spilling on the dark floor. He knelt and grabbed one, managing at last to light it. It flared, blinding him, then extinguished itself.

'Sylvie!' he called, louder this time. 'Sylvie, it's me – I've come back. Where are you?'

He lit another match and this time succeeded in lighting the wick of the candle. The flame bloomed and steadied, and Yul held the candlestick away from him to look around. The bed was empty and unslept in. It suddenly occurred to him that maybe Sylvie hadn't come back to the Hall after all. Perhaps she'd remained in the Village – gone to see if the children were alright in the Nursery and then stayed there. Which meant that he was now alone in these apartments. The thought made him shudder again.

Shielding the candle's fragile flame, he retraced his steps back through the empty bathroom and children's playroom and into the enormous sitting room. The flame did little to illuminate the vast area, dazzling his eyes and making the shadows even blacker.

'Sylvie?' he called softly, wanting more than anything the reassurance of her voice. The flame flickered and Yul's heart lurched as he saw her cloak lying across the back of the chair. So she was here – but where had she gone? Cursing the power cut and wishing the candle was more effective, he crossed the room to the fireplace. On the mantelpiece under the gigantic mirror was a candelabra. Carefully Yul started to light the candles but then a movement in the mirror caught his eye and his skin erupted into bristling terror as in the reflection before him, something sprang up behind him in the darkness and screamed and screamed.

Yul spun round, the candle-flame in his hand almost extinguishing, to see Sylvie standing by the window, her hands to her cheeks and her eyes and mouth gaping wide in absolute horror. The screams poured from her and as quickly as the flame allowed, Yul hurried across the room to comfort her. She was beside herself, her body convulsing and hair rippling as she shook, her hands clamped to her face and the nails digging into her cheeks. Juggling the candle and trying to put his arm round her was impossible, but then suddenly the power came back on and the room was flooded with light.

Blowing out the flame Yul took Sylvie in his arms and held her tight, waiting until the terror subsided. She could barely speak but shivered compulsively, shaking her head and apologising, clinging to him and crying softly.

'Did you smell it?' she whispered.

'Smell what?'

'When you came in here first, did you smell anything?'

123

'No,' Yul shook his head, 'no I didn't. What was it?'

'Why did you say you'd come back? Why did you keep saying that?'

'Because I had come back,' he said. 'I don't understand. Why were you so upset?'

But she wouldn't answer and after calming her down a little more, he ran a hot bath. An hour later they were both in bed, warm and dry and sipping tea. Sylvie couldn't tell him what had scared her so much and he was loath to push it – whatever it was had now gone. She was reluctant to turn the light off and Yul teased her gently about this, getting out of bed to put a light on in the bathroom and leaving the door ajar, so their bedroom was softly lit.

'Silly old thing,' he murmured into her hair as at last they stretched out, lying in each other's arms. 'It's me that's usually spooked at Samhain, not you.'

'I was so frightened when you were stumbling about in the dark,' she mumbled, almost asleep. 'And you said that you'd come back . . .'

They both drifted off to sleep, exhausted from their earlier fear and the long day, but during the night Yul awoke and reached for her. She smiled sleepily, drowsy but welcoming, and pulled him towards her. Propped on an elbow and half asleep himself, Yul kissed her deeply while he caressed her, knowing her so well. Soon she was gasping, wanting him urgently.

But as he braced himself above her on the point of making love, her eyes suddenly shot wide open. In the faint light, hovering above her, she saw her worst nightmare. This man poised over her didn't have dark curls, but straight silver-blond hair. He smiled down at her, eyes gleaming darkly.

'Sylvie, my beautiful Sylvie,' he murmured.

She shoved him away with a scream of absolute terror, the heel of her hand catching him hard on the jaw. She rolled to one side and out of bed in almost one movement.

'Get away from me!'

Chest heaving in panic, she backed away to the door. The dark shape in her bed sat up groping wildly for the light switch and the lamp crashed to the floor.

'Sylvie! What's the matter?'

'Keep away from me! Stay away!'

Sylvie flung the bathroom door wide open, heading for the girls' bedroom, wanting only to escape.

'Sylvie!'

She turned and caught a glimpse of Yul kneeling up on the bed with the quilt all tangled around him. He reached out towards her, his face twisted in anguish.

'Sylvie what is it? Don't go!'

She shook her head in complete confusion – this was now definitely Yul. Sobbing, she stumbled into the other bedroom and slammed the door shut, climbing into Celandine's empty bed with all the lights blazing. Yul tried to come in but she shouted at him to leave her alone, and recognising the hysteria in her voice, he returned to their bedroom. He spent a fitful night, worried sick. Sylvie sat bolt upright with Bluebell's quilt around her shoulders trying to stay awake. Every time her eyelids closed she'd jolt awake until at last she gave in to exhaustion and dozed restlessly. It was a long night and morning couldn't come soon enough.

Sylvie sat hugging her knees and stared absently at the ragged trees outside, still holding on to brown leaves that longed to let go. Her breakfast sat untouched on the table, as did Yul's. She closed her eyes and tried to swallow the sharp pain in her throat, a pain that also prickled at the back of her eyes and made hot tears well up suddenly and spill from under her closed eyelids. What was happening to her? What had happened last night?

She felt vulnerable and scared and worried about Yul. What must he be feeling? She'd never rejected him like that, not even during her illness. But she was sure it hadn't been him in bed with her last night. She was certain it was Magus and not a figment of her imagination, just as his strong scent had been real a little earlier. Somehow, Magus had returned. She sat in a state of misery, unsure of what to do or say for the best. How could you tell your husband that in the middle of the night, just as you were about to make love, he'd transformed into his late and hated father? In the cold light of morning it seemed utterly ridiculous.

Yul had gone now, presumably down to his office. He'd tried to talk about it this morning but Sylvie simply couldn't tell him what had happened. She'd stayed silent and withdrawn, resisting all his attempts to talk or just hold her, and eventually she begged him to forget the whole thing and leave her be. He'd looked so upset as he left but she was terrified of telling him what had really happened. She started to clear away the breakfast things, putting them in the dumb-waiter to go down to the kitchens. Her hands shook and the crockery rattled as she told herself firmly that her husband was not a shape-shifter and it couldn't possibly have been Magus who'd come to her bed and almost made love to her last night. That was the stuff of madness.

Yul stomped around the Stone Circle feeling the anger rise within him.

'*Desecrated!*' he spat and kicked at the remains of the funeral pyre, filthy on the soft earth floor. Another great patch of scorched earth very close to the Altar Stone showed where the lightning bolt had struck the night before at Samhain, during the Dark Moon. It was as if the very elements themselves had turned against Stonewylde, striking at her heart. Yul shuddered at the memory of the lightning strike, recalling the terrible sensation when he'd felt his whole being switch polarity and jolt in agonising spasm. He looked up and the black crows and white skulls painted on the great stones leered down, mocking him.

'Clear it up!' he roared, kicking viciously again at the ash with his riding boot. 'I want every single trace of this sacrilege removed! This is a place of life and energy, not death! Never, ever again ... and wash the stones.'

The men who'd come up on the wagon to tidy the Circle looked at one another nervously.

'But the paintings . . .'

'Wash them off!'

'But Yul, sir, it's the custom to leave them until the Winter Solstice,' said one of the men tentatively.

'I don't give a damn about the custom! That custom is finished! I want every single reminder of this awful Samhain ritual removed. If I find just one sign of it, there'll be big trouble. *Do you all understand?*'

He glared at the group of men belligerently and they nodded and kept their eyes down. Yul was formidable when he was angry.

Without a backward glance he strode across to where Skydancer was loosely tethered and swung up into the saddle in one powerful motion. A nudge from his heels and the great horse launched into a canter down the Long Walk, also sensing his master's anger and pent-up rage. They rode hard away from the Circle and up towards Dragon's Back. Once on the ridgeway, Yul gave Skydancer his head and man and horse flew, sweat gradually drenching them both despite the cool November breeze. Eventually they slowed down many miles away, with the green hills of Stonewylde all around them and the soft grey skies above. Yul slumped in the saddle, his shoulders drooping as Skydancer ambled along getting his wind back, cropping occasionally at the short turf.

Yul gazed, without seeing, at the curved beauty of the landscape. His deep grey eyes were clouded with inner turmoil and his mouth, usually so firm, quivered. He fought back the tears, but lost the battle as great heaving sobs overwhelmed him. Sylvie was the person he held above all others. She was the brightness to his darkness, his counterpart and balance – how could she not want him? What had happened last night? He tried but failed to push away the terrible thought – was this a return to her illness?

A few days later, Leveret stood above the springhead looking down. The hill was almost vertical here and very short grass struggled to survive on the thin soil that barely covered the rock. Although she couldn't actually see it, Leveret knew that just below her, under the craggy outcrop of rock at her feet, the spring gushed from a cleft in the rock-face. The clear, pure water tumbled down, seemingly a small fountain but quickly gaining in volume and velocity as it surged down the hill towards the distant Village.

It was joined on its journey by other small springs until it became the river that flowed past the Village, full of otters and kingfishers and overhung with weeping willows. An ox-bow next to the Playing Fields formed a great fresh-water pool with beaches where the children played and swam in the warm months. Yul had taught her to swim there many years ago. The river flowed on, past the mill where the flour was ground, the tannery where the skins were cured, the clay beds where the potters worked, and into the reed beds where the thatchers gathered their materials and the wading birds nested, before finally reaching the sea. Looking now at the thin trickle just visible through the undergrowth, it was hard to imagine such a small source creating such a body of water.

None of this occurred to Leveret as she stood listening to the water tinkling below. She'd come here unintentionally, wandering out of the Village along the river bank and then taking a detour when the spring became too small and steep to follow upstream any longer. She'd walked in the early morning half-light up into the springhead hills, feeling a need to be somewhere high and quiet. She stood on the rock above the watershed and gazed at the beauty all around her. Wisps of mist clung to the lower hills in the clean November morning. The sky was palest blue, with streaks of gold and pink to the east where the sun would soon rise. The morning star was fading fast, and a late fox slunk past her heading for its earth. The sound of joyous birdsong was all about. A pair of great buzzards circled overhead, mewing and calling mournfully. Their enormous wings were spread on the air currents, the white stripes and splayed end-feathers clearly visible as they drifted.

Leveret sighed deeply and the breath caught in her throat. She felt unutterably sad as she looked down at the boulders below. As she'd done so many times before, she questioned the point of it all. Her life was a misery and everyone was against her. The one thing she wanted to do – roam Stonewylde freely so she could learn about the plants and fungi, collect them and make concoctions to heal – was forbidden, and instead it was all duty. She must go to school, must work hard to get good exam results, must help with all the jobs at home, must join in the Village activities and be like everyone else.

But she wasn't like everyone else. The other girls of her age – Tansy, Linnet, Bryony and Skipper to name a few, and even the younger ones like Cecily and Faun – they all belonged to something she didn't even begin to understand. They were interested in the same things, laughed together, fancied boys openly, talked about all the boring stuff that they found fascinating and Leveret wasn't a part of that. She couldn't care less who said what, the clothes everyone wore, or whose hair was longer or prettier. She had her deep secrets and would rather have died than share these with such fatuous company. Although there was someone special she found attractive, this too was dark, forbidden territory where nobody trespassed. The only person she actually enjoyed being with was her friend Magpie and even he could be hard work at times – besides which, she wasn't allowed to see him anymore either.

The glimmer of hope that had kept her going was the dream of contacting Mother Heggy at Samhain and of one day being the Wise Woman of Stonewylde. She'd completely messed that up, and then had another terrible fight with her mother after the fiasco at Samhain. Maizie was now adamant that Leveret would never be allowed to become a herbalist, but should instead go to university in the Outside World and become a doctor. Her future seemed as bleak as her present.

Since Samhain she'd felt as if she were walking a tightrope. Her mother was furious with her for disappearing from the Barn without saying where she was going, and had been threatening to talk to Yul. She'd also scolded Leveret for misleading Clip about her brothers. Once again, Sweyn had managed to twist the facts and avoid punishment for the apple-bobbing incident, and Leveret despaired of her mother ever listening to the truth. Rosie had taken her aside and called her selfish and unfeeling for spoiling Samhain for their mother, saying how ashamed she was to have such a nasty little sister. Sweyn and Gefrin had hinted darkly at some horror in store for her which filled her with dread, and she had to constantly manoeuvre herself into situations where she wouldn't be alone with them. Magpie was upset with her too because she'd vanished at Samhain and not been with him.

Even Clip, whom she now thought of as her wise silver owl, had given her a stern talking to about the dangers of mushrooms and especially Fly Agaric. He'd made her promise never to take anything like that again when she was alone. She was still experiencing after-effects and Clip said that the hallucinations may continue sporadically for some time. She didn't want to lose his good will too, and was grateful that he'd squared her absence with Maizie and tried to explain about Sweyn's cruelty. It wasn't Clip's fault it fell on deaf ears – how was he to know that Maizie never ever stuck up for her but always took her brothers' side?

Leveret looked down at the boulders and imagined how she'd actually die if she jumped. The quickest end would be if her head split open and her brains spilled out. The worst would be breaking a limb and being unable to move, to die slowly of exposure, as nobody would think of looking for her up here. Neither option was inviting and she decided that if she were to end her life it would have to be more controlled and less down to chance. She'd make herself a strong concoction – she knew several natural poisons – and ensure there was no doubt about the outcome. Not that she wanted to kill herself – life was difficult, but she wasn't ready to pass on to the Otherworld yet. Magpie loved her even if nobody else did, and how would he manage without her friendship?

She dragged her gaze from the dangerous rocks below and looked up to the blue skies. The buzzards had disappeared, but ahead she saw a sight that made her heart lift. A lone kestrel, golden in the rising sun, hovered overhead. Its tail feathers fanned out and its wings were perfectly balanced to keep it almost motionless in the air. Leveret's thin face broke into a rare smile – maybe the kestrel was an omen.

The early morning walk didn't make her too late for school although Maizie was angry that she'd disappeared again and had missed breakfast. It was during Religious Studies, when she was grappling to understand how anyone could worship such strange gods in such bizarre ways, that the intercom phone buzzed and the teacher informed her she was to go to Yul's office immediately. Tansy and Skipper whispered at this and several people looked at her strangely. Many forgot that she was Yul's sister, which was just how she wanted it. But incidents like this reminded everyone and then she had to put up with more ostracism. It wasn't that the young people of her age didn't like their magus; rather it put Leveret into a different league to them.

Leveret stood in the doorway, her heart thudding. She wasn't scared of Yul but of the power he had over her, over what she could and couldn't do. He'd never hurt or torment her the way Sweyn and Gefrin loved to do, but ultimately he could make or break her life with just a few words. He held all the power and she had none.

Yul stood with his back to the door, looking out of the French windows at the gardens beyond. Leveret observed how his broad shoulders drooped. He still wore his riding clothes and she'd noticed lately how he was out and about very early every morning on Skydancer. Several times she'd had to hide in the bushes to avoid him seeing her. He seemed even taller than usual, although maybe he'd lost some weight. His dark hair was quite long now and she saw how it curled exactly the same as hers did with tiny bits of twig and leaf caught up in it.

There was something quite desolate in the way he stood lost in reverie, so large and powerful and yet so very defenceless. Leveret felt a sudden rush of her old love for him, for the big brother she'd once adored. He was still the same Yul. She had an entirely unexpected urge to run over and fling her arms around him, hug him very tight, kiss his cheek and gaze into his deep grey eyes just like she used to. To tell him that whatever was the matter, she still loved him and always would.

He turned, his eyes sad and mouth vulnerable. But when he saw Leveret his expression changed abruptly and he glared at her.

'Stop lurking in the doorway, Leveret! Come in and shut the door – you and I need to have words.'

Her rekindled affection was promptly extinguished. She shoved the heavy door closed and stomped across the room to stand before him. He looked down at her, his face hard and closed. She glowered up at him through her mat of curls, green eyes insolent.

'Well?' he barked. 'Do you know why you're here?'

'Because you sent for me.'

He nodded slowly, the lines around his mouth sharper than ever.

'So that's how you want to play it – fine by me. That's exactly the attitude that has upset Mother so much. She's at her wits' end with you and it's going to stop. You have to start behaving yourself as of today.'

She continued to stare up at him, not lowering her gaze, not looking contrite or in the least bit scared. He felt his fingers flexing and was shocked to realise he wanted to slap the insolence from her face, to grab hold of her shoulders and shake her hard. How dare she defy him like this? What could he do to stop her, to make her fear him and scare her into submission?

Then it hit him like a blow between the eyes – this was exactly how Magus had felt when, as a boy, he'd shown neither respect nor fear. Yul took a deep breath to steady himself at the enormity of this revelation. He'd never, ever even contemplated hitting a child. How could he have considered it now? It hadn't been a conscious thought – his hands had started to move of their own accord. Was he turning into a sadistic bully like his father?

Yul shook his head and looked away, gazing once more out of the window at the clear November morning. He was tired, having been up since long before dawn riding like the devil along Dragon's Back. He'd eaten no breakfast and had been sleeping very badly on the sofa; the last thing he'd needed was his mother upset and worried, nagging at him to sort Leveret out and make her behave when she couldn't.

He closed his eyes for a moment and could feel himself trembling – with exhaustion, hunger or both, he wasn't sure. That was why he'd felt that momentary urge to physically punish this small and pathetically defiant girl who was no threat to him, nor to the fabric of Stonewylde. He must keep this in proportion and not let his personal problems impinge on his judgement or handling of this situation.

He looked again at Leveret and saw her properly this time. She was still small for her age and always had been. She was remarkably like him, dark-haired and scowling, with winged eyebrows, a straight nose and full mouth. Her cheek bones were sharp and her jaw a softer female version of his. Her skin was olive like his, tanned from so much time spent outdoors and this made her clear sea-green eyes, so long-lashed and slanted, all the more striking. She wasn't pretty but was attractive in an unusual, quirky way. She was also a little dirty and clearly not interested in her appearance, for her hair was wild and messy and her clothes very basic Stonewylde work-clothes of coarse linen, dyed a muddy green.

He thought suddenly of another half-sister, Magus' daughter by Rowan, whom he'd noticed only yesterday as she ate lunch in the Hall. Faun must be two years younger than Leveret but she was clearly very self-aware. She was already taller than this dark-haired girl before him, long-limbed and quite plump, curvy where Leveret was slight. Faun had the silver-blond Hallfolk hair, which she tossed over her shoulders at every opportunity. Her pretty, smooth face was the complete opposite to Leveret's pointed, secretive one.

Yul felt a surge of affection for this dark sister, whom he remembered had loved him fiercely as a small girl. He recalled her climbing all over him, begging him for more stories as his reading improved, riding on his shoulders for miles when he took her up into the hills. She'd always been naughty and defiant, never respected the rules. He remembered finding her once out in the back garden amongst the raspberry canes, the fruit all gone and a guilty look on her face. She'd run circles round the two brothers closest to her in age; Yul had made puzzles and played games with them and Leveret, so much brighter, always beat them. She'd been a delightful little girl, independent and fierce but very affectionate. What had gone wrong? Why was she so awful and sullen nowadays?

'Come and sit down, Leveret,' he said wearily. She followed him to the old leather sofa and sat stiffly on the edge whilst he sank back into the softness of it, his long body stretched out. 'I'm going to call for some breakfast. Will you join me? Mother says you missed it again today.'

She shook her head.

'Leveret, I know you. You're kind and loving and I'm sure you don't want to upset Mother deliberately. The way you're behaving is really getting her down. I want to work this out with you for Mother's sake. You love her too, don't you? Will you listen to me? We can sort this out if you'll meet me halfway.'

But she couldn't. She couldn't climb down from her position of stubbornness and defiance. If she did she was scared she'd capitulate totally and burst into tears, agreeing to everything he said and giving in to what Maizie wanted. Yul was very patient at first, trying hard to get through to her. The kinder he was, the stiffer she became. She refused to communicate, hating herself for being so difficult but not knowing how to compromise.

At last he fell silent, defeated, and she relaxed a little. He was being so nice and she ached with pity for him – for the sadness in his eyes, the tired lines on his face, the way he sighed and looked as if his world were falling apart. Deep inside, a little piece of her started to melt. Maybe she could tell him everything: her dream of being Stonewylde's Wise Woman, her need to be free to roam, her fear of Sweyn and Gefrin and their cruel treatment. Maybe he'd understand and be on her side. They'd been really close once – maybe it could be like that again. She sat back a little on the sofa and turned to face him. His eyes were closed and his mouth soft, and she longed to hug him tight like she used to.

'Yul, I—'

The intercom phone buzzed and he wearily opened his eyes and rose to answer it. Leveret sat there thinking of how to begin. She felt as if a great weight had been lifted. She should've come to Yul before – they'd always loved each other and maybe he'd only shut her out because he was so busy and preoccupied, not realising how much it hurt her. He slammed the phone down hard and strode back to stand before her. The sadness had vanished and his face was now taut and angry.

'Right, Leveret. I've tried but have clearly not got through to you. So—'

'Yul, I want to talk! I think—'

'No! I've wasted enough time. You've had your chance to talk but we've been going round in circles here and now I've missed an important call, and you've managed to miss the rest of your lesson, which is probably what you wanted. I hear that you're not working hard any more. Mother told me you don't want to continue your studies after your exams, but be assured that you will. You're blessed with intelligence and by goddess you'll use it. I'll be checking up on you at school regularly from now on, Leveret, and if I see you're not working hard I'll start breathing down your neck. You'll start co-operating with Mother and do all the work you have to do at home just like every other person at Stonewylde. We grow our food and we make our clothes – it's part of our lives here and you're no exception.'

'No, but you are,' she muttered, her throat constricted with unshed tears at his sudden volte-face from the kind brother to magus.

'WHAT?'

'You don't grow your food or make your clothes. Neither does your wife.'

'Don't you *dare* answer me back like that!'

She shrugged and stared ahead, her body once more stiff and defiant.

'You *will* toe the line, Leveret, or suffer the consequences.'

'Which are?'

Yul could bear her insolence no longer. He yanked her up from the sofa and gripped her by the shoulders, his fingers digging into the delicate bones, stooping so his face was level with hers. Flashing grey eyes locked onto rebellious green ones. She wouldn't drop her gaze but sent out pulses of anger at him. His face darkened dangerously and she felt him tremble, struggling to control his rage. She almost wanted to laugh out loud at the power she had over him – she'd never seen him this angry before. He saw the exultation in her eyes and for a second she thought she'd gone too far, pushed him beyond control. She almost had. But Yul's past was the most powerful factor in all that he did. Slowly and carefully he let go of her shoulders, straightened up and took a step back. He breathed deeply, consciously unclenching his jaw.

'We'll discuss the consequences at the end of school today – come back here then. Return to your lessons now and apologise for your absence. That's all.'

Dismissed, she walked stiff-legged from the room and spent the rest of the morning worrying herself silly about what he was going to do. It made her angry that this was exactly what he'd intended.

At lunch time, she trooped into the Dining Hall and queued with everyone at the big serving tables for her food. She really didn't want lunch but knew she needed to eat; she'd felt dizzy and weak all morning. The noise was terrible in here and she contemplated just walking out and skipping school completely for the afternoon. She could go home, get some bread and cheese and spend the afternoon out in the open. But Leveret knew that would only bring down more trouble on her head, especially if Yul wanted to see her later after lessons.

Feeling utterly despondent, she shuffled along in the queue with all the other students, slowly reaching the serving tables. Marigold stood here, sporting a large colourful apron and flushed cheeks. She was supervising the students on work detail who were busy serving up lamb hot pot and mashed potato.

'Not that much, Bee! We'll run out afore we're halfway through! And don't slop it everywhere!'

The students served the food from steaming vats, which were replaced at intervals from trolleys pushed in from the kitchen. The whole operation went like clockwork for Marigold was more than accustomed to feeding such large numbers, even if her latest band of helpers had little idea about portion control. Cherry, meanwhile, kept a close eye on the students clearing away the dirty plates and keeping the tables clean.

Leveret finally received her plateful and looked for a space to sit. The long tables were laid with cutlery, water and bowls of pears. Everywhere teemed with teenagers and she eyed the teachers' corner warily, not wanting to sit anywhere near the large, secluded alcove where the adults were served their lunch. She scuttled down the long rows to a slightly emptier spot in the corner and quickly began to eat.

There may just be time to go outside to visit to the herb garden before afternoon classes began. Leveret knew that next September, the start of her final school year, she'd move up here and join the other boarders. She really hoped to get in Cherry's good books and influence her when the work detail rotas were drawn up every week. If she could get herself rostered to work regularly in the herb garden, life would be a bit more bearable.

'Can I sit here, Leveret?'

She scowled up through her mat of curls and was really surprised to see ginger hair. Rufus – the only person at Stonewylde, apart from his mother, to be blessed with truly red hair. Her scowl deepened. The last thing she wanted was to make conversation with a silly boy, who'd doubtless attract his mates to the table too. She knew it was Rufus' first year at Senior School, although he lived in the Tudor Wing with Miranda. She'd seen him daily when they were at the Village School together, but had never really had much to do with Rufus. However as offspring of two of the key Council Elders and siblings of Yul and Sylvie, they'd been thrown together on occasions in the past. Leveret grunted noncommittally and continued eating quickly. If he thought she'd be friendly he was wrong.

'I saw you coming out of Yul's office at break time,' said the boy, sitting down opposite her. He picked up his cutlery and started to eat, his table manners far neater than hers. Rufus watched her carefully from beneath his thick fringe of silky red hair. Like his half-sister Faun, he'd inherited his father's deep brown eyes. Combined with the bright hair and pale skin, he was striking and Leveret had always thought of him as a red squirrel. Not that she thought of him much.

'Did he ask to see you, or did you ask him?'

His voice was quiet and a little hesitant, and he nervously blinked at her through his fringe.

'None of your business!' she retorted. 'What's it to you?'

'Sorry. It's just that . . . I know you're Yul's half-sister and I'm his half-brother, and—'

'Yeah, but different halves. I'm no relation to the old magus.'

'No, I know – you're lucky. Everyone hates him and I don't like people thinking I'm going to turn out like him.'

'Doesn't seem to bother Yul. Or Faun.'

'No, I suppose not.'

Leveret had almost finished her lunch and took a great gulp of water, anxious to be off. She'd take a pear with her to the herb garden.

'Leveret, do you think . . .'

He stopped and she frowned at him. He was pretty hard work and she'd never asked him to sit here.

'Spit it out, Rufus. Do I think what?'

He knew she was about to get up and leave, and it came tumbling out in a rush.

'I really want Yul to teach me to ride and I want to go and ask him but I'm scared he'll say no or just laugh or something and—'

'Why on earth are you telling me this?' she asked. 'I can't ride. Well, not very well.'

'I just thought . . .' he paused and looked at her in anguish.

Their eyes met for the first time and Leveret felt an unexpected surge of sympathy. He had beautiful deep brown eyes, like soft velvet, and his hair reminded her of new conkers. But it wasn't that – it was his wistfulness that got to her. So she smiled encouragingly; he'd been brave to come and sit with her and his mates were probably all laughing at him.

'Tell me, then,' she said more gently. 'What did you think?'

'I wondered as you're so close to Yul if you might kind of … ask him for me? Or at least see if you think he'd listen if I asked? He's so brilliant, such a fantastic rider and if he'd just take me out and—'

Leveret felt another rush of compassion. Poor kid – she needed to put him straight about his half-brother.

'Rufus, I'm sorry but I don't think I can help you. You've got the wrong idea about me and Yul. He never usually speaks to me at all and I was only in his office this morning to be told off.'

'But you're so close to him! I've seen you loads of times. I remember the day when he came on his horse – that beautiful Nightwing – to collect you from Nursery and he sat you up on the saddle in front of him and you galloped away together across the Village Green. And him giving you piggy-backs up to the Stone Circle for the ceremonies, and when he took you home from school that time you were sick all over the floor. And on the beach in the summer, you used to hold onto his neck when he swam out to the rock, and—'

Leveret felt a lump in her throat as his words spilled out. Poor Rufus; she'd never realised. It'd never occurred to her how Rufus must've felt watching her as a little girl with her wonderful big brother, who was also his big brother. She doubted it'd ever occurred to Yul either. She couldn't actually recall one incident when she'd seen him even talk to the little boy, let alone make him feel special.

'Oh Rufus! It's true, Yul was lovely when I was young, before he went away to university and then came back and was handfasted. He was lovely and I adored him. But … but he's not like that anymore. He's horrible, really awful. He's just been shouting at me in his office and I actually thought he was going to hit me!'

Rufus looked doubtful at this.

'No, really! He grabbed me and his face was red and he was shaking with fury. He's not a nice person anymore and really, you're far better off without him. I'd steer well clear of him and not ask him about riding. He'll just drop you when other people muscle in and he gets bored with you, and then ...'

She couldn't go on. Rufus stared at her, trying to gauge her expression under the curtain of black curls.

'Leveret? Are you okay?'

She shook her head, keeping her face down.

'Well ... thanks for warning me. I might still ask him if I get a chance, but I won't expect too much. Sorry if I've upset you.'

Rufus got up in embarrassment, taking his half-eaten lunch away. He'd never intended to make anyone cry.

9

Squatting alone at the end of a muddy lane, on the very edge of the Village, was a desolate cottage. It seemed to slither into the surrounding brambles and briars, the filthy, cracked window-panes staring out like dead eyes. The front garden was untended and choked with tall weeds and inside was no better. The sitting room was dark and squalid with unidentifiable piles of mess everywhere, all furred with greasy dust. A fire burned in the hearth but other than that it was a cheerless place. The furniture was similar to that in all the other cottages but it was all heavily worn and soiled. Unlike Maizie's scrubbed table and well-stocked dresser, the table was littered with stale scraps of food and mounds of dirty crockery. Acrid smoke from three pipes hung heavily in the air. Clustered around the fire on battered rocking chairs sat three women, two elderly sisters and one enormous, slack-bodied daughter, all drinking tea and smoking, engaged in desultory conversation.

Violet and Vetchling were wrapped in dirty shawls, their feet clad in ancient boots, whiskery faces lined and grimy. They were an unfetching pair, their faces permanently creased in expressions of dissatisfaction. Vetchling's daughter, Starling, was little better. Long, greasy hair hung down her back, which was slabbed with fat. Her face could've been quite pretty – and once it had been – but her belligerent scowl and dark-stained teeth put paid to that. She drew deeply on the clay pipe and toasted her great rolls of stomach and side-sagging breasts in the heat of the fire.

The three could be found like this most days. They were close-knit; the events of years ago when Vetchling's son Jackdaw had been banished from Stonewylde bound them together. The whole community had ostracised them, but even before that they'd lived on the fringes. Diligence and sheer hard work were prized by the Villagers and these three were not good examples of such virtues. Starling had never been hand-fasted, but as a young woman had enjoyed the company of many of the Village lads, especially when they'd been drinking and weren't feeling fussy. Unlike most Village women, Starling had conceived Magpie late in life. She had no desire for a child and thanks to her mother and aunt's knowledge, had managed to avoid falling pregnant until his conception. His father could've been one of many and Starling made no secret of her indifference to the unwanted baby, neglecting him shockingly.

The three women sat now in companionable silence, sucking on their pipes and slurping at their tea. Just as they always avoided the Stonewylde doctor, they'd also rejected the services of the Stonewylde dentist. Consequently Violet and Vetchling were now almost toothless and Starling would be following just as soon as her puffy gums gave up their hold on her remaining dark stumps. They treated their ailments themselves as the two older women had a good knowledge of herb lore. Even today, Violet and her sister cultivated a diversity of unusual plants. Stuffed in the dresser drawers were paper twists bursting with various seeds, all gleaned from this year's gathering. The back garden of their cottage, where fruit and vegetables were supposed to be grown, bore harvests unlike those of the other Villagers. The dense weeds and undergrowth were merely a blind. Nobody ever examined the nature of the rank fecundity of Violet and Vetchling's plot, and an abundance of strange plants thrived there undisturbed, producing crops not grown elsewhere at Stonewylde.

'Fire needs stoking,' muttered Vetchling, grunting as she leant forward to fling another log into the flames. 'More wood, Starling.'

'He's out there now chopping,' replied her daughter. 'Can't you hear him?'

Vetchling was a little deaf but could just hear the rhythmic thud of axe on wood coming from the lean-to outside. She nodded.

'Taking his time about it,' she grumbled. 'Always does, lazy clout. If there's a job to be done, he'll make it last all day, that one. Bone idle.'

'Aye, sister. Listen, he's stopped again.'

'Magpie!' bellowed Starling. 'Hurry up with them logs!'

The back door crashed open and Magpie tramped through the kitchen into the sitting room bearing a great basket of newly cut logs. The three women eyed him malignantly as he shuffled between them with his burden, trying to place it on the hearth whilst avoiding their feet. His coat hung in filthy folds about him and his nose was running. He kept his dull eyes down.

'Lazy good-for-nothing!' spat Starling, aiming a solid kick at his bent form. He yelped like a dog. 'Is that all the wood cut now?'

He stood there in their midst with his head hanging, greasy hair covering his face, and nodded.

'About time too – it's taken you all morning. Now get the water, boy. WATER! D'you understand?'

He nodded again miserably and stood there waiting for any other instruction.

'Well get on with it then, you half-wit!' Starling screeched, picking up the heavy stick she kept propped by her chair for just such a purpose and lashing out at him. He could have avoided the blow but didn't, and it caught him soundly on the hip. He'd learnt over the years that dodging the blows and kicks only made them rain down harder; it was best to take them stoically from the outset. He began to shuffle away, sniffing hard, and Violet's boot shot out to connect with his shins.

'Don't dither about fetching the water, boy,' she said. 'I've an errand for you myself and I'm not waiting all day. If you take too long there'll be no dinner. You'll come back to an empty bowl and 'twill serve you right.'

He regarded her mournfully then left the room, collecting the water cart from outside to pull down the lane to the nearest pump in the heart of the Village.

Starling chuckled and stuffed another pinch of the herbal mixture into the bowl of her pipe.

'He ain't getting no dinner anyway, the stupid git. I already told him that this morning when he spilt the ashes all over the hearth. Mind you, he's probably forgot. What did I ever do to deserve such an idiot?'

'He has his uses,' muttered Violet. 'If he were normal like Jay, he'd be up at the Hall now. Terrible custom that, taking our young 'uns away from us. Jay should be living here with his family, not up there.'

She spat into the fire and rocked harder on her chair.

'Aye, sister, but our Jay comes back most days to see us, don't he? Likes his pipe too much to stay away long,' cackled Vetchling. 'That boy does love a good smoke. Don't know what we'd do without him popping in to see us. He's a fine young man, just like his father were.'

'Aye, just like our own Jackdaw.'

'I saw that busy-body Maizie yesterday,' said Starling. 'Did I tell you?'

'Aye, daughter, you did. That one's got ideas above her station. Who does she think she is?'

'She knows well who she is,' muttered Violet grimly. 'She's the mother of that upstart whelp. 'Tis why she thinks she can come poking her nose into our doings.' She spat again, more violently. 'She'll get her come-uppance, that one, and pay for her high and mighty ways. She'll fall along with the rest of 'em.'

'Aye, sister, she'll fall, and that bastard of hers with his black locks. Blond is the magus, not black – any fool knows that. He'll fall alongside his whore of a mother, and that Outsider runt of a wife too. They'll all suffer, right enough, and we'll be sitting pretty.'

The three cackled in unholy unison and sparks shot up the chimney.

A while later, Starling heaved herself out of her chair and waddled over to the range. She poked at the bubbling contents of a large iron pot and the aroma of rabbit stew filled the cottage. The two crones smacked their lips. Starling began to ladle portions into chipped bowls and Vetchling rose creakily to get the spoons and bread. Soon all three were tucking into their dinner, still rocking gently by the fire, sucking and champing at the very tender stew that never came to an end but was added to daily. The bread, collected from the bakery by Magpie earlier in the day, was dipped into the rich gravy until it disintegrated. Starling helped herself to several portions of stew and generous amounts of bread, but the crones had smaller appetites. At last they sat back replete, and all belched loudly before reaching for their pipes.

'She wanted to know why the boy weren't at school,' said Starling, resuming the earlier conversation as if there'd been no break. 'I told her he was poorly with a head-cold. She said he must see that bitch-doctor if he were ill and he must be back at school tomorrow.'

'Interfering busy-body,' muttered Violet. 'Sniffing in our doings. Why should she tell us what to do? Who is she anyway?'

'Nobody, sister, nobody. She got no right to interfere with us. We'll do as we like with that boy. 'Tain't up to her.'

'I'll have to send him back to school tomorrow,' said Starling. 'We don't want that doctor poking about examining him, do we? Maizie gave me a right old talking to about the boy – don't know what's suddenly got her all of a-fuss about him! Ain't none o' her business and I told her so. She didn't like that, but then she said I got to take him to the bath house too afore he goes back to school.'

'Pah!' cried Violet. 'The worst thing to do to a body if it's got a cold. He don't need a bath anyway. 'Tis unnatural, all this bathing.'

'I know, Aunt, but I'll have to take him. She'll just make trouble if I don't.'

Just then they heard the sound of rickety wheels on the lane; Magpie had arrived back with the tanks on the cart full of fresh water. He dragged the heavy cart up to the back door and positioned it so the taps were to hand. Then he came in and stood in the doorway sniffing hopefully. The three turned to regard him, Starling smiling.

'Can you smell the dinner, boy?'

He nodded and looked towards the corner where his empty bowl lay on the floor.

'Are you hungry?'

He nodded eagerly.

'Do you want some dinner then? Nice rabbit stew?'

He nodded again, his eyes more alive than they'd been that day.

'Ah, but what did you do this morning, Magpie?'

He looked puzzled, then began to mimic the action of wood chopping.

'No, dim-wit, before that. What did you do?'

He looked completely dumbfounded.

'What did you do that made me angry? Goddess he's stupid! What did you do and I said you'd get no dinner? Aye that's right, remembered now, have you? So will you get any of this nice dinner now? No. That's right, you'll go hungry. Now get in your bed!'

Whimpering, he scuttled over to the corner and flung himself down onto the fetid rug on the floor under the stairs, the dirty alcove serving as his bedroom. He was treated like a dog, even down to the bowl on the floor. He sat there rocking backwards and forwards, curled in misery as the three women laughed.

'Shall I tell him about the bath?' whispered Starling gleefully.

Magpie's reaction was as they'd imagined, and it was only the threat of a sound beating from Jay that persuaded him to leave his bed and follow Starling down the lane. He shuffled behind her, whimpering the whole way, terrified of the ordeal that lay ahead. She laughed and scolded in turns, frightening him further and enjoying his terror. At the bath house she kicked him into a cubicle and began to fill the bath with hot water. Magpie snivelled noisily until she'd had enough; picking up the metal jug used for rinsing hair, she clouted him over the head with it.

Half an hour later they re-emerged, Magpie much cleaner but still smelling disgusting as he'd had to put on the same filthy clothes. Starling waddled grimly to the centre of the Village and entered the food stores. She might as well get more supplies now she was here with Magpie to carry everything. The boy did have his uses.

Leveret was delighted to have Magpie back at school because she'd been lonely without him. There were many students of her own age at school as she'd been born towards the end of the baby boom, but by nature, Leveret had no close friends. She was prickly and secretive and rejected any tentative invitations to join one group or another. Lately she'd been worse than usual, skulking about the Hall under her own black cloud, unable and unwilling to confide in anybody about her dark unhappiness.

Magpie wasn't in any of Leveret's teaching groups. She was one of the high fliers whether she liked it or not, and he bumped along at the very bottom of the non-academic group, learning basic literacy and numeracy skills and a practical trade. When Magpie had first arrived at the Hall School four years ago, it had been difficult for Miranda to place him anywhere. She tried her best, but he was kept at home a great deal with various ailments, and when he did turn up his attention span was short and his communication non-existent. He spent most lessons gazing out of the window vacantly, or if he had any paper, drawing tiny sketches.

On a practical level Magpie was often sent into the huge kitchen gardens to learn about growing vegetables and fruits. There he was an asset when it came to undertaking the very mundane, repetitive tasks that others hated, such as planting peas; he'd take the same slow care with the last pea as the first.

He never skimped or rushed a task but would continue doggedly until it was completed, provided the instructions were very clear and simple.

On his return to school after this latest absence, Magpie slouched into the Hall along with all the others who walked up every day from the Village. But unlike them, he didn't stand around in the main entrance hall talking in groups as he had no friends and couldn't talk. Nor did he go to his first class to leave his bag as he didn't have one. Instead he went straight to the Galleried Hall where morning assembly was always held. He'd looked for Leveret on his walk to school and was sad not to have found her, but he loved this great room and it cheered him up.

The stained glass was beautiful, especially in the morning with sunlight streaming through. He was also fascinated by the carvings up on the roof bosses and particularly liked the faces of the Green Men and the triple hares. He stood still on the ancient stone flags, neck tipped back as he studied the vaulted roof. It was too early for assembly so he had the place completely to himself. After a while his neck ached so he lay down on the floor on his back and found he could see the carvings perfectly in this position. Assembly was held standing, just a brief coming together to start the day, so there were no chairs in the way and he could stretch out in comfort. Magpie smiled at his discovery of a better way to view the ceiling, his turquoise eyes dreamy with pleasure as he lay there in his filthy coat gazing upwards and grinning.

Gradually other students started to arrive, stepping round to avoid the prone figure and giggling at his incongruity. Soon the hall was full of youngsters with an island of space around Magpie, who still lay on the floor oblivious to the mocking laughter and jibes. Sweyn was one of the more vociferous and even managed a well-aimed kick, which set some of the others off. Magpie sat up, confused and distressed, and by the time the teachers arrived there was a great deal of noise and jostling. Miranda was furious to find such a disturbance going on before assembly, which was usually a peaceful and orderly start to the day. When everyone parted to reveal Magpie sitting on the floor crying, she rolled her eyes in exasperation.

'Get up, Magpie!' she called. 'It's time for assembly, not a rest!'

This set everyone roaring with laughter, which made Magpie howl in fear.

'Goddess but he's an embarrassment!' Swift hissed to Sweyn, flicking his hair aside in a gesture of contempt. 'Wait till I tell Granny Violet about this. They should keep him at home – he's too stupid for school anyway.'

'Too bloody stupid for anything,' growled Sweyn in sympathy. 'We'll tell Jay when he gets back from college tonight. He'll sort the bugger out.'

Miranda was still trying to restore order so she could begin assembly. The other teachers waited around the dais and the students pushed one another to get a glimpse of the hilarious sight of Magpie having a rest. He continued to sob noisily, snot dripping from his nose.

'Magpie!' Miranda called firmly. 'Get off the floor and stand up this minute! You're making a complete fool of yourself!'

'But it's what Magpie does best!' called someone, and the whole place erupted into laughter, even some of the adults joining in.

Leveret had arrived late as usual but heard the final exchange. With cheeks burning scarlet, she elbowed her way to where Magpie sat hunched up in utter confusion, his eyes frightened.

'BE QUIET, THE LOT OF YOU!' she shouted, her voice raising to the high rafters. She bent to one knee and put an arm around Magpie and several people wolf-whistled at this.

'SHUT UP!'

She talked softly to the sobbing boy and taking his arm, helped him to stand up.

'Come on, Maggy, we'll go for a walk outside.'

He followed her docilely, head bent and still sniffing noisily. Leveret glared at everyone as she led him out. The hall had fallen completely silent and at the exit she stopped and turned, her cheeks flushed and eyes flashing green sparks. Her voice shook with disgust.

'I hope you all feel ashamed of yourselves,' she cried, 'mocking and upsetting poor Magpie. *Especially those of you who should know better!'*

She looked daggers at Miranda up on the dais and there was no mistaking her intended insult.

'Leveret!' called Miranda over the many heads. 'Come back here!'

But the girl turned and then, shockingly, made the ultimate gesture of contempt at her head-teacher. With a sharp downward flick of her flexed hand, the ancient Stonewylde sign meaning 'Go to the Otherworld!' she marched out with Magpie.

Of course there'd be a price to pay for her insolence, but Leveret ignored that. She spent the morning with Magpie walking in the woods and then up on the hills, not caring if she got into trouble. They went up to Hare Stone and sat with their backs to the great monolith, soaking up the mild November sunshine. Magpie was so distressed it took Leveret a long time to calm him down enough to communicate.

Eventually she understood from the vivid and shocking set of images that he flashed before her, what had happened the day before. He'd barely eaten and was so hungry, and he'd been forced to have a bath. Later, Jay had beaten him with Starling's stick because he'd tried to take some bread when he thought nobody was looking. She understood that the three women had laughed at this, egging Jay on to further brutality. This morning he'd been pushed out of the house early and shouted at to get up to school, where he hadn't been for ages. Magpie was bewildered and hurt and Leveret's heart ached for him. He panicked sometimes and she worried that if there were more incidents like the one today he might one day turn and lash out at someone, and then be blamed for that as well.

They went back to the Hall at lunchtime because poor Magpie's stomach was rumbling so badly, but rather than face the mass of people in the Dining Hall, Leveret took him through the walled kitchen gardens and straight to the kitchens. Yul had taken her as a small child to visit Marigold when Maizie and Miranda had spent so many hours interminably discussing their new-found leadership. Marigold was one of the few at Stonewylde who actually liked the odd dark-haired girl, but her plump face crumpled in disapproval at the sight of Magpie on the door step in his filthy coat.

'No, Leveret, I'm sorry my love but I'm not having him in the kitchens.'

'But Marigold, he's starving!'

'I'll give him some food but he must eat it outside. He's crawling with dirt and goddess knows what else.'

'He can't help it. Everyone's so cruel to poor Magpie and it's not his fault. He's the gentlest, sweetest person I know.'

'I'm sure he is, dear, but he's not coming in my kitchens.'

She brought a great plate of rabbit pie, potatoes, vegetables and gravy to the door, and a spoon, remembering that he had trouble with any other sort of cutlery.

'You're wonderful, Marigold – thank you. He told me you're kind to him when he's working in the kitchen gardens and that you feed him sometimes.'

'That's right, dear. Poor mite – he always looks so lost and hungry. But he didn't tell you that, surely? He's mute.'

'Sign language,' she said quickly. 'We use sign language.'

Marigold shook her head at this.

'I'd have thought that were beyond the poor boy. Still, he trusts you and you're a kind maid. I do look out for him and I will whenever I can. I feel sorry for the lad, all filthy and frightened and no one to care for him. Makes me wish I could take him under my wing and clean him up, teach him how to live proper. That mother of his is a really nasty piece o' work, and as for them two old crones ...'

She broke off and fearfully made the sign of the pentangle on her chest.

'Just look what they done to my Lily's son! Jay's turned out bad, just like his father and 'tis all their doing. If Magus'd let me look after that little boy from the start, when my poor Lily were murdered, Jay would've grown up very different. But oh no, not Magus. "Marigold," he says, "you're needed here in the Hall kitchens. I can't lose you just to bring up a little boy when he has another granny about." Well! If that's not—'

'Thanks again!' said Leveret cheerfully, taking the laden plate across the courtyard to where Magpie sat waiting patiently. Marigold was kind, but she was also infamous for her moaning sessions about the loss of her grandson Jay to her rival Vetchling.

Later Leveret braved the Hall, knowing her rudeness wouldn't go unpunished. First she had to face Miranda, who was still furious. Leveret adopted her usual tactic of sullen silence, refusing to apologise or try to make amends. She knew she was in the right and saw any kind of climb-down as tantamount to condoning Miranda's treatment of Magpie. Her punishment was work detail every night at the Hall for a week. The boarding students had work detail only twice a week so this was a harsh punishment, especially as Miranda said she'd make sure the work was nothing easy.

'Window cleaning, grate polishing, stone floor scrubbing – I shall make sure Cherry gives you the hardest jobs. I am very, very angry with you for your rudeness, Leveret. You know our fundamental laws as well as anyone, and children don't ever behave so rudely towards their elders. To show such contempt and insolence towards me, especially in front of the whole school, was unforgivable.'

Leveret was pleased that Miranda felt she'd lost face, and still felt perfectly justified.

'I think it's unforgivable the way Magpie's treated,' she retorted.

'Oh come now, Leveret – I was trying to make light of the situation in assembly. I could see he was becoming distressed and I was —'

'No!' cried Leveret. 'It's more than that. Nobody cares about him! Nobody makes sure he has enough to eat or looks after him! I'm sick of everyone laughing at him and —'

'But that's Maizie's role, surely? Haven't you spoken to your mother about this, if you're concerned for his welfare?'

Leveret flashed her a look of scorn.

'Of course I have! And all Mother says is that his family are a law unto themselves and she can't interfere.'

'I can't believe that Maizie hasn't said anything to them, if there really is a problem,' said Miranda firmly. 'And anyway, looking at Magpie, he's tall and well-grown for a sixteen year old, isn't he? So he obviously is fed reasonably well.'

'But he's so dirty, and —'

'Yes, I'll give you that. And we can insist that he washes properly – I'll have a word with Maizie about that. But Leveret, his family aren't the easiest of people, as you know. They remind me of how it was when I first moved here from the Outside World all those years ago. Some of the Villagers seemed really filthy but it was just a way of life here, living close to the land and not worrying about a bit of dirt.'

Leveret shook her head in despair.

'You don't understand and you're doing just what Mother always does when I try and say something! You just don't know how Magpie's really treated. And as for Jay, his cousin – he makes Maggie's life a misery.'

Miranda frowned at the stubborn girl.

'Seeing as how Jay goes off to college in the Outside World every day, and boards at the Hall, I don't really see that he gets much opportunity to interact with Magpie. And anyway, Leveret, how come you know all this? We're all aware that Magpie's mute, so how do you know what goes on in his home? I think you're just getting yourself all worked up about nothing much, and —'

'I don't know why I ever expect anyone to listen,' said Leveret bitterly.

'I think you'll find I have listened, actually,' said Miranda sharply. 'I've listened and told you I'll speak to Maizie about Magpie's lack of personal hygiene. I don't believe the other issues you've raised to be valid. And besides, we're here to discuss your rudeness this morning and your complete lack of contrition or apology.'

Leveret sighed heavily and Miranda glared at her.

'I'll have to tell Yul about this and I know he'll be as dis-appointed as I am. You've really let your family down with such behaviour. Maizie will be equally upset.'

'As you're punishing me already, do they really need to know?' asked Leveret, trying to keep the dread from her voice.

'Yes, they certainly do need to know – exactly as I'd want to know if Rufus had behaved badly. You two have to set an example to all the others. Rufus knows that and I'm sure you do too!'

Leveret rolled her eyes at this, having heard it a hundred times before from her own mother. It was no fun being related to the leaders of Stonewylde.

'Now you're being rude again, Leveret! What's the matter with you? I know Maizie's a good mother who brought you up properly so there's no excuse for this sort of behaviour. Do you want me to make it two weeks instead of one?'

Leveret merely shrugged at this, her eyes stonily glazed into an expression of bored contempt. Miranda was reminded of some of the fights she'd had with Sylvie at this age. Leveret was four-teen, going on fifteen, just the age that Sylvie had been when they left the Outside World and moved to Stonewylde. Sylvie had argued and flounced about during their arguments so they always had a good fight and cleared the air. But this girl was far more insolent and something in her eyes said that she knew she was above all this and bored by such mundane engagement. It was difficult to ignore the deliberate disrespect.

'Right, two weeks it is! Go back to your lessons and wait to hear from Yul.'

Yul had exploded and actually reduced Leveret to tears, which was some feat given her normal defensive tactics. His anger was formidable. He seemed to glow with it, sparking fury with every flash of his eyes. He said that for the next two weeks while she was on work detail, she'd move into his family apartments and sleep in one of the bedrooms further down the corridor so he could watch over her. She'd not be allowed to leave the Hall for the whole time – no roaming around Stonewylde and no wandering off and disappearing. As Leveret thought of the Moon Fullness that night and then the Dark Moon in two weeks' time, her heart plummeted. Now she wouldn't be able to gather anything for her collection and there was a whole list of things she needed to prepare. She'd intended to try her spell at the Winter Solstice having missed her chance at Samhain. She bowed her head in misery.

'Good, I see I've finally got through to you! We'll find Mother and tell her what's happening.'

He smiled triumphantly as Leveret gazed at the floor in tearful despair. Maizie stood with her arms folded and nodded.

''Twill be strange being on my own in the cottage,' she said, 'but you do what you think best, Yul. I'm pleased you can all see now what I'm up against. Good to know 'tis not just me. She's become a nasty young girl and let's hope that this punishment sorts her out once and for all. Sweyn and Gefrin were only asking today what's to become of her, and could they help at all. Those two are really turning out well after all – I feel proud o' them.'

Leveret let out a strangled cry at this.

'Do you have something to say?' asked Yul coldly.

'None of you know!' cried Leveret. 'The things they've done to me . . .'

'Sweyn and Gefrin? What things?'

'All sorts, always, all my life!' she shouted, her voice cracking with emotion. 'They've hurt me, broken my things, mocked me, shouted at me, almost drowned me—'

'So why didn't you tell Mother?'

'I did!' she wailed. 'I've always tried to tell her!'

'Aye, she's a great one for telling tales,' frowned Maizie. 'But after a while I took no notice. If even half of what she claimed were true, they'd be complete monsters. Don't believe her, Yul. She tells lies to try and get them into trouble, I reckon.'

'No I don't!'

'This "drowning" is a good example,' said Maizie heatedly, her cheeks flushing. 'She told me Sweyn had tried to drown her in the old apple-bobbing barrel at Samhain! She'd even managed to convince Clip and he came telling tales too! I spoke to our Sweyn and he laughed. He admitted it straight away, dunking her head in the water, but he said 'twas only a quick bob to bring her back to her senses, seeing as she were in some sort o' trance . But o' course Clip got the wrong idea and took her away with him up to the Dolmen of all places! It ruined my Samhain, worrying myself about her and all the time she were fast asleep up in that cave!'

'You *always* take their side! You never believe me even when someone else backs me up. And last time they came round to babysit I almost died of suffocation!'

'Don't be daft!' said Maizie sharply. 'I recall you were told to do the weaving and you didn't. 'Tis just another of your —'

'It's *true!*' Leveret was crying now, a terrible combination of anger and frustration. 'They told you I'd fallen over but they'd locked me in the cupboard for hours.'

'Which cupboard?' asked Yul. 'I don't—'

'The one in your old bedroom! Under the eaves.'

Yul stared at her, any half-conviction he may have harboured turning to cold disbelief.

'Now I know you're lying, Leveret. That cupboard's tiny – you'd never fit in there.'

'*But I did!*' she screamed. 'They shoved me in so hard I thought I was going to die! They *are* monsters and they make my life a misery! Why won't anyone believe me? *I hate you all!*'

Leveret became hysterical, screaming and flinging the things on Yul's desk to the floor. She wanted to destroy everything in her frustration at their indifference to her suffering. Yul restrained her, kicking and screeching, pinning her flailing arms to her side and lifting her bodily onto the sofa where he held her down.

'Get Hazel, with something to calm her down,' he commanded. Maizie was paralysed with shock at the sight of Leveret so out of control; the girl had lost all reason. She tried to phone through to the hospital wing but Hazel wasn't there. Then abruptly the screaming and thrashing stopped and Leveret's eyes rolled up to reveal the whites. She started to shake.

156

'Oh goddess, she's having one of her turns,' moaned Maizie.

'What's the matter with her? Have I hurt her?'

'No, no she does this sometimes. Remember? How she used to go blank when she were little? She still does it sometimes, never grew out of it as we thought she would. Let go of her, Yul. She'll come round in a minute.'

'Can you find Hazel anyway? She should see this.'

Whilst Maizie was out of the study looking for the doctor, Yul stared down at his youngest sister in consternation, smoothing the curls back from her ashen face. Her breathing became deeper and then the shaking stopped. Her eyes rolled back down and she gazed up at him in complete confusion.

'The darkness and the brightness will be torn asunder,' she whispered. 'Stonewylde will tremble – the magic will die and the earth and the moon will dance here no longer. The sacred spirals will unravel and all will be eclipsed by the evil that comes. It's already started.'

'*What*?' he gasped. 'What are you talking about, Leveret?'

All he'd really taken in was the part about the darkness and the brightness being torn asunder, which was a little too close to the truth to be dismissed. But Leveret merely shook her head and, by the time Hazel arrived with her bag, no longer remembered saying anything at all. Leveret was taken to the hospital wing for the night but seemed fine, other than sobbing for several hours into the alien pillow at her isolation and the injustice of her treatment.

157

10

Sylvie was unaware of the commotion in Yul's office. She was busy supervising the girls' tea and keeping an eye on the clock. It was the Moon Fullness tonight and she could feel faint pulses of excitement in her fingertips; she intended to walk up to Hare Stone before the sun set and watch the Owl Moon rise. It was quite a while since she'd seen it.

'Eat your boiled egg nicely,' she said to Bluebell, who was getting into a mess as usual. 'I'm just going to see if Granny Maizie would like to bath you both tonight and put you to bed.'

'Why Granny Maizie?' asked Bluebell. 'Why not you?'

'I'm going for a walk,' she replied. 'It's the Moon Fullness and I want to watch the moon rise. I won't be very long.'

'Can I come?' asked Celandine.

Sylvie regarded her elder daughter, who was such a serious little girl.

'Not this time, darling. Maybe in the spring when it's warmer, I'll take you up to Hare Stone and we can watch together.'

'I'd rather dance.'

Sylvie looked sharply at the girl. Was this moongaziness coming out? Or merely the fact that Celandine was devoted to dancing and danced all the time.

'Dancing at the Moon Fullness is something I used to do,' she said quietly. 'With my moon wings and a magical silver dress.'

'Like a faerie?' asked Bluebell. 'Were you sparkly, Mummy?'

'I expect you were beautiful,' said Celandine.

'I certainly felt beautiful, and yes, I was sparkly, Bluebell. It was the best thing ever – the moongazy hares and the barn-owl would join me, and your father would, too. He'd sit with his back to the stone and watch me dance.'

The girls stared at their mother in fascination, awed by her tone of wistfulness. Sylvie's eyes were faraway, remembering moonlit landscapes and magical spirals and Yul's adoration.

'Why did you stop, Mum?' asked Celandine. 'If it was the best thing ever, why did you stop?'

There was a silence as Sylvie thought about this, then she sighed deeply.

'*So we'll go no more a-roving, so late into the night,*
Though the heart be still as loving, the moon be yet as bright.'

'Mummy?' cried Bluebell in consternation at this strangeness. She jumped down from her chair and ran round to Sylvie, burying her eggy face in her mother's skirt.

'It's alright, Blue,' said Celandine. 'I understand, Mum.'

'Do you?   It's strange – I don't know why I feel this need to go tonight but somehow . . .'

'When did you last dance for the beautiful Moon Goddess, Mum?'

Sylvie thought about this, shocked at just how long ago it was.

'I stopped going every month when I was expecting you, Celandine, during the winter when it was cold and icy and Father said I may slip and fall. I started again after you were born but only for a while, and then I was expecting Bluebell, and then . . .'

'Why not after I was borned, Mummy?'

'Because I was ill, darling. Remember I've told you about this? I was very ill for a while and I had to go to a special hospital in the Outside World to get better again. But after I came home, somehow I never moondanced again. I never felt the need to, not until tonight . . .'

'You should go tonight – go quickly. You need to go,' said Celandine, her deep grey eyes full of concern and love.

Sylvie smiled across at the dear little girl, touched by her instinctive understanding.

'I will, darling. I'll just see if Granny Maizie's still up here or if she's gone home to the Village already. If she has, maybe one of the big girls from school will sit with you until I get back.'

The light was fading as she walked swiftly towards the woods and the hill. It felt so good to be out in the open, alone in the evening. There were a few clouds clustered around the setting sun but the night was clear and fresh. Sylvie wore her beautiful green cloak, decorated with tiny glass beads. It had been a birth-day present sewn for her by Maizie. She breathed deeply and smiled – why had she left it so long, when she was born to moondance? She almost broke into a run as she reached the woods leading up to the hillside. They seemed dark but she entered without fear, knowing the path well – it wasn't like those early days when Yul had worried for her safety. Nor was she in a trance like she used to be, unaware of anything except the over-riding compulsion to honour the rising moon – although there was no doubt that she did feel an echo of it. Her heart raced and her fingers tingled strongly. Surely it wasn't just from the exertion of hurrying?

The wood was full of noises in the twilight; flapping wood-pigeons that made her jump with their sudden panic, the cry of a jay, noisy rustling from squirrels in the dead leaves that carpeted the ground. She smelled wood-smoke and knew the charcoal burners had been nearby that day. Twigs brushed her and several times she had to duck suddenly or lose an eye. Once she heard the unmistakable grunting bark of deer and was reminded of so many things she'd forgotten about Stonewylde. Cocooned in the Hall, she'd lost touch with the wildness and the greenness of life.

Then Sylvie was out of the wood and climbing up through the long, damp grass towards the stone at the top. She passed several rocky outcrops and felt a stirring of memory from that night so long ago, when the three hags had huddled here in wait for her, determined to mark and taint her. She'd never been able to pass this spot without remembering them and their horrible, evil intentions. She'd been up here many a time in daylight to look for the little pouch that Mother Heggy had given her for protection. It had snapped that night on Winter Solstice Eve, when the crones had grabbed her and thrown her to the ground. Try as she might, Sylvie had never found the little leather bag and had given up her search eventually, assuming the crones had found it and kept it for themselves.

The sun had already set, the sky glowing golden blue to mark the point of its departure, and Sylvie thrust all nasty thoughts of the crones aside. She reached the stone, a little out of breath, and placed a hand on its ancient skin. She felt a stream of comfort emanating from it. Then she turned to where the moon would rise, the point opposite the setting sun, and realised that she was just in time for here was the pink rim just peering over the horizon. She felt a wild elation in her heart, an echo of her moongaziness, and began a few tentative steps moon-wise around the stone. She sensed the hares in the gathering darkness and greeted them. Her spirit rose in her body giving her wings and, for the first time in years, Sylvie began to dance.

Just as the full moon cleared the tree tops around the Village Green, Kestrel and his mates were thrown out of the Jack in the Green. George told them they'd all had quite enough and as he ran the pub and was a beefy man, they left without too much protest. They settled themselves on a couple of benches and watched the moon rise higher.

'Aren't you meant to be meeting Sorrel tonight?' asked Jay. 'You said you'd arranged it all for tonight.'

'Yeah, that's right – hayloft after moonrise.' Kestrel produced a bottle of mead from his jacket and took a swig. 'No harm in keeping her waiting a little though.'

Swift watched Kestrel carefully, as always learning and storing away the knowledge for possible future use. Kestrel was very good-looking and in his second year at college, destined to be one of the few Stonewylders so far to go on and study at university. Edward, his father, had very high hopes for him. Kestrel's smile was ready and charming, his features perfect, and he treated the Stonewylde girls as a list to be worked through.

'She's had her implant then?'

'Of course! I'm not going to risk anything, am I? How about you lot, then? Got any little honeypots lined up for the Moon Fullness?'

They all shook their heads.

'Though that Becky at college – she'd be up for it if she was here,' said Jay. 'Pity we can't bring Outside girls back here. She's gagging for me.'

Kestrel laughed at this.

'Yeah, gagging would be the best thing for her, mate, with the mouth on her. Or better still, a paper bag over her head.' He ducked as Jay made a half-hearted swing at him. 'Only joking! She's alright. Maybe we could arrange for some girls to visit. Not that I've noticed a shortage of home-grown ones, mind you. That little Sorrel ... phew! She's so keen. And there's Daisy too, all ready to be picked. I've got my work cut out for me. I can't understand what's wrong with the rest of you.'

Kestrel knew perfectly well that the others in his gang didn't share his success with girls. Jay was too aggressive, too quick to fly off the handle. Gefrin was a fool, though Kestrel knew he was keen on some gormless girl at the farm where he now worked every day. Sweyn was probably terrified of girls and wouldn't know where to begin, which he hid behind a great show of indifference. And Swift ... Kestrel wasn't sure about him. Swift was a bit of a dark horse and he was far too clever for his own good. The older boy decided he'd have to watch Swift in case he turned out to be a rival. He'd noticed girls giving the blond-haired boy the eye, despite his slight build. Kestrel, being tall and muscular, couldn't understand what any girl would see in a slim, smaller lad. But Swift wasn't quite an adult yet, in the Stonewylde sense, so Kestrel dismissed any threat from him. He took another gulp of mead and gazed up at the bright moon. Sorrel could wait another ten minutes or so – do her good.

'Have you heard what happened with that sister of yours?' Swift asked Gefrin and Sweyn.

'Stupid bitch, what's she done now? Apart from making an idiot of herself this morning in assembly,' said Sweyn. 'I was bloody embarrassed, I can tell you.'

'Yeah, and that half-wit cousin of mine,' agreed Jay, cracking his knuckles. 'Thank goddess I wasn't there to see it. Is he going to get it tonight when I drop by at the cottage later on for a smoke!'

Gefrin giggled at this.

'So what happened with Leveret then?' asked Kestrel. 'I heard she was rude to Miranda, wasn't she?'

'That's right – flicked her in front of everyone. So Miranda told her she was on work detail for two weeks,' said Swift.

'Hah! No less than the old cow deserves,' said Jay. 'I'd have liked to give her the flick myself many a time.'

'Yeah, miserable old bitch,' agreed Gefrin. 'But two weeks' work detail just for flicking?'

'Seems a bit steep,' said Kestrel.

'Then Yul started having a go at Leveret as well,' said Swift.

'Good,' grunted Sweyn. 'About time he did something useful. He ought to bring back whipping like they used in the old days and start with her.'

'No chance of that,' said Swift. 'But she did try to snitch on you two. Screamed at Yul about some of the things you've done to her.'

'Little bitch!' hissed Gefrin. 'So now we're in for it!'

'No, not at all. Maizie stuck up for you both and then Yul joined in. He told Leveret he didn't believe her.'

Both brothers burst out laughing at this.

'Did you really stuff her into a tiny cupboard?'

'Too right! Didn't think we'd get the door shut, but we did. She weren't very happy in there.'

'Well, when Yul said he didn't believe her she totally flipped and he had to get Hazel in to deal with her.'

'Hazel? Was Lev ill then?'

'She went crazy and passed out – all very dramatic.'

Jay whistled.

'She really is mental, ain't she? They should put her in a strait-jacket and lock her in a padded cell. Just like they did to Sylvie.'

They all laughed at this.

'So where is she now?'

'In the hospital wing. She'll go to Yul's rooms when she's better.'

'I bet Mother's upset – the little cow always upsets her. Just wait till I get my hands on her!' said Sweyn grimly. 'Especially now nobody believes her.'

'Well you'll have to wait until she's allowed home. Yul said he'll be watching her closely for the next two weeks while she's on work detail and staying at the Hall,' said Swift.

Kestrel looked speculatively at Swift, whose blond hair was gleaming in the moonlight.

'How come you know all this?' he asked. 'How come you heard everything?'

Swift smiled and winked.

'Just in the right place at the right time,' he said. 'Are you going to share that mead or what?'

Kestrel laughed at this.

'No chance! I need something to keep my strength up – I've a long night ahead of me.'

Sylvie finished her dance, feeling full of energy and magic. For the first time at this sacred place she'd been fully conscious of the rising moon and its beauty, and was glad that her days of going into a complete trance were over. As she danced around the great stone she'd felt a glimmer of the spirals that swirled on the site. They weren't exactly under the ground – it was more complex than that. She was part of the spirals herself and felt them gyrating inside her, and yet they were also outside, weaving around the stone, marking strange patterns into the earth and the air. The barn owl had visited – surely not the same one that joined her all those years ago – and its ghostly white wings had whispered through the night as it floated towards the stone. Perching there, it had raised its exquisite heart-shaped face towards the silver moon and stared, black eyes fathomless in the dark night.

Now Sylvie leaned against the stone soaking up its energy. She tingled with life, with excitement – this was how it should be, what she was born for. She felt that a new era was beginning and she could put the past behind her. She'd forget that terrible experience in bed with Yul, when she'd genuinely believed that Magus had returned to haunt her. She felt strong now, ready to take on the challenge of the year ahead; ready to work with her powerful husband, not against him. And ready to guide Stonewylde through the difficult months as Clip prepared to leave.

Sylvie raised her arms to the moon and poured out her soul, receiving an equal measure of quicksilver magic in return. Then remembering her two little girls who may still be awake and wondering where she'd got to, she began to make her way down through the wet grass towards the woods. She was just skirting a group of boulders that protruded from the hillside when she stopped in her tracks, heart beating erratically. She'd caught the faintest whiff of scent.

And then the voice, soft and deep, filled her head.

'*Sylvie, Sylvie, my moongazy girl . . .*'

She sank onto a boulder, her eyes wild with panic.

'*I love to watch you dance. You're as beautiful now as you ever were.*'

She looked around frantically. Where was he? This was real, this wasn't just in her head. He was really here, and close by.

'*But Sylvie, you should be at the stone on the cliffs. I'm hungry for your moon magic.*'

Her eyes swivelled desperately, catching the moonlight in their silver irises. She peered all around, then up at the stars glittering like scattered diamonds in the cold night air.

'*I've come back for you, my moongazy girl, and this time you'll be mine.*'

Her chest heaved in panic and her hands trembled violently. Where was he hiding? Then she heard a low chuckle from behind a boulder and she sprang to her feet screaming, clutching at her head to block out the terrible laughter. Her feet moved of their own accord; she was off, running down the hillside, stumbling in the tangled grass, crying at the nightmare to go away and leave her alone.

Sylvie almost missed the entrance into the wood where the path began, but at the last minute spotted the dark archway amongst the trees and swerved into the shelter of the trees. She raced along the path, sobbing in terror, oblivious to the birds that squawked out of their roosts at the unwelcome intrusion. Several times she tripped over tree roots, once falling flat on her face on the soft earth and pushing herself up desperately to continue her headlong flight. She thought she heard a deep voice calling her name, again and again, which spurred her on even more. Then she felt strong arms around her holding her tight, twisting her round so she could run no further. She screamed and screamed, shaking her head from side to side, long silver hair rippling in a wild halo.

'Sylvie, Sylvie it's me! Stop it! STOP IT!'

Gradually she ceased her struggles and frantic efforts to escape, held fast in the strong grip of his arms. She dissolved into heart-breaking sobs, all control and reason lost. Yul stroked her hair, whispering soothing words, holding her close now rather than restraining her.

'It's alright, my love, everything's alright. You're safe now, you're safe, Sylvie.'

Her wild sobs slowly subsided and became normal crying, though she still trembled like a captured bird. He bent and kissed her forehead tenderly.

'What is it? What's wrong?'

But she couldn't speak, couldn't explain her terror.

By the time they got back to the Hall she'd stopped crying. They managed to cross the entrance hall without being questioned by

166

anyone, although halfway up the stairs they met Martin coming down.

'Good evening,' he said politely. 'Did you have a good walk?'

'Not now, Martin,' said Yul curtly. 'Sylvie's had a bit of a shock and she needs to get to bed. Send up some brandy, would you?'

'Brandy? Yes, of course. Should I find the doctor too? Is she injured?'

'Yes . . . no, don't send Hazel, although you could ask her to be ready if I need her.'

'I don't need Hazel,' whispered Sylvie. 'Yul, I'm fine.'

Yul nodded over her head at Martin, who smiled his understanding.

'I'll send the brandy up in the dumb-waiter so as not to disturb you. Goodnight, Miss Sylvie. I hope you sleep well and make a quick recovery.'

'I'm not ill,' she muttered. 'I'm fine, thank you.'

Martin merely raised his eyebrows and continued down the stairs, the polite smile still on his lips.

Despite Sylvie's protests and refusal to drink any brandy, Hazel did visit their rooms and insisted on something to calm her. Sylvie became very distressed at the sight of the syringe but Yul brooked no argument. Hazel administered the drug grimly, trying to soothe her at the same time, repeating again and again that it was just to help her relax so she could sleep. When she'd left, Yul helped his wife undress and carefully tucked her into bed, sitting on the edge next to her and stroking her hair back from her face in a gentle, rhythmic movement. Sylvie's eyes became cloudy and her body lost its tenseness as the drug kicked in.

She gazed up at her husband whose handsome dark face was full of love and concern. She could see it in his beautiful grey eyes and it made her feel safe and cherished. But as she gazed into his eyes she saw something else that made her shrink. Yul hadn't come near her since that awful night and she'd been dreading the first time he did, terrified there'd be a repeat of the previous events. She'd tried to steel herself for the inevitable advance he must make, for Yul could never go very long without making love with her. But not tonight, not after what had happened up at Hare Stone.

'No, Yul. Please no,' she mumbled.

'What?' he asked gently, still caressing her forehead and temples, running his long fingers very slowly through the silky hair that flowed onto the pillows.

'I can't make love with you tonight. I'm sorry, I can't.'

She saw him flinch, rejection darkening his eyes.

'That's okay, my darling, I wasn't intending to. I just want you to feel calm and safe, and then you can tell me what happened up at Hare Stone.'

'I don't know ... I just want to sleep.'

Her eyelids were heavy and her body felt like a lead weight on a bed of clouds.

'We'll talk in the morning then,' he said softly, aching with longing for her. She looked so beautiful as she drifted off to sleep, so serene and defenceless. Tonight he couldn't sleep in his office as he'd done since that night, waiting until she said she wanted him again. It would be torture lying next to her all night, but he must sleep by her side and take care of her.

He slipped into the bathroom and then, anxious not to disturb her, climbed carefully into the great bed, the scene of such passion in the past. Yul smiled bitterly in the darkness. He ached with frustration and need for her and just for a second, the terrible notion swam through his head – she was heavily drugged and would never remember anything in the morning. He took a deep, shuddering breath. What'd gone wrong between them? How had this estrangement happened? And the thought occurred to him again, as it had done several times since her outburst in this very bed nearly two weeks ago – was Sylvie falling ill again? Was her psychosis beginning all over again?

That night Sylvie had the familiar dream that had haunted her for so long. She lay in her private room, the patch of blue sky and tree tops visible through the barred window. Soothing smells drifted in the air, aromatherapy being part of her treatment. She

168

was floating somewhere above her bed in a state of disassociation, her body no longer her own. There were so many strange hands invading her privacy – regular shots, soothing baths, deep massage, gentle exercise on toning tables, but worst of all, the electro-convulsive therapy in the special room downstairs. All this was standard treatment for her severe puerperal psychosis – not that she was aware of that.

Most of the time Sylvie wasn't aware of anything much. She was docile and hovered just above her body, but occasionally she'd slip back into herself and understand. Then she'd cry for her little Celandine and tiny baby Bluebell, her beloved husband and her life at Stonewylde. Sometimes she'd remember the last time she saw them all. She'd recall the horror of being forcibly wrenched from her screaming children, the hidden knife clattering to the ground, the voices from Quarrycleave calling her name, begging her to come quickly with her little girls. Hazel and Yul, Miranda and Clip, the grim-faced nurses in the private ambulance, faces, faces, all shocked and frightened ... and then she'd forget again.

Sylvie entered the recurring dream at the usual place. She was floating over her bed watching the young woman who lay there, pale and weak as a wraith. Her thin wrists and ankles were strapped into the restraints to prevent her from harming herself and she'd been sedated after her earlier thrashing about. The door opened and a visitor walked in, strange in normal clothes. It was a man, tall and well-built, with short blond hair and bright blue eyes the colour of robins' eggs. He moved with the controlled tread of a heavy man who worked hard to keep in shape. His suit was beautifully cut and he smelt of expensive cologne; she noticed every detail, down to the heavy gold wedding band on the thick finger of his well-manicured hands.

The man approached the bed and gazed down at the figure strapped helplessly there. Her eyes stared up at him, unfocused and blank. A smile stretched his full mouth. She knew this man – he was from the past and she should remember who he was. He took one of her fragile hands, then noticed the resistance as the restraint prevented him from raising it.

'Sylvie,' he said softly, his gaze brushing over her body purposefully. 'Finally, after all this time. You know who I am, don't you?'

She couldn't respond. Her tongue was heavy and numb and her lips parted with an effort but no speech came forth.

'Oh, Sylvie, what have they done to you? I never thought our reunion would be like this, in such a place.'

He stood silently for a moment, drinking in every detail of her whilst she gazed up at him like a life-size doll. He traced the sharp planes of her face with a heavy finger and even in her drugged state, she felt a prickle of revulsion crawl over her skin. She stirred ever so slightly but could manage no more movement than this as slowly, deliberately, his hands explored her.

'I had to see for myself,' he said thickly. 'I wonder if you'll remember this visit? I've so much to tell you but it'll have to wait until you're better. I'll be back for you one day, Sylvie, even if it takes years. You're in my mind constantly, in my dreams and my fantasies. I've never forgotten you and one day you'll be by my side, where you belong.'

He bent to plant his lips on hers. She felt their smoothness and the taste of mint, with only the slightest moist pressure. But then, shockingly, he carefully licked her mouth, coating her lips with his saliva which remained long after he'd left the room.

Bluebell had finally stopped wailing and was once more asleep, along with Celandine who'd been disturbed by her sister's noise. Sylvie's restlessness and whimpering seemed to have passed and she now breathed peacefully under the soft quilt. Yul found the brandy sent up earlier and, sitting by the window in their shadowy bedroom, poured himself a generous shot. What a night – what a day, in fact.

He looked out at the bright moon. First his sister having hysterics and then his wife – what was the matter with everyone? Sylvie's behaviour had really alarmed him and tomorrow he'd have a proper consultation with Hazel. This time there'd be no delay; if Sylvie was becoming ill again they'd nip it in the bud and get help now, before it could spiral out of control.

As for Leveret ... he thought back to the morning's violent scene in his office, her face scarlet and her breath ragged. And suddenly he had a clear flash of memory – tiny Leveret red-faced and screaming in his arms whilst two little boys looked guiltily at their feet and refused to own up. It was Lammas all those years ago and they'd not watched the cricket match because of it. Was he missing something here? Despite Maizie's assurances that Leveret was lying about her brothers, Yul resolved to speak to the pair of them soon. Leveret was rude and insolent and she constantly disobeyed Maizie and avoided her tasks. But maybe she wasn't a liar. And as for the fit ... was it serious? Did she need treatment too?

Sighing, Yul swirled the remains of his brandy in the glass before tossing it down his throat. Owl Moon – and with it the memories of tree cages and rope. Why couldn't life ever be easy, he wondered gloomily, climbing back into his cold marital bed next to his forbidden wife.

11

Yul decided to make his announcement just before the Frost Moon, which fell in mid-December this year. He chose dinner time in the Dining Hall to do this; all the boarders would be there, including the college students.

'If I can have your attention please!' he called, standing at the head of the huge room. It was as noisy and crowded as ever, teeming with all the youngsters and many adults who lived at the Hall. Slowly the voices died down as people noticed Yul standing. It was unusual for him to be there at all – he generally ate privately with his family in the evenings.

'Following a request from Kestrel,' he began, scanning the eager faces before him, 'I've decided that we'll throw a special party just after Yule. It'll be a Yule dance, different to anything that's been done at Stonewylde before. The party is just for our young people – everyone who boards at the Hall – and we'll also include the year group below who'll be moving up next year.'

There was a huge swell of noise at this. Yul raised a hand for silence.

'Anyone at college in the Outside World is welcome to invite their Outside friends to come along and if—'

The explosion of voices completely drowned him out. He waited, grinning at the group of teachers who nodded wisely, showing that they already knew all about it.

'We'll hire a coach for the evening to bring guests into Stonewylde and then return them afterwards,' Yul continued. 'The dance will be held in the Great Barn, and for the first time we'll hire a sound system and lighting to make the evening special for you all. This is an experiment, so don't mess it up. If you have any questions then ask Miranda or one of the Senior School teachers, and give them any names for the invitations. Let's hope the dance goes really well!'

Yul sat down again and sipped his water, scanning the horde of excited faces before him. Martin approached and murmured discreetly in his ear. Yul frowned.

'No, I didn't put it before the Council of Elders first! You know Clip is handing Stonewylde over to me and this was my decision to make.' He glared at the older man, who looked back stonily. 'I'm sorry if it doesn't meet with your approval, Martin, but times move on. Could you locate my youngest brothers please, Gefrin and Sweyn, and tell them to come and see me in my office when dinner's over.'

'Bloody hell – we're really going to get it now!' groaned Gefrin as they made their way slowly to the office.

'Just don't panic and blurt anything out,' said Sweyn. 'Remember what Swift said – they didn't believe her. If we deny everything it'll be alright.'

'Yeah, but what—'

'Let me do the talking,' said Sweyn. 'I ain't scared of Yul.'

'Yeah but—'

'If he were that bothered he'd have said something ages ago when she had that fit in his office. Just agree with everything I say and don't admit nothing.'

Yul was having a discussion with Harold when they knocked on the door.

'Good, I need to talk to the two of you. Sit down and I'll be with you in minute.'

They sat on a sofa, staring at their feet. Yul and Harold resumed their conversation at one of the desks, both looking at a screen.

'So what exactly do you need?'

Harold tapped at the keyboard, his serious face intent. His fingers flew as he concentrated.

'We need more labour every day this week up at the warehouse,' he said after a minute. 'See all these orders? We just can't pack and despatch them in time with the people available. I'm trying to get these smaller orders out before next week and the Christmas post deadlines. The big ones'll be couriered but even then there's a cut-off date if they're to be with our customers in time for Christmas.'

'But why this sudden crisis? Surely you've been aware of the postal deadlines for some time.'

Harold looked across at Yul, his round glasses reflecting the columns of figures on the screen. He grimaced and looked embarrassed.

''Tis my fault. I decided to do a special promotion last week, after what you said at the last meeting about Stonewylde really needing more money. I sent out a marketing e-mail to all our previous customers just to see what'd happen. Some of 'em go way back to when we only sold honey and cider – they didn't know we'd expanded our range. I didn't realise the response I'd get. Honestly, Yul, it's incredible! They can't get enough of our Stonewylde stuff! The new felt hats especially! They're unique and so colourful – we sold out o' them within hours, and—'

'Okay, Harold, put it in a report for me so I can see everything clearly. I need to speak to these two lads now. So bottom line – what do you need?'

'Six extra people in the warehouse – quick, bright ones – for the whole o' this week. That should do it. If they work hard, we'll get all the orders picked and packed and out in time then. And if we could have any more of those hats made up quick . . .'

'I'll see what I can do and I'll let you know what I've sorted out in the morning.'

When Harold had left, Yul came to sit opposite his two youngest brothers. Gefrin fidgeted and wouldn't meet his eye; Sweyn lifted his jaw and met Yul's gaze squarely.

'Thanks for coming to see me. You're aware of the problems

Mother's been having recently with Leveret?' Yul began.

'Yeah, we've been helping out,' said Sweyn. 'Keeping an eye on Lev for her.'

'She's been really bad!' said Gefrin. 'She won't even—'

'We don't like seeing Mother so upset,' interrupted Sweyn. 'We want to help any way we can.'

'How admirable,' said Yul drily.

'Yeah, well, Rosie's busy with her family, Geoffrey and Gregory have little ones on the way too, so it's down to us. You can't help out, can you?'

Yul tried to conceal his dislike as he regarded his youngest brother. It wasn't Sweyn's fault that he looked so like his father.

'I do what I can but it's not easy when I have so much else to deal with. Leveret's going through a difficult stage at the moment and it's important we all support Mother.'

'Yeah, we know that. We—'

'So what I wanted to talk about was something Leveret said the other day. She became very upset, really distressed, and she said that you two were to blame.'

'She's just—'

'Hear me out, please, Gefrin. She said that you'd locked her in a cupboard.'

'*A cupboard?*'

Sweyn's pugnacious features were puzzlement itself.

'The one up in my old bedroom – that little cupboard under the eaves.'

'But nobody could fit in there!' said Sweyn firmly, shaking his head. 'Oh . . . hold on, I know what she's on about! Yeah, we did try to put her in there once, but that were years and years ago. We were bad when we were little – you probably remember – and Mother left us on our own a lot, being so busy. And we'd just lost our father too. We were horrible to Leveret as little ones, weren't we, Gef?'

'Well, yes, a bit, I suppose.'

'No, let's be honest – we did tease her a lot. But 'tis all in the past, and we'd never lock her in a cupboard now. That was just stupid kids' stuff and anyway, she'd hardly fit in that little place, would she?'

Yul nodded slowly, watching them both carefully.

'I thought so too. So when she said—'

'It just ain't true – honest, Yul. Why'd we do something daft like that? We only want to help Mother. Though if you want the whole story, we did have a go at Lev that night when we went round to keep an eye on her. We told her off for being so selfish and upsetting Mother and I shouted at her, but I were so angry! And she had that funny turn too – she's always a bit weird afterwards.'

'That's the other thing I wanted to ask you both about. She had one of those turns in here, and she said some strange things when she came round.'

'She's always saying strange things – maybe that's where she got the idea about the cupboard from? Maybe she dreamed about it when she passed out? Mother said Lev looked like she'd taken something she shouldn't have at Samhain. Her eyes were really weird. But I don't know . . .'

'Okay, that's sorted out then,' said Yul briskly, relieved to have got to the bottom of it all. 'I must say, I did wonder when she said about the cupboard. I remember it as being really small.'

'Well, either she's dreamed it or else she's lying and trying to dump us in it,' said Sweyn. 'She does that, don't she, Gef?'

'Yeah, she's always telling tales and making things up,' he agreed. 'Lucky for us Mother takes no notice o' her.'

'Okay, boys – I'm sorry to have got you in here like this but I had to be sure. I've kept Leveret at the Hall for a couple of weeks to give Mother a break but now she's back home, maybe you can both help out if needed? I'm sure that we can sort Leveret out together, and now I know what she's up to, I won't take any notice of her lies in future.'

Yul was just thinking he may have a few minutes to himself when there was another knock on the door. His heart sank when Clip appeared in the doorway – just what he didn't need tonight when he was so busy. Yul sighed wearily and gestured to the sofa.

'It's about this Yule dance for the youngsters,' began Clip. 'Martin came to see me and—'

'Oh for goddess' sake! Why all this damn fuss? It's only a dance!'

Clip nodded and leaned forward slightly, his pale grey eyes strained. Yul thought he'd never seen Clip looking quite so old and worn.

'Believe me, Yul, I don't want to get involved. But Martin came to find me especially and he's very upset. You know that he and I have never enjoyed a ... close relationship, so that alone's an indication of how strongly he felt.'

'Why the hell didn't he come to me himself?' asked Yul angrily. 'Why try to go over my head?'

'He said he did try to speak to you but you wouldn't listen.'

'That's ridiculous! He said something to me a few minutes after I made the announcement in the Dining Hall, in front of everyone. It was hardly the right time or place for a discussion!'

'Of course not. He should've come to speak to you another time. But he thought you wouldn't listen so—'

'So he came running to tell tales to you instead! Well it won't make any difference, I can assure you.'

'Yul, I don't want to take sides. I'm just warning you about how he feels, and according to him, many of the older ones too. Apparently since you announced the dance at dinner tonight, Martin's been dashing around doing a straw poll amongst the older Stonewylders and they all agree with him. I thought you should be aware of it.'

'Fine. Thank you – is that all?'

Clip sighed heavily and raked a hand through his wispy white hair.

'Yul, don't treat me like the enemy. I'm not against this dance.'

'Well that's good! Because the dance will go ahead regardless of Martin or anyone else whinging about it. I have to look ahead for our young people – our lifeblood. It's all very well sticking to traditions and following the old ways, but our society at

Stonewylde will implode if something drastic isn't done soon.'

'Yes, I realise—'

'Our gene pool is tiny. We *have* to do something about this huge generation my father encouraged. Our youngsters can't find partners within the community – we're in danger of inbreeding already and it's a constant worry to me. That's one of the reasons I've really encouraged this age group to go on to college in the Outside World, even though some of them are clearly more suited to manual labour on the estate. I've pushed them into college just so they'll meet partners who aren't Stonewylders. And in that spirit, this Yule dance is an important step forward.'

'I can appreciate that, Yul. As I said, I'm not against the dance. All I would say is firstly, expect some backlash from Martin and the older Stonewylders, the ones who grapple with any changes. All the members of the Council whom you didn't consult when you made the decision to hold the dance. Think how you can make this easier for them to accept rather than just forcing them to do so.'

Yul bridled at this but Clip continued doggedly.

'And secondly, think through how you intend to handle an influx of Outsiders to Stonewylde. I don't mean now at the dance, but in the future if your plan is successful. Would they take part in our rituals? Would you allow them to bring Outside artefacts, clothes and gizmos into Stonewylde? You need to plan very carefully, to consider how it would work. Otherwise the whole thing could backfire and make a hell of a mess.'

Yul looked at his watch, eager to get on with his work. It was growing late and since Sylvie's upset last month he was loath to sleep downstairs and leave her alone with the children all night.

'Okay, Clip, I'll bear it in mind. Now I'm sorry, but I really must—'

'There was one more thing. How's Sylvie?'

'Sylvie? She's fine.'

'I'd heard some rumours ... just gossip really, but I gather she had some kind of anxiety attack last month? And you may recall

I was worried about her at Samhain, when I told you I'd step down this year?'

'Just gossip, as you say. Nothing to worry about, but if you're so concerned, why don't you ask her yourself?'

After Clip had gone, Yul poured himself a drink and stood in the French window looking out at the garden beyond. The moon was almost full and the grass gleamed brightly, the crystals of dew on every blade reflecting the moonlight. Would Sylvie tell Clip what the problem was, he wondered? Because she certainly wasn't telling him. She'd refused to discuss it, trying to gloss over both the incident at Hare Stone during the Owl Moon, and before that, the awful night at Samhain when she'd suddenly turned on him just as they were about to make love.

Memories of that night still haunted him. One minute she'd been eager and welcoming, kissing him and murmuring encouragement. And then suddenly, without any warning, she'd screamed and hit him in the face, rolling away and leaping out of bed. Apart from the horrible sense of rejection, she'd frightened him that night. Since then they'd managed to make love a few times but both knew it wasn't right. Their beautiful love-making had turned into something mechanical and tense, and Yul longed for a return to their normal spontaneous and abandoned passion.

He'd tried to get Hazel involved, talking to her in detail of Sylvie's irrational behaviour during both incidents. He was so worried that she was becoming psychotic again and had told the doctor that if this was the case, he thought they should act immediately this time and get help from the outset. Hazel, however, had remained non-committal and this had infuriated him. If she'd been more decisive last time, maybe they'd all have been spared the pain of seeing Sylvie falling apart before their eyes as the voices she claimed to hear became louder and more demanding, and her sense of reality dimmed. But here was Hazel once more advocating caution, once more telling him they must wait and see how it developed. Yul drained his glass and abandoned any further notions of work that night. He'd better take

179

himself upstairs and make sure that Sylvie was alright. Harold and his warehouse packing issues would have to wait until morning, as would the shortage of felt hats.

'I wish Auntie Leveret was still here,' said Bluebell at breakfast. 'I miss her now she's gone back to the Village with Granny Maizie.'

'So do I,' said Celandine. 'Auntie Leveret's very magical.'

'We can write some more of our story for her!' said Bluebell. 'She'd like that.'

Yul stared at his daughters in surprise.

'I thought Leveret hardly spoke to you two!' he said. 'I never saw her being friendly in all the time she stayed here. Not that I saw much of her, I suppose.'

'She wasn't friendly at first,' said Celandine. 'She's never really said much and we always thought she just didn't like us. But this time . . . Auntie Leveret's really nice and I think she was a bit shy.'

Sylvie smiled at her eldest daughter; Celandine could be very perceptive for a six year old.

'I think you're right – she was a bit shy and also quite unhappy,' Sylvie agreed. 'I'm so glad you girls were kind to her and made her feel welcome. You cheered her up, I think.'

'Yes, we did, Mummy!' cried Bluebell. 'Once when you were in the Village and Auntie Leveret was looking after us and putting us to bed, we found her crying and—'

'Blue!' said Celandine warningly. 'That was private!'

Yul frowned at them, helping himself to more scrambled egg.

'Crying? I hope she didn't upset you girls.'

'No, Father,' Celandine said patiently, 'it was Auntie Leveret who was upset. We gave her a cuddle and read her our new story, the one about the hares, and she really liked it. It made her much happier and after that she wasn't so shy anymore.'

'No, she was smiling and I expect it's 'cos she loved our story! And her name means "Baby Hare" so we're going to make a new hare in our story who's actually our Auntie Leveret!' giggled Bluebell.

'I'm really pleased you cheered her up,' said Sylvie. 'I must get to know Leveret better myself. I always thought she didn't like me much either, but maybe I was wrong too. From now on I'll try to talk to her more even if she doesn't seem very friendly.'

'I wouldn't waste your time,' said Yul. 'She can be very difficult and rude and she'll probably just snub you.'

'Well she wasn't rude to us!' said Celandine hotly. 'She was very kind and we'd like her to come and stay again.'

'Yes, again!' said Bluebell. 'Tonight! Can she come tonight? It's the Frost Moon and we can make up another chapter in our book. "The Hares at Frost Moon", we'll call it, and Auntie Leveret can help us with all the spelling.'

'Are you going moondancing again tonight, Mum?' asked Celandine. She'd been practising a special dance all month, desperate to go up to Hare Stone next spring as promised. She was disappointed when her mother merely shook her head.

'But why aren't you going tonight?'

'Your mother didn't enjoy it last time and she won't be doing it again,' said Yul curtly.

'Is that true, Mum?'

'Of course it's true!' he snapped. 'That's enough, Celandine.'

The girl looked at her mother with puzzlement.

'But it used to be the best thing ever, you said. And you told us it was magical at the Owl Moon last month.'

'It wasn't magical, it was terrible,' said Yul, glowering at Sylvie and the girls. 'And your mother was ill afterwards, remember? She couldn't have breakfast with us because she was all sleepy in bed in the morning.'

'I wasn't ill,' said Sylvie quietly, the issue still not resolved because they'd both been skirting around it. 'You know full well why I was sleepy the next morning. The moon dancing was magical and I loved it. But I had a bit of a fright afterwards in the darkness and I panicked.'

'You were totally hysterical.'

'Only because I was frightened.'

181

'What frightened you, Mummy?' asked Bluebell through her toast. 'Was it the barn owl?'

'No, darling, not the barn owl. I thought I heard something.'

'What?'

Sylvie's eyes met Yul's over the table and she knew he was waiting to hear her answer too.

'What was frightening, Mummy?' repeated Bluebell. 'Not the hares?'

'No, not the hares either. I just ... I don't know, I thought I heard a voice and it scared me. It sounds silly now. It was all a lot of fuss about nothing and I certainly wasn't ill.'

She glared at Yul, still upset that he'd called for Hazel and forced the injection on her.

'It wasn't a lot of fuss about nothing,' he said firmly. 'It was very unwise of you to go up there alone in the darkness. Luckily you'd told the girls where you were going so I was able to come and find you. I dread to think what would've happened if I hadn't been there.'

Sylvie remained silent at this, abandoning her toast. She knew exactly what he was thinking; hearing voices had been one of the symptoms of her illness. He should understand why she was so reluctant to talk about this business now.

'I don't think it was unwise of her to go up there,' said Celandine bravely. 'I think it's just what Mum needs, some moon magic. I'll come with you tonight, Mum, if you're scared to go on your own.'

Yul slammed his cup down onto the saucer so the tea slopped onto the tablecloth.

'Your mother is not going anywhere tonight!' he said. 'And neither are you, Celandine. No, nor you, Bluebell.'

Sylvie felt really annoyed now. She hadn't intended to visit the stone that night, being far too frightened of the possibility of hearing Magus' voice again. But that was her choice to make, not Yul's.

'Your father's forgetting that I make my own decisions,' she said coldly. 'If I wish to go moondancing I will. I'll decide later on. But it'll be much too cold at the Frost Moon for you two. As I said last month, I'll take you in the spring. You can watch the moon tonight from the sitting room window and you'll be warm and cosy.'

She stood up abruptly and folded her napkin.

'Hurry up now or you'll be late for Nursery. Go and brush your teeth and then we can get going.'

She looked across at Yul who was frowning, keeping quiet in front of the children. Doubtless he'd bring it up again later on. She almost wanted to moondance just to spite him ... but Sylvie was still terrified of who might be waiting up there for her.

Leveret sat at a large table in the Great Barn, letting the tittle-tattle wash over her. All the talk was about the dance to be held just after Yule, but Leveret had far more pressing things on her mind. Tonight she faced a serious dilemma. She desperately wanted to gather things for her spell at the Moon Fullness, things that must be harvested tonight when the magic was strong. But her two weeks spent at the Hall, working for hours on end after school and at the weekends, scouring enormous pots and pans, scrubbing floors, washing the banister spindles of obscure stair-cases, made her reluctant to risk more trouble. She'd hated staying in Yul's wing, knowing he was constantly close by and watching her. The only highlight of the fortnight had been her little nieces; Leveret smiled to herself at the thought of them.

She was now back home and trying to behave herself. She looked forward to the celebrations at the Winter Solstice and Yule, and realised that if she toed the line, everyone would ease off her a bit. She avoided her brothers' unwanted attention by coming along to help Maizie at the endless meetings. Leveret had never appreciated just how much preparation and hard work went into Yuletide. She was down in the Great Barn every night with her mother, who was making never-ending rotas of jobs and lists of food. Leveret found herself getting roped into the tasks and was enjoying being helpful and earning her mother's praise.

Tonight she was involved with making decorations for the Great Barn. These were mostly different types of evergreen twisted into garlands and wreaths, and candles placed in tiny silver lanterns. But her problem remained: how to collect the holly twigs and mistletoe sprigs she needed, and how to do it tonight. The spell she'd found in the Book was special to the Winter Solstice and required items sacred to this time of year; as tonight was Frost Moon it was now or never.

Leveret sat with the large decorations group at trestle tables in the Barn. They were all using snips to cut out shapes from thin pieces of metal, which were twisted into little lanterns to be hung on wires around the Barn. There was already a good supply from previous years but there were never enough of the tiny lanterns. Families liked having them in their cottages too as the Solstice was a festival of light. Already the great Yule Log had been selected from the orchard and seasoned, and lay in the Barn waiting for its beautiful decorations. The children in the Village School made tiny fir-cone people and animals to adorn it, along with small star wreaths of holly, ivy and mistletoe. The Yule Log was lit after the ceremony in the Stone Circle, and smouldered in the hearth in the Barn for the whole twelve days and nights of Yule. On the thirteenth day, everyone took a little of the ashes and charcoal to bury in their gardens to ensure fertility for the coming year.

A generous portion of the Yule Log ash was always taken to the orchards for the Apple Wassail in early January. Everyone in the community gathered amongst the apple trees, hung with lanterns and small pieces of bread, and toasted the trees and their spirits with a specially brewed cider, again ensuring fertility. There were many such rituals at Yuletide and they were as much a part of the peoples' lives as eating, drinking and making love.

But this year the time-honoured traditions would be changed to accommodate the Outsiders' Dance, as it had come to be named. The dance itself wouldn't affect any of the normal cele-brations, falling between Yule and the Apple Wassail of Twelfth Night, but nevertheless, feelings were running high. Leveret had no intention of taking part in the dance herself but she knew that most of her contemporaries could think of nothing else.

'So what'll happen to all these here decorations and the like?' asked one whiskery old woman busy cutting the metal. 'Will they all have to come down for that night?'

''Twould be a complete waste o' time, that,' grumbled her daughter. 'I don't understand what this thing is they're putting up. Sound system, I heard. What's that then? Martin said 'twould be a shocking mess and he reckons it will shake the old place in its roots!'

'Aye, but the young 'uns need something special, don't they? Now they're going to the Outside World and making new friends and such. We need to give it a chance.'

'What do you think, young Leveret? I reckon you're jumping in your boots for this dance, aren't you?'

She smiled and shook her head.

'Oh no, not me! I don't like that sort of thing. I can't bear the thought of Outsiders coming into our Village and—'

'Well, there you have 'un! See, not even all the youngsters want this thing! Oh, our Yul's made a mistake here and Maizie should be doing something about it.'

Leveret glanced across at her mother, sitting with another group on the other side of the Great Barn making lists of who was going to bake what for the week-long celebrations. Maizie's cheeks were flushed and she was totally immersed in her task. She was a natural organiser and loved this kind of challenge. Leveret smiled, feeling happier than she'd been for a long time. It was so good to be getting on with her mother at last, after Maizie had said they'd put the past incidents behind them and start afresh. Leveret was trying very hard to please her by offering to help and not waiting to be asked.

She was frightened of being left alone in the cottage with Sweyn and Gefrin, who'd cornered her in the Hall one day. They'd reminded her that as far as they were concerned she hadn't got away with it and would take her punishment from them at the earliest opportunity. She shuddered at the thought of them. Yul hadn't been as forgiving as Maizie either. His final words, as she'd left her bedroom in his wing, were that he'd be keeping a very close eye on her and the first sign of trouble would see her back again. She got the feeling that there were other things on his mind too, and that she was bearing the brunt of his dark mood.

Leveret judged it must be around eight o'clock or so. The groups generally disbanded by ten o'clock at the latest for people rose early at Stonewylde and needed their sleep. If she were going to slip out it was now or never. She considered asking her mother if she could go and collect the things she needed. She'd much rather tell the truth if she could, for Maizie was being so kind to her at the moment and Leveret felt guilty deceiving her. But would Maizie let her go out into the night – especially the moonlit night when the magic was strong?

Her mother had a wasp in her shawl about the Moon Fullness, always going on about girls getting into trouble and boys being wild. It was true, of course – the Moon Lust still coursed through everyone's veins as strong as ever despite girls not falling pregnant under the full moon any more. There'd be couples out there tonight in every sheltered spot honouring the moon in traditional fashion, and Maizie would never agree to her wandering out into the bright darkness, however innocent her mission. Leveret would have to deceive her.

'I've got my own pair of snips at home which are much better than these,' she said to the people sitting nearest to her in the group. 'I'm just going to nip back and fetch them.'

'Aren't those any good then?' asked one of them. 'You can swap with me if you like, Leveret.'

'No, it's alright thanks – I like using my own. They're nice and small. I won't be long.'

Feeling very guilty and with a final glance at Maizie sitting engrossed amongst her group, Leveret got up. Grabbing her cloak from the pegs by one of the back doors, she slipped out into the night. Her heart pounded at her treachery and she almost turned back to the Barn, prepared to abandon the idea of collecting the things for casting a spell at the Solstice. But she felt compelled to continue with her plan. She'd had the Book for almost two years now and was desperate to cast. She knew Mother Heggy was watching her, waiting for contact and she had to go through with this – she had no choice.

12

Leveret had concealed a draw-string flaxen bag and the special gathering knife in the large inner pocket of her cloak. She'd found the knife in Mother Heggy's cottage at the same time she discovered the Book of Shadows and it seemed ancient; Leveret suspected it was much older than the crone herself. It was compact, fitting nicely into a small female hand, with a very smoothly-worn white horn handle – probably made from deer antler. The blade was of tempered steel, engraved with strange symbols, slightly curved and very sharp. Leveret had found a worn whetting stone inside the carved box with the knife and she was careful to keep the blade sharp. It was perfectly designed for a herbalist to harvest her ingredients and necessities, and when Leveret had made her find on her thirteenth birthday she'd been happier than at any other moment in her life.

The gathering knife was very different from the third object she'd found on her birthday; a ceremonial athame, wrapped in soft linen with an outer layer of oilskin. Leveret intended to use the gathering knife to collect the materials she'd use for her spell, and to use the athame during the spell-casting ritual. She knew how special tools became linked to those who used them, especially when the purpose was sacred and magical. Using the crone's tools would create a strong bond between her and Mother Heggy and make contact easier. It also felt right deep inside, as if she were continuing the long tradition of magic passed on from woman to woman.

Leveret took an appreciative breath of the cold night air and looked up at the blazing stars twinkling in thick clusters across the velvet sky. The great Frost Moon, its face daubed with grey shadows, had cleared the Village Green treetops and was radiating magical light, bathing all in moon-dusted quicksilver. Leveret felt a thrill of energy, soaking its radiance and feeling the magic coursing through her veins. She was not especially moongazy but who could be immune to it on such a night as this? She ran lightly over the damp grass which would later be brushed with sparkling frost, towards the orchards.

Leveret knew exactly which tree bore the mistletoe she'd collect, for she'd been carefully planning this for a while. She'd noted the footholds and branches which would help her climb and ran now like a young deer, fleet and delicate of foot, to the gates of the vast orchards. The trees rose in moon-brushed blackness towards the starry heavens and Leveret felt another rush of emotion at such beauty. She loved this – she loved the night, the moon, the magic and the sheer poetry of Stonewylde at the Moon Fullness. Her breath caught in her throat and she thanked the goddess for giving her life and showing her such wonders. She thought of Mother Heggy who'd once walked these lands and had gathered sacred ingredients under the same moon with the same knife.

'I'll do everything right,' she whispered into the silent darkness. 'I work with love for the goddess in my heart, and honour for you and your wisdom, and I ask you to help me, Mother Heggy. Help me be a Wise Woman such as you were.'

Climbing the gnarled tree wasn't too difficult for she'd selected a good one, and soon Leveret was up in the branches, as sure-footed as her oldest brother had once been. She paused for a while, feeling the spirit of the apple tree around her. It was a strange sensation, almost impossible to explain; there was a sort of aura that pervaded the whole tree, wreathed around the trunk and woven about the branches. It was a life-force, an energy that swirled slightly, ebbing and flowing as if the tree were breathing. It was a benign force and she greeted it respectfully, making the sign of the pentangle in the air.

Leveret sat in a cleft of branches for a while just feeling the energy and aligning her own energy with it, so they worked in harmony. Then she rose and reached up to the mistletoe, growing thickly in a huge clump. She knew the relationship between the apple tree and mistletoe was a strange one; she'd read that mistletoe was a parasite, but she knew instinctively it was a more complex partnership. She muttered the words she'd memorised from the Book for cutting the sacred plant; they meant nothing to her, for they were words from a different language that she'd never seen or heard before. Leveret wasn't to know just how ancient these words were, passed down orally through the generations and only recorded in the Book of Shadows comparatively recently. She hoped she'd remembered them correctly and, just for good measure, added her own words of honour to the mistletoe, asking forgiveness for the cut.

Taking the white-handled knife from her pocket she made a clean, sharp cut and removed a good piece of the white-berried, sickle-leaved plant. She kissed it and carefully put it in her flaxen bag. Then with a farewell stroke of the tree trunk Leveret jumped down from the tree and ran silver-footed from the orchards back towards the Village Green. She'd become so engrossed in her mission that she'd forgotten all about Maizie and her own deceitfulness. She was heading for an ancient holly tree that grew slightly back from the Village Green on the far side. It was a beauty, its trunk silvery-grey and pimpled with tiny growths, enormous branches sweeping down to the ground all around it. It was covered with jewelled red berries at the moment and although they were not specified in the spell, Leveret thought they'd add to the potency if she gathered some with the deep glossy leaves.

She skipped lightly across the huge expanse of grass and felt a tingle of something ancient, some pattern that must be traced and grounded. She began to leap and twirl, following a blueprint laid by many feet several millennia ago in this ancient woodland temple. It was the dance of the moon, the earth, the life force – the Dance of the Goddess.

Leveret was not a natural dancer but she moved gracefully around the empty ground as if in a trance, her feet stamping and pointing, jumping and tiptoeing to the ancient pattern. She heard a primeval drumbeat reverberating in her soul, a rhythm that marked the dance, and it felt so good to be alive, so powerful. She raised her arms and shook her wild dark curls in joy, spinning with her cloak billowing out around her. She felt the energy from all the different trees crowding around the Green, the eddies and swirls of tree spirit energy that flowed around her almost giving her wings. Here too was the potent spirit of the Green Man; Leveret sensed the myriad energies and felt herself becoming part of the whole ecstatic dance of life.

Inside the Barn, Maizie had finally completed the baking rota to her satisfaction. The labour was fairly shared and nobody felt put upon or left out, which was no mean feat. She looked across to the trestles where people still worked busily on the Yule decorations. The huge Barn interior was alive with the buzz of conversation and the lilting sounds of a group of musicians practising some of the Yule jigs. They'd recently been persuaded to record some of their songs, and Maizie had heard that Harold and Yul were trying to arrange something for them in the Outside World.

Maizie couldn't see Leveret's distinctive dark curly head amongst the people working diligently at the lanterns, but assumed she'd simply gone to the privy. She rose a little stiffly and went over for a word with Rosie. Her elder daughter's cottage was right over the other side of the Village so they rarely bumped into each other in passing, especially as Rosie worked full time at the dairy. Maizie was proud of what her daughter had achieved. Her handfasting with Robin was a good one and he'd proved to be a fine husband. Their two children, Snowdrop and Edrun, were happy in the Nursery every day with all the other little Stonewylders whilst their parents worked.

Robin was in charge of the enormous dairy which had become a huge enterprise, particularly since the cheeses had taken off at Stonewylde.com. Rosie had risen to the challenge of helping to breed a large herd of goats and she supervised the production of goat's milk and cheeses as well, which were in high demand amongst Outside World customers. The kid-skin products had recently become another profitable side-line along with goats' meat and Rosie was keen to develop this offshoot of the dairy, wanting to do her bit to help Stonewylde's economy. But consequently mother and daughter had little private time together for a quiet chat, primarily seeing each other in the Barn when they were involved in community events like this one.

'Who's sitting with the little ones tonight?' asked Maizie, looking at the Yule socks Rosie's group had been knitting. They were still making up for lost time at the Dark Moon at Samhain.

'Robin's sister has them staying at her cottage,' said Rosie. 'She really don't mind and they're good company for her two.'

'You know Leveret would come and sit with them, don't you?' said Maizie.

Rosie grimaced at this and shook her head.

'I don't think Robin'd allow that,' she said. 'He don't think too highly of her and to be honest I'm not sure I trust her either.'

'Oh Rosie! How can you say that about your sister?' said Maizie in dismay.

Rosie shrugged and began casting off stitches, as deft at handicrafts as ever.

'I'm sorry, Mother, but she's been awful lately and I wouldn't want to leave my little ones in her care.'

'Well Sylvie told me that Celandine and Bluebell think the world o' her,' said Maizie stoutly. 'And she's been very helpful lately. I can't speak highly enough of the effort she's been making since she came back from her stay with Yul and Sylvie.'

'Where is she now? Are Sweyn and Gefrin keeping an eye on her for you?'

'No, Rosie, our little Leveret has been here all evening making lanterns! I'm surprised you didn't notice her. She were over there . . .'

'So where is she now?'

'I expect she's in the privy. She'll be back any minute now I'm sure, and then I'll take her home. She's been peaky lately and she needs her sleep. The girl's worked hard tonight and I'm proud o' her.'

'Well I got here a good half hour ago and I've not seen her,' said Rosie. 'Are you sure she's not out gallivanting in the Moon Fullness? You told me she were with that daft Magpie last month and . . .'

Rosie trailed off guiltily at the stricken look on her mother's face.

Leveret reached the other side of the Green following her circuitous, spiralling route, not hearing the sounds of merriment spilling from the Jack in the Green, and not noticing the light blazing from the windows of the Great Barn where people were still busy with their Yuletide preparations. She was oblivious to everything except her quest to harvest some sprigs of holly. She ran through the special words for the holly tree in her head, hoping again that she'd remembered them correctly. It wasn't until she'd almost reached the edge of the Green where the trees stood in a deep fringe of protection that she heard the sound of high-pitched terror. She stopped dead, the spell broken and her heart suddenly hammering.

The sounds were coming from under one of the many sweet chestnut trees, set back from the Green as the holly was, in the thicker part of the wood that surrounded this far end. She started to walk towards it, feet dragging and scared of what she'd find but knowing she had to investigate. With a feeling of dread she recognised her brothers' voices amongst the jeers and laughter and then realised with horror that the squeals of distress were Magpie's.

She broke into a run but then slowed again, trying to see what was going on and what they were doing without being spotted herself. Still standing on the Green with her back to the distant Barn and the pub, she peered into the darkness ahead. In the gaps between the thick trunks she made out lights and movement under the hanging boughs of an enormous chestnut tree. There were several youths, all contemporaries of her brothers, along with Jay, of course. They crowded around something which she guessed must be Magpie but they were blocking him from view. A couple had candle lanterns and there were also Outside torches, powerful ones that created harsh spotlights that arced about as the youths moved. There was a flickering fire too and she could smell not only the woodsmoke but also roasted chestnuts and the sweet smell of cider. They'd obviously been having some sort of a party – and Magpie must be their entertainment.

There was a great deal of raucous laughter, the horrible, primitive laughter of young men engaged in something cruel; something that involved a gang and a victim. She saw the small barrels of cider being passed around, the spouts open and liquid pouring into gaping, tipped-back mouths. She still couldn't see Magpie, only hear his continuous whimpering and distress. Her stomach knotted with pity and anger and she stepped closer. Then she heard Jay's deep, harsh voice full of taunting cruelty.

'But I thought you was hungry, Magpie! I thought you was so hungry you had to steal food from the pantry and gobble it down in secret like the dirty animal you are. What's wrong with this food then? I know you love rabbit.'

There were shouts of laughter at this.

'Give him some more!' called Gefrin, his voice slurred. 'Make him eat some more, Jay.'

'Your friend here thinks you'd like some more,' said Jay. 'Would you like some more rabbit, Magpie?'

There was a terrible screech.

'Sorry, can't understand you. Yes or no? More rabbit or not? If you don't say no then it must be yes. Well?'

Another desperate screech.

'Looks like he wants some more. Are you ready, Sweyn?'

The bodies parted slightly as Jay moved forward and Leveret

was transfixed at the spectacle before her. Magpie was on his knees with Sweyn standing directly behind him, holding him down. Magpie's upper body was upright and bent back slightly, his hands tied in front of him. Sweyn grasped a handful of his hair and forced his head backwards mercilessly. Leveret let out a mew of horror when she saw that Magpie's face was covered in glistening blood. But as Jay advanced she realised it wasn't Magpie's blood she was looking at. It was worse than that. In his hands Jay held the bloody carcass of a skinned rabbit, pink and raw as a new-born baby, which he began to jam into Magpie's mouth. The boy struggled, fought and squealed but the bloody flesh was shoved in his face, with Sweyn behind making sure he couldn't move.

'Eat!' yelled Jay. 'Eat it, you moronic, half-witted bastard! Eat it I said!'

He kicked Magpie hard and continued to force the dead animal into the boy's mouth. Magpie was gagging, his body convulsing, but still the raw meat was rammed into his mouth which was then held shut, forcing him to swallow or choke.

'STOP!' cried Leveret, unable to watch any more. She knew she should run and get help but she couldn't leave Magpie with them like this. 'STOP IT NOW!'

They spun around and she heard the awful sound of Magpie vomiting again and again. The flushed, sweating faces stared at her in shock and then Sweyn broke into laughter.

'It's our little sister come to save her boyfriend!'

They all roared with laughter and hands grabbed her and yanked her forward. Sweyn let Magpie go and kicked him over so he toppled into a heap on the ground next to his puddle of bloody vomit, whimpering and sobbing between the retching. Sweyn advanced and grasped the front of her cloak, pulling her up onto tiptoe so their faces were close. She could smell the cider on him and the rank odour of his sweat. He looked more pig-like than ever, spittle flecking his mouth.

'What are you doing out tonight, Hare-brain? I thought you were being a good little girl helping Mother.'

'I am,' she said, her voice shaking. 'I have been helping her.'

'So what are you doing out here in the woods?'

'Nothing.'

He laughed and let her go, looking down at her and breathing heavily, his small eyes alive with excitement.

'Hold on to her, Gef,' he commanded, and turned to Jay for a whispered conference.

'She said she were going to get her own snips,' said one of the women at the table. 'But that were a while back and she never showed her face again.'

'Well, I expect she felt tired and stayed on at home,' said Rosie quickly, putting an arm around her mother.

'But Rosie, what—'

'Come on, Mother, let's get you home and we'll see if she's there,' said Rosie. 'If Leveret's been so good lately and really turned over a new leaf, I'm sure she will be. And if she's not, we'll come back here and wait for her. There's bound to be a good reason why she's disappeared like this so don't fret.'

They fetched their cloaks and made their way out into the brilliantly moonlit night, their breath clouding around them. Their boots clattered on the cobbles as they walked along the wide paved area outside the Barn. When they reached the Jack in the Green, the noise and brightness flared out at them. Many men helped out with the Yule preparations in the Barn, but others felt they'd earned a few tankards of cider after a day's hard physical labour and left the ceremony provision to those who still had some energy left in the evenings.

The two women walked past briskly to the darker, quieter lane ahead, radiating out of the heart of the Village like a spoke on a spider's web. An owl flew past, it's white wings ghostly in the darkness, and everywhere the moon cast her silver glance. Her beams were caught in the shadowy thatch of the cottages, glinting off the little panes of glass in the windows, dancing back from any shiny surface she could find. The Bright Lady walked the night in her silver shoes and the dew turned imperceptibly to glittering frost. It was a beautiful, magical night.

'Oh, Rosie, what you said about her gallivanting out with Magpie ...'

'I wish I'd never said that! This is our Leveret we're talking about. She's not a bad girl, not in her heart. I'm sure she'll be curled up at home by the fire with her nose in a book and the Yule decorations completely forgotten.'

'I hope so, Rosie,' said Maizie dejectedly. 'She promised to be good for me and I trusted her. If she's let me down again ...'

A minute later the other youths were told to untie Magpie, who lay in a heap apparently unable to move however much they encouraged him with their boots. One of the small barrels was brought across and the spout tipped over Magpie's face so the cider washed him, removing the rabbit's blood.

'Take him back to his cottage,' said Jay to the youths. 'Don't disturb the women as they'll be busy during the Moon Fullness. Just kick him through the gate – even that idiot can find his own way from the garden gate. We don't want him wandering around like this on the Green in case any questions are asked.'

The youths nodded, staggering slightly, and hauled poor Magpie to his feet. He could barely stand as they prepared to frog-march him home. He didn't even seem aware of Leveret's presence but was making a horrible noise – a combination of sobbing and screeching.

'Oh, one more thing before he goes,' said Jay casually. Entirely without warning he bunched his great fist and punched Magpie full in the stomach. It was a mighty blow and the grunt of air escaped from the boy's lungs in a sickening burst. Magpie jack-knifed instantly but the youths on either side wrenched him back upright, retching and groaning, and began to drag him home, skirting around the edge of the Green. Which left Leveret alone with Jay, Sweyn and Gefrin.

'Shall we give her some delicious rabbit as well?' asked Gefrin, who still had her arm twisted up behind her back in a painful grip. 'I reckon she needs feeding up, skinny little runt that she is.'

The other two laughed but Sweyn shook his head.

'What have you been doing, Leveret?' he asked again. He seemed to have calmed down from his earlier excitement and she wondered if maybe he was going to let her off lightly after all.

'I was helping Mother in the Barn,' she replied, trying very hard to keep the fear from her voice for she knew it only egged them on. 'I just went home to collect some snips for cutting the lanterns. That's all.'

Jay surveyed her with narrowed eyes. His face was beaded with perspiration despite the cold night and like Sweyn he stank of sweat and cider. His belligerent face loomed closer and peered into hers.

'She's lying. She ain't been home at all.'

'No, I don't think so neither. Let's see what she's got hidden under her cloak.'

Leveret began to struggle then, terrified they'd take the sacred knife from her, and she moved so suddenly that Gefrin lost his grip. She managed to wriggle free and stood with her knees slightly bent, eyeing all three like a cornered animal ready to launch into flight.

'Don't even think about it!' warned Sweyn, edging closer to cut off her retreat. But she did. With a sudden sideways leap she darted off, jinking across the grass with the three young men hot on her heels. There was a moment when she thought she might get away but it was short lived – she didn't stand a chance against them. Jay brought her down hard, launching himself into a tackle that knocked her flying. He landed squarely on top of her, crushing her so she couldn't breathe, and laughed triumphantly.

'Any other girl lying under me on the grass at Moon Fullness would be fair game,' he said, his breath wafting over her in foul waves. 'But this one – eugh! She's got to be the ugliest girl at Stonewylde and she's more like a boy than a girl. So not tonight, darling – sorry to disappoint you.'

He shifted his weight and pushed himself off her, still pinning her arms to the ground.

'I'd kill myself before I went with scum like you!' she hissed. 'You stink like a torn cat and you've all the wit of a farmyard animal. I'm not into bestiality – sorry to disappoint *you*.'

With a swift swipe he clouted her hard around the side of the head so she saw violent colours and her skull rang with noises.

'Bitch!' he spat. 'Don't you speak to me like that!'

'No!' cried Sweyn. 'For goddess' sake, don't hit her hard or there'll be proof.'

'Never hit her very hard,' added Gefrin. 'You got to do things that don't leave marks.'

They dragged Leveret to her feet and took her back to the fire that still smouldered under the chestnut tree.

'I'll search her,' said Jay, eyes still dark with anger at the way she'd insulted him. He'd never been spoken to like that before, enjoying a certain elevation amongst his peers. The fact that it had come from such a small, young girl only made it worse. He wrenched her cloak open and began to frisk her roughly, deliberately poking her hard and offensively.

'Get your hands off me!' she growled through clenched teeth. 'I'll tell Yul that you've assaulted me.'

He jabbed her ribs at this.

'Don't flatter yourself! You got the most disgusting body I ever seen. Nobody in their right mind would assault *you*, you ugly little bitch. And Yul wouldn't believe you anyway.'

He'd found nothing, of course, but then her cloak fell to the floor and he saw the way she glanced at it.

'There's something in her cloak!' he said triumphantly, whisking it off the ground, and when she began to struggle in Sweyn's grip they knew he was right. She closed her eyes in sorrow, knowing they'd desecrate the precious gathering knife. Finding the big pocket sewn inside the cloak, Jay rummaged and then pulled out the flaxen bag with a flourish and a whoop of delight. Sweyn and Gefrin laughed in anticipation and all three crowded round the torchlight to see inside the bag.

'Mistletoe!' he exclaimed incredulously. 'Is that it?'

Her heart sank as he turned again to the pocket; she knew the knife was nestling in there, tucked into the seam. But after groping around inside, he shook his head.

'That's it.'

'This is good!' said Sweyn. 'She's been out on her roaming again, gathering things. Fancies herself as a bit of a witch, does our Hare-brain, and Mother told us she wants to be the new Wise Woman. Competition for Old Violet!'

'Mother'll go mad with her!' said Gefrin gleefully, following his brother's train of thought. 'Lev'll be in big trouble now!'

'Yeah, just when Mother thought she could trust her little girl too. She's going to be so angry and disappointed when we tell her.'

To her dismay Leveret burst into tears at this, sobbing but unable to hide her face in her hands for they were pinned behind her by Sweyn. He jeered as she cried, and the others joined him in his mockery.

'Pathetic little cry-baby!' said Gefrin. 'Just like you've always been.'

'Was that a bit close to the truth, Leveret?' laughed Sweyn. 'I think we should get her back to the Barn right now, boys, and let Mother see what sort of a daughter she's got.'

'What, and that's it? Aren't we going to do anything to her first?' asked Jay, unable to contain his disappointment. 'Not have any fun with her at all?'

'No ... unless ... lie her down on her back a minute. I've got an idea.'

Jay held her down on the ground, prickly with fallen chestnuts cases, whilst Sweyn picked up the barrel and began to pour cider into her mouth. She kept it shut and twisted her face to one side so the sticky liquid ran off into her hair and all over the grass. But then Gefrin grabbed hold of her head to keep it still and Jay sprawled across her, pinning her arms painfully to the ground by her sides. He held her nose shut and grasped her chin. She could barely breathe anyway and had to open her mouth, her

eyes wild and pleading. Sweyn poured the cider in steadily –
although much of it still ran down the sides of her face – and she
started to choke.

'Mother'll be upset Lev's been up to her old tricks again, sneaking about in the night. But when she sees Hare-brain drunk as well . . .' he chuckled. 'I reckon our little sis might even have to miss Yuletide for this.'

13

Yul sat cross-legged on the Altar Stone waiting for the sun to rise. It was two days before the Winter Solstice and the Stone Circle was almost ready. The bonfire was huge, with a hollow centre and ladder reaching to the tiny crow's nest on top. Here the Herald of Dawn would wait with his unlit torch for the first rays of the rising sun to appear. This year Yul had chosen his half-brother Rufus for the role and Miranda had been so pleased, not realising it had been Sylvie's suggestion. Miranda tried not to push her son forward for special treatment, but she also wanted to ensure he didn't miss out on something just because he was Magus' posthumous last-born child.

Yul glanced around at the vast standing stones, noting how the decorations weren't quite finished yet. There was holly, ivy and mistletoe painted beautifully on every stone in an intricate design, and several deer leaping gracefully across them, for the deer was the totem animal of this festival. All that remained to be done were the golden discs of the sun, the fiery emblems always present at the two solstice festivals. Doubtless the artists would be back today to finish them off.

Yul looked at his watch, wishing impatiently that the sun would rise so he could get back to his office. He hadn't been up here for a while to mark sunrise or sunset and had realised, as he faced the ordeal of yet another restless night, that he was losing touch with what really mattered. He should be up here every day receiving the Earth Magic and honouring the goddess as he'd always done in the past. It was just that he was so very busy all the time and there were so many demands on him.

But the thing that was really affecting him so adversely was the breakdown in communication with Sylvie. This, more than all the work piled on him, made him tired and irritable and unable to function properly. He'd always taken their happiness for granted, basked in the harmony of their love and passion without realising that at some point it could come to an end. Had it come to an end? He didn't know – Yul thought she still loved him, but things had gone very wrong between them. He was terrified that she was becoming ill again; that the present problems were an early indication of the return of her psychosis. He loved her so much and couldn't bear the thought of watching her slowly disintegrate again before his eyes. Last time it had started with irrational behaviour and the hearing of voices, and history seemed to be repeating itself.

Yul hung his head – he couldn't cope without Sylvie by his side and if she wasn't there, he wouldn't even want to. She was so much part of Stonewylde that the two were inextricable. He felt unutterably weary, exhausted by worry and lack of sleep. There was also the problem of his damn sister to contend with. The morning after the last Moon Fullness Maizie had marched up to his rooms early in the morning with a puffy-eyed Leveret in tow. The girl had obviously been sobbing her heart out for she could barely see and her breath was still catching in convulsive gasps. But he'd never seen Maizie so hard-hearted and cold towards her daughter, ignoring Leveret and speaking as if she didn't exist.

'I wash my hands o' her, Yul. I've had enough – do what you like with her. I don't care if she stays with you in this wing or joins the other boarders – just keep her out o' my sight.'

'What happened?' he asked, shocked at the way she was speaking. It really was as if she didn't care any more. She was dull-eyed and the lines around her mouth were sharp. Maizie shrugged, glancing at her stricken daughter with dislike.

'She let me down. Again. I really believed that this time she were going to behave. I trusted her and I was so proud of her . . .'

She broke off as Leveret began to cry again, sounding small and pathetic, uncomforted by either her mother or brother as she stood sobbing into her hands.

'She's kept up this blubbing for most of the night but quite honestly I don't believe it,' said Maizie. ''Tis all for effect – she's a liar and a deceiver and I'll never trust her again. I feel nought but dislike for her and I never thought to say that about one o' my own children.'

'But what did she do?'

Yul couldn't believe this was Maizie, the most loyal, caring mother in Stonewylde.

'We were working in the Barn last night – I were on the food committee working out the baking rota and she were with the group making Yule lanterns. I'd only said earlier how proud I felt that she were helping me every night with such a cheerful heart. Since the boys left home I'd been looking forward to just the two of us spending time together, me and my last child without all the bustle of a big family around us. And I thought—'

'Mother please don't! I'm sorry – I love you, I really do!'

Maizie completely ignored the heart-wrenching words of despair as if Leveret hadn't spoken.

'Anyway, then I noticed that she weren't with her group but I never thought she'd deceived me again. Then I began to wonder because she still wasn't back and they said she'd gone to fetch her snips so Rosie and I started to worry and went home to see if she were there.'

'And was she?' asked Yul.

'No she weren't!' said Maizie bitterly. 'She'd never been there at all – that was just more of her lies. So Rosie and I went back to the Barn, and I were starting to worry all the more what could've happened as I *still* didn't think she'd let me down again. And then Sweyn and Gefrin came marching in, with Jay as well, dragging her all screaming and kicking. She were making such a noise! Like a pig at slaughter, all that squealing and wriggling she did! I nearly died o' shame in front of all those people in the

Barn – all my friends, all the committees, all the people I have to work with day in and day out. I wished the earth'd swallow me up to see my daughter hauled in like that in such shame!'

Yul eyed Leveret with the same look of disgust as his mother had.

'I don't believe I'm hearing this,' he said, his voice turning curt with cold dislike.

'She'd sneaked out when I weren't looking and she'd been collecting mistletoe in a bag, when I'd particularly told her she was *not* to roam about the estate, she was *not* to collect things for her remedies or whatever it is she makes, and she was *never* to go wandering off at the Moon Fullness. Neither were she to meet up with that Magpie, but she did! There was no denying it – she were caught red-handed by her brothers with a flaxen bag full of mistletoe, skulking around under the trees in the Village Green with the boy. And somehow she'd got hold of some cider and she were drunk! That must be Magpie's fault, for Jay said he's known to knock back the cider whenever he can. We all know he's not right in the head but this girl should know better.'

They both turned to look at her as if she were something nasty on the sole of a shoe. Leveret was as white as a swan and seemed unable to speak, her breathing raw and convulsive.

'And worse still, she's tried to deny it all and blame her brothers! She *always* tries to wriggle out of it. She told me the most terrible lies about them last night that nobody in their right mind could swallow.'

'I find it extraordinary that she's behaved like this,' Yul said, shaking his head, 'after all the promises she made to us both last time.'

'I know! You see why I don't want to deal with her any more. She'll be fifteen at Imbolc and I know 'tisn't the custom to board until September when she's in her last year at school, but I want you to arrange for her to move up here now. I don't want her at home.'

'I'm not surprised – who would, after the way she's betrayed your trust? Of course she can move up to the Hall. She'll have me to answer to and I won't make her life easy. I'm so sorry, Mother.'

He put his arms around the plump, dark-haired woman who barely reached his chin and gave her a big hug. She squeezed him back gratefully and left the room without a backward glance at her sobbing daughter.

So now Yul was lumbered with Leveret too, who moped about like the world was coming to an end. He really didn't need that as well, not just now. And tomorrow was the Rite of Adulthood day and he must spend it up in the Wildwood with the boys ... Yul sighed, his head in his hands, and then realised with a jolt that the sun had come up and he hadn't even noticed. He leapt to his feet on the stone, frowning with puzzlement and shock. He'd felt nothing at all, no Earth Energy, no green magic flowing through him. What on earth had happened? He felt a clutch of fear at his heart – was this the beginning of the end for him? He recalled how Magus' power had waned and shivered at the prospect of Stonewylde rejecting him too.

'Don't leave me now, Goddess!' he called out loud in anguish. 'Please don't you abandon me as well!'

The cart full of paints and brushes, lanterns and evergreens arrived at this moment and the men and women who came with it stared at their magus strangely. Yul barely noticed them but strode distractedly out of the Stone Circle and back down towards the Hall.

'And bright blessings to you too, Master Yul!' muttered one of them.

Clip wandered out of the kitchens with a bag of fruit and some hazelnuts, the provisions he intended to take with him that evening to the Dolmen for his personal Solstice feast. It was early morning but he needed to bathe and prepare himself for the Solstice tomorrow. He crossed the entrance hall, absent-mindedly brushing into a small person on the way.

'Sorry,' he said. 'Oh, Leveret!'

He'd barely recognised her – she looked terrible and seemed to have shrunk in on herself. Her pointy little face was even sharper than usual, the usual healthy glow replaced by a wan waxiness. Her black curls were bedraggled and unkempt and she regarded him with sunken eyes, the green dulled.

'Blessings, Clip,' she muttered.

'What's happened to you? Are you ill?'

She merely shook her head and tried to continue across the hall. He took her arm and noticed how thin it was.

'Leveret, tell me what's the matter? You look awful. Have you been eating?'

She shook her head again.

'But you mustn't fast too much, never more than a couple of days. Especially not at your age when you're still growing.'

She shrugged and looked listlessly at the floor.

'How long since you ate anything?'

She shrugged again and he stared at her perplexed, at a complete loss as to what to do. Then he led her to a large oak settle by the fireplace and sat down with her. She sat next to him like an automaton.

'Does Yul know you're not eating?'

'He doesn't care. He hates me,' she whispered. 'Everyone hates me and I'm nothing. Worse than nothing.'

'Oh Leveret, you know that's not true. What about Maizie? I know your mother cares about you.'

Her face crumpled at this but no tears came. She shook her head. Clip frowned, then awkwardly put an arm around her narrow shoulders, pulling her into his side and holding her gently.

'Leveret, I'm sure they care. I know everyone's busy at the moment but they do care.'

'No they don't! Mother said she's finished with me once and for all and she sent me to live up here. She won't let me stay in the cottage and she wants nothing more to do with me, ever. Rosie won't speak to me at all – she thinks I'm nasty and selfish. Yul said I'm a thorn in his flesh and he hates me because I upset Mother. Then Sweyn and Gefrin said they're going to do something really awful to me, worse than they've ever done before. Now no one cares about me at all, they know they'll get away with it. And Jay says he wants to join in as well.'

'I spoke to your mother about Sweyn,' said Clip. 'I told her what he did to you at Samhain, with the apple-bobbing barrel, so—'

Leveret laughed bitterly at this; a horrible sound entirely devoid of mirth.

'That was kind of you, Clip, but pointless. Mother confronted him and of course Sweyn told his usual lies and she believed him. She always chooses to believe him and Gefrin before me.   Why's that? Why does she love them and not me? What have I ever done so she won't believe me but always —'

Her voice cracked and Clip squeezed her shoulders, feeling so inadequate.

'Leveret, you mustn't think that way. I'm sure she loves you as much as your brothers. I'll speak to her again and convince her you're telling the truth about them. I know what I saw in the Barn.'

Leveret shook her head and sighed heavily.

'Really, there's no point. Mother isn't interested in the truth. She's only interested in what she wants to hear. She said some horrible things about me and Magpie too. There's nothing – absolutely nothing – I can do to make her see the truth. Poor Magpie ... '

She broke off, her voice fading to nothing.

'What about Magpie? He's Starling's son, isn't he? The mute boy? I thought he was your friend – I know I've seen you together.'

She nodded.

'I'm forbidden from seeing him. The things they did to him ... he can't eat now. They forced him to eat raw rabbit but nobody believes me. And the only thing they cook in his house is rabbit stew and now he can't eat it at all. He's so hungry but nobody will listen to me and he's getting sick. If Magpie can't eat then neither can I so we're both going to die.'

Clip shook his head.

'No you're not going to die, Leveret. That's silly. How old are you?'

'I'm fourteen. And it's not silly – you just don't understand, Clip.'

'Look, it's the Winter Solstice tomorrow and you'll be taking part in the ceremonies and having such a good time at the party in the Barn. You'll forget all this misery and woe.'

'I won't,' she said mournfully. 'I won't be taking part in any-thing. I won't even be here. Thank you, Clip, for being so nice to me. I like you and I'm sorry if I've ever done anything wrong to you. I must go now – I have things to do.'

She stood up, unsteady on her feet.

'You were very kind to me at Samhain and I wish I'd had a father like you to teach me. All I ever wanted to was to learn about plants and magic and to be the Wise Woman. I never wanted to hurt Mother or do anything bad. But everything's gone wrong and I can never make it right again. Magpie and I ... our lives are a misery and everybody hates us. We're at everyone's mercy and we can't go on like this anymore. I just wish I could've been a Wise Woman.'

Clip had no idea what to do with her. She was clearly very distressed – maybe he should tell Maizie, or even Sylvie. But then he remembered it was the start of the Rite of Adulthood today and they'd both be under the willow tree with the women and the girls. Yul would be out too, in the Wildwood with the boys. There was nobody about today who could talk to the girl and help her. Nobody but him and he didn't have a clue where to start.

'Would you like to come up into the Solar with me?' he asked. 'Up in my tower? You've never been there before, have you? The views are really stunning and you could look at some of my books – I've a vast collection of them. And I'll play you my gongs if you like. There's nothing like a sound bath to put things in perspective.'

But she shook her head.

'I've got to get some food from the kitchens for me and Magpie to take with us.'

That sounded more promising – at least she was intending to eat.

'Are you going on a picnic then?'

'We're going on a journey and we'll need some food or we'll never make it there. It's a long way to walk in the cold. I've been dreaming about it every night and I know Magpie and I must go there – it's where we belong.'

Clip looked at Leveret in consternation. She really did look terrible and all the light had gone from her eyes.

'You're not running away, are you? Because Leveret, if—'

She shook her head impatiently, and stood up.

'No, Clip. I've never wanted to leave Stonewylde and that's half the problem. My life isn't my own anymore – everyone else makes all the choices for me and I've had enough of it. I'm taking control of my own destiny and I've decided what we have to do. It's the only thing we can do, with everyone hating us. Sorry but I must go, Clip. You're a kind man and I liked you a lot.'

She left then, stumbling across the hall into the passage leading to the kitchens. Clip watched her go with a sad heart, thinking how he must do something to help her after the Solstice. Before he left Stonewylde he'd take her under his wing and try to nurture the magic he knew she possessed.

It was mid-afternoon when Magpie and Leveret finally reached their destination. The trek had been horrendous and many times Leveret doubted whether they'd actually make it. Even though they'd stuffed themselves with bread and cheese in the empty kitchens before they left, both were weakened by their lack of food over the past few days. She suspected that Magpie had at least one broken rib and he was limping badly too. Jay had obviously given him a good going over before the rabbit scene that she'd stumbled on, and then they'd all laid into him when he couldn't get up. Poor Magpie – her heart ached for him.

He'd retreated into himself after that terrible night, gone to a place where nobody could hurt him anymore. He was filthier than ever and she thought he must have just been curled up on his blanket under the stairs ever since that night, unable to do anything for the pain and unable to eat the food that was tauntingly offered by his mother, who probably knew all about the raw rabbit torture. Leveret realised how lucky she'd been to grab Magpie as he hobbled outside to use the lavatory at the bottom of the garden. She may not have had another chance.

They approached Quarrycleave slowly, both exhausted. The wintry sun was hazy behind thin cloud and the air was cool but mild for the time of year. A flock of rooks flew overhead noisily; Leveret saluted them and dragged Magpie on.

'Come on Maggy, nearly there now. Look, there's the quarry, the Place of Bones and Death they call it, and it's where the old Magus died. It's a very special place of death and I've been dreaming about it ever since I decided what we must do. Quarrycleave has been calling to me and I know this is where we belong – at least we're wanted here.'

They approached the shallow end of the sprawling quarry and as they got closer Leveret made the sign of the pentangle. She felt a trickle of fear in her throat; it truly was a place of death. She knew where they were heading – she'd heard all the talk and stories over the years, as had every other child at Stonewylde. Magus had died falling from Snake Stone, a huge pillar different to the Portland limestone in the quarry. Made of a sparkling rock, it was carved with writhing serpents and was the site of a battle between her eldest brother and his father on the eve of the Winter Solstice, thirteen years ago tonight.

Leveret had never visited Quarrycleave before – it wasn't exactly forbidden, but very strongly discouraged as it was a dangerous place. She'd heard the place was haunted by evil spirits but she wasn't sure whether that was just superstition. Nevertheless she felt an uneasiness here that surprised her, a constant feeling of being watched and even being followed by something. Several times as they struggled through the quarry, stumbling down the long corridors of rock and brushing past the

211

sinuous ivy, she'd felt as if something were just around the corner behind them, stalking them. Once the feeling had taken hold it was difficult to ignore and she found her heart beating faster. Magpie was whimpering and struggling along but sending her no messages even though she was holding his hand. He seemed incapable of even the limited communication they usually managed.

'It's not far now, Maggy,' she said encouragingly. 'Can you see that great rock up there? We just have to get there and then we can rest.'

They came to the place where the labyrinth of stone ended, at the head of the quarry where the hill rose sharply above in a high cliff of stone. Now they must climb up the side of the quarry along the narrow path. It was their last ordeal and a difficult one, especially as Leveret couldn't hold on to Magpie. By the time they reached the point where the stepping boulders led up to the top of the Snake Stone she was crying tears of frustration and exhaustion. Her chest was heaving and Magpie's near continuous moans of pain and distress upset her terribly. They sat together on a boulder to catch their breath before attempting the final climb.

'Is it really hurting? Poor Maggy – it's your ribs. If things were different I'd have put on a poultice and bandaged you up. You should be lying in a warm, soft bed, looked after and cared for. But there's no chance of that, not for either of us, is there?'

Magpie hunched next to her in his filthy old coat, his breathing still laboured. She took his dirty hand in hers and rubbed it against her cheek. He laid his head on her shoulder, almost knocking her over.

'I tried to tell them you were hurt and in danger but nobody would listen to me,' she continued sadly. 'Nobody believes anything I say. So we'll take our chances, you and me, Maggy. We'll leave this place and move on to the Otherworld. Mother Heggy'll look after us there, I know she will, and they say it's a wonderful place with none of the horrible things here. I can feel Mother

212

Heggy waiting for us just on the other side. Come on then – we're almost there now.'

She pushed, dragged and cajoled Magpie up onto the great boulders that acted as steps to the Snake Stone. She was so small compared to him but also very determined, and eventually she heaved him onto the stone platform, the stage for Magus' final moments of life. Leveret looked down over the quarry; the shadows were deepening on this very short day and she felt another jagged thrill of fear. She was sure there was something lurking down there. Maybe it was just a wild animal – a dog or fox, or even one of the big cats that were rumoured to inhabit the Wildwoods to the east. Whatever it was, she was very pleased to be out of the dark pit below.

She tried to dismiss her dread and gently helped Magpie to sit down, not wanting him to topple over the edge to a slow death of broken limbs. It was a truly gigantic pillar with a very steep drop, but there was room for both of them to stretch out on its top.

'Look at these carvings, Maggy. Can you see the great snake here, coiled up? And here are the cups – I heard they used to hold moon eggs made of this special sparkling stone. It has magical properties, you know; it stores up moon energy channelled by a moongazy maiden. Mother told me all about this and what happened to the old Magus.' She paused, the memories of her mother telling her stories as a child difficult to bear. 'Let's just rest now and get comfortable and then we can do it.'

Magpie lay down on the rock and curled into a foetal position, whimpering softly. Leveret sat next to him, cross-legged, stroking his face. He was filthy and his hair crawled with lice, but she was beyond caring about things like that. She loved him – she was the only person in the world who loved him – and if things had been different she'd have cared for him and made sure that he was happy, as much as he could be. But she had no power and she couldn't stand by and watch him suffer any longer. If she did he would die, at the hands of either Jay or his mother, and it would be a slow and brutal death involving much suffering first.

This was kinder. At least this way they could go together and it would be peaceful and relatively quick.

Leveret nodded, sure she'd made the right decision. What point was there in living? Her mother would never trust her again and couldn't bear to be near her. Yul couldn't stand the sight of her and Rosie wasn't speaking to her. She had no friends at school, nobody liked her, and she was now in effect an exile in her own community. And as for Sweyn and Gefrin – she was truly terrified about their threats. They'd made it very clear that together with Jay, they had something really awful in store for both her and Magpie; after witnessing the rabbit incident Leveret knew this was no idle threat.

She knew her mother would be upset that she'd made the choice to pass on to the Otherworld, but in the long run it was for the best. She and her mother could never rebuild their relationship. The trust had died and couldn't be revived and it was just too painful to carry on like this with her mother despising her. She thought of the other people who might be affected. Marigold in the kitchens was generally very kind to both her and Magpie, and she'd be sad. Clip, who was so wise and different from anybody else she knew – he'd be a little upset perhaps. Leveret thought briefly of her two nieces, Celandine and Bluebell.

Until she'd been banished to Yul's apartments, she'd despised them as silly, spoilt little girls. But she'd started to get to know them recently and knew that if things had been different, she'd have maybe grown to love them. They certainly seemed to be very fond of her and she'd enjoyed their sweetness and affection. They'd been so distressed by her sadness and depression during this last week, since Maizie had dumped her at the Hall, that Yul had prevented her from seeing them. Leveret had been confined to her room at all times when she wasn't actually in class or doing chores, and had been banned from any contact with them. Yul had shouted at her for upsetting his daughters but she hadn't meant to at all. Not that he had believed anything she said.

Yul had been so angry with her, yet again, after Maizie had abandoned her, shouting at her, pushing his face into hers and really frightening her. He'd lectured her endlessly about how selfish and cruel she was and told her how Maizie's life had been terrible for sixteen years until her father Alwyn had died. This now was their mother's chance to be happy and content, not feel betrayed by someone she loved. On and on he'd ranted until she could take no more. Leveret didn't need to be told what an awful person she was – she already knew. She hated herself and knew she was worthless; why else did nobody like her? She'd no friends and was the ugliest girl at Stonewylde, skinny and hideous. Nobody would ever want her. Nobody would even talk to her.

She cringed with embarrassment at the ridiculous hopes she'd nursed about the boy she'd liked. He was perfect – so handsome and popular, so clever and kind, with loads of girlfriends. She'd been stupid to dream that one day he might notice her and ask her to be his girlfriend. She hung her head in shame and self-loathing. Her life was a misery and there was no end in sight. She'd had enough and longed only to leave this place and enter the Otherworld. Once they were there, everything would be better and they could start again. Perhaps Magpie would even have the power of speech.

Leveret rested her hand gently on his bruised and swollen cheek and looked down at him just as he opened his lovely turquoise eyes to gaze deeply into hers. She could feel his thoughts again, thank goddess, for he'd even locked himself away from her. But now he was back and she smiled at him, returning his love.

'You're a beautiful boy, Magpie,' she said softly. 'Your life has been terrible and you don't deserve it. You know Levvy loves you too. That's why we're going to the Otherworld together. Are you happy to go there with me?'

He nodded, his eyes blazing his need to always be with her.

'Alright then – let's do it now before it gets dark.'

She shifted slightly and fished in her cloak pocket for the small bag. Opening the draw-string Leveret pulled out the shrivelled mushrooms. There were four of the dull beige caps – two each. Death Caps – lethal and final.

14

The light was fading amongst the trees as the men and boys in the Wildwood cooked their feast on the fire, the meat on a spit and large potatoes wrapped and baking amongst the glowing charcoal. There were other treats spread out on rough trestle tables and a great barrel of cider too. Some of the men were drumming and everyone was laughing and enjoying themselves. Yul sat on a log slightly apart from everyone, his back against a tree trunk. It had been a very long day, as these days always were, joining in all the activities alongside the youngsters destined to become men in the morning.

All day Yul and some of the men had kept the boys in the Wildwood, away from the community, and engaged in physical endurance challenges. Yul was exhausted from the stealth games, tree climbing and archery, and he longed for a hot bath and bed. But there was the evening of feasting, singing and drinking to be got through first and more male bonding with the youngsters. They were all very excited about becoming men and receiving new ceremonial robes from their families and pewter pendants from their magus.

Yul fingered the pewter pendant on its leather thong around his own neck. He'd chosen the Green Man as his personal totem, and the other side was embossed with a sprig of mistletoe just as all these youngsters would have too. Tomorrow was his birthday – twenty-nine years old. Thirteen years since he'd become a man, although the occasion hadn't been marked in this way. He hadn't even taken part in the customary ritual up at the Stone Circle because he'd wanted to wait for Sylvie to reach her sixteenth birthday.

It had been a terrible day overall, though it had started well enough with the wonderful sunrise ceremony. The relief that his lifelong battle with Magus was finally over had been overwhelming, but all day he'd been haunted by the thought of that broken body lying at the foot of the Snake Stone amongst the boulders and stone rubble. Edward had dealt with that – and the other two bodies at Quarrycleave – and Clip and others had stepped in too, wanting to protect the boy from further distress. Yul distinctly remembered the strong sense of unreality that had clouded everything that Winter Solstice, and the feel of new beginnings for everyone at Stonewylde.

When the sun had risen over the Village Green and the community had arrived at the Great Barn for a Solstice breakfast, someone had discovered old Professor Siskin's body curled up on the ground, all rimed with frost. Sylvie had been devastated; convinced his death was her fault. But worst of all, for Yul at least, had been the discovery of Mother Heggy's death. He and Sylvie had walked to her tumble-down cottage later on that morning, still in their beautiful Winter Solstice robes, hoping to persuade her to come to the Barn for the festivities. Yul remembered noting the lack of smoke trickling from the crooked chimney, which was an ominous sign in mid-winter, and had pushed the door open with trepidation. He'd never forget the sight of the tiny crone still hunched up in the centre of her circle of salt, the five points of the pentangle marked with symbols of the elements, the little fire-cauldron cold and dead.

Mother Heggy had looked so small and helpless then, but she'd been so very strong for him. He'd cried on seeing her, great sobs of anguish and sorrow, and Sylvie had done her best to comfort him just as he'd comforted her a little earlier by Professor Siskin's body. His sixteenth birthday had been a day like no other and he wouldn't wish it on any of the boys here today. They seemed so young and carefree, yet they all knew so much more than he had at their age. He smiled wryly; if nothing else, he could feel a sense of achievement that the youngsters of Stonewylde were now educated properly and had many choices and opportunities open to them.

He sat there gazing at the revelry around him and wondered what Sylvie was doing now. She would have left the girls' Rite of Adulthood events under the willows by the river and was probably back at the Hall putting their daughters to bed. Leveret could've been told to babysit of course, and Celandine and Bluebell would've loved that. Yul couldn't understand why they'd formed such a strange attachment to their disgraced aunt and he was sure it wasn't reciprocated in the least. Leveret had proved far too selfish to feel anything for them. He didn't want her hurting their feelings and was determined to keep her away from them; she was hardly a good influence in any respect and seemed to constantly upset them with her ridiculous moods and dramatics.

Once Yuletide was over he'd move her into a dormitory with other boarders – why should she have special treatment? Sylvie had said she felt sorry for the tragic teenager and wanted to talk to her about her side of the story, but Yul had been angry at the idea and forbidden her to talk to Leveret. The last thing he needed was his over-emotional and unpredictable sister setting off his unstable wife's depression. Sylvie had given him one of those looks and he'd felt the resentment seething inside her. He knew she thought he was too dominating but he couldn't help it; it was just his way and she'd known that all along from the start. She used to joke about it and call him the lord and master – now she seemed to hate it, but it was too late for him to change.

Yul admitted, reluctantly, that he was like his father in this respect. Magus had been dominating too, but how else could the leader of such a large community be? It was no use being weak and indecisive like Clip – surely Sylvie saw that. Everything he did was for her, with her comfort or happiness in mind. He didn't want her getting involved with his wayward sister because it would only cause her heartache in the end. Sylvie was so kind, so gentle and soft-hearted, and she'd only get hurt. Leveret had turned out badly and she was his problem, not his wife's. He needed to put his sister straight by whatever means he thought fit and it wasn't Sylvie's place to get friendly and act as if Leveret had done nothing wrong. In Yul's books, upsetting their mother was one of the worst things anyone could do.

'Meat's cooked, Yul!' called Edward, his face red and glistening from the heat of the roaring fire. 'Are you going to help carve?'

'No, I think Tom should help you,' said Yul. 'I'm after some cider. It's time to get rat-arsed, as they say in the Outside World. It's been quite a while since I did.'

Edward chuckled at this and lifted the roasting meat off the fire. Yul needed to let his hair down a bit, he thought. He'd seemed so distant and bad-tempered lately. Maybe with a few drinks inside him he'd forget his worries and go back to that lovely wife of his to end the day with the perfect celebration. He grinned at the thought and decided that maybe he'd do exactly the same when he got home. That's what all this male bonding was about anyway – reaffirming the status of the man in society, or so he'd read somewhere. And there was nothing wrong with that at all.

'Swift, take the magus a tankard of cider, would you, boy? And have one yourself – you're far too solemn. This is your big day remember? You'll be a man tomorrow and I expect my Kestrel will be leading you astray over Yuletide. That boy's so popular with the girls – I wish I'd had his success at that age!'

Swift smiled politely and carried a dripping tankard over to where Yul sat against the tree. When the magus downed it in one he refilled it ... and then made it his mission for the evening to ensure that the tankard was always full. He realised he'd never seen Yul drunk before and it would be interesting to watch.

Back in the Hall, Harold sat at his desk in the office as always, tapping away at the keyboard. It made no difference to him that it was Solstice Eve and everyone else was either drinking and making merry or preparing for the next day's events. He'd been invited to join the youngsters at their Rite of Adulthood get-together in the Wildwood with some of the other men but he'd naturally refused. Harold wasn't a physical sort and had grown from the nervous youth of the old days into a rather anxious and intense man, almost the same age as Yul. He hid behind an owlish pair of glasses and spent most of his life behind a screen in this room.

Harold jumped as Martin suddenly appeared – he hadn't knocked and moved silently on the thick Aubusson carpet. Pushing his glasses back up his nose Harold swung round in the swivel chair to face the tall, silver-haired man who stood near the door staring at him.

'Martin! You scared me for a minute,' he said awkwardly. 'Can I do something for you?'

'I doubt it,' said Martin, moving into the room and coming closer to the screen. Harold's instinct was to try to block it as he was working on some rather confidential figures at the moment, but that would've been very rude. Martin's wintry grey eyes flicked over the screen but showed little interest.

'If you're looking for Yul he's out with the youngsters,' said Harold.

'I know,' Martin replied coldly. 'My son Swift is there. 'Tis his Rite of Adulthood this Solstice.'

'Ah yes, I'd forgotten.'

There was a pause and Harold wondered what Martin wanted.

'Didn't you want to join them?' he asked eventually. 'I thought the fathers usually—'

'I'm far too busy on Solstice Eve to go off drinking in the Wildwoods,' replied Martin stiffly. 'There's work to be done and I can't rely on these youngsters and their rotas to do things properly. 'Tis not like in the old days when staff were trained properly, is it? Not that you ever finished your training, did you?'

To Harold's astonishment, Martin sat down in the other leather swivel chair – Yul's chair.

'Well, no I didn't, but then . . .'

'I know – everything changed and you started school again.

221

Pah! Though I seem to recall they found you could already read and write a bit, didn't they?'

'A little,' said Harold. He had no idea why Martin was here and talking like this to him. Normally the older man maintained a dignified and formal distance.

'Always did have ideas above your station,' muttered Martin. 'And look at you now; in on everything, thinking you control it all—'

'No!' said Harold, pushing back his glasses and jerking his long wrists in dismay. 'I don't think that, Martin. I do what I can to help, that's all.'

'You were just a pot-boy,' said Martin bitterly. 'Someone to clean out the fires and polish the Hallfolk's shoes. And now you're sitting in the magus' office with all his private things at your fingertips thinking you rule the roost. I know what you're up to, young Harold!'

'No, that's not it!' cried Harold, his voice squeaking. 'I don't—'

'If you recall, it were on this very night thirteen years past that I asked you to help me as I lay on the floor in Magus' chambers bleeding. This very night that you refused to help and locked me in there, left me for dead!'

'No, Martin, I—'

'Yes you did! They didn't find me till the next morning and I were almost dead! 'Tis a wonder I didn't die in the cold night with that head-wound. I haven't forgotten, Harold, don't think I have. Every Solstice Eve I think on it, and tonight's no exception. I warned you at the time there'd be consequences. As I said, I know what you're up to and I shall put a stop to it. You won't get away with it.'

Martin rose and glared down at the younger man whose Adam's apple was working furiously in his throat.

'The vipers will be cast out!' Martin muttered, leaving the room. Harold stared at the door long after it had closed, trying to make sense of his words.

*

As darkness fell, Clip hunched over the kindling in the Dolmen and nursed the small fire into life. He fed sticks into the flames, gradually adding larger ones until the warmth spread and permeated his thin limbs. The back of the Dolmen was shadowy, the bracken and rug that Leveret had slept on at Samhain still there. He sat down on a log next to the fire, making sure he could still see outside; it was important to see the stars if he could. He took a swig of water from his bottle and glanced at the bag of fruit and nuts. But he had a journey ahead of him tonight and had been fasting for three days as he generally did – food would have to wait until the Solstice tomorrow. Clip was so used to this aesthetic lifestyle that it was no hardship at all. His body had long since learned that sending hunger signals to his brain would make no difference. His abdomen was hurting right now, though not with hunger. This pain had begun to gnaw at him regularly and he thought of it as the serpent within his belly. He was learning to live with it and even spoke to it sometimes, but tonight it would be easy to ignore. Once he'd left this realm, he'd feel nothing anyway.

Clip knew this would be his last Winter Solstice at Stonewylde. By this time next year he could be anywhere in the world – maybe in the Australian Outback or with a tribe in North America. He wanted to visit Peru and the Steppes, Tibet and the Amazon; Clip had been captive here for thirteen long years and longed to be free to roam. He'd only ever been the custodian – never the guardian – of Stonewylde, always haunted by the bad things that nobody else seemed to notice. He knew of the evil up at Quarrycleave that lay waiting for new victims. He knew too of the corrupting influence of power and he wanted nothing of it.

Clip didn't remember his own father, but he recalled the terrible way his Uncle Elm had lived, debauched and utterly selfish, spoiling everything around him. He'd heard of the rape that had resulted in his own conception up at Mooncliffe and the torment his mother had suffered every single month, with his brother also born out of such brutality. The taint of power had all passed on to his brother and Clip knew only too well just what an evil man Sol had been. The sophisticated, charismatic persona had been a mere mask which had slipped alarmingly by the end of his life.

Clip acknowledged that he too had behaved very badly, although Miranda had told him kindly it was just as well or she'd never have had Sylvie nor her wonderful life at Stonewylde. But that didn't detract from his own wicked act. And now Yul seemed destined for the same fate. Today he was a far cry from the passionate, idealistic boy who'd fought his father thirteen years ago. Clip sighed – he'd done his best and stayed here all these years from a sense of duty and guilt. It had to be enough. Stonewylde and her demands had bled him dry and now he wanted to wander the world and honour the Goddess in all her guises, not just her Stonewylde robes. That's all he'd ever wanted to do – to be free of this place.

He settled into his customary position and began to clear his mind; usually the process was quick. An empty, clear mind, a bright shining radiance filling his head ... his totem, the silver wolf, would appear and lead him through a strange, symbolic landscape, feeling a sense of heightened perception. There'd be some sort of entrance – maybe a cave, or passing beneath a waterfall, or even through a foxhole – and then they'd be in and the journey could begin. Clip fidgeted, his bony bottom uncomfortable.

He glanced into the shadows at the back of the cave again, seeing only the bracken and blanket where Leveret had slept. Should he be acknowledging another presence tonight? Had a spirit joined him? No, it wasn't that. He stared deep into the heart of the fire, trying again to clear his mind. Empty, just a bright, shining radiance ... he glanced again into the cave's shadowy depths. Something was pulling at him, nagging at his subconscious – something he should understand. He sighed again and stared into the dark shadows, letting his mind wander freely.

All was bright and here was his silver wolf at last, slinking through the trees, his eyes so wise as he led Clip towards a great cave-mouth. Clip walked, one hand on the wolf's head and the other holding his ash staff. As they approached the mouth, Clip felt a tingle of fear and looked around. The landscape was bizarre, huge, pale boulders and outcrops of Fly Agaric, the brilliant red startling against the white rock.

Clip hesitated at the entrance, frightened to go inside. He looked up and saw two huge pointed stalactites of stone curving down from the roof. Passing between them he shivered, thinking they looked like fangs, but the wolf urged him onwards and Clip followed ... into the darkness of the cave and then, too late, he understood. He was inside a serpent, and travelling deeper, down into the long tunnel of its body. This wasn't a journey he wanted to make and he halted, reluctant to continue deeper into the snake's body, which had become labyrinthine in its twists and turns.

'I don't want to go any further,' Clip said to his spirit guide. 'This place is evil and it frightens me.'

The wolf turned his silvery eyes to Clip's and looked deep, deep into his soul.

'The time has come,' said the wolf, 'to face all those things that you fear the most. Now is your chance to right all wrongs, to prove yourself a man of honour. You're the saviour and you must act now.'

Clip looked ahead, peering into the long tunnels and saw a tiny hare crouched in the shadows. He felt a tug at his heart and stepped towards it, wanting only to scoop it up and keep it safe.

'Now awaken,' commanded the silver wolf. 'You know where she is and what she will do. Don't let the evil claim her for its own.'

Clip's eyes flew open and he lurched to his feet in the entrance of the Dolmen, almost stumbling into the small fire. He poured his water onto the embers, and taking up his staff, hurried down the hill in the deepening dusk.

'Can you sit up, Maggy? We need to eat our special mushrooms now.'

He struggled upright, groaning at the pain in his ribs but wanting to do as she asked. He leaned against her heavily and she almost toppled over, the mushrooms dropping from her hands onto the stone.

'No! Oh, here they are. Be careful, Magpie – we mustn't lose these. They're going to take us to the Otherworld.'

Leveret peered at the dried and shrunken caps in the gathering gloom, hoping desperately they were the right ones. She knew how potent Death Cap was; there really was no escape, no antidote. She wanted the end to be quick although she knew there'd be some pain as the lethal toxins entered their nervous systems, destroying their livers and kidneys. It could take some hours. She'd done her research on the Internet and learned far more details than the Book of Shadows had offered her.

She held the four caps in her cupped palms and thought carefully. Was she doing the right thing? For herself, she was absolutely sure. She no longer wanted to live. She had no future – the heaven of Stonewylde wasn't meant for her. She wished that she was good enough and had so desperately wanted to be the Wise Woman one day. But she'd failed in every sense and this was the only way out of the misery she'd endured these past few days. All her life she'd suffered at the hands of her brothers and she could see it stretching away endlessly into a bleak, loveless future. Inside she felt cold and blank.

And Magpie – did he have a future? Was there any way his life could become worth living? She knew that without her the answer was no. Without her he'd be at the mercy of Jay and Starling. Even when alive she had no power to protect him. So yes, this was the right thing for both of them and best to get it over and done with now. She squeezed the dried caps and felt their sponginess. This was it – this was the way their world would end. No more life, no more Stonewylde, but at least they'd find peace in the Otherworld.

Leveret looked at where the sun had gone down in a bloody puddle of glory. The darkness was crowding in and once more she sensed something down in the quarry. She peered below, sure she could hear a rustling noise in the ivy. Well, if it was a carnivore it would be welcome to their carcasses, and if it was something else, something less tangible – they'd soon be gone into the Otherworld and oblivious to anything in this one, however frightening it was. She felt the mushrooms in her hands – they were so light. Would they work? How could something so small and insubstantial do something so immensely powerful? There was only one way to find out. So why was she feeling so reluctant to do it when she knew it was the right thing?

'Mother Heggy, speak to me, please! Is this right? Should we do this?'

But there was no answer, only more stirring in the quarry below. A cold shiver began to spread over her skin despite the warmth of Magpie propped against her. Leveret sensed a deep hunger all around her that craved and craved.

'Mother Heggy, will you be there on the other side of the veil waiting for us? Please give me a sign that this is the right thing to do.'

She felt the thing below creeping closer and had a sudden image of death, of broken and bloody bodies lying amongst blasted stone and thick choking clouds of stone dust, of something feeding on the death. And then there was another image of weapons – piles of bloodied weapons and more bodies, mutilated beyond recognition, and more feeding. But the hunger couldn't be satisfied. She saw a man with silver hair and black eyes laughing, but then the hunger devoured him too.

Leveret shuddered, knowing that they had no choice now – Quarrycleave had them and they too must feed this hunger with more bodies, poisoned ones. This was why she'd been called here and it was the right thing to do, to join her Stonewylde ancestors at this special place.

'Maggy, you must eat both these caps quickly now so we can go to the Otherworld together and find Mother Heggy. Look, see Levvy doing it? Mmn, delicious. Eat yours too – good boy. Swallow! Is that both of them gone? I know they taste a bit funny but never mind. Have you swallowed them both? Now we'll curl up together here and go to sleep.'

He squeezed her hand and she felt the radiant love in his heart.

'I love you too, Magpie. We'll be together in the Otherworld, don't you worry. I'll always look after you, I promise.'

Strangely, as she closed her eyes she thought she heard the long, anguished cry of a wolf howling in the winter's night. But that was ridiculous. Leveret smiled with relief – they'd done it and now they were free. There was no turning back now.

By the time Clip arrived in the old Land Rover they'd been asleep for a good couple of hours. He'd first had to get back down to the Hall from the Dolmen and find a vehicle. The place was deserted – many of the senior adults were involved with the Rites of Adulthood events, others were observing the Solstice Eve at the Stone Circle and most of the young people who lived in the Hall were down in the Village, presumably helping with the final decorations around the Village Green. Clip had no idea what he'd find when he reached Quarrycleave, but he threw in a first aid kit just in case he wasn't too late and could do something to save them. He also brought blankets and water, and then thought of torches too.

Clip stood in the kitchens frantically wondering if there were anything else he should bring. His heart was pounding and he felt scared, knowing the urgency of the situation but not used to acting so decisively. He phoned up to the hospital wing hoping to find Hazel but she was down in the Village, so he raced around to the barn near the stable block where the vehicles were kept. He spotted Tom's son, Fletch, and asked him to come along to help. Luckily the keys sat in the Land Rover; Clip felt very strange sitting in the driver's seat. It was so long since he'd driven but Fletch had already had a couple of glasses of cider and was worried about driving all the way to Quarrycleave, especially over the rough ground. Soon they were bouncing up the track and then turning onto the ridgeway, Clip calling on the Goddess to save the youngsters' lives and not let them die. He should've known! Leveret had as good as told him and he hadn't listened. If he were too late he'd never forgive himself.

After an interminable journey the Land Rover pulled up at the quarry mouth and Clip and Fletch jumped out. They hurried through the quarry calling Leveret, their voices bouncing strangely off the rock faces.

'How do you know they're here?' asked Fletch. 'Did Leveret tell you?'

'Not in so many words,' replied Clip, 'but I know they are. I can feel it . . . and something else too. Come on, we need to get to the head of the quarry and climb up to the top of the Snake Stone. That's where we'll find them.'

The relief Clip felt at discovering their bodies on top of the Snake Stone was short-lived. At first he thought they'd merely meant to jump but had changed their minds and were now sleeping here for the night. But when he tried to awaken them and found them drowsy and confused, he feared they'd taken an overdose. Magpie woke up fairly easily but he couldn't speak, and Clip tried desperately to wake Leveret up enough to find out what exactly they'd taken.

But then a mushroom rolled out of Magpie's hand and Clip realised: of course Leveret would choose something natural like mushrooms. He peered at the shrivelled cap in the torchlight but it was impossible to identify. He knew enough about mushrooms to understand that death was not instant, even with the most lethal ones, and several hours could pass before symptoms manifested. He guessed at this stage they were only sleeping, exhausted from the long walk here and probably very hungry and cold too. He carefully put the remaining cap in his pocket – there was one person at Stonewylde who could identify it, if she had a mind to co-operate. Then he set about trying to wake Leveret, whilst Magpie cried into his hands in fear and distress, scared by the turn of events and the bright light in his face.

Leveret was groggy but furious when they managed to rouse her. The next person she'd expected to see was Mother Heggy, not Clip and certainly not Stonewylde. But he and Fletch managed to get them both into the Land Rover eventually, after a nightmare trek in the dark back down the boulders and through the black labyrinth of stone. All around then the quarry breathed and sighed its disappointment and by the time they reached the Land

229

Rover all four of them were completely spooked.

They sped along the tracks, Leveret and Magpie bundled up in blankets, and Clip questioned Leveret as he drove.

'What have you taken?'

'Death Cap,' muttered Leveret. 'It's no use, Clip. There's no antidote and you shouldn't have interfered. I wanted us to pass on to the Otherworld at the Place of Bones and Death with our ancestors.'

'I don't think it could've been Death Cap,' said Clip. 'You'd be feeling some symptoms by now. You're not in any pain, are you?'

'No,' said Leveret. 'But maybe it's still too soon. I'm sure they're Death Cap. I checked . . .'

She huddled miserably in the blanket, cuddled up to Magpie who was moaning with terror at the ride in the vehicle and pain from the bumpy track.

'Well I think you've taken something else. Thank goddess – and my silver wolf!'

They soon arrived at the Hall. The youngsters were taken straight to the hospital wing where a nurse was on duty keeping an eye on a couple of elderly patients with bronchitis. Having left Leveret and Magpie in safe hands, Clip drove fast down to the Village. Hazel was soon located in the Barn whilst Maizie was just leaving the girls' Rite of Adulthood party under the willow tree to see to her baking for the morning. She went completely to pieces when she heard what had happened, screaming with distress and clutching at Clip desperately. He tried to reassure her that he thought Leveret had taken something other than the fatal mushroom, and Hazel quickly took over as Maizie was becoming hysterical. Clip left the two women to drive back to the Hall in the Land Rover whilst he hurried down to the dirty cottage at the end of the lane. He hoped Old Violet was in a good mood.

She peered at the shrunken cap and sniffed it.

'Leveret said it was Death Cap. Is she right?' he asked anxiously. The crone continued to examine the dried, spongy fragment with her twisted and blackened fingers. 'Is it Death Cap, Violet? Could it be something else?'

'Death Cap, Death Cap,' she muttered. 'Good old Death Cap. Quite slow, she can be, but always brings the Dark Angel with her, though he may have to wait a while at the door.'

'Aye, sister,' chipped in Vetchling. 'The Dark Angel never leaves her side unsatisfied.'

Clip stood there with fear in his pale eyes, his wispy hair sticking out wildly. He was feeling very strange himself, having fasted for three days and then rushed about all over the estate. He should be in a peaceful trance right now.

'But is this mushroom a Death Cap, or did Leveret get it wrong?'

'Did she get it wrong? There's a thing – did the girl get it wrong? She worked alone, you can be sure.'

'Doesn't it bother you that Magpie has taken it too? They're both in the hospital wing right now.'

'Pah!'

She spat viciously into the fire.

'Please, Violet, is it Death Cap or not?'

'Don't know why you're in such a bother,' she said grumpily, eyeing him through her tufted white eyebrows. 'If 'tis Death Cap, there's no remedy, none at all. Not even in your fancy hospitals.'

'Aye, not even them fancy hospitals can banish the Dark Angel,' croaked Vetchling. 'He'll come with his burning eyes if 'tis Death Cap and no use you fretting.'

'If you can tell me what this mushroom is, I'll make sure you're rewarded.'

'What with?' said Starling, still sitting by the fire and apparently unconcerned that her son had tried to kill himself. She shifted her great bulk to break wind. 'What'll the reward be?'

'Oh Goddess, I don't know! What do you want?'

'Mead!' she replied. 'We want mead and we want it for the Solstice. Three bottles o' good stuff like you lot have up at the Hall. Strong stuff.'

'Of course. So—'

'And pastries and cakes, them special ones they make at the Hall for Yule, with lots o'—'

'Yes, yes – you can have any food or drink you want! Please, Violet, is it Death Cap?'

She stared at him, her crumpled face malignant.

'No.'

He stared back.

'Are you sure?'

'Aye.'

'What is it then?'

''Tis False Death Cap – not poisonous at all. Stupid girl! She should've come to me and I'd have given her Death Cap, no mistakes. Old Violet knows.'

'Aye, sister, you know Death Cap. Stupid girl – Maizie's daughter, what do you expect?'

'Bring the mead in the morning,' said Starling. 'And a whole basket o' cakes and pastries. Send it all up with Jay and he can have a drop o' mead too.'

Clip turned and stared at her, dizzy with relief that it wasn't a poisonous mushroom. His heart was hammering in his chest now the terrible tense moment of truth had passed.

'Your son could've died tonight, Starling. Don't you care at all?'

'No – a dog's got more sense than him. And at least a dog can bark.'

She smiled at Clip as he stood there staring at her incredulously. As her lips stretched the crooked brown stumps behind them became visible.

'I remember you when you were a young man,' she leered. 'Not looking too good now, are you?'

Violet leant forward in her rocking chair and to his dismay, placed her gnarled hand on his abdomen.

'Been hurting, has it? If you need something for it, Violet can help.'

'Aye, Violet can help,' cackled Vetchling. 'For a price, mind you. Nice little remedy to take the pain away, sure enough. We know, we understand. A nice little remedy can make you feel good, so you come to us and forget them fancy hospitals when it gets too bad. Old Violet can help.'

The three of them sat laughing as Clip stumbled out of the stinking cottage and out into the starry Solstice Eve. Once more he was reminded of the crones' power and it shook him to the core. How on earth had they known about the serpent that writhed in his belly?

15

It was dark in the Stone Circle and people were gradually arriving via the Long Walk, adults in their ceremony robes, children in their tunics and cloaks, all wrapped warmly against the early morning chill of December. Everything was ready; cakes and mead set out on the flat stones around the Altar Stone. Rufus stood with Greenbough next to the great bonfire ready to climb up the ladder to the top, although it was not yet time. The pewter pendants were laid out carefully, ready to be presented to the new adults, and the families had come with the brand new ceremony robes they'd prepared. The stones were beautiful with their Yule decorations: holly, ivy, mistletoe, deer and the golden suns, although it was still far too dark to appreciate them. No sign of dawn yet streaking the south eastern skies.

It was a dark, cloudy morning and Greenbough was whispering instructions to Rufus about using the watch and getting the timing just right, for it looked doubtful that the sun's rays would be visible with such cloud obscuring the sky. It was a shame; nothing beat the magic of the long golden rays hitting the magus as he stood resplendent in glittering gold robes up on the Altar Stone, chanting in the full glory of the Solstice. But it couldn't be helped and at least they had the watch and didn't have to guess. The red-haired boy was very nervous, shaking with fear, and Greenbough put a steadying hand on his shoulder.

'You'll be fine, lad – take a deep breath and stay calm. Mind your step on the ladder coming down when you're holding the torch. Just do it like we've practised.'

Rufus nodded, his velvet brown eyes scared. He knew how important it was that the Herald of Dawn did his task perfectly and was terrified of letting Yul down.

Yul stood behind the Altar Stone watching people arrive. He felt really awful, his mouth dry and his head throbbing. He closed his eyes and fought the dizziness and nausea. Cider didn't usually affect him like this but he'd drunk so much last night, seemingly bent on self-annihilation. He remembered Swift constantly at his side, bringing him more cider every time the tankard was getting low. He liked the blond-haired boy, so quiet and attentive, who'd asked him all sorts of intelligent questions and was so respectful and deferential. Swift had shown such admiration and regard for him which was a pleasant change after all the rubbish others had been dishing out lately. But Yul knew he shouldn't have drunk so much, especially not when he had this ceremony to lead.

There were great blanks in his memory. He knew he'd been sitting against a tree trunk for a long time with Swift by his side. He remembered the singing and the drumming, the deep reverberating beat entering his body and making him feel so good. He'd wanted to get up and dance to it, join in with the youngsters and the other men who'd put on the antlers and started a tribal dance around the fire and the remains of the feast. Swift had helped him up, staggering under the weight of such a tall man for the boy was lightly built. He'd flicked the straight, silvery hair from his eyes and grinned at Yul, helping him to stand steadily as everything swayed around him. For some reason they had both found this hilarious and Yul remembered roaring with laughter, feeling better than he'd done for a long time.

But later ... he cringed now at the thought of it, not wanting to explore the memory but unable to stop it. Eventually they'd decided to return to the Hall for they must be up early for this ceremony. The youngsters were reeling about merrily, all except for Swift who'd probably been the only sober one there. Swift had helped Yul crawl into the cart which had been there all day, the horses tethered to the trees. Most of them had managed to walk back, the physical effort helping them to sober up. But Swift had insisted that Yul ride in the cart, along with the nearly empty cider barrel, drums and bows and arrows. Yul wasn't in any fit state to argue and had spent the rolling journey home trying to hold on to the contents of his stomach. When they'd arrived back at the Hall Swift had helped him down and taken his arm to lead him inside.

'Can't remember the last time I came home like this,' slurred Yul, leaning heavily on the boy.

'Well, why not? You're the magus after all. If you can't have a few drinks when you want, who can? No harm in that,' said Swift.

'Sylvie won't approve,' muttered Yul.

'I don't see why not. Why should anyone not approve? It's the man's night after all, isn't it? Nothing to do with the women – they've got their own party. I thought that was the whole point of the separate Rite celebrations. A man's gotta do what a man's gotta do and the women have to accept that.'

'Yeah,' giggled Yul, trying hard to climb the wide stairs and stumbling all over the place. 'If she doesn't like it, she can lump it.'

'Show her who's boss,' laughed Swift.

'That's right. Who's the lord and master.'

Sylvie had been waiting up, sitting in a chair by the dying fire. She frowned at the state of him, glancing at the smirking boy by his side who clearly found the sight of his incapacitated magus highly amusing.

'Now don't start having a go at me!' Yul had mumbled when he saw the look on her face. 'I'm not taking any of your nagging tonight – I don't wanna know. And why aren't you in bed waiting for me?'

'Thank you, Swift,' she said curtly to Martin's son standing quietly by, watching the scene. 'Good night.'

'Thanks, Swift!' called Yul, far too loudly. 'I won't forget what a good drinking companion you've been. See you in the morning!'

'Sssh!' hissed Sylvie. 'You'll wake the girls!'

'Don't shush me! I'll make as much noise as I like. I'm the magus and it's about time you remembered that.'

When Swift had gone, she tried to make Yul sit down and listen.

'Something awful happened tonight,' she began, attempting to manoeuvre him into a chair.

'I don't want to know,' he muttered indistinctly. 'I'm sick of all the worry and trouble. I've had a great night and all I want now is to get to bed – with you, my darling. Always want you, constantly. It's been too long. Come on, Sylvie, come to bed.'

'No! You must listen, Yul. It's Leveret, she tried to do something terrible tonight. She—'

'What?' he roared. 'That bloody girl again! I'll sort her out once and for all. Where is she?'

He lurched towards the door but she grabbed his arm.

'Yul, I know you're drunk but please, you must listen. She's not here – she's in the hospital wing. She's fine now, but she tried to kill herself tonight. And her friend, Magpie – they tried to commit suicide.'

Yul stared at her, his addled brain trying to make sense of what she'd told him.

'Tried to kill herself? No – she's not that stupid.'

'Not stupid, Yul, just deeply unhappy. Why else would a young Stonewylder try to go to the Otherworld before their time's up? I told you I wanted to talk to her. I could see there was something terribly wrong but you wouldn't let me.'

He turned on her and glared belligerently.

'Oh right, so it was all my fault! Everything's always my fault, isn't it, Sylvie? Blame me for this as well.'

'Don't be ridiculous – it's nobody's fault. It's just very sad that she felt desperate enough to try and take her life. But she's fine, no harm done. She's sleeping now and Maizie's with her.'

Yul shook his head, his eyes still unfocused and confused.

'Poor Mother! The things that girl has put her through, and

now this. Leveret probably didn't mean it anyway – just trying to get more attention. I've got to sort her out.'

'No, Yul. You've got to listen to her instead of shouting at her, but not now. You're right – you need to get to bed. We'll think about this in the morning.'

She started to guide him towards the bedroom. He leered at her and she suddenly felt as if she didn't know this dark-haired, handsome man one bit. This wasn't her Yul.

'Keen now, are you? About time too! Come on then, Sylvie – I'd better make the most of it, hadn't I?'

The rest of the night was something he didn't want to think about now, not with the ceremony about to start soon. He looked around and saw Sylvie, beautiful in her dark green and silver robes with patterns of Yule evergreens embroidered in fine detail, the mistletoe and holly berries picked out with fresh-water pearls and red garnet. She was completely ignoring him and he didn't blame her. He just hoped she'd excuse his behaviour on the grounds of drunkenness, because he'd never, ever have treated her like that if he'd been sober. He shook his head at the thought of it and wished he hadn't, for it felt like his brain was rattling about in his skull.

The great Circle was now packed with bodies and there was a feeling of expectancy and hush. It would soon be time for the Herald of Dawn to light the torch but before that happened, Yul should be up on the Altar Stone chanting the sacred words to invite the sun. Words that seemed to have escaped him right now. Stumbling slightly he climbed up, swaying as he found his balance, and the drums began a soft beat. He caught sight of Swift's silver hair as he stood amongst the other youngsters waiting to be acknowledged as adults. The boy grinned at him and Yul grimaced back. Then he began the tortuous task of remembering the chants.

The ceremony was not one of the better ones and everything that could go wrong did. Yul tripped over the words and there were even embarrassing silences whilst he desperately tried to recall what came next. The damn ceremonies were too long, he thought irritably. Rufus caught his mood and panicked up in the crow's nest, forgetting what time he should look for on the watch and Greenbough's hissed commands were audible to everyone, destroying the magic of the moment. Then the boy slipped coming down the ladder with the burning torch and his cry of alarm was heard in the silence, making some of the children giggle irreverently.

There were no bright rays to gild the glowing magus and Yul only felt a tremor of Earth Magic spiral up from the Altar Stone, not the great rush he normally experienced. There was no green fire, no power blazing from his finger tips and filling his soul with joy. Sylvie looked as sour as an unripe apple and refused to meet his eye at all. When the moment came to pass the energy on to his people, to share his magic with the community, he could tell from their bewildered faces that they'd felt nothing at all. He wasn't surprised – he had nothing to give them. The queue of folk waiting to take his hands and receive their customary share of the Green Magic looked on in surprise as people in front of them left the Altar Stone muttering and complaining. Yul stood there dejectedly feeling as if the Goddess had jilted him.

Sylvie, meanwhile, was also having a bad time. She was trying very hard not to dwell on the awful night she'd spent with Yul. The only way she could deal with it was to put his brutality down to the cider; he'd never behaved like that before. Today she felt sore and soiled, like damaged goods, and it would take a long time to forgive him for that. She knew he was struggling with the ceremony but hearing him stumble over the words filled her with a certain amount of satisfaction – served him right.

She thought back to that glorious Winter Solstice sunrise thirteen years ago when she and Yul had stood together on the Altar Stone like bright angels, locked in an embrace so fierce and eternal that nothing could have broken them apart. She recalled the sizzle of green Earth Magic that had spiralled around her handsome Yul, radiating from within him so that every single person in the Stone Circle was blessed with his luminosity. And now she gazed at him with candid eyes and didn't like what she saw. He looked terrible, pale and waxy, his eyes blood-shot and puffy. He'd made a complete mess of the beautiful ritual, reducing it to a meaningless jumble of words and phrases with no heart to it. And as for the so-called communion of energy . . .

Sylvie felt the restlessness within the Circle and the surprise at just how lacking in the usual magic this ceremony was proving to be. People around her were muttering and fidgeting and there was an atmosphere of real disappointment. Martin stood by the Altar Stone and had been helping with the cakes and mead, as he always did, but the look he gave Yul was one of contempt. Sylvie couldn't really blame him because she felt the same way. How could he have let himself get so very intoxicated last night, knowing how important this ceremony was to everyone? How could he spoil the youngsters' Rite of Adulthood like this?

Then Sylvie got the shock of her life. She stood near the Altar Stone, having her own part to play in the rituals. The youngsters were getting ready for the presentation of their robes and pendants, jostling about and lining up. Miranda was trying to ensure Yul had the pendants ready in the right order, and he was swaying and looking even paler than before. Sylvie felt a throb of anger towards him for ruining the rituals, and looked up across the Circle for a moment. She had the strangest sensation of being watched, which was ridiculous as many people were watching. But something was making her skin prickle.

There, standing right at the back of the crowd leaning against one of the stones, she thought she saw Magus. It was too far away and murky to be sure, but it looked so like him – tall and well-built with glinting silver hair. Her heart leapt in her chest and at the same time she felt panic rise in her throat. She also felt a strange, sinking feeling of inevitability as the crowd spun dizzily in front of her. Events were spiralling out of control, things were falling apart, and her love for Yul was at an all time low.

*

Leveret lay on the narrow hospital-wing bed and gazed out of the window. It was a cold, grey dawn and she imagined the rest of the community all up at the Stone Circle right now, the bonfire blazing and the drum-beats echoing in everyone's souls. This was the first ceremony she'd ever missed in her life and it felt very strange not to be a part of the heartbeat of Stonewylde. She looked across to Magpie's bed and was alarmed to see it stripped and empty. Her heart jolted but then with a sob of relief, she saw that he lay underneath it, all the bedclothes crumpled up into a nest, sleeping peacefully. She doubted he'd ever slept in a proper bed before. His bruised and filthy face was child-like in its innocence and she thanked the goddess she hadn't killed him after all.

She looked across to the other bed where Maizie lay asleep, her dark curls spread on the white pillow. As she gazed at her mother's plump face, relaxed at last after last night's frantic worry, Leveret felt a great lump in her throat and the ready tears prickled her sore eyes. She'd cried so much and felt emotionally wrung out, drained and exhausted. She also felt like a complete fool.

Her mother's reaction as she'd come barging into the wing not long after Leveret and Magpie's arrival had proved that Maizie loved her as much as ever. Maizie had crushed her in such an embrace, scooping her daughter onto her lap as if she were still a little girl, cradling her tight and planting endless kisses all over her face, interspersed with breathless, sobbing entreaties.

'How could you do that, Leveret? Don't you know how precious you are? Don't you realise how much I love you? What were you thinking? You silly, silly girl! Oh – please Goddess say 'tis not Death Cap! It can't be – you'd be suffering by now if 'twas. Don't you ever, ever do anything like that again, do you hear me, girl? To think I almost lost you. I might still but – oh, no 'twill be some other mushroom, I'm sure! Oh, Leveret, how could you so such a thing? You're my special child, my very special little one, and I nearly lost you!'

On and on it went, rocking her like a baby, washing her with tears. Leveret had cried uncontrollably too, clinging to her mother and basking in the comfort of her soft, warm bosom. The nurse left them to it for a while as she tried to undress Magpie and get him into bed. But he'd screeched in panic and made such a fuss that Hazel and the nurse had given in and concentrated on putting him into bed fully-clothed. Then they'd done the same with Leveret, prising her from her mother's grasp and giving everyone a warm, soothing drink.

Leveret sighed deeply, feeling safe and warm and so very pleased that the suicide attempt hadn't worked. She was amazed at how suddenly the prospect of entering the Otherworld had become the worst thing ever, when only yesterday it was what she longed for most. The huge crushing weight of misery that had sapped her will to continue had lifted instantly the moment she realised just how much her mother truly loved her.

Leveret should have been lying on the Snake Stone right now, chilled and sluggish with hypothermia after a night out in the midwinter cold, the poison inside her body attacking her vital organs irrevocably. She may even have been dead by now. One of the reasons she'd chosen Death Cap above other poisons was because she knew there was no antidote. The victims always, without exception, died ... except that, like an idiot, she'd used the wrong mushroom.

She remembered Clip's triumphant entrance into the room not long after Maizie's hysterical arrival, shouting at the top of his voice that it was *False* Death Cap they'd taken, which was completely harmless. Although she was so relieved now that it hadn't worked, she felt stupid for making such a mistake. Everyone accepted Old Violet's identification, although Hazel had been on the phone to Guy's Hospital to verify the details and possible symptoms. Somebody had been despatched from Stonewylde with the remaining mushroom, instructed to drive through the night to the Toxicology Department for scientific identification. But Leveret knew she hadn't poisoned herself – she'd have felt it by now. All she felt was hungry, exhausted and very embarrassed at the thought of facing the community. As far as she knew no young Stonewylder had ever tried to take their own life before.

*

Much later in the day Leveret watched a crow flapping about in the cold, wintry air and eventually landing on a branch outside the window. The crow fixed her with its beady eye and let out an enormous croak. She stared intently at the clumsy, scruffy bird as it struggled to balance. Then it began a song of unholy cacophony making such a noise that the nurse came rushing in and banged on the window to frighten it off. Leveret smiled to herself – Mother Heggy hadn't left her after all.

She looked across at Magpie, still amazed at his transformation. They'd had to sedate him that morning in order to get him into the bath. He'd been soaked and scrubbed clean, the head lice eradicated, and he now wore a warm Stonewylde nightshirt. His ribs were bandaged and all his injuries dressed. She hardly recognised him – his hair was a lovely shade of rich butterscotch and his eyes glowed turquoise in a clean face. His fingernails had been cut and teeth given a thorough clean and everyone was amazed to find that underneath all the dirt Magpie was really a lovely young man, despite the bruises on his face. He was so very proud of himself, constantly stroking his own skin and hair and beaming at her.

'You mustn't send him home,' Leveret said to Hazel when the doctor visited in the lull between events in the Village.

'Absolutely not,' Hazel had agreed. 'He's quite badly malnourished and many of the injuries aren't recent, so he's clearly been abused for some time. I feel terrible that I hadn't realised before. I think half the trouble is that it's Martin's family who are responsible – nobody likes to interfere.'

Leveret thought grimly of the many blind eyes that had been turned at Magpie's plight all his life. But today wasn't the time for blame and recriminations, not when Magpie was at last being given the care and treatment he'd needed all along.

'We'll keep him in the hospital wing over Yuletide whilst his ribs heal,' Hazel continued, 'and then Yul will have to make arrangements for him to move up to the Hall. Magpie certainly won't be going back to his mother's house, I promise. I can't understand why he hasn't come to live here already. He's sixteen, isn't he?'

'Yes, but his mother insisted she needed him at home to help with the heavy work because they don't have a man in the house, and nobody's ever stood up to those women. They've always got away with treating poor Magpie badly and he's been nothing but a work-horse all his life.'

'Well it's going to stop now. I remember Magpie as a little boy, the tests I did trying to find out what was wrong and why he couldn't speak. I should have pursued it further and kept a closer eye on him but it was always difficult. I can see why now – his mother was clearly covering up the ill-treatment. I do feel bad about it.'

Hazel's kind brown eyes were downcast.

'Because he can't speak, he's been ignored,' said Leveret sadly. 'I've tried so many times to tell everyone what's been going on ...'

'Don't worry, Leveret,' said Hazel firmly. 'From now on I'll be looking out for Magpie's welfare.'

Clip too came for a visit, his wispy white hair and twinkling eyes a welcome sight. Leveret had surprised herself by flinging her arms around him and hugging him for a long, fierce moment, much to his delight. Nobody had ever really shown him a great deal of affection.

'You're determined to muscle in on my journeying, aren't you, Leveret?' he'd said when she released him, slightly embarrassed at her spontaneous burst of emotion. 'First Samhain and now the Solstice. I'd planned a peaceful couple of days up in my Dolmen away from all the fun, but you've plunged me right into the action.'

'I'll never forget that you came to rescue me,' she said. 'Even though the mushrooms weren't lethal, the long night in the cold air could've killed us, being so hungry and exhausted. And Quarrycleave itself, that feeling there ... I'm so pleased you worked out where we were and what I was intending to do.'

'It was my silver wolf who led me to you. You have to promise me you'll never do it again, Leveret.'

'Never! I've seen what it did to Mother – I wouldn't put her through that again no matter how bad I felt.'

'And you're feeling better now?'

'Oh yes! Although nothing's really changed, I somehow feel that I can deal with it all now. Magpie's going to be safe now that Hazel's aware of the problems he had at home, and hopefully Mother won't always take my brothers' side. I'll just have to try and win Rosie over in time.'

'I'm sure you will,' Clip smiled, relieved at her change of heart. 'And I hear you're going home tomorrow? Maizie's keen to have you back now?'

Leveret nodded happily.

'We're really going to start again. She knows I must gather what I need sometimes, and in return I'll always tell her what I'm doing rather than sneak off.'

'That's good. I don't expect you wanted to deceive her to begin with, did you?'

'No, it made me feel very guilty. It's just I felt this ... this compulsion to go ahead. I wanted to start practising magic, you see.'

'And you still want to be a Wise Woman one day?'

'I do, definitely, but I'm not making a fuss about it now. There's ages till I have to leave school and I'm hoping by then Mother will come round to my way of thinking.'

He looked at her carefully, noting how the sparkle had come back into her green eyes. She was an extraordinarily beautiful girl, while being strange and different, and he felt a real affinity with her.

'I'd like to help you, Leveret, if you're agreeable. I'm not that wise myself but I have a lot of knowledge. I can guide you when you start journeying and give you books to read to help you on your path. I've collected a great deal over the years. It may not be the sort of knowledge Mother Heggy had and you will need herbalist knowledge like hers too, but you live in a different time and you need to know things she didn't. Would you like me to help?'

'Oh yes please! I need a guide, a mentor. I'm always groping about in the dark and I never know if I'm on the right track.'

'Well I'm pleased you were wrong about the mushrooms at least. Someone was looking out for you last night, I'm sure.'

As he left Clip patted her arm affectionately.

'One more thing, Leveret – don't mention this to Yul, will you? I'm sure he wouldn't approve of any guidance I might give you. I don't think Yul likes me much.'

'I'd never tell anything to Yul. I don't like *him* much, to be honest. He's not the person he used to be.'

The next day Marigold came to visit bringing a great tray of Yuletide treats. She hugged Leveret and gave her a thorough telling off for being so silly, then she went to Magpie's bed and sat there stroking his hand.

'This poor boy! You look so different now, Magpie. You're all clean and scrubbed, aren't you?'

He beamed at her, pulling her hand onto his head to feel his soft, shiny hair.

'He's very proud of himself,' said Leveret fondly. 'I think with a bit of encouragement he'll learn to enjoy baths. Have you heard he's going to be moved up to the Hall, away from those evil women?'

'About time too! I always said they was evil, didn't I? Wicked and cruel, and Goddess knows what they done to him over the years, the poor boy. I always said—'

'I'm a bit worried about how he'll cope with boarding here, though. You know how everyone teases him and I want to keep him well away from Jay. Jay's the one who broke his ribs and beat him up.'

'Aye – less said about him the better, I'm ashamed to say. But Leveret, I been thinking about this carefully,' said Marigold slowly, scanning Magpie's guileless face and still stroking his hand. 'I'm going to ask Yul if Magpie can come and live with me in my cottage. I've an empty room and Cherry can help me look after him. I reckon he needs a bit of mothering, poor mite. What do you think?'

. Leveret was practically speechless with joy at this suggestion. Cherry and Marigold, their families long grown up and in their own homes, lived together in one of the small cottages that tucked into the Hall near the large kitchen courtyard. The homes were for people who worked full time in the Hall and it would be an ideal solution for Magpie. The two women would really care for him in the maternal way he needed and she needn't worry about his welfare any more.

'And just think,' said Marigold as she left. 'Wouldn't those three hags just hate my having him? Sweet revenge for their taking Jay away from me all them years ago!'

The one visit Leveret was dreading was Yul's, for she knew how angry he must be with her. She confided in her mother, who promised to keep him away until he'd calmed down. Yul had been stalking around under a black cloud all through the festivities, upsetting people without thinking and generally dampening the spirits of those around him. Even he didn't know what was the matter with him. Everything he did seemed to go wrong, starting with the first Solstice celebration and going on from there. He couldn't get the Yule Log to light. He'd dropped the flaming torch during the evening ceremony at the Circle, reminding himself forcefully of the ceremony when Magus had done the same thing all those years ago at the Summer Solstice. The Earth Magic was very weak and he knew there was something wrong but didn't know how to put it right.

During the Yule party he'd managed to get really drunk again without planning to at all. Swift had come over for a chat, building on the relationship forged between him and the magus on the night of his Rite of Adulthood. Before he'd realised it Yul was knocking back mead by the bottleful, assisted by the sober young man. Luckily there hadn't been a repeat of the previous fiasco with Sylvie, but only because he'd stayed down in his study and virtually passed out on the sofa. Even then he'd woken at some point in the night and considered going up to their bedroom to make love with her, telling himself that he was her husband and she had no right to be so cold and frigid. Fortunately he fell asleep again before he could do anything about it.

The whole holiday was terrible with Sylvie avoiding him at every opportunity and his own daughters eyeing him warily. He wasn't sure if he was imagining it, but he sensed a certain hostility amongst some of the folk, which he could only put down to the disappointing lack of Earth Magic at the festival. People seemed to avoid him, or at best watched their tongues when he was around. Yul had never felt so cold-shouldered by Stonewylders before, but without anything tangible he wondered if perhaps he was simply being a little paranoid. Whatever the case, it did nothing to improve his bad temper.

The unwanted visit came when Leveret had gone back home with Maizie, having first been promised by both Hazel and Marigold that they'd look out for Magpie and keep Jay well away from him. Leveret was now back in the cottage where she'd lived all her life and basking in Maizie's affection. She had yet to face the rest of the community and was dreading it, feeling so ashamed of herself and what she'd tried to do. She made excuses when Maizie tried to persuade her to come and join in the fun at the Barn, saying she still felt wobbly and tired. She actually felt very well indeed having caught up with her sleep and eaten fit to burst.

It was whilst Maizie was organising the children's treasure hunt around the Village that Yul arrived unannounced. Leveret was reading a book by the fire, curled up in one of the old leather armchairs. The door swung open and her eldest brother stood on the threshold, tall and filling the doorway with his muscular frame. She looked up startled, her heart starting to skip with fear. He triggered a memory from way back in her past – of an enormous man standing on the threshold looking in. Had that been the old Magus?

Yul frowned down at her and she was struck by how changed

he looked. Although he was still very handsome – the chiselled face and deep grey eyes would always ensure that – his hair was unkempt, falling into his eyes, and his mouth hard.

'Good! I was hoping to find you here.'

He stepped in and firmly shut the door behind him.

'Can I get you something to drink?' she asked politely, knowing the kettle was bubbling gently on the range.

'No . . . yes, some mead if Mother's got any. It's cold out there.'

She was a little surprised but duly poured him a glass which he sipped slowly, watching her all the while. She felt very uncomfortable under his scrutiny.

'You're looking well, Leveret.'

'Thank you, I feel fine now.'

'I can't help but think you came out of this too lightly. Violent stomach pains or cramps might've put you off ever trying it again.'

'I won't ever try it again.'

'Really? Even though it's proved so effective this time?'

She stared at him in puzzlement. Surely he didn't think she'd just done it for effect? That had never even occurred to her.

'Hit a nerve, have I?'

'No. I thought I was going to die – that's what I wanted.'

He rolled his eyes at this and scowled at her.

'I just can't make you out, Leveret. You've got everything you could ever wish for. Your life is so easy, so comfortable – why would you want to end it? No, you might have hoodwinked Mother and everyone else but you can't fool me. This was carefully planned and orchestrated – the act of a clever but completely selfish teenager.'

She was silent at his words and he sat forward to bring himself closer to her. His slanted eyes were beginning to darken with anger.

'If you could've seen the state of Mother when Clip came and found her in the Village that night . . . I'll *never* forgive you for putting her through that.'

'I'm so sorry about that,' she whispered. 'But I thought she

249

didn't love me anymore so I didn't think it'd matter to her if I passed on to the Otherworld.'

He laughed harshly, his eyes cold.

'Don't be so stupid! You know full well she loves you. You've always been the special one – perhaps even her favourite, which is why Sweyn and Gefrin have always resented you.'

Leveret frowned at this – surely not?

'You were just trying to manipulate her and everybody else and it's worked, which is what makes me so furious,' continued Yul. 'Everybody might be fooled but be assured, Leveret, I'm not. I know your game, and if you ever, *ever* do anything like that again, I'll make you wish you'd never been born. Do you understand?'

'Yes,' she nodded. 'I swear to you I won't.'

Yul got out of his chair in one fluid motion and she shrank back, not knowing what he was going to do. She used to feel safe with Yul but she certainly didn't now. He was taut as a bowstring ready to be released, pent up with suppressed energy and anger; he was very frightening. But he strode into the kitchen and brought back the bottle of mead, refilling his glass and gazing into the fire. She sat quietly so as not to antagonise him.

His face in profile was so powerful, the nose and cheekbones perfectly carved, jaw and brow strong. His mouth was drawn into a line of bitter tension and Leveret wondered if once again she were taking the brunt of his anger over something entirely different. She noticed his long, square-tipped fingers drumming on the side of the chair impatiently and then he looked up at her, his grey eyes full of something wild and driven. She found it impossible to look away.

'You're to work very hard at school too. I'll see all your books and all your marks every week. Any slacking and you'll stay at the Hall again so I can make bloody sure you study.'

'Yes, I promise I'll work really hard.'

'And you'll help Mother in the house too. I expect you to do a lot of the work. She should be slowing down a bit and taking it easier now, and you can ease the burden for her. Have you noticed how old she's looking? How tired? There's grey in her hair and lines on her face that weren't there until very recently, and that's your doing. So make sure you take the pressure off her by doing the housework, fetching the water, cooking and tending the vegetables. Is that clear?'

'Yes Yul, I'll help her as much as I can.'

'Hmmn.'

He poured himself another glass and drank it steadily, his boot tapping on the hearth.

'You were once a really sweet little girl, Leveret, and I loved you.'

His use of the past tense cut her to the quick. He stared at her again, his eyes boring into her.

'You're not anymore. Somewhere along the line you've turned into a selfish, lazy and heartless young woman. I suppose it's in your genes – your father's nastiness had to come out some time. You remind me of him, the way you've upset Mother, and that's why I'm determined to crush this self-centredness out of you.'

Leveret could think of nothing to say to this; she hated to be reminded of her father's cruelty. She'd heard enough about him to know he'd been a terrible man and the last thing she wanted was to turn out like him.

'Well? Say something!'

'I'll try hard not to be like him. I'm very sorry, Yul, really I am, for everything. I'm turning over a new leaf.'

'You'd damn well better be. And another thing – Mother says you won't go down to the Barn to join in the festivities. Why is that?'

She shrugged uncomfortably.

'I ... I didn't feel well enough.'

'Rubbish! You ate some harmless mushrooms. There's absolutely nothing wrong with you at all.'

He poured the last of the mead into his glass and examined it, staring at the gold liquid.

'Do you know what I think, Leveret? I think you're embarrassed to go and face everyone after what you did. But I think a bit of humiliation is just what you need. So you'll join in everything from now on – I insist.'

She gazed at him mournfully but nodded her obedience, having no real choice. He drained the glass suddenly in one gulp and turned to smile at her. His eyes were still dark but not quite so intense and focused any more. His smile made her go cold – it was a smile without any warmth, a cruel smile. Leveret felt she was looking at a stranger.

'I'm pleased we had the chance to talk alone,' he said, standing up. He swayed ever so slightly but quickly righted himself. 'Remember what I've said. I expect you to be perfect and if you're not, I'll deal with you personally.'

He opened the door and breathed deeply of the cold air outside, then turned and fixed her once more with his steely glare.

'Bright blessings at Yule, little sister.'

16

The next day Leveret walked up to the Hall to see Magpie, very nervous about leaving her sanctuary and facing everyone. As she stomped down the lane, she realised she had a choice now, a significant one. She could skulk around as if she were embarrassed and ashamed, or she could take control of her situation and brazen it out. So she made her decision and felt much better for it. She met several people along the way but smiled and greeted them as if nothing had happened, and apart from a few stares, people were fine. In the Hall a group of older girls were standing in the entrance hall pulling on gloves and hats. They fell silent as she walked in and she felt awkward, feeling their eyes on her.

'Blessings, Leveret,' said one.

'Blessings,' she replied, smiling brightly at the whole group. It felt strange; normally she kept her head down and never looked people in the eye, wanting to avoid unnecessary contact. There was a pause whilst they all watched her.

'We ... we heard about what happened,' said Iris, the elder of Kestrel's two sisters and Leveret nodded. 'You must've been feeling awful to have done that. Was it very frightening?'

'No, not really frightening. I was just so unhappy I wasn't thinking straight, I suppose. But it's in the past now.'

'Yes of course. I expect you just want to forget it ever happened.'

'That's right.'

'Well, we're sorry anyway. If you're feeling down again don't bottle it up, will you? There's always someone to talk to if you need it.'

Leveret looked at them in astonishment and blushed with pleasure at the kind words.

'Thank you,' she said. 'I'll remember that.'

Magpie, still in the hospital wing, was doing very well. He sat in a chair by the window with a sketch pad and pencils, drawing the rooks flying around like bits of black ash in the grey skies. His smile was radiant when he saw Leveret and he leapt up, scattering pencils, and engulfed her in a great hug. She hugged him back and for the first time it was a pleasant experience; he didn't smell horrible and she wasn't worried about catching head lice.

'You're looking wonderful, Magpie. Let me see what you're drawing? That's fantastic!'

Her praise was genuine for he was a truly talented artist. Using just soft graphite pencils he'd captured the wintry scene perfectly. The rooks were exquisite, as if he truly understood rooks and what made them rooks rather than starlings or blackbirds or crows. He'd captured their essence in the way they flew, the angle of their wings, the way they positioned themselves in the sky. She could almost hear them calling.

'You're such a good artist, Magpie. We must make sure you get the chance to develop it, now your life's all new and exciting. Who gave you the sketch pad and pencils?'

Using their special way of communicating, Magpie let Leveret know that it was Hazel and that she'd promised him paints too. She held his hand and looked at him and the image of the doctor came into her mind in minute detail, down to the cut of her blond hair and the pattern of the cable stitch on her pink woollen jumper. She also got a sense of Hazel's kindness and concern, which Magpie had obviously picked up. The image of the paints wasn't quite so vivid as Magpie's knowledge and experience of these was smaller, but she saw a framed picture very close up with oil paint daubed thickly and guessed that was what he meant.

'Hazel's promised you oil paints?'

Magpie nodded happily and squeezed her hand. More than anything she sensed his exhilaration and joy at being free from daily fear and physical abuse. They sat together for a while, Leveret still marvelling at how he'd changed so quickly. She'd always known he was a sweet person from when they'd first met in the Nursery as tiny toddlers. She'd sensed the goodness in his soul even then, seen beyond the revolting, mute boy who could manage very little and made such a fool of himself all the time. Now maybe others would see it too and he'd have a proper place in Stonewylde's society. Just as long as she could keep Jay away from him, but she had plans to protect Magpie.

While he continued drawing rooks, Leveret took a small pair of scissors from her pocket and showed them to him.

'You know about scissors, Magpie. I want to cut a little tiny piece of your hair. See? I'll do it to myself first and it doesn't hurt. Now a piece of Maggy's hair.'

To her relief he allowed her to snip off a lock of his golden brown hair, which she carefully wrapped and put in her pocket. That was the first part – but there was lots more to be done. She was just about to leave when Swift came in, looking as surprised to see her as she was to see him. They stared at each other.

'What do you want?' she asked finally.

He raised his eyebrows at this, looking down at her and enjoying the sensation. As he was a fairly small youth, looking down on someone else was quite rare.

'That's not very friendly, Leveret,' he said smoothly. 'I just came to visit Magpie and see how he's getting on.'

'He's fine, no thanks to your mate Jay.'

'Nor to you! Jay may have been hard on him but I gather you actually tried to kill him.'

She flushed at this and looked away. Swift took the sketch pad from Magpie, who'd stopped drawing and was gazing up at them both in consternation.

'Very good, Magpie! Clever boy!'

'Don't talk to him like a dog – he's not stupid.'

'Really? Sorry, I didn't realise.'

'Why are you here? Did Jay send you?'

She knew Hazel had forbidden Jay to come anywhere near the hospital wing. But she also knew Swift was in league with Jay and her brothers, although she didn't realise the true extent of it for Swift was very careful to be seen with the right people at the right time. He smiled sweetly at her and flicked his fringe aside.

'I don't get sent anywhere by anybody, Leveret. I only wanted to see how Magpie was doing. We are related, you know – our grannies are sisters and we're old mates, aren't we, Magpie?'

He put a hand on the boy's shoulder but his body blocked her view so she didn't see how Magpie flinched at his touch and curled into himself. Swift turned and gave her another charming smile.

'Don't make an enemy of me as well, will you, Leveret? You've got enough to contend with surely, with your brothers and Jay. I know what they're planning and it's not pleasant. You know, I could be a good friend to you if you're nice to me.'

'What are they planning?' she asked, her mouth dry. This was exactly what she'd been trying to escape from when she swallowed the mushrooms. Leveret couldn't face more bullying – she'd have to get her mother to put a stop to this and hoped she'd be more prepared to listen now.

'I don't know if I want to share that information with you, Leveret. You've only ever been hostile towards me so let's see how it goes, shall we? Anyway, good to see Magpie's on the mend. He'll be living next door to my father, I hear, so I expect I'll be seeing a lot more of him.'

'I thought you were a boarder.'

'Of course I am. But with my family's cottage so close I'm always popping in. Father likes to hear all the news.'

'I'd have thought Martin already knew all the news.'

'Oh he does. Let's say, we pool our knowledge. Well, I must be off. Bye, Magpie – keep up the drawing.'

When he'd gone, Leveret gazed at the door thoughtfully.

'I don't know if he's alright or not,' she said. 'He isn't as bad as Jay, is he? But they're friends and I'm just not sure about him.'

Magpie shook his head and she ruffled his clean, golden hair.

'You're not sure about anyone, are you? But you'll learn to trust people, I promise you, and I'll still be looking after you. That's what I'm off to do now.'

When she left the Hall, Leveret turned up the narrow path that led towards the cliff but branched off before she got that far and made her way to Mother Heggy's cottage. She hadn't been here since the day before the Solstice when she'd rushed in to collect the Death Cap mushrooms. She looked around the tiny place wishing that she could do it up properly. The dried mushrooms and herbs hung rather forlornly from the low rafters, and everywhere was layered with dust and cobwebs. Leveret decided she'd come up one day soon and really tidy it up.

But now she had something else to do. Making sure the door was securely shut, she went over to the hearth which took up most of one wall and climbed into the empty grate. Ducking down, she positioned herself under the chimney and reached up. Her groping hands found the alcove, up high inside, and she carefully retrieved the heavy Book of Shadows. She blew the dust and cobwebs off the piece of thick, waxed linen wrapped around it, and took it over to the ancient table where she opened it up and started to leaf through the pages.

As always when she touched the Book, Leveret felt a dark excitement race through her body. She also felt Mother Heggy's ghostly breath on the back of her neck and she began to horripilate, rubbing her arms to stop the goose-flesh.

'Blessings, Mother Heggy. Thank you for giving me the wrong mushrooms and for sending Clip to find us.'

There was no answer of course but some dried leaves by the door drifted slightly across the stone flagged floor, making a soft, whispery sound.

'Now I need your help, dear Mother Heggy. I'm going to cast

257

my first circle at the Dark Moon. Bring the magic to me please, Mother Heggy. Bring the dark magic to make my spell work.'

She bent her head and started reading the spell she'd found. This was the one she needed now, not the silly love spell she'd considered trying before. She found much of the writing hard to read for the ink had faded and it was spidery and badly spelt. She was just grateful that Mother Heggy had grown up in the time when Villagers were still taught to read and write, albeit at a basic level, otherwise there'd be no legacy of the crone's wisdom. Taking a school notebook and pencil from her pocket she began to carefully copy out the words and list of things she needed. She smiled as she worked, feeling truly content. This was what she was born to do.

Leveret's happiness was short-lived however, for when she returned home to her cottage in the Village, Maizie was waiting for her and dropped a bombshell.

'Sit down, Leveret. I've something to give you.'

Her mother was very excited and Leveret felt intrigued. She guessed it was a Yule present as her mother hadn't yet given her one but always made something special each year. Last year it had been a beautiful pair of soft mittens knitted with lamb's wool. She sat back and smiled at her mother, who clumped up the stairs and then came down again slowly.

'Close your eyes, Leveret!' she called. 'Close your eyes and put out your hands ... there!'

Leveret opened her eyes and saw a garment of very soft, fine linen dyed a deep ivy evergreen.

'Can you see what it is? 'Tis a dress, a very special dress.'

'It's lovely, Mother,' said Leveret in a puzzled voice, trying to sound enthusiastic. Her mother knew she hated dresses. 'Thank you very much.'

'No, you don't realise, Leveret. 'Tis a party dress to wear to the Oustiders' Dance tomorrow night!'

Leveret looked up at her mother in horror.

'But Mother, I'm not going to *that*!'

'O' course you are! Everybody over the age of fourteen is going.

Yul told me he'd specially invited you when he dropped by to see you. I started making this way back in November when Yul first told me he were thinking of holding the dance, long before he announced it to everyone. I knew you'd nothing pretty to wear and you'd feel awkward, so I wove this special piece o' linen from the finest flax and dyed it this lovely colour to bring out your green eyes. And I been sewing it ever since, trying to keep it hidden from you. Do you really like it?'

Her voice faltered and Leveret had to make a quick decision. Argue and insist she wouldn't go, which was what she wanted but would hurt her mother dreadfully, or agree to go and make her mother happy, but practically die of embarrassment in the process. Given the recent events, there was little choice. She stood up and unfolded the dress to get a proper look.

'Mother it's beautiful – I love it! Thank you for all the love and time you've put into it for me. Especially when I know you've been upset with me.'

She kissed her mother soundly and then looked again at the dress. It was beautiful indeed; tight long sleeves with points that would fall over her hands like a Tudor gown, a sweetheart neckline that wasn't too exposed but would show her slim neck, and tailored so it would cling to her body, making the most of her slenderness. The skirt was slightly flared and when she held it against herself, came to just below the knee. It was lovely and would flatter her well. But she hated dresses and she knew just how she'd feel in it – like a sparrow in kingfisher's plumage, out of place and ridiculous.

'That's not all!' said Maizie excitedly, delighted that Leveret was pleased with it. She'd been worried that she was wasting her time for nothing, that the girl would flatly refuse to wear it or go to the party. 'Look, these are to go with it.'

From the bottom of the dresser she produced a box from the Outside World. Inside were a pair of delicate ballet pumps made of dark green suede, a perfect match for the dress.

'Wow! How on earth did you get these, Mother?'

'I didn't – they're from Yul and Sylvie.'

'Really?'

'When I told them I were making you the dress, Sylvie said she'd get shoes to match. She found them on the Internet for you – I hope they fit.'

Leveret couldn't believe it.

'I'm amazed Yul still wanted me to have them,' she said. 'He's so angry with me.'

'Yes ... he'd wanted to burn the lot after the mistletoe mis-adventure. Thank the goddess I said no – I couldn't bear to destroy such lovely things, though I never thought I'd give 'em to you, especially when you were to be kept in your room at the Hall over Yule. But let's not dwell on that. You'll look beautiful tomorrow night and I'll be the proudest mother in Stonewylde!'

Leveret regarded her steadily and swallowed.

'Mother, it's the Dark Moon tomorrow night and I'd planned on celebrating it. This is something I really must do – it's very important to me.'

Maizie frowned, remembering their new compromise and not wanting to break it so soon.

'Right enough – where did you want to go?'

Leveret thought about this. She wanted to do it in Mother Heggy's cottage but that was impossible. She couldn't tell her mother how she used the place and she couldn't sneak up there either – that would break their new trust.

'I don't mind. Tucked away in a corner on the Village Green maybe?'

'Alright ... does it matter when you do it?'

'Not really. After nightfall, but not so early that there are too many people about to see me – and before midnight, of course.'

'That's fine. Go to the party first and then later on you can slip out to the Green and dance or whatever 'tis you have to do. You'll be safe on the Green with the Barn so close by. Is that fair enough?'

'Yes, Mother, thank you. It's so good not lying to you.' She gave Maizie a hug. 'But there's one more thing.'

'What?' asked Maizie warily, thinking she'd now push it too

far and make an unreasonable demand. 'What do you want now?'

'I'm really, really scared of going into the dance with all the Outsiders there and that strange music. Would you come in with me for a while at least? Please?'

On the morning of the Dark Moon Leveret rose early and went down to the river as the sun was rising. It was a beautiful sunrise that would've been perfect for the Solstice. The cold water glinted as the sun rose higher, glittering over all it touched with a pink-gold light. A water rat swam towards the river bank and then disappeared into its hole, and a crowd of mallards quacked loudly at Leveret's intrusion as they bobbed about searching for an early breakfast. She stood on the river bank and drank in the beauty and peace, making the sign of the pentangle. Earth, fire, water, air – and the spirit in me, she thought. The shimmering water eddied past her, heading out to sea. She breathed deeply, her breath clouding out around her as she exhaled. Then she turned to the great willow that overhung the river, the same one that had sheltered the girls on the day of their preparations for the Rite of Adulthood.

Leveret stroked the lined and deeply fissured bark of the tree, calling on the spirit that lived there. The willow was a feminine tree and the spirit was ancient and powerful. She stood with her hand on the trunk, looking up into the tangle of branches that canopied overhead. She felt the energy all around her, alive and vibrant even though it was the heart of winter and trees were dormant. This one only slept and even in sleep its magic was strong.

'Sister Willow, I greet you. I honour your spirit and ask forgiveness for the cuts I'm about to make. They're done with goodness of intention and love in my heart for another. I only take what I need and no more. Blessings, Sister Willow.'

The whispered words hung around her as her breath had done. Taking a small kitchen knife from her pocket she began to cut pieces from the fine branches, wishing it were spring when the tree would be covered in whippy little shoots, so much easier to work with. Leveret felt an overwhelming sadness at the loss of the white-handled gathering knife, for even though she'd spent as much time as she could searching the Green she'd had no luck in finding it. Maybe somebody else had spotted it and picked it up. She grieved for its loss deeply but tried not to think of it now. This willow must be gathered with the right feelings in her heart and so she concentrated on that and shut out her sad thoughts.

At sunset she was out again, this time with a bag containing everything she needed for the spell and the circle tonight. She'd kept it very simple in the end, nothing like she'd planned to do when gathering at the Frost Moon. That bag had been confiscated but maybe that was for the best, the way things had now turned out. The spell she intended to cast tonight would be very basic but hopefully all the more powerful for it. Leveret planned to leave her bag containing all the necessities hidden somewhere on the Green, so she could just slip out of the party later and pick it up. She did a circuit of the clearing, looking for a likely spot. The trees were bare and although darkness would soon fall, she didn't want to risk somebody finding her bag. She ended up under the only evergreen tree there – the great yew, the tree special to Yul and Sylvie. She felt its intense, powerful magic as she approached and knew it was a fitting choice, for the yew was the tree of the crone and Dark Magic.

But strangely she felt something else as she stepped under the low boughs and stood in the gloomy shelter. She felt love so strong it took her breath away. She felt passion and desire, adoration and ecstasy, an intermingling of souls that time couldn't destroy. Leveret felt it winding around the branches, mixed up with the eternity that the yew represented, the phoenix-like ability to regenerate and grow again from the ashes and withering. She'd never felt anything like it and realised that it was Yul and Sylvie's love she was picking up – their union of darkness and brightness into one.

Leveret had never before thought about the beautiful relationship between her oldest brother and his moongazy wife.

She'd only ever seen it as a nuisance, something which had taken Yul away from her. Now she sensed a little of the magic of their partnership but realised that recently there'd been little evidence of their love. Both of them were miserable; perhaps they should come here and be reminded of what they'd once shared? Not wishing to intrude on this shrine to their unification, Leveret quickly hung the bag on one of the small branches that protruded from the pink flaking bark of the enormous bole. She bowed to the tree and slipped out back onto the Green just as the evening star was blooming.

At home Maizie was feverish in her excitement.

'You better get down to the bath house now, my girl, else all the hot water will be gone.'

'Mother, most of the people going tonight live up at the Hall and they'll be using those bathrooms. There'll be plenty of hot water in the bath house. It doesn't start till eight o'clock and that's practically four hours away.'

'Alright, but don't leave it till the last minute, will you? I want to help you get ready and I got to go to the Barn in a while to set out the food. I'll be back in good time but have your bath whilst I'm gone. Are you feeling excited yet?'

'I suppose so – but I'm more terrified than excited.'

'You'll be fine, Leveret. You'll look so pretty in your new dress and all the boys'll be wanting to dance with you.'

'I doubt that very much,' muttered Leveret, remembering Jay's words only two weeks ago at the Moon Fullness. The ugliest girl at Stonewylde, he'd said, with a body like a boy's. If anyone looked at her this evening it certainly wouldn't be because she looked so pretty – they'd be gaping at how stupid she looked in such a lovely dress. A sparrow, not a kingfisher. She thought of all the unkind taunts her brothers had made over the years about her unattractive looks, and her recent resolve to enlist help to stop their bullying. She decided to try and broach the subject with her mother now but felt nervous, not wanting to spoil the new harmony by making her mother choose between her children.

'Mother, I know you've always said I'm a tell-tale . . .'

Maizie eyed her warily and sighed.

'Let's not start on all that, Leveret. 'Tis forgotten now – I know you never meant to tell lies about your brothers.'

'But Mother, I—'

'The thing is, my girl, I do understand they've tormented you over the years. O' course I've always noticed that. It started when you were only a tiny little thing, but you see, they lost their father and 'twas a very difficult time for everyone but especially Gefrin and Sweyn. The other four were older but they were only little boys theirselves and they didn't understand what were going on. Then what with our Yul becoming the new magus and me being out every hour o' the day and night trying to help organise the community . . . 'twere a difficult time for us all. You were lucky – you were too young to understand anything.'

Leveret nodded – she'd heard all this before and knew it was part of her mother's justification for believing her two youngest sons weren't really so bad.

'The thing is, Mother, that over the years they—'

'Oh I know, Leveret, I know it's gone on a long time. You don't need to tell me that. But really, 'tis normal for brothers to torment a little sister. You ask any girl with a big brother. But they're older now and I know they've become much more kind and responsible. So let's not dwell—'

'But it hasn't stopped! Really, they're even worse now and they've said they're going to—'

'Leveret, you know this isn't true. Please don't spoil—'

'Mother it *is* true! Clip saw what Sweyn did to me at Samhain!'

'I know what Clip thought he saw – he came and told me. And I took it up with Sweyn and he explained everything. He were angry with you, right enough, for messing about and upsetting me. He did bob your head in the water – he admitted that. But he weren't trying to *drown* you! You've just got into the habit over the years of making it all out to be much worse than it really is.'

'Please, Mother, why—'

264

'Leveret ... this is a special night. Let's not spoil it with any more o' this talk. Let's put it all behind us now. Please?'

Leveret hung her head. This is what always happened every time she tried to tell her mother; nothing had changed at all. She'd just have to find someone else to help her. Maizie went into the kitchen to check on her fruit pies baking in the oven and Leveret sat down at the table and started teasing out a pile of wool for felt-making. She'd taken Yul's words to heart and was trying very hard to help her mother more. Yul had been right – Maizie did look tired nowadays.

Just then the door crashed open and in walked Sweyn and Gefrin. Maizie called out to them from the kitchen to sit down and she'd bring them in some mulled wine in a minute. They both stared at Leveret.

'We just heard you're going to the Outsiders' Dance tonight, Lev!'

'That's right.'

'Why?'

'Why not?'

They both laughed.

'I can think of lots of reasons why not,' said Sweyn, his voice low so Maizie, clattering in the kitchen, couldn't hear. 'You'll stand out amongst all those lovely Outside girls and we'll be so embarrassed if anyone realises you're our sister. You're an ugly little bitch and—'

'Wine's warming up!' called Maizie. 'Won't be long.'

'And we don't want you there cramping our style,' added Gefrin. 'Showing us up.'

He sat down opposite her and kicked her hard under the table. She flinched from the pain but carried on pulling at the clumps of raw wool, teasing it to fluffiness, keeping her head down. Sweyn came and stood behind her, putting his hands on her shoulders. His thick fingers dug cruelly into her collar bones making her gasp.

'And Jay's really got it in for you,' he warned. 'I mean *really*. He said you insulted him at the Moon Fullness. He don't take that from no one but especially not you. Jay can be ... well, put it this way, he's a vicious bugger when he gets going. Don't expect us to stick up for you – we'll just walk away and leave him to it.'

Gefrin giggled.

'We've seen Jay in action and it's not pretty. I've heard people say his father Jackdaw was the same and he killed his wife, didn't he? Like father like son. So watch out, Hare-brain, 'cos he's out to get you. He'll be specially looking for you tonight.'

Maizie came in triumphantly, rosy-cheeked from the oven heat, bearing a tray of cups and a jug of steaming wine that smelt of blackberries, cloves and nutmeg.

'Have you heard that Leveret's coming to the party tonight?' she said brightly, pouring the mulled wine and handing it round. 'She's got a lovely new dress and she'll look so pretty.'

Sweyn choked into his wine and grinned at his brother.

'We was just saying we'll look out for her tonight, make sure she's alright.'

'Ah, that's really nice of you boys – thank you. She's very nervous, you see, and though I'll be there at the beginning to help serve the food, I can't stay all night. 'Tis for the young people and Yul says we must leave you all to it once the party's found its feet. If you'll be looking after her I won't need to worry.'

'No problem, Mother,' said Gefrin. ''Tis our pleasure.'

'See, Leveret?' said Maizie cheerfully. 'Your brothers'll make sure you have a special evening.'

'We certainly will, Mother!' said Sweyn, putting his arm round Leveret's shoulders and squeezing her hard. She cringed at his touch. 'We'll make sure it's a very special evening for her.'

Leveret stood outside the entrance to the Great Barn trembling like a kitten.

'I can't go in there, Mother!'

'Don't be silly – o' course you can!'

'Everyone'll stare and laugh at me.'

'No they won't. If they stare at you 'tis only because you look so lovely.'

266

It was true. Maizie was amazed at just how lovely Leveret looked. She'd always been such a tom-boy but tonight she'd blossomed into a beautiful young girl on the cusp of woman-hood. The dress fitted like a dream, the tight bodice emphasising her surprisingly rounded breasts and tiny waist whilst the longer skirt gave her a bit of extra height, perfect as she was so small. They'd tied a scarlet ribbon round her neck with her silver charm – the crescent moon or bow of the Huntress – hanging from it. Most young people wore their Naming Ceremony charm until their Rite of Adulthood when it was replaced by the pewter pendant; it was a way of showing whether or not they were adults.

Maizie had insisted on sweeping up her long glossy curls and pinning them in a knot. With her wild hair swept back, Leveret was transformed. The sharp, pointy face with slanted green cat's eyes became elegant, even delicate, and her eyes were stunning without dark curls constantly falling into them. Her neck was a slim white column accentuated by the scarlet ribbon and she looked like something from a fairytale.

'Cinderella, you shall go to the ball!' Maizie had laughed, overwhelmed by her daughter's almost exotic beauty.

'It's the ugly step-sisters I'm worried about,' Leveret had muttered in reply.

Now they both stood outside the Barn, Maizie with her arm around her trembling daughter.

'See – the coach hasn't arrived yet,' said Maizie. ''Twill be better to go in now while it's still quite empty, then you won't feel so self-conscious. You can come and help me check on all the food.'

So they went in, feeling the alienness of the Barn. There was a disco set up with mixing decks, machines and electric lights and two strange men stood behind it busy with large head-phones over their ears. The music was very loud and full of bass compared to the fiddles, drums, guitars and flutes normally heard in here. But Maizie was right – there weren't too many people around yet. Leveret hung up her cloak and stood in her dark green dress feeling very strange, as if she were another person.

And it seemed as if everyone else thought she were another person too. Bryony, Linnet, Skipper and Tansy, who were in her class at school, stood and stared at her in disbelief. They all looked nice but none of them were in Leveret's league. The group of older girls who'd been so kind to her the other day actually came over to compliment her.

'Leveret, you look absolutely stunning!'

'Wow – I barely recognised you.'

'Talk about the ugly duckling! Look, you're a swan!'

Leveret giggled at this and began to relax just slightly. Maybe she did look quite nice and maybe people wouldn't think she was hideous. Maybe – just maybe – Kestrel might notice her tonight?

17

Understanding that her daughter was terrified, Maizie kept her close while she talked to other adults behind the laden trestle-tables of food. The last thing she wanted was Leveret to bolt back home in panic. Maizie was immensely proud of her, beaming at the Village women who shook their heads in amazement at the little tomboy's transformation. Leveret stood quietly and gradually the Barn grew busier as groups of boys who'd been messing about outside on the Village Green started to drift in. Then there was a call from the Gatehouse to say the coach had arrived and was on its way down. Many more youngsters still outside piled into the Barn and the disco lights were switched on, strangely colourful and flickering to people only used to lantern and candlelight in the place. The volume of the music was turned up and everyone waited expectantly. Leveret, her heart pounding with nervousness, looked around to locate Sweyn, Gefrin and Jay – and Kestrel too, if possible – but she couldn't see any of them.

The coach pulled up outside the Village as the cobbled tracks weren't wide enough for such a vehicle, and almost fifty teenagers from the Outside World tumbled out in an excited, noisy throng. They were all from the local college and were intrigued to be here. The kids from Stonewylde were renowned for being an odd bunch, strangely quaint and different from them in many ways, and nobody in the coach party knew what to expect now they were in the Stonewylders' stronghold. In fact the guests had no idea just how honoured they were. Inviting such a large group of Outsiders into Stonewylde had never been done before in living or recorded memory – not since the days of tribes and settlements when visitors would come to trade, and that was a very long time ago.

The young people in their party clothes huddled round the familiar coach and looked about in bewilderment, trying to make everything out and wondering why, even for rural Dorset, it was so very dark here. There were no street lights although lanterns hung from the buildings and shed just enough light to intrigue them further. They recognised a pub and a village green – that much was familiar to them. But then Kestrel arrived in their midst, a handsome recognisable face in an alien world, and ushered them all towards the open double doors of the Great Barn.

The crowd of Outsiders heard the familiar boom-boom-boom of music and saw the flashing coloured lights and lasers, and felt more at home. They poured into the vast building, taking in the tiny twinkling silver lanterns and evergreen decorations that hung from its massive rafters. They liked the old-fashioned Christmas decorations, which had been left up in the end, and were amazed at the size of the barn. They noticed the tables of food that lined one wall and the bar with its wooden barrels, rows of bottles and jugs of juice and water. After the wild speculation that had been rife during the coach ride, everything seemed quite civilised after all.

Coats were taken and put into a side room for later. People hung around in small groups eyeing the central stone-flagged area that was clearly a dance floor, and the bales of straw, upturned logs and wooden benches dotted around for seating. Those Stonewylders who attended college began to mingle, shouting welcomes over the music, taking their friends to get drinks from the bar. And so the first ever Outsiders' Dance began.

Leveret hid behind the food tables in terror. She was one of the youngest there; no one from her year-group had yet visited the Outside World and wouldn't until February. She was aghast at the sight of so many unfamiliar faces. Growing up in a closed community meant that every single person she ever saw was known and recognised. Their clothes were so strange, so completely different. Even though the Stonewylders who went to college wore Outside clothes sometimes, theirs were fairly ordinary, everyday outfits. But most of these visitors wore incredible, bizarre party things. Leveret couldn't understand why some of the girls' shoes were so contorted. How could they possibly walk when their feet were tilted and crushed like that? And the make-up – it was as if they'd painted themselves to act in a drama. She stood and gawped in pure disbelief.

Kestrel was acting as the host, feeling responsible for the evening. It had been his idea in the first place and Yul had warned him that should anything go wrong, he'd be held responsible and the event would never be repeated. But rather than worrying about it Kestrel was revelling in his role, loving being at the centre of attention and the leader of the event. He'd rejected Outside clothes and decided to make a feature of his difference, being smart enough to realise that to Outsiders he must seem rather exotic. He wore the traditional festival clothes: narrow black linen trousers, black leather Stonewylde boots with their unique shape, and a flowing white shirt of the finest material.

Kestrel looked devastatingly handsome with his hazelnut-brown hair and laughing blue eyes and every girl in the place was aware of him. Leveret was no exception. She'd located him and now watched him carefully; he was the sort of person impossible to ignore and was doing the rounds, ensuring all the visitors had drinks and food. Leveret shrunk into the shadows as a group approached the food table she hid behind. She slipped off to one side in case she'd have to serve anyone, not wanting any contact with the strangers.

As she stood huddled by the wall, her eyes wide with curiosity and shyness, Swift spotted her and came over. Although she still was unsure about him she was relieved to talk to someone familiar

'I didn't recognise you, Leveret,' he said, standing close enough that he didn't have to shout. 'What a transformation!'

She gave him a sideways look and smiled slightly.

'You'll turn a few heads tonight, I expect,' he continued.

'Hardly, with all these amazing Outsiders – they're the head-turners.'

'Only to those who haven't seen them before. They're quite familiar to the Stonewylde college people and even I recognise a lot of them from my visits.'

'Will you be going on to college next autumn?' she asked.

'Without a doubt, and probably to university too like Kestrel.'

'He's leaving then next year?' Her heart sank although she'd always known it was likely; he was one of the highest fliers of his year group.

'Yes – Kes is very clever. And what about you, Leveret – what are your plans? I know you're a high achiever too.'

She grimaced and shook her head, and Swift was quite fascinated by the delicacy of her jaw and neck, the plane of her cheekbones. Leveret had spent her entire life hiding behind the mass of dark curls. Whoever would've thought there was a real beauty, invisible up until now, dwelling in their midst.

'I don't ever want to leave Stonewylde,' she replied and he laughed.

'You'll change your mind once you've visited the Outside World – we all do.'

They stood quietly for a while watching the groups of people laughing and shouting over the music, drinking and eating. A few had started dancing already, including Kestrel.

'Just look at Kes!' mused Swift. 'He's in his element. He's got the girls lined up and waiting for him tonight as ever.'

Leveret swallowed at this. She knew she wasn't alone in wanting him.

'He's very popular,' she agreed.

'Too right! He could have any girl he wanted in this place tonight, and no exaggeration, he's probably had at least half of them already. He's been working his way through the Stonewylde girls, picking them off as they turn sixteen. And then there're all the college girls too. He'll have a challenge when he gets to university though. Even Kestrel couldn't manage that many, though he'd love to die trying.'

Leveret couldn't bear to hear talk like this – Kestrel was popular but not so promiscuous, surely? Her throat felt tight with jealousy at the thought of him with so many girls.

'Let's go and get a drink, Leveret – come on.'

Not allowing any refusal, he took her arm and tugged her away from the safety of the shadows right out into the open where the coloured lights played brightly. Leveret was terrified, her mouth dry and hands trembling. She walked beside Swift with a straight back, her head high and not daring to look around or catch anyone's eye, just like a stiff-legged cat self-consciously picking its way along a high, exposed wall. She knew people were looking at her, lots of people, and she shook with terror. She'd been right all along – she was ridiculous, hideous, the ugly, skinny bitch her brothers had always told her she was, the ugliest, most boyish, girl in Stonewylde.

'Hey, Swift! Who's this? I don't think ... Sacred Mother! It's our Leveret!'

Kestrel stood before them smiling incredulously. He was sheened slightly with perspiration from dancing which merely accentuated his good looks. His eyes were alight with fun; they'd been sparkling with pleasure and now widened in sheer surprise. He removed Swift's hand from Leveret's sleeve and turned her around slowly, looking her up and down. Then he gazed into her face, tilted her chin and swivelled her head slightly to see her profile. He grinned and she felt the full blast of his charm.

'I just don't believe it! What happened to you? Where's my grubby little girl with the mop of curls and the scowl?'

Leveret smiled shyly, lowering her eyes and then glancing up at him through her lashes, completely unaware of just how exquisitely alluring that was. She could think of nothing remotely intelligent to say so kept quiet.

'Exactly how old are you?' he asked, glancing at the silver Huntress' bow hung on the scarlet ribbon around her throat.

'Fourteen,' she replied. 'Fifteen at Imbolc.'

'Pity,' he smiled, chucking her cheek with a gentle finger. 'But you'll be worth waiting for.'

Then he was off and back on the dance floor with the girls he'd been with, whilst Leveret practically glided on wings after Swift to the bar, tingling with wild joy.

Sylvie stood by Yul's side watching the party warm up. More people were dancing now, the food plundered but by no means finished as Stonewylde feasts were always abundant. She hadn't wanted to come to the event but Yul had insisted. They were the hosts and should at least make an appearance although he realised the last thing their young guests wanted was to make polite conversation with adults. Sylvie stood sipping a glass of cordial and felt all her sensibilities recoil from the scene around her. The sight of the garish Outside clothes and make-up, the overt sexual display in the dancing and music all brought back memories of her visits to Yul at his university, when she'd had to endure such events.

Sylvie remembered the curiosity and hostility she'd encountered when meeting Yul's peer group. She'd attended an agricultural college in Dorset which enabled her to return home frequently as her health and allergies had always been a concern. Yul, however, after sailing through his exams with amazing grades for someone who'd only learned to read and write at sixteen, had gone to one of the big city universities. Clip and Miranda, practically the only ones at Stonewylde who knew about education in the Outside World, had been sure that broadening his horizons was what Yul needed most, before returning fulltime to Stonewylde. They didn't want him getting restless in the future or feeling he'd missed out on anything the Outside World had to offer.

So Yul had spent three years at an enormous, busy university where he'd encountered a life completely and utterly alien to anything in his world. He'd missed Stonewylde terribly and Sylvie in particular, and had loved nothing better than coming home in the holidays. But he'd also had a great time, soaking up all the place had to offer socially and culturally as well as academically, and had clamoured for more. He was very popular amongst his peers although Sylvie knew he'd been faithful to her whilst he was away studying. She trusted him absolutely for he was passionately and obsessively in love with her. It had been hard for her letting him go like that as her small agricultural college was a far cry from his huge and exciting university; not that she'd ever wished to go somewhere like that herself.

During the term time he frequently asked her to come and spend the weekend with him, wanting her to meet all his new acquaintances and see his new lifestyle. Sylvie was very reluctant, knowing she'd be an object of curiosity. She understood that his peers were keen to see the cause of his fidelity and devotion; his faithfulness to her certainly wasn't from lack of interest amongst the girls there. When she'd visited he'd been so proud of her, showing her off to his wide circle of friends, not understanding their lack of enthusiasm towards her. To them she was the boring girl from home, unsophisticated and old-fashioned in her tastes. Nobody could understand what on earth the exotic and exciting Yul saw in her.

Sylvie glanced at him now as he drained a tankard of cider, his throat moving as he tipped back his head and swallowed. Like Kestrel he too was wearing traditional Stonewylde clothes which accentuated his long powerful legs and slim waist, the breadth of his shoulders and chest. Despite the recent events she felt a familiar pulse of desire for him which she quickly squashed. That terrible night when he'd forced himself on her so roughly was still fresh in her mind and imprinted on her body. She bruised as easily as ever and the marks from his rough, grasping hands were still visible, livid against her white skin. She'd had to be careful the girls didn't see such graphic evidence of their father's new brutality.

'Doesn't Leveret look beautiful?' she said, watching the girl as she stood apart sipping a glass of dark liquid.

'Where? I haven't seen her yet.'

She pointed towards the slim girl with her elegant hairstyle and svelte dress.

'That's Leveret?' he gaped. 'I didn't recognise her! Goddess, she looks so different. Who'd have thought it? I'll have to watch her with the boys – see the attention she's attracting? Do you think she even realises?'

'Probably not – I don't think she's interested in boys yet. It's so good to see her looking happier now.'

'Yes, she got exactly what she wanted and Mother's eating out of her hand . . . but let's not talk about her now. I think I've sorted Leveret out and she won't be playing up again. Do you want another drink?'

'No thanks, I've had enough.'

She watched him go to the bar for a refill.

And so have you, she thought to herself.

Leveret refused to join in the dancing despite being asked by several people. She loved to dance at the festivals to the wild drums and she loved to jig to the fiddles and flutes, but this was different and she didn't feel comfortable with it. So she stood and watched, sipping elderberry wine and only talking when people joined her for a conversation. She was quite enjoying herself, basking in the compliments and praise, but most of all in the elation that Kestrel's interest had inspired. She remembered the Dark Moon outside and her elation turned to a tingle of excitement as she thought of her planned ritual on the Green. Soon she'd slip away unnoticed; it'd be good to get out from this noise and heat too.

She'd managed to avoid her brothers and Jay so far although they'd spent some time standing across the barn from her staring, whispering together and clearly discussing her. She felt the waves of hostility emanating from them, especially from Jay who seemed unable to take his bulging blue eyes off her. She moved closer to one of the exits, knowing her cloak was on a peg nearby and thinking maybe this was a good time to collect her bag from under the yew tree and get started. She'd no idea of the time but knew she must perform the spell before midnight, for this was the time of the Dark Moon and after midnight it'd be tomorrow.

Leveret was near the door and the pegs when suddenly she saw the three youths heading her way, like large henchmen closing in on their victim. Maizie and most of the adults had already left but she tried to move back into the safety of the crowds. She was too late – they surrounded her and her brothers positioned themselves on either side of her, each taking an arm and holding her tightly.

'Well, well, fancy seeing you here!' giggled Gefrin, squeezing her upper arm hard.

'Mind my dress!' she hissed. 'Mother made it.'

Sweyn jabbed her sharply in the back.

'Don't start getting uppity, Leveret,' he growled. 'You know where that leads.'

Jay stood in front of her, towering hugely and sweating profusely. He reeked of cider, as did the others.

'Look at you all tarted up,' he sneered. 'Did I upset you the other night? Tried to do something about it, did you? You're still an ugly, skinny little bitch and don't you forget it!'

'Kestrel doesn't think so!' she blurted out, her cheeks burning.

'Kestrel? Was Kes sniffing around then? What did he say?'

'None of your business!' she retorted, wishing fervently that she hadn't mentioned him at all. She should've just kept quiet and let them get the tormenting over and done with.

Jay glared at her in surprise, then punched her in the stomach. It wasn't a hard punch, nothing like he'd given Magpie, but it made her grunt in pain as the air was forced from her diaphragm.

'Careful,' warned Sweyn. 'No bruises or marks, Jay – we said about this.'

'Yeah, yeah, I know, but she ain't talking to me like that. So I'll try again, Leveret – what did Kestrel say that made you think you're not the ugly little weasel we all know you to be?'

She hung her head, still gasping for breath from the blow that had winded her and not wanting any more pain tonight.

'He said I was worth waiting for,' she said quietly.

'HE SAID YOU WERE WORTH WAITING FOR!' crowed Jay at the top of his voice, laughing raucously. 'And you took that as a compliment, did you? Stupid little bitch! Kestrel pokes anything that moves; of course he'll get round to you when you're old enough. That doesn't mean a thing so don't flatter yourself! Anyway, if he thought you were that bloody hot he wouldn't want to wait at all, would he?'

He looked at her and shook his head mockingly.

'Are we going to take her outside then?' asked Gefrin. 'Like we said.'

'Too many people about,' said Sweyn. 'And we've better things to do tonight, haven't we, with all these girls here? Let's leave it for tonight – Leveret's still going to be here tomorrow. And the next day and the one after that. We can sort her out any time we want.'

'Yeah, you two go on and get some more cider in – I'll be with you in a minute. I'm just going to have a quiet little word with Leveret on my own.'

'Alright but remember what we said. If there's any marks to prove her snitching, we're all in big trouble.'

'I ain't going to hurt her, not tonight. Don't worry – no marks.'

Sweyn and Gefrin ambled off towards the bar and Jay turned to Leveret, who was filled with a plummeting dread. There was something really nasty about Jay. He was worse than her brothers who, all said and done, were just thick bully boys. But Jay was something else – he had an edge of viciousness that she found terrifying and she remembered the warning her brothers had given her earlier in the cottage. He leered down at her and took her hand in his.

'Come on – outside, girl! I got something special for you.'

He tugged on her resisting arm and led her out into the cold night. It was shockingly quiet after the booming of the relentless music. The stars spangled in the black sky, filling the heavens. Leveret looked up and hoped Mother Heggy was somewhere out there still watching over her welfare. She was terrified of being alone with Jay who didn't share her brothers' concern about their mother finding out. Jay wouldn't care less – his family had been in dispute with Maizie for a long time and she knew there was bad feeling between them stretching back many years.

He pushed her along the side of the Barn until they reached a buttress which blocked the view from the door. A lantern hung from a hook to guide anyone using this way as an exit and she could see his face clearly. He was bullet-headed with a massive neck peppered by a nasty rash where the bristles had only been roughly shaved. His face was ugly and pugnacious, his prominent eyes sparking with aggression, and now he shoved her hard into the corner where the buttress met the wall. He leant his hands on either side of her against the stone, trapping her in a human cage of muscle and sinew. His breath washed over her in foul waves as he stared down at her.

'I got a bone to pick with you!' he began. 'It's *your* fault they moved that half-witted cousin of mine up to the Hall.'

She said nothing and kept her head down.

'Now my auntie and the two old ones have no one to do all the heavy work. They expect me to come and chop the wood and get the water every day. AND I'M NOT VERY HAPPY ABOUT THAT!'

She felt his spittle spray her face and involuntarily raised her hand in disgust to wipe it off. He grabbed hold of her wrist and yanked it away.

'What's the matter, Leveret? Don't like me getting too close, eh? Scared of me, are you?'

Still holding her wrist he edged his body forward even closer to hers so they were almost touching and she felt the heat pulsing off him. She was completely trapped by his bulk and increasingly frightened of what was he was going to do to her. He was so huge and she felt very vulnerable indeed. She held her breath, gazing straight ahead at his chest and hoping desperately that someone would come along and find them – although to the casual observer they'd simply look like a couple canoodling in the darkness. She raised terrified eyes to his and he chuckled.

'Yeah, you should be scared, girl. You're right to be scared.'

As he glared down at her she saw something different in his eyes and he chuckled again, giving her wrist a cruel twist.

'But that'll wait for now. I got a present for you – something you're going to need in the future. And I got the same present waiting for Magpie when I get the chance to give it him.'

With his free hand he pulled a small package from his pocket and placed it in her hand, closing her reluctant fingers over it.

'It's from Old Violet, so next time you'll be able to do the job properly.'

'What is it?' whispered Leveret, looking down at the dirty piece of cloth in her hand. Whatever was wrapped inside was very light indeed.

'Death Cap – the one you should've taken but messed up. Keep it safe, Leveret, because soon you'll wish you were dead all over again.'

Laughing, he turned and stomped back into the Barn.

The stars blazed down on the girl standing straight-backed in the centre of a circle of salt. The elements were represented on the points around the circumference – a tiny lantern for fire, a stone for earth, a feather for air and a rough clay dish filled with water. The fifth element, the spirit, she'd symbolised with a little wooden hare that Yul had carved for her as a child. At the head of the circle lay a small and very rough altar, simply a large chunk of bark, decorated with mistletoe, holly and ivy as befitted the season. There was also a tiny cake and an egg-cup of elderberry wine. Everything was representational and the gifts showed that she gave back to the goddess what had been freely given to her – the fruits of the earth.

Leveret had whispered the words she'd memorised from her notebook as she'd sprinkled the salt, calling for protection from any spirit or person wishing her harm. Holding Mother Heggy's athame in both hands, she now stood pointing it to the stars and calling the power of the elements to join her in the circle. She summoned each element in turn, asking that it lend its energy to her for the magic and indicating the symbol she'd used to represent it. The element of spirit, last to be summoned, she called from within, the blade at her chest. Then she invited the spirit of Mother Heggy to join her if she would.

Once the protection was in place and the elements summoned, she began to raise the energy she needed. With tiny steps Leveret started to walk widdershins around inside the circumference of the circle, the athame in her right hand pointing skyward and her left hand pointing to the earth. Leveret was acting as a conduit, a conductor of the energy which must pour down through her into the circle to create the magic. She called upon star-fire, for the dark skies were ablaze with it. She called upon the spirit of the Dark Moon, the crone, and especially Mother Heggy. She called and called, circling and circling, her entire being summoning, inviting and drawing it down.

Gradually she felt it coming, building into a cone of pure energy. There was a change inside the circle, an excitement and force that hadn't been there before. Still she circled, one arm skyward and the other earthward, her face raised to the diamond stars in exaltation. Finally she stopped – it was enough. The air around her was thicker, quivering and crackling with invisible force. She bowed and sat down cross-legged on the frosty grass with her cloak wrapped around her, facing the altar she'd built.

Now she pulled out the willow she'd cut earlier and had woven into a rough sphere. She placed it carefully on the altar and asked the Dark Goddess to bless it and for the spirit of the willow tree to act as guardian. Then she took out a twist of paper and very delicately unwrapped the precious contents – the lock of Magpie's butterscotch-gold hair. She raised it to her lips and kissed it gently, concentrating on a bright and happy image of her friend. She thought hard of Magpie, the kind soul within the simple body; the gentle soul she loved so dearly, blessed with a creative gift and a love of all things natural. She thought of the innocent soul that had been tormented and abused almost from the day it entered his body and this world, that had suffered constantly at the hands of others yet still shone with goodness. Leveret concentrated until she felt the essence of Magpie's soul was with her. Then she poured it into the soft lock of hair resting in the cup of her palms, which she held now up to the heavens.

I call upon the five elements summoned here to my pentacle,
I call upon the power of the Dark Goddess, the secret magic of the Dark Moon,
I call upon the wisdom of the Wise Woman who once walked these lands,
I call upon the spirit of every tree gathered around this sacred place,
I call upon the mother-love of the great willow by the river,
I call upon the energy of this land, the green magic of Stonewylde,
I call you all together into this circle to witness my spell!

I ask you to bring magic tonight for my spell of protection,
I ask you to give me power to weave a spell of protection for Magpie,
I ask you to be guardians to my friend and protect him from mortal danger,
I ask you to bind those who'd hurt him and create a shield of protection
I ask you this with love in my heart – protect Magpie!

I will do what you will in return,
I will do your bidding, whatever it may be,
I will be your vessel and serve you, in return for this spell of protection.
May Magpie be safe from all harm!
Blessed be!

Leveret took the willow sphere from the bark altar and deftly pushed the lock of hair inside through a gap. She took some loose strands of willow from her bag and wove them into the ball, closing the larger gaps and gradually making the whole thing ever more solid and substantial. The hair was now locked within safely. Leveret cupped the willow globe gently in her hands and then held it to her heart. She threw her head back and looked up at the stars blazing in the velvet skies. She wished with every fibre of her being upon the stars. Then she hung her head, suddenly exhausted. She'd done it – her first spell. And she realised with a start that she'd used none of the words so carefully copied out from the Book of Shadows. The words for her spell of protection had been entirely her own, drawn straight from her soul. She hoped they were good enough.

Standing stiffly, Leveret raised the athame to the skies once more and dismissed the elements she'd summoned. She sent the energy she'd raised out of the circle and back into the starry night and then she bent and scattered what she could see of the salt with her hand, breaking the ring of protection. She'd finished and she'd done her very best. She could now feel the absence of the power that had gathered around her in the darkness. She blew out the tiny lantern and began to pack all the things away into her bag. Carefully she wrapped the sphere in a piece of cloth ready for its resting place tomorrow. Finally she lifted the chunk of bark that had served as a rough altar, but as she did her hand touched something which made her jump back with a cry. The hair on her arms rose in fear. Gingerly she reached forward again, groping in the freezing grass, and her fingers closed around the smooth bone handle of the gathering knife. Leveret knew for certain that it hadn't been there when she started – Mother Heggy must have been with her all along.

18

The festivities of Yule were finally over and life at Stonewylde felt a little bleak. Days were short and nights long and it seemed ages until the next festival: Imbolc at the beginning of February. Folk used the dark evenings productively; the flax weaving and dyeing was completed and the bolts of new linen cloth cut and sewn into clothing and bedding. Patchwork quilts were started so no scraps were wasted and the carded wool was knitted into yet more garments. A lot of felt was made too and used to line coats and boots as well as make lovely bags, hats and slippers. The Stonewylders were industrious and took pride in their crafts. Leveret was surprised to find she enjoyed helping Maizie and learning more about how to make functional but beautiful things.

But there was dismay when it was announced that every household must contribute a set number of specific items for Stonewylde.com before the growing season began. Harold had made lists of what was required to keep the warehouses well stocked for the season ahead, and these were posted in the Great Barn and the Galleried Hall. Young people boarding at the Hall spent the long evenings sewing quilts and whittling figurines and candlesticks, whilst those Village women gifted at embroidery decorated the delicate and much sought-after white linen nightdresses. Slippers and hats made from Stonewylde's thick, high-quality felt were in great demand and every evening Villagers gathered in the Laundry House to make more felt, whilst others worked in the Barn on the finished material, cutting and sewing.

Harold had commissioned a Stonewylde logo which was put on every product – a beautiful curly S that looked like a snake. Harold was really proud of his branding and the Internet mail order company was growing amazingly fast. Selling out of so many products before Yule had whetted the public's appetite and there were now waiting lists for many of the goods. A feature in a quality Sunday newspaper alluding to a mysterious private estate deep in Dorset that produced hand-made, organic goods for the luxury market had only added to the interest. Harold became increasingly excited at the prospect that Stonewylde.com was about to become something huge and he warned Yul that they must be ready for it.

The high quality leather produced in the tannery was tremendously popular, and Harold urgently requested that more people learn the craft of leather work. Orders for shoes, boots, jackets, belts and bags were pouring in and demand far outstripped supply. Meetings were held with Edward to discuss the economics of raising more cattle for their hides, and of the impact the extra beef would have on the balance of agriculture that had always been so stable in the past. Yul threw himself into the logistics of organising the economy, glad of the extra work to fill his interminable evenings while things were so difficult between him and Sylvie.

They'd reached a careful truce after the events of Samhain and Yule, knowing they couldn't carry on like this indefinitely but both unable to make it better. Yul deeply regretted the terrible night on Solstice Eve when he'd drunkenly forced himself on Sylvie. He'd apologised at length, his remorse genuine and profound, and they'd skirted around the issue that had led to his need to do it in the first place. Sylvie had toyed with the idea of telling him the truth, but how could she explain that Magus was haunting her? She knew how ridiculous it sounded and, worse, she knew Yul would assume she was slipping back into mental illness. So she offered some vague fabrication about the hormonal implant upsetting her body's natural balance.

Yul knew this wasn't the full story and wondered if she'd lost interest in him because there was someone else. It was ages since she'd left Stonewylde so it'd have to be someone living in the community. He went through every male over the age of twenty or so but could think of no one who could've captured his wife's interest, let alone get her into bed. But it still preyed on his mind despite knowing in his heart that it was a ludicrous notion, and made him irritable and depressed.

Yul tried to reconnect with the magic of Stonewylde, the other issue that was making his life miserable. He took Skydancer up to the Stone Circle every morning for the sunrise, and tethered the great grey stallion whilst he sat on the Altar Stone and tried to spiritually realign himself with the energy that used to flood through him. He spoke to the Goddess, pouring out his troubles and worries, raising his arms in supplication as the sun appeared over the horizon. Sometimes he felt the familiar throb of green magic, although never as strongly as before. But often there was barely a flicker and he'd leave the sacred place disconsolate, tired and disillusioned.

Then every day he'd ride hard along the Dragon's Back, sometimes heading west towards the hills where the sheep grazed in summer, and sometimes to the east towards the great Wildwood. He'd arrive back at the Hall trembling with exertion and bathed in sweat, clattering into the stable yard where Tom or a stablelad would be waiting. Yul was surprised to see Rufus there one morning, the boy's bright auburn hair as distinctive as ever. The boy smiled shyly as Yul dismounted and came forward tentatively to stroke Skydancer.

'I wouldn't do that,' said Yul rather brusquely, loosening the girth. The stallion was dark with sweat for they'd ridden harder than usual that morning and Yul didn't want the boy to be on the receiving end of the horse's exhausted bad temper. Rufus' face fell and he snatched his hand back. Yul tossed the reins to Tom and strode up to the Hall for a much-needed shower. He noticed Rufus there on several occasions after that and wondered idly why the boy had started visiting the stables in the mornings before school. Rufus wasn't chatty and Yul recalled Sylvie telling him how shy the boy was. He skulked around in the shadows, probably getting in Tom's way and upsetting the horses, and he always seemed about to say something but never actually did. Yul found his nervousness irritating and found it easiest to ignore the boy.

After breakfast in his office with Harold, which they found was the best time for a daily liaison, Yul would settle down to the day's work which increasingly took place not out on the estate but in his office, either on the phone or at the computer. He ate lunch in the Dining Hall, trying to mix with the youngsters at school and the other adults living there. He made an effort most afternoons to go down to the Village and call in to the Village School, the Nursery or the Barn. He knew how important it was to keep in touch with the heartbeat of Stonewylde and not become a distant figurehead, however busy the logistics kept him. He spent some time with his daughters later, sitting with them whilst they ate their tea and played until bath time.

He and Sylvie dined together in their apartments once the girls had been put to bed, but then the long evening stretched ahead of them. This was the difficult time for him. In the past, although he was always busy and often had to work in the evenings, he loved to spend the evening with Sylvie, talking, reading, cuddling up on the sofa. He never tired of her company. But now they were awkward together. She was silent for much of the time and he found it difficult to talk to her; he found himself actually making conversation, trying to think of things to speak about, which was an utterly ridiculous situation.

So rather than endure that, Yul would return to his office and work, or increasingly watch the television in there and drink a bottle of mead, which helped him sleep. The sofa bed became his permanent sleeping place. He couldn't bear the pain and embarrassment of Sylvie's possible rejection of him so he very rarely risked it. The longer the situation continued, the more difficult he found it to approach her. Unhappiness lodged in his heart like a chip of ice, permeating everything he did and affecting everyone around him. Yul's darkness of spirit was all-pervading, made worse by the waning of his ability to channel the Earth Magic.

Sylvie kept herself busy and progressively threw herself into the crafts that everyone else around her worked on, and which were becoming so important to Stonewylde's economy. As she became more adept she would sometimes ask a couple of the girl boarders to babysit so she could join other women working in the cosy sitting rooms downstairs, or even down in the Village. She felt herself gradually become more integrated into the community now she was no longer so totally wrapped up in Yul. She was more receptive to others and found people starting to relax in her company and talk more openly; it was the one positive thing that kept her going during the long dark days and nights.

She found the evenings difficult too and as the hour for bedtime approached she'd become withdrawn, quiet and worried. Although she longed for Yul, ached for the warmth and closeness they'd always shared, another part of her had begun to hope he'd stay downstairs and leave her alone. He drank more now than ever before. Instead of a glass of wine with dinner he now finished off the whole bottle before going down to his office. She knew he drank mead in the evenings while he worked, for she'd smelt it on him and seen empty bottles being taken away. The rare times when he had come to share her bed she heard his speech slur and stumble and noticed his grey eyes lose focus. She knew he was trying to blur his disappointment at her coolness, but she dreaded a repeat of that drunken assault and hated the thought of Yul being anything less than in full control of himself.

Bluebell had been always a poor sleeper and now often woke during the night. In the past Yul had been very firm about her staying in her own bed, but now Sylvie found it easier to let the little girl climb into her large empty bed for the rest of the night. It helped keep her ghosts at bay, too. Magus continued to haunt her subtly, usually at night, and Sylvie wondered every day whether it was real or just a figment of her imagination. She'd catch the faintest whiff of his scent which would send her heart racing in panic, terrified to open her eyes in case his smiling face loomed over her. Several times, in the moment between waking and sleeping, she saw a shadow move in the darkness, and Sylvie was sure she heard the creak of a soft footstep in the next room on more than one occasion. Once she'd caught the glimmer of silver hair in the reflection of her mirror and had spent the rest of the night curled up in a ball under the bedcovers, terrified of what else was in the room with her.

There were many small and seemingly insignificant events that began to accumulate into a terrifying catalogue. Sometimes, despite not touching a drop of it since that awful December thirteen years ago, Sylvie awoke with the sweet taste of mead on her tongue. Often, for no logical reason, she'd feel a draught whispering on her skin or stirring her hair, as if Magus were touching her with gentle fingertips. Each one of her senses picked up on Magus' presence and, as the incidents increased, her fear fed itself, making her jumpy and tense even during the day. There was nobody she could confide in about this; one of her biggest fears was that everyone would believe she'd relapsed back into psychosis.

The rift between Yul and Sylvie didn't go unnoticed by Miranda, who grew more and more concerned. Only a few months ago everything had been fine, their passion for each other had been almost embarrassingly evident. Many a time she'd intercepted their smouldering glances during public events, sensing the almost tangible synergy that existed between them. But not now. Their discord was palpable and it affected everyone living in the Hall. They'd previously been a beacon of harmony but now shed misery and tension as a dog sheds itself of water, and it was painful to watch.

Miranda tried to speak to Sylvie and see if she could help but she hit a brick wall. Sylvie merely replied that they were both tired and one bad patch in thirteen years wasn't so bad. Sylvie was close to her mother in many ways but her relationship with Yul had always been private, and it was her very obsession with him that had prevented the mother-daughter bond from deepening. Miranda wondered about speaking to Yul instead, but he'd wrapped himself in an impenetrable black cloak of unhappiness that brooked no intrusion. She was wary of him in his present state of mind; he was like an unexploded bomb and she didn't want to be the one to detonate him. So Miranda kept her peace and hoped it'd all blow over in the spring, when everyone livened up and there was plenty of sunshine and laughter at Stonewylde.

In the meantime, Miranda had an idea how to cheer her daughter up. After consultation with Harold – as she had to use the Stonewylde account – she went online and bought a pair of tickets for a ballet being performed in Bournemouth. She also booked a luxurious hotel room for the night, thinking that some special time alone may help bring the couple back together. But when she told Sylvie about the treat she didn't get the expected reaction.

'Oh Mum, that's very sweet of you but I couldn't possibly go.'

'Why on earth not?'

The thought of spending a whole night alone with Yul in a strange place filled her with dread. She didn't know what to say to him anymore and if he made any moves in bed she'd feel embarrassed and awkward. But she couldn't tell Miranda that.

'He's too busy at the moment. He works all hours – you know that.'

'All the more reason to take a night off and spend some time with you! I realise it's not the most romantic destination but a night alone together away from Stonewylde and all the pressures here is just what you both need. You can enjoy a lovely meal out, enjoy the ballet, go back to the hotel . . .'

Sylvie knew it was exactly what she didn't need. Yul would probably drink himself silly and then turn all maudlin on her or, worse still, become aggressive.

'I'm sorry, Mum, but I really don't think so. It was a lovely idea though.'

'So what should I do with the tickets then?'

They both thought about this.

'Why don't you go instead?' suggested Sylvie. 'I know – you

could take Celandine. You know how she loves to dance and she'd adore the ballet, especially *The Nutcracker*. Oh yes, do that!'

But Miranda really wanted Sylvie to have a break so they finally agreed that she'd take the little girl herself. Once she'd grown used to the idea Sylvie became very excited at the thought of going to the Outside World. Apart from a brief shopping trip last year with Yul she hadn't been out for ages. But Yul was very against the whole thing and tried his best to stop her from going.

'Give me one good reason why not.'

'I don't want you to go. I don't . . . I don't like the thought of you away from Stonewylde.'

'So I'm a prisoner here?'

'Don't be ridiculous, Sylvie. It would just be very strange for you to be away for the night.'

'What difference would it make? You sleep downstairs every night anyway.'

'Only because you don't want me anywhere near you!'

They glared at each other over the dinner table, the food forgotten. Now they'd reached the heart of the matter but both stepped back from the subject, unwilling to face it. Yul reached for the wine bottle and poured himself another glass, watching her face carefully. She took a deep breath.

'If you could explain to me why I can't take our daughter away for one night for a very special treat, I'd listen. But there's no reason other than your selfishness, so I'm sorry but we're going.'

'No you're not.'

'I think you'll find, Yul, that you can't forbid me to go. Who the hell do you think you are?'

'I'm your husband, a fact you seem to have forgotten in your efforts to cut me out of your life. Anyway, it wouldn't be fair. What about all the other children at Stonewylde? Don't you think they deserve a visit to a ballet too?'

'I'm sure they do and next time I'll arrange a party booking and take them all. But this time I'm going with Celandine and that's it.'

Sylvie's cheeks were flushed and her lips quivered with anger –

this was so typical of his high-handedness. He regarded her with equal anger – she was the one being selfish.

'Children don't leave Stonewylde until they're fourteen,' he said stubbornly.

'Then this will be the exception – and anyway, maybe they should. You're always on about how we need to mix more with the Outside World and encourage more interaction. You can't have it both ways. I shall tell Celandine in the morning and you'll see how much it'll mean to her. Think of that, if the idea upsets you so much – think of how she'll love it.'

'I don't want you to go, Sylvie.'

His eyes were flashing dangerously and under normal circumstances she'd have backed down as she always did and let him have his own way. But that, she thought, was the problem – he'd been getting his own way for far too long.

'I realise that but I'm still going.'

She stood up from the table and started to clear it, stacking the dishes on the trolley to wheel to the dumb waiter. The youngsters downstairs on work detail that night would deal with them. Yul rose too and took his glass and the bottle over to the sofa, where he flung himself down bad-temperedly. He watched her walking back and forth with the trolley and dishes. She was as gorgeous as ever, he thought moodily. Her silver hair swung down her back in a great silky swathe, almost brushing her buttocks. He surveyed those too, noticing how the material of her dress clung to every slim curve. He felt his desire for her growing by the second which only added to his fury. The clearing done, she stood before him watching as he drained his glass.

'Are you intending to stay up here for a while or will you be disappearing downstairs?'

He shrugged.

'Why not? Are you trying to banish me from this room as well as the bedroom?'

'Not at all! I'd love you to stay here for the evening because—'

'Well in that case I will. It makes a change to be wanted.'

'—because then I can go downstairs and help with the quilts. We're padding them tonight.'

He sprung up and took her by the shoulders, his eyes blazing into hers.

'What's the matter with you?' he shouted. 'Why are you treating me like this?'

'I'm not! But I want to help the other women and I can't leave the girls on their own.'

'For goddess' sake! You can rig up an intercom, the way I've suggested countless times. One of those baby alarm things they use in the Outside World.'

'No I can't! This is a huge house – even if I heard them crying it could take me ages to get up here and they'd be frightened in the meantime. You can't leave young children on their own like that. Have you any idea how often Bluebell wakes up with nightmares? How she cries and needs comforting straight away, not in five minutes' time when I've finally heard her and run half a mile to get here.'

'You've spoilt her,' he said coldly, dropping his hands and turning away. 'You shouldn't let her sleep in your ... our bed.'

'How do you know she does?' She thought then of the footsteps and shadows in the dark and grabbed his arm. 'Are you the one who comes into my room at night? Are you the one who sneaks about in the darkness and terrifies me?'

'What? What are you talking about?'

She let go of him, unsure of herself.

'Nothing – forget it.'

'Has someone being coming into our bedroom at night?'

'No! No, that's not what I meant.'

He stared at her and she looked away and wouldn't meet his eye. Maybe he'd been right all along – maybe there was somebody else. The thought, even though he knew it was irrational, stabbed him like a shard of glass.

'I know Bluebell sleeps with you, Sylvie, because she told me. She said now I've gone to live downstairs she looks after you at night when you cry in your sleep.'

Several times over the next few days Sylvie almost gave in and cancelled the trip. It was such hard work standing up to Yul. But Celandine would've been devastated so Sylvie stuck to her intentions and at last the time came to leave. She and the little girl stood in the stone-flagged entrance hall with their overnight bag waiting for the car to come round. They were being driven to the station where they'd catch the train to Bournemouth. Celandine was almost beside herself with excitement, hopping from foot to foot and pirouetting around on the parquet floor and old Wilton rug until she was dizzy. Sylvie peered out of the window wondering where the car had got to. It was freezing cold outside – a horrible grey January morning – and she didn't want to miss the train and have to hang about at the station waiting for another one.

She heard the sound of sobbing and then Yul appeared on the staircase carrying a distraught Bluebell in his arms.

'Oh Yul! I'd told her to wave from the window-seat upstairs with Granny Miranda. This'll only make it worse for her.'

He glared at her, still furious that she was going.

'She wanted one more kiss,' he said coldly. 'At least she got one earlier. You didn't even say goodbye to me.'

Sylvie took the distressed child from him and hugged her tightly, regarding Yul evenly over Bluebell's shoulder.

'You stormed out of the room, Yul. You weren't there to say goodbye to.'

They stared at each other as Bluebell's sobs turned to gulps and then stopped. Sylvie's gaze roamed over him, as ever struck by his sheer handsomeness; the mop of black curls falling over his angry face, his slanted deep-grey eyes hurt, his mouth hard.

'Put her down,' he commanded.

Frowning, she did so and Bluebell ran over to join Celandine by the window.

'Come here,' he said, and reluctantly she stepped forward. He reached and enfolded her in his arms, holding her tight and hard.

'I'm sorry, Sylvie,' he whispered in her ear. 'I'm really, really sorry. I don't know what's the matter with me – I guess I'm just jealous. I love you! I love you so much it hurts. I'll miss you terribly and that's the only reason I can't bear you going. But I do hope you have a lovely time – I just wish it were me you were going with.'

She felt a lump in her throat at his softly spoken words which she knew came straight from the heart. It took a lot for Yul to climb down like this. She suddenly wished she'd never suggested taking Celandine. Her mother had been right all along – a romantic night away together was just what she and her husband needed.

'I love you too, Yul. And I'll miss you.'

He started to kiss her gently on the lips, but with a rush of their old passion it developed into a kiss of major proportions, deep and long. Celandine and Bluebell rolled their eyes at each other – they were used to this. There was a beep outside and reluctantly Sylvie pulled away. Yul's eyes were blazing with want and need, his cheeks flushed and breathing rough.

'Just five minutes?' he pleaded huskily. 'Please?'

'We'll miss the train,' she smiled, stroking his hot cheek, her voice full of promise. 'But when I get back tomorrow ...'

Sylvie and Celandine sat in their plush seats listening to the orchestra tuning up. The little girl's eyes were brilliant with joy and exhilaration. She wore her best dress of fine, pale yellow linen, with her namesakes – bright yellow starry flowers – embroidered on the bodice, and the white satin ballet shoes they'd bought that afternoon in the shopping centre. Celandine clutched a programme and was torn between wanting to look at the photos of the dancers and gazing around the theatre in wonder. This was her first time away from Stonewylde in the Outside World and it was almost too much excitement for her to bear. The bell rang and she jumped in her seat like a frog.

'It's just to warn the people the ballet's starting soon,' explained Sylvie, smiling down at her. 'They won't let anyone in once the ballet's begun in case they disturb everyone and make too much noise finding their seats.'

Celandine nodded.

'We ought to do that when we have our dramas and dances and the Story Webs,' she said. 'People always come in late making too much noise.'

Sylvie laughed and smoothed her daughter's long silvery curls. This had been such a good idea and despite wishing Yul were here, they were both having a really lovely time. When they'd checked into the grand hotel earlier she'd found a huge bouquet of flowers waiting in their room. It was a really sweet gesture of Yul's and not one that she'd imagined him making. The little card had read *'To my beautiful Sylvie – I can't wait to carry on where we left off. See you soon xxx.'* She wished the four of them had come here together as a family, although Bluebell was probably still too young. Next year, she thought with pleasure.

The final bell rang and the lights started to dim; Celandine squeaked with excitement, fidgeting in her seat. Just then someone started to push down the row. The only empty seat was the one next to Sylvie and she took their coats off it and held them on her lap, waiting for the person to squeeze past her. There were whispered apologies and a *'ssh'* from behind as he plumped down into the vacant seat. Sylvie glanced at Celandine as the red velvet curtains with their gold tassels glided slowly open, smiling to see her open-mouthed rapture at the scene on the stage. The music exploded into such a great noise that the little girl jolted with fright, never having heard a full orchestra before. She gaped at the brightness of the costumes and the leaping feet of the dancers as they began the colourful opening scene of *The Nut-cracker.*

But Sylvie jerked violently when without warning, pushing under the coats that still lay on her lap, she felt a hand on her knee. She swung around in the darkness and in that heartbeat second realised that Yul must have engineered this and carefully planned such a surprise. She began to smile, amazed at his ingenuity, but when she saw the face next to hers her heart leapt in her chest with horror. She couldn't see him clearly in the semi-darkness but the heavy jaw was the same as was the well-cut blond hair. He smiled at her shock and squeezed her knee.

'We meet again!' he whispered.

Sylvie was speechless, her mouth dry. Her heart pounded like a piston and then she realised what he was doing and tried to push his hand away under the coats. He gripped her tightly.

'Don't make a silly fuss, Sylvie,' he whispered.

'Get your hand off me!' she spat, and was shushed by several people in front and behind. She glanced desperately at Celandine, who fortunately was totally engrossed in the vivid scene on stage. Sylvie tried again to push him off, wriggling her leg and shoving at his arm.

'Don't jig about, Sylvie, or you'll get me worked up. Just sit still like a good girl and watch the ballet. I'm not doing you any harm and I won't go any further – unless you want me to, of course.'

She sat in numbed misery throughout the first act. True to his word, Buzz kept his hand on her knee, his fingers like branding irons on the thin nylon of her stockings. Several times Sylvie thought she should just get up and whisk Celandine away, but every time she glanced at her daughter and saw her breathless joy she didn't have the heart to ruin such a perfect experience. She battled with herself over what to do for the best – cause a huge upset and disturbance or keep quiet until the first interval – and the longer she allowed the situation to continue, the more difficult it became to stop it. She felt Buzz turn to watch her on several occasions but she looked resolutely ahead, her cheeks burning and throat dry, determined to ignore him. She decided they'd leave during the first interval, not wanting to engage in any kind of skirmish with him.

As Tchaikovsky's wonderful music filled her head, Sylvie remembered her terrible recurring dream where Buzz assaulted her in the hospital bed as she lay strapped down and helpless. She felt ashamed to have dreamt such an awful thing and couldn't stop thinking about it with the man himself so close to her. She was acutely aware of everything about him – his bulk, for he was a big man, the smell of his expensive aftershave, the brush of the soft material of his suit against her arm. Her flesh crawled at his proximity and the feel of his hand on her leg, lying there so intimately but casually while her daughter sat beside her, innocent and unaware of what was going on.

The curtains swished across the stage and the lights went up.

'Celandine, we have—'

'Oh Mummy, it's the best, *best* thing I've ever seen! I love it so much! Thank you, thank you!'

'I know, darling, but—'

The hand clenched hard on her knee under the coats and Buzz leant across, forcing her to sit back in her seat.

'Hello! You must be Celandine. Delighted to meet you!'

'Hello,' replied the girl, looking puzzled. 'Who are you?'

'I'm an old friend of your mother's. Are you enjoying the ballet?'

'YES!' she gasped. 'Isn't it *beautiful*? I want to be a ballet dancer when I'm grown up and dance on my own in the Great Barn and up in the Circle for all the people to watch.'

'Spoken like a true Stonewylde child,' he said, smiling at her. 'I wish my little girl could be the same.'

'Do you have a little girl too?'

'Oh yes, she's a bit younger than you, almost five. Like your sister Bluebell.'

'You know about her?'

'I know everything about you all,' he replied. 'Every detail. And now, I was wondering if you'd like to go over to that lady there and buy us all a nice ice-cream?'

Sylvie tried to remonstrate but was smoothly over-ridden, and Celandine was despatched down the aisle clutching money.

'How did you know we'd be here?' she hissed as soon as the child had left. 'Why are you doing this? And if you don't remove your hand now I shall get up and leave! I mean it, Buzz.'

Chuckling, he slid his hand off her leg and kissed his own fingers where they'd touched her.

'Mmn! You didn't complain last time, did you Sylvie? Not when I came to visit you in hospital?'

Her mouth dropped open and the warm theatre spun crazily around her. Her vision went black around the edges and there was a fizzing noise in her ears. Buzz gently leaned her forward to bring her head down and she felt the blood rushing back. Sylvie struggled to sit up and remove his hands from her shoulders. She turned to face him, still white with shock.

'Was that real?' she whispered in horror. 'I thought it was a dream.'

'Oh yes, Sylvie, it was very real. I relive it every single night as I lie in bed with my wife, wishing that it were you and not her beside me. It was real alright – I remember the pattern on your nightdress, the restraints, the apricot-coloured roses by the bedside. I remember every single tiny detail. It was such a very ... intimate experience.'

She blushed scarlet and hung her head in misery. She felt horribly sick and couldn't believe this was really happening. How on earth had he known they'd be here in this theatre and in these very seats? She looked over towards the aisle suddenly remembering her daughter whom she should be looking after, not neglecting because of this unwelcome ghost from the past.

'Celandine's fine. Look, she's coming back now with the ice-creams. What a dear little girl she is.'

'Please, please leave, Buzz. This is meant to be her special treat and you're ruining it.'

'Hardly! She'll only feel it's ruined if you make a fuss and start complaining – that certainly would spoil it for her. So sit still and be quiet. You know you're enjoying it really.'

Celandine nipped along the row, so pretty in her lemon coloured dress with her white-blond curls flowing down her back, and handed out the tubs of ice-cream. She gave Buzz the change, looking at it in bemusement.

'I gave the lady the note for the ice-creams and she said I must take these as well, so here you are. Thank you very much. I've never had an ice-cream like this before. Only the frozen juicelollies we have in the summer when it's hot. I love these little cups and these tiny spoons tucked into the lids. Can we take the spoons home, Mum? Bluebell would love them. Isn't this wonderful? Oh!'

She tasted the cherry and vanilla ice-cream and closed her eyes in ecstasy, her excited chatter silenced for a moment.

'You're not eating yours, Mum. It's lovely! Do try some.'

'I'm not hungry, Celandine. You can have mine if you like. Sit down, now – the second act's about to start.'

'Not leaving then?' asked Buzz, his pale blue eyes gleaming.

'Of course we're not leaving!' retorted Celandine. 'There are still two more acts, Mum said, and I wouldn't leave for the world. This is the best thing I've ever done in my whole life!'

Buzz's lips stretched into a broad smile.

'One of my best things too,' he said smoothly, his hand sliding across as the lights dimmed.

Sylvie spent the night on the alien hotel bed in sleepless despair. Next to her Celandine slept soundly, exhausted from the multitude of new experiences she'd had that day, and Sylvie tried hard to keep her crying silent and still. Eventually she got up and sat by the window looking out over the city, wishing she'd never come here. Imagine if she'd come with Yul! She shook her head at the thought; the two men would've been at each other's throats within minutes, the thin veneer of civilisation dissolved by their long-standing mutual hatred. The ordeal she'd endured in the theatre, keeping quiet for the sake of her daughter who'd have been devastated to miss the ballet, was horrendous and sickening and she felt ashamed of herself for not putting a stop to it. Why had she let him do that?

But worse still – far worse – was the knowledge that her terrible dream was actually a memory. Buzz really had come into the nursing home and assaulted her whilst she lay drugged up to the eyeballs and strapped to her bed. How had it been allowed to happen? Had he talked his way in or maybe even bribed someone? And tonight – how had he known which seats they'd have? Or that they'd be there at all? And the hotel – how had Buzz known about that? For he'd deftly found them a taxi after the performance and told the driver where to take them.

It suddenly occurred to her – the bouquet must be from him too! She grabbed the card and re-read it in the orange sodium light glaring into the room, shuddering at the true meaning the message carried. And then she started thinking of all the implications of what had happened, both tonight and four years ago in her private hospital room. After all these years Buzz was still bent on revenge for his banishment. And somebody at Stonewylde, somebody who knew her well, had been feeding him with the details to do it. Somebody whose intent was absolutely malicious. The thought made her blood run cold.

On the train home the next day Sylvie sat silently staring out as the heathland of east Dorset turned to the hills of the west, the landscape changing gradually but dramatically. She'd been unable to eat the delicious buffet breakfast that Celandine had devoured so enthusiastically and was now feeling sick and exhausted. Her daughter chattered non-stop, reliving the whole experience – the shops, her new shoes, the hotel and meals, and most of all, the ballet. Sylvie realised she was fighting with a decision and, much as she hated it, would have to ask Celandine to lie. She'd toyed with the idea of telling Yul everything but knew he'd explode with rage and probably do something rash and dangerous.

'Darling, I know we don't normally keep secrets from each other in the family but I'm going to ask you to be very grown up and understand something important.'

Celandine fixed her with an intent stare, her eyes as deep grey as her father's and just as intelligent.

'It's about that man in the theatre, isn't it?'

'Yes! How did you know?'

'You didn't like him even though he was very polite and kind. I didn't realise at first as I was watching the ballet. But you wouldn't look at him and you were all stiff and quiet.'

'That's right and I didn't like him being there but I couldn't make a fuss in front of all those people and spoil the ballet. You see, he used to live at Stonewylde a long time ago, when Father and I were still young like Auntie Leveret is now. He and your father really hated each other and had a terrible fight. Magus, the man in charge at the time, banished him from Stonewylde. And that man has never forgiven your father and still blames him for it. So if Father knew he was there last night he'd be so, so cross I don't know what he'd do.'

'We don't want him any crosser than he already is, do we?' said Celandine. 'He's bad enough now, always grumpy and he doesn't even sleep in our rooms any more. Does he still love us, Mum?'

'Oh yes darling. But he's not very happy at the moment. So please don't mention anything about that man when we get back. I hate asking you to not tell the truth but I don't want your father to be angry and upset.'

'That's fine, Mum. I understand and I won't say anything at all about him. What's his name anyway?'

'Buzz, short for Buzzard.'

'I've never actually liked buzzards much – they're predators, you know.'

19

There was something wrong at the heart of Stonewylde, and like a malignant disease it pervaded everything around it. Everyone felt it growing and spreading, touching their lives in one way or another. Like a canker it was invisible to the eye, impossible to isolate and cure, but growing all the time and tainting everything with its poison.

As the Council of Elders sat in their circle, the discontent spilled out.

'I've never before encountered such rudeness and restlessness amongst the students,' said Miranda irritably. 'It's appalling the way they're behaving and it reminds me of the school where I taught in London. There's so little respect or deference towards adults and I really don't like it.'

'I warned everyone about this,' said Martin. 'I said if we let in all them Outside folk there'll only be trouble. They led our youngsters astray with their wild clothes and coarse dancing. I seen them myself and—'

'I seem to recall your son Swift enjoyed it as much as the next one,' snapped Yul. 'I don't think we can blame the poor behaviour at school on one small party, surely?'

'No, I don't think it's that either,' said Dawn. 'We've had problems in the Village School too – fighting and aggression on an unprecedented scale. The children are so defiant! Thanks for sorting out those boys I had to send up the other day, Miranda. I've never had to do that before.'

'No problem,' she smiled. 'Thank Tom, not me! He had them mucking out the stables all afternoon – that cured their cheekiness.'

'Aye,' Tom growled. 'Cocky little buggers the pair o' them. Would've had the strap in the old days, but . . .'

His voice tailed off as he glanced guiltily at Yul.

'Things haven't been too good in the Nursery either, have they, Rowan?' said Sylvie quickly. 'That awful chesty cold and cough that's been going around?'

Rowan nodded but failed to offer any more information.

'It's a nasty bug,' agreed Hazel. 'So many of the little ones are poorly with it. We don't normally keep them indoors whatever the weather, but with the high temperatures they've been experiencing I've had to advise mothers to keep them at home in their beds. I've got a whole ward full of older Stonewylders in the hospital wing, all with this dreadful chest infection. I really think the idea of re-homing some of our frailer folk in the Hall would be worth pursuing.'

Yul nodded at this.

'Hazel, maybe you and Martin can look into how we might organise this? Martin, you need to look at which rooms could be available for use and Hazel – you and Martin can then discuss what sort of renovations or changes would be needed to make the accommodation suitable for the elderly. Can I leave that with you two initially, and then bring me your report?'

Martin muttered under his breath and Yul's cheeks flushed.

'Sorry, Martin – did you say something?'

''Tis just I don't have time to be worrying about rooms for the old folk,' he grumbled. 'I'm too busy as it is.'

'I could get together with Hazel and—'

'No thank you, Sylvie – it needs to be someone who's involved with the accommodation and who knows all the issues. Cherry, maybe you could help?'

'Aye,' she nodded, 'I'll lend a hand but truth be told I'm rushed off my feet too. What you all been saying about the youngsters' rudeness – I'm feeling it too. None o' the work's done proper no more, not to my standards. But when I tell 'em off or point it out – phew, you should just hear the back-chat I get and the looks they give me!'

'I were only saying this the other day,' said Martin, shaking his silver head. 'No training – how can you expect youngsters like that to do a proper job? There's no discipline and no standards and I don't like it! In the old days we—'

'I'm sure things'll improve when the weather gets warmer,' said Sylvie. 'It's the Wolf Moon tomorrow night and then only a couple more weeks to Imbolc. It always feels brighter somehow after Imbolc.'

'Aye,' said Maizie, 'the birds know that spring's on its way after Imbolc. Let's hope our young folk buck up their ideas too. But I need to talk about the Village now.'

Yul sighed heavily, not liking to stop his own mother from speaking but wondering for the hundredth time why they even bothered with a formal agenda when everyone ignored it.

'If it's about the quotas —' Martin began ominously and Maizie nodded vigorously at this.

''Tis about the quotas, right enough. I'm sorry to speak out about this, Yul, because I understand what was said at Samhain about Stonewylde needing to sell things to make money. But it's gone too far.'

Several of the Council Elders nodded at this and murmured agreement.

'My goodwife said everyone's grumbling like a bunged-up wasps' nest,' said old Greenbough. 'Got to make this, got to make that ... she said folk are fed up being told they got to make stuff they used to make for the love of it. 'Tis no pleasure no more.'

'Aye, however many bits o' linen she embroiders, my goodwife says Harold's list says she must do more and more!' said Hart indignantly. 'Every blooming night she's at it, and my daughters and all, and they're right fed up.'

'Everyone's happy to do what they can,' said Maizie, 'and everyone gives o' their time willingly. But now 'tis beyond that – the loving care's gone out of it and 'tis done grudgingly. Though

I've tried to smooth things over many a time, when the folk complain about being told what to do by a jumped-up boy who—'

She stopped abruptly, seeing Harold's ears burning scarlet.

''Tis true there's grumbling and moaning in the Village,' agreed Cherry, 'but I'd rather see them lazy youngsters in the Hall having to work in the evenings making things for Harold than watching television every night and playing their horrible music so loud! And as for that there Internet ... all that fiddling about and clicking 'tis not right and I know I sound old-fashioned but I still don't like it! The one good thing about Harold's damn quotas is it keeps them work-shy lazy lot o' youngsters busy and ...'

Yul clapped his hands angrily to call the meeting to order, glaring around at everyone present. Clip was away with the fairies as usual but everyone else looked grim and discontented.

'Come, where's your loyalty to Stonewylde and the community?' he said sharply. 'You all know why we need these goods – that's not up for discussion today. As the Council Elders it's your responsibility to explain to the folk why we need everyone to work extra hard in the next few months, and to quell the complaining. Enough! Edward – what news on the agricultural front?'

'Very poor,' said Edward sadly. 'I wish I had good news to cheer everyone's hearts but I don't. One o' the big tractors broke its axle last week, as many of you've already heard, and that's affected the work badly. We're way behind and 'twill be at least another fortnight afore it's mended, 'cos the new parts have to be shipped over and all. We had a fire in a hayrick up at Tall Trees Farm and now one o' the grain silos over at Old Meadows Farm is riddled with rats. There's a right plague o' them and the all the grain there's tainted now. We put in traps and cats and old Feverfew bought his terriers in too, but them rats are everywhere.'

'Tell 'em about the cows too,' said Robin sadly.

'Aye, one o' the best dairy herds broke through a fence – don't ask me how 'cos I don't rightly know how the silly girls managed it. Several o' them drowned in the slurry pit afore we could get 'em out.'

Everyone nodded – this was common knowledge and had been very upsetting.

'Then there's that horrible mite that's got into our chickens – we never seen it afore and we called in a new vet now. We could do with our own vet, you know, Yul. We always had the knowledge how to deal with sicknesses – our cunning men could do most o' the healing and remedies for the livestock – but lately there's been some strange stuff going around. We found a whole batch o' prime wheat ready for milling has got the mildew and rotted away. And of course this damn cough and cold has got to many o' the workers too. I never seen so many grown men take to their beds afore, but 'tis a genuine ailment and they're as weak as kittens with it.'

Edward stopped, shaking his great head in dismay.

'I'm sorry, Yul, that it's all bad news. As Sylvie says, maybe after Imbolc things'll pick up a bit. I hope so – couldn't get much worse.'

The circle of people all sat quietly for a moment reflecting on Edward's words. Yul scratched around for something positive to raise everyone's spirits but couldn't think of anything – he felt horribly gloomy himself.

'Well, despite Martin's doom-mongering, the Outsiders' Dance was very successful,' he said eventually. 'I thought everyone did a splendid job of organising it and the feedback from the youngsters is very positive.'

'Aye, but how long till they're climbing the Boundary Walls to get into Stonewylde now?' said Martin hotly. 'How long till—?'

'I've already told Kestrel – who I must say, Edward, was a real credit to you that evening – that if everyone behaves themselves we'll have another Outsiders' Dance at the Midsummer Holiday.'

Martin shook his head, his thin face pinched with anger.

'I'm sorry, Martin, but you'll have to get used to this. Outsiders are going to be a part of Stonewylde in the future. Every young person here needs to look outside the community for their future partner and—'

'NEVER!' shouted Martin, and everyone stared at him in shock.

'We've reached a critical point genetically,' said Hazel quietly. 'I'm sorry that it goes against our old principles, but Stonewylders are simply too closely linked now. Reproduction could be dangerous, I'm afraid. I've spoken about this with Yul at great length and done a lot of research, and bottom line is that we need to bring in new blood.'

'I don't want to discuss this right now,' said Yul, 'because it's a tricky and sensitive issue and I appreciate feelings may run high. But be warned, everyone – Outsiders *will* be coming to Stonewylde. We've had to introduce the compulsory contraceptive implant to curb the population explosion. The next step may have to be some control over who partners whom within Stonewylde, after extensive DNA tests. The simplest solution to this problem is to encourage our young people to find partners from Outside – which is what I'm attempting to do.'

'On that note,' said Dawn, 'I'd like to bring up the question of Rainbow again. I replied to her e-mail after Samhain and said we were discussing her coming here on sabbatical, but at Imbolc it'll be three months since she sent her request and I wondered if anyone's had any more thoughts on it? She's still very keen to come and stay for a few months and, as I said, more than happy to pay. I thought perhaps if we're going to start bringing in Outsiders it wouldn't be such an issue allowing her to come?'

Once again Sylvie felt a sinking of her heart. Rainbow – and with her the memory of all those horrible Hallfolk. The terrible problem of Buzz had yet to be resolved and the thought struck Sylvie – was Rainbow's request part of a strategy of Buzz's to get back to Stonewylde? And worse – was Dawn in on it too?

'I don't want her coming here,' said Sylvie abruptly. 'I don't like the idea and we should say no to her.'

Everyone stared at her and Yul frowned.

'We need to discuss it first,' he said. 'You can't just make that decision, Sylvie.'

'Actually I think I can. I'm sure Clip will back me, if I really don't want her here. Won't you, Clip?'

He'd been almost completely silent during the meeting so far, listening to the arguments and complaints going back and forth and longing to be anywhere but here in this meeting. He was dreaming of freedom and had decided not to get involved in anything today. But looking up at his daughter, he saw a woman who was deeply distressed and wondered yet again if he were doing the right thing by leaving this year. He'd already set the ball rolling by making an appointment with a solicitor in the spring, about his will and signing over the estate. Now Sylvie's haunted wolf-grey eyes met his and he wondered if he should still go ahead. Tomorrow was the Wolf Moon, his special one, and maybe he'd be given an answer when he journeyed.

'Ultimately of course I'd back you, Sylvie. As everyone's aware, I'm planning to leave Stonewylde this year and signing over the inheritance to Sylvie. So—'

'I think you mean to *me* and Sylvie!' said Yul furiously. 'And this isn't a topic up for discussion today so let's leave it at that, shall we? And as for Rainbow—'

'I don't want her here!' Sylvie cried.

'As for Rainbow,' he continued, giving his wife such a venomous look that she visibly recoiled, 'we'll discuss her rationally and calmly at our meeting next month and not make illogical decisions without thinking things through properly first. Won't we, Sylvie?'

Sylvie and Yul were at the very heart of the general malcontent that pervaded Stonewylde. Their relationship was deteriorating steadily, the great reunion that Yul had hoped for after Sylvie's trip to Bournemouth in ashes around them. He'd been so hopeful after their kiss in the hall as she left, and had spent her night away in a fever of anticipation. He'd driven to the station the next day to meet them himself . . . but one look at her pale, drawn face as she got off the train had set his misgivings in motion. Although she insisted they'd had a wonderful time, he could see she was tired and depressed – with an edge of something else that he couldn't place.

The passionate night together he'd dreamt of was a complete failure. He'd been loving and patient with her and she'd tried so hard to respond to him with the joy and eagerness he longed for, but it was no good. She'd flinched as he touched her, no excuses able to negate that involuntary movement of denial. After a while he'd withdrawn from their mechanical love-making and stumbled downstairs in a haze of grief to spend yet another night on the sofa bed with a bottle of mead. Sylvie had cried herself to sleep, too wrung out to care whether Magus haunted her that night or not. Just knowing that Outside, Buzz was plotting and waiting for an opportunity to get his revenge on Yul and that inside somebody – she still had no idea who – had turned traitor, was more than she could cope with. The worst thing was that she felt unable to share any of it with Yul or indeed with anyone. She felt totally alone.

One of the few positive things in this difficult time was Magpie's rehabilitation. He'd moved into Marigold and Cherry's cottage tucked in by the kitchen gardens in the lee of the Hall and next door to Martin's home. The sisters were shocked when Magpie automatically took his food to a corner of the room and crouched on the floor to eat it messily with spoon and fingers. He didn't know how to wash himself, brush his hair or clean his teeth, and every night would make a nest of blankets on his bedroom floor. All his old clothing was burnt including the horrible coat, but he hated having to change his new clothing every day, feeling comfortable only in soiled and dirty clothes. The two women were patient and kind with the poor boy who'd been treated as an animal all his life, and their loving care was a revelation to him.

Leveret was a welcome visitor after school every day. She'd take his hand and smile at him, then look into his eyes and speak – and he appeared to respond. She was a strange one, the two women agreed, cocking her head as if she were listening to him, answering him when he hadn't said a word. She tried to explain that over their years of friendship they'd found a way to communicate with thoughts and images instead of words. That made no sense to them but they appreciated her help – she'd more influence on him than they could hope for and she was useful in interpreting his thoughts.

Magpie was in his final school year when non-academic pupils mostly engaged in practical training, so he spent every morning working in the huge kitchen gardens which he loved. Instructions must be precise and unambiguous – it was no good telling him to pick some sprouts; he'd meticulously pick every single one. He liked the protection of the high walls and knowing his cottage was tucked safely inside. One side of the kitchen wing overlooked the gardens with a wide door leading out to a cobbled courtyard, and Marigold kept a constant eye on him. Magpie would look up from his weeding or planting and glance towards the kitchens and there she'd be, smiling and waving. He still refused to touch meat and after Leveret's explanation, Marigold embraced his vegetarianism with enthusiasm. He put on weight steadily and grew taller almost by the day. At sixteen he was undernourished and lanky but at this rate he'd be fit and healthy by the summer.

Magpie's afternoons were spent in the art room with the new teacher David, and he was given his own corner and a range of materials to work with. Before, he'd sat silently during all his lessons and drawn tiny images which he refused to show, never listening to the teacher and taking no interest in what was being taught. But Magpie was a naturally gifted artist and now David was able to show him techniques and materials he'd never encountered before. Magpie loved to sketch, rapidly filling pads with beautiful pencil and charcoal drawings, but he also loved to paint and was introduced to oils, watercolours and acrylics. He quickly produced an amazing semi-abstract painting of a sky filled with swallows and David was very excited at his raw talent. Magpie's subject was always nature and he loved to roam outside with a sketch pad, gaining inspiration from what he observed with his artist's eye.

His evenings were spent in the cottage by the fire with Marigold and Cherry, looking at picture books from the Village school or listening to stories. Whilst they read to him he made tiny animal figures from a great lump of clay David had given him from the clay beds by the river. Although he'd attended school in the past, Magpie had shut himself off into his private world; he knew none of the fairy stories or folk tales that the children heard daily. He was enthralled now when one of the women read to him and showed him the pictures, and would get excited as the stories drew to their conclusion. The women reckoned he had the mind of a four-year-old and he was a pleasure to have around. His dancing turquoise eyes gave them all the reward they needed for their devotion to his welfare.

Leveret was delighted with his blossoming, her only remaining worry being Jay and the Death Cap mushroom. She'd stowed hers away safely in Mother Heggy's cottage, but thought often of Jay and his threat to Magpie. She told him constantly that if ever Jay gave him a mushroom he must never put it in his mouth – he must save it and give it to her. She was worried he'd remember her giving him mushrooms at Quarrycleave and think it was alright. She warned Marigold and Cherry too.

'Don't worry, we'll look out for Jay,' they assured her.

'He's never yet tried to come here looking for our Magpie,' added Cherry.

'I'd give him a piece of my mind if he did!' said Marigold, quivering with indignation at the very thought of it. 'I saw the marks on that poor boy's body and the way he can't eat meat and gets upset anywhere near rabbit. I can't believe any grandson o' mine could behave so cruel! I wish you'd let me tell Yul or Clip about what happened, Leveret.'

'Please Marigold, you know it would only make things difficult,' said Leveret with a frown. 'I wish the whole gang could be punished for what they did – they certainly deserve it – but my brothers were there and Mother would be so upset if I got them into trouble. And of course it's only my word against the whole gang's anyway – there's no evidence and Magpie can't tell them anything, can he? They'd all just deny it and then I'd get into trouble again for telling lies.'

'Aye, well, it makes my blood boil to think on it. That Jay is evil just like his father, and if my dear Lily's watching through the veil she must be bowing her head in shame. 'Tis all that Starling's doing, her and those two old sows.'

'The only visitor Magpie gets is Swift and he seems kind enough with the boy, but 'tis hard to say. Where Magpie don't talk you can't always tell if he's upset or not.'

'I'm not sure about Swift,' said Leveret, remembering Swift's friendliness to her at the Outsiders' Dance – unlike the other three bullies. 'Does he come over much?'

'Well Martin likes him to come by every evening for a visit and while he's there next door he sometimes pops in.'

'Aye but don't you worry, little maid. We'll make sure our Magpie's safe from all harm.'

The day before January's full moon, when the Council of Elders' meeting and the school day were over, Leveret received a message from Clip inviting her to visit his tower. After popping in to Magpie's cottage she made her way back into the Hall again through the kitchens and the maze of corridors and passages towards the tower. She'd never been inside before and was a little nervous, for it was drummed into every Stonewylde child that the shaman's tower was private.

Clip took her up to the solar on the top floor and brewed some rosehip tea, trying to put Leveret at ease. They sat talking, the fire burning in the grate at their feet, and Leveret stared around completely spell-bound. She was fascinated by his collection of objects from all over the world but most of all by the walls of books, some of them ancient and leather-bound, others very modern. There was an antique globe, a telescope and a computer; it was a juxtaposition of old and new, ancient and modern, and Clip told Leveret this was how she must see her learning.

'You need the old wisdom of Mother Heggy,' he said, gazing into the flames and toasting his toes in the heat. 'You need to know the old ways, the cunning ways and the healing power of plants. There's much to learn there, Leveret, and you must continue with your gathering when the growing season starts and make your notes and illustrations. You must also observe the seasons and watch how the goddess changes her robes during the year. See the creatures and the birds, how they behave, whether they're giving clues about events that have happened or are about to happen. You must learn so much about nature, including human nature – you don't have to be a crone to be the Wise Woman but you do need a great deal of wisdom and that's hard when you're so young.'

Leveret nodded at this. She'd wondered how it would work, being only a young girl.

'I wish there were someone to teach me all the herbal lore,' she said. 'There's only Old Violet and—'

'No!' said Clip forcefully. 'On no account get mixed up with her!'

'Never,' agreed Leveret. 'She's evil and after the things those three women put poor Magpie through, I'd never trust myself near her.'

'There are many old ones in the Village who know herbal tradition,' said Clip. 'Don't be afraid to ask. Seek them out and talk to them – I'm sure you'll find they'll be delighted to share their knowledge with you. You'll need to write it all up, create a—'

'A Book of Shadows!' she interrupted happily. 'Yes, Clip, that's exactly what I want to do, more than anything in the world! I want to record my remedies, my own discoveries and wisdom, and create a detailed encyclopaedia of plants, bark and fungi. I hadn't thought of asking some of the old ones for help but that's a really good plan.'

'Nobody will have old Mother Heggy's knowledge,' said Clip, 'nor even Old Violet's. But if you ask enough people you'll build up facts and information. There are plans afoot to move the most

314

elderly and frail people up to the Hall, which is a good idea, so why don't you get involved with that? Once they've made the move it'd be easy for you to sit regularly with a group of them and make notes, that sort of thing.'

'That's a brilliant idea!' she said.

'But Leveret, you need to do more than that,' said Clip frowning. 'I don't know – I have the strangest inkling . . . I think you're destined to be far greater than simply the Wise Woman, for all that's a special role.'

'Really? But that would be enough for me,' she said. 'Please don't suggest I study to become a "proper doctor" like Mother wants. I'm not leaving Stonewylde.'

'No . . . it's something else. You're a magical girl and you need to feed that part of you too. I want you to learn about other cultures and how they celebrate life. You must read and study the writings of wise people from all over the world and of every religion and spirituality.'

'Okay,' she said with a gulp. 'If you say so but it sounds like hard work.'

'From what I've heard you're very clever,' Clip said with a smile. 'You've the gift of a fine intellect and a good memory and you must make full use of those gifts. Because there's another role you need to fulfil at Stonewylde other than healing the sick.'

'Is there?'

Leveret began to prickle all over, knowing that she was stepping along a path of no return. Clip's words were leading her towards her destiny and he took her hand in his gently, gazing into her green eyes.

'I think you know this in your heart already, Leveret. You need to start your own inner journey towards spiritual knowledge from the divine. You must learn to be a shaman – to be Stonewylde's shaman. I think it's what you were born to do.'

As he spoke, Leveret felt a great rush of emotion and her eyes filled with tears. Hearing Clip spell it out in real words made all those bizarre feelings and longings she'd experienced her entire life suddenly slot into place. This was right – this was her destiny.

Leveret sat and cried quietly at the profound sense of relief and truth that Clip had released in her heart and soul.

They continued talking for some time and Leveret confessed to finding the whole idea very daunting – much more complicated than gathering a few herbs and casting a spell. Clip wished he'd started to teach her earlier because if he kept to his plan to leave by Samhain, she must learn very fast. He selected three books for her to begin the education she needed.

'You're going to be working incredibly hard,' he said. 'You mustn't let your conventional school-work suffer, and you need to be out in the open watching and learning, but you'll also need to do this extra, heavier study too.'

Leveret nodded, hoping she was up to it. There was also the problem of helping at home too – she didn't want to upset her mother and was keen to keep her promise to Yul and take on some of their mother's burden of work.

'There's also the other side, the most important side of course – journeying. I've always found it easiest at the Moon Fullness,' he explained. 'Others find different times better – but tomorrow's Moon Fullness is the Wolf Moon and it's very special to me. My spirit guide and totem is the silver wolf, you see. I think we should journey together and see if the time's right to begin the search for your spirit guide.'

'Oh Clip!' Leveret said excitedly. 'So you think I'm ready?'

'I think so, yes, and if I'm to be your mentor we need to make a start, especially as you probably won't make contact with your guide until you're a bit more practised. I believe you travelled during your experience with Fly Agaric, which was uncontrolled and dangerous for a novice like you. I want to train you to go on a safe journey where you're always in control and where you can ask questions and find answers – that's what being the shaman is all about. You're the interpreter for your community, the link between this reality and other realms. I've been a very poor shaman, I'm sorry to say, but you, Leveret – I think you'll be a truly great one.'

*

Clip wore a silver robe, well-worn but beautiful, decorated with a Native American wolf design. He gave Leveret a plain white robe of soft wool, as befitted a novice, and a bowl of sweet-smelling rose-water for bathing her hands and face. She'd fasted for the day as instructed, and now they sat in the solar in front of the fire. It was still only late afternoon but the sun set very early at this time of year. They sat on comfortable cushions on a round woven rug of many colours that she hadn't seen here yesterday. In the middle was a dish of herbs, a small drum, and a black cloth covering something. Leveret felt nervous but excited and Clip smiled at her, patting her hand comfortingly.

'First,' he said softly, 'we'll sit and empty our minds, focusing on nothing at all. I shall play my gongs to help this process – the waves of sound will help your mind to clear itself of everything that tries to crowd in and allow your mind's eye to open. When we're both peaceful and calm – for playing the gongs is as spiritually uplifting as listening to them – we'll go out on the roof and watch the light fade from the sky and the stars and moon appear. Then when we feel ready we'll come back in here and begin our journey. Is there anything you wish to ask before we start?'

'Yes – why are we in here and not up in the Dolmen or somewhere sacred?'

'Because it's too cold out there for you, Leveret. Wolf Moon is cold and icy and it takes years of experience to be able to ignore your body's clamouring for warmth and leave it behind. Years of self-discipline and self-denial and even then it can be difficult. As soon as the weather warms we'll journey outside, but not now.'

He was silent for a while, then rose and stood behind her where the gongs hung on their stands like golden suns. Very softly, very slowly, Clip began to beat the bronze discs into quivering, magical life.

'Stare into the flames,' he instructed, 'and empty your mind of everything but this glorious sensation of sound.'

Leveret looked into the crackling heart of the fire, mesmeric in its continuous flickering dance, and let the beautiful dome of resonance and reverberation engulf her. Thoughts came rushing in but she gently pushed them away; they sneaked up again but she sent them back, and slowly she found her mind full of cloudy greyness that absorbed the dancing flames and the heartbeat of the shimmering gongs. Her breathing slowed right down and became as soft as the ebb and flow of gentle waves over shingle.

The quivering music slowed, quietened and stopped, the final shred chasing around the circular room until the air was free from vibration. Clip came over and took her hand, helping her up. He fastened a thick woollen cloak around her, an embroidered Stonewylde felt hat on her head, and a pair of warm mittens on her hands. Leveret felt calm and dreamy, her spirit awakened by the voices of the magical gongs, though perfectly conscious of everything around her. Clip wrapped himself in a dark cloak and led her out through the oak door onto the roof. The cold air hit her skin like an icy flannel and she was pleased for the warm clothing.

They stood looking to the south-west where the pale blue sky was striped with golden shreds as the sun disappeared. Leveret breathed deeply and felt so very peaceful. A flock of birds flew overhead and she heard a cow lowing in the distance. She stood perfectly still as gradually the light dissolved from the skies and the first star began to twinkle, faintly at first, then getting brighter and brighter as more stars appeared. They turned towards the north-east and the darker horizon and watched silently, in deep reverie, until eventually a deep gold moon started to rise. It was streaked with low cloud that wisped around its perfect beauty; slowly it emerged from its place of slumber, slowly it rose in the sky as a great golden orb.

Leveret thought then of wolves, of black pointed noses and silver eyes, the streaking of grey and silver in the thick coat of fur. She felt wolf all around her as the moon rose, losing its golden glitter and becoming yellow and then more subtly white. There were soft grey shadows on its face and she thought again of wolf, a nose pointed up to the sky, a throat opening and the mouth letting out a long note of celebration. She breathed in the

Wolf Moon magic, feeling the cold prickling around her just as the stars prickled the velvet sky.

Clip's hand slipped into her mittened one and he led her back into the warm, glowing solar, where they removed their outer clothing and sat once again on cushions on the woven rug. He picked up a handful of the herbs and tossed them into the flames – they released a powerful aromatic scent and the fire crackled blue and green. Leveret breathed deeply of the heady smoke, feeling her head become lighter. Her cheeks and fingers tingled with the heat, throbbed with it, and she felt strange. Clip began to drum very softly an insistent, summoning rhythm.

'Remove the cloth,' he said, 'and take up the ball. Feel it and look deep into its heart.'

The ball was of smooth polished crystal and danced with firelight under her hands.

'We're emptying our minds once more and seeing only the brightness within. Everything is touched with soft radiance and we see only brightness and light.'

She felt the light inside her head softly glowing and the smoothness of the crystal ball under her palms was soothing. Clip continued to drum for some time until her breathing slowed right down and the drum beat entered her soul, became part of her being.

'We're waiting now in this place of limbo, in this liminal space, for our guides to appear. Our guides are our friends and they'll look after us as we journey, always bringing us back safely. If we feel frightened or threatened they'll bring us back to this place of brightness. They'll always be by our sides as we travel and they'll protect us.'

It was peaceful waiting patiently for the guides, who were coming but from a distance and couldn't yet be seen.

'Now I see my guide. The silver wolf slinks into the brightness and his eyes are all-knowing as he stands and waits. Maybe your guide will appear, but probably not this time and we don't yet know what form it'll take. We must wait calmly and perhaps get a glimpse, if the time is right. If not, we'll both travel with my wolf.'

Leveret couldn't see the wolf or anything else. Nothing was coming – it was just warm and bright.

Suddenly there was a great black presence. It crowded out the brightness with its blue-blackness, its glossiness, its quills and barbs. There was a great pointed beak and a knowing eye and then it shrank into clear focus – a great crow! No – it was a raven! Leveret smiled and her heart welcomed her raven, her spirit guide. The massive bird bowed its head and then she saw the wolf too, silver and lithe, standing next to her raven. Together the wolf and the raven moved forward into the brightness and then she saw two shadowy figures following – herself and Clip, insubstantial compared to their vibrant guides. Their steps were steady as they walked towards the source of the radiance.

And then they were in a wood – all around them the birds sang and squirrels leapt from branch to branch. It was green and fresh, every plant and tree sparkling with crystal droplets of dew. There was an archway amongst the trees made of boughs that arced together over-head. Feathers hung from the archway and the wolf and raven brushed past them through the gap.

'Only follow if you will,' said the raven, although its beak didn't move and the voice was soft but sweet.

The shadowy Clip took Leveret's hand and together they stooped and went through the archway into the realm of dreams.

They journeyed far in that strange place and Leveret saw things which amazed her. It was a wondrous place, not frightening in the least, but so different from the world of reality. They saw sights and tasted scents that were so far removed from the everyday as to be magical. They journeyed far but then it was time to return, and up ahead they saw the archway with its hanging feathers. By the curved boughs the wolf and raven paused. The raven grew large again, filling her vision with its blue-black glossiness.

'You may ask one question,' it said gently. 'But I may be unable to answer and you may be unsatisfied. Ask me now.'

Leveret thought swiftly, for time was trickling rapidly out through the arch.

'Will Mother Heggy return to guide me in the world of reality?'

The raven cocked its head.

'She cannot return who's not truly departed. She's waited long for you and she's ready – it was you who wasn't ready.'

They bent and passed again under the arch into the place of brightness. All around was radiance but gradually it dimmed into greyness, and then the fire appeared and the shadows of the room were all around. The flames had died down to a deep red glow illuminating Clip's smiling, joyful face.

'I knew you were the special, magical one, Little Hare,' he said softly. 'I felt it in my bones. You're here to succeed me and now I know that the spirit of Stonewylde will be in safe hands.'

20

On the Village Green, the young men were practising their marksmanship with the bow. Several groups had gathered in the bright sunlight and a gaggle of girls stood around watching and making a lot of noise. The scene was quite idyllic with the Village Green surrounded by mature trees, mostly skeletal in mid-winter, but displaying their different textures and colours of bark in the low winter sun. The Great Barn stood behind them like a massive mother, golden and ancient, a haven and gathering place for all. The smaller building, the Jack in the Green, nestled close by and all the cottages clustered nearby like chicks around a hen. Smoke trickled from most chimneys promising cosiness inside and something tasty bubbling on the range. A woman walked by with two small children in tow, all wrapped up warmly in bright woollen jackets and thick felt hats. A youth pulled along a great trolley of logs and a man clattered by on a horse, whilst a crowd of children played on the cobbled street in the wide area outside the Barn, chasing each other and laughing.

The targets had been set up at the far end of the ancient clearing in front of the trees, just as they'd been for centuries and centuries – great woven circles of thick straw with a small star made of card in the centre marking the bullseye. The air was full of the sounds of arrows being released from the powerful bows, zinging through the sunlight to thwack into the straw. Each youth had a quiver on his back, a special belt with a socket for the arrow to be loaded, and a leather glove to protect his firing hand. Edward was over-seeing the practice, signalling when the latest volley of shots had been completed and the excited boys could run to their group's target to see the evidence of their marksmanship. Stars that had been pierced were proudly removed and labelled as proof of expertise, although there were few of these for the central star was small and difficult to hit.

Kestrel was in his element. He was a strong archer, very accurate, and at eighteen this was his final year to compete for the honour of being the Archer of Imbolc. He'd done it last year and fully intended to win again this year. He was an almost archetypal figure, tall and strongly built, handsome and youthful. His powerful arms pulled back the string and made an extended line with his tilted jaw. His back rippled with sinew and muscle; legs apart and slim hips twisted, his chest opened up when he aimed and his blue eyes held the gleam of victory. He loved the attention of the girls watching and the admiration of the other boys. He wasn't showing off – he knew he was the best there and was merely enjoying his position of supremacy.

Not all the youths took part as some were no good at archery and others just not interested. Sweyn and Gefrin were two such as this, but they stood with Kestrel's group watching and praising him. Jay and Swift were taking part, both being reasonably adept if not in Kestrel's league. Jay found failure difficult; if his arrow missed the straw target altogether he'd become angry and abusive and find some excuse for missing.

Swift was a better sportsman and accepted his poor shots with equanimity even though success mattered to him. He was very aware of the crowd of girls hanging around his archery group and knew they must find Jay's aggressive bluster very trying. So Swift only laughed if he missed, flicking his fringe and looking sideways at the girls, and going for their sympathy. Kestrel caught one such exchange and thought again that he must watch Swift, who was becoming a bit too popular for his liking.

'Stop showing off, Swift!' he said loudly. 'And where's Sorrel anyway? You shouldn't be making up to all these girls, not when you're walking with someone. These little beauties are all mine, aren't you, girls?'

There was much giggling and wriggling at this, all eyes back on Kestrel again which was how he liked it. In fact most of the girls watching had been his at one time or another and they all knew it. Swift gave him a long look, his grey-blue eyes slightly narrowed.

'Sorrel's helping her mother set up the lunch for us,' he replied. 'And I'm not walking with her – we may do in the future but not at the moment.'

'Oh go on, Swift!' said one of the girls. 'You know she's mad about you and you went with her at Yule for your Rite of Adulthood. She thinks you want to walk with her.'

'I might do. I'm thinking about it,' he replied, smiling charmingly.

'You should,' said Kestrel. 'She's good and I should know – broke her in myself.'

'Kes!' shrieked the girls.

Swift eyed him carefully then pulled an arrow from his quiver, nocking the fletching into the bowstring.

'So you did,' he said evenly. 'And what a good job you made of it.'

'Naturally,' laughed Kestrel. 'It's what I do best, isn't it, girls?'

Jay scowled at the pair of them; no girls were interested in him at all. He was too belligerent and his clumsy, arrogant overtures made girls run off in alarm. He'd had slightly more success at college where he wasn't so well known but Stonewylde girls were very wary of him, particularly with his family history.

The practice was drawing to a close and the boys had been given ten minutes' notice of lunch in the Barn; after that would come the actual competition to determine the Archer. The youngest boys there, at fourteen, knew they wouldn't be picked but it was good to practise now to improve their chances when they were older. Just to get one arrow in the star was a great achievement and the little cards were pinned on display in the Barn until after Imbolc for all to see. The group of girls went off to help in the Barn and Edward blew the whistle for the archers to stop firing and go to collect all their arrows, making sure their quivers were full for the competition later.

As they strolled towards the targets Swift regaled them with the latest news of Magpie.

'He was screaming this morning, Father said – making that awful screeching noise. Apparently he'd trodden on a dead rabbit outside the front door when he went out.'

Jay roared with laughter, his bullet head turning almost crimson with mirth.

'I knew that would set the bugger off!' he shouted with glee.

'You put it there?' asked Gefrin. 'That was a good idea.'

'Yeah, I caught six of 'em yesterday, too much for even my fat Auntie Starling to eat. So I took one round last night for the half-wit and left it by his door step. I knew it would get him going.'

'Be careful though,' warned Swift. 'Cherry and Marigold are on the look-out for you anyway.'

'Do you think I care? I like winding 'em up, stupid old bags.'

'Yes but they'll tell my father and then he'll have to have a go at you.'

'So?' said Jay belligerently. 'What's he going to do?'

'Well if you won't take it from him, he'll probably tell Yul.'

'And? What'll Yul do – banish me? I don't think so!'

Swift shrugged. He'd warned Jay – he couldn't do anymore. They'd reached the target and Jay began to pull his arrows from the straw boss.

'Looks like you missed the star again,' teased Kestrel, pulling a couple from the ground that had missed the straw target altogether.

'Yeah, it's these arrows – they're shit.'

Kestrel laughed. 'My father gave me these at my Rite of Adulthood,' he said, tapping the quiver on his back.

'Well I ain't got a father, have I? Some bugger had him killed off – some bugger set a crow on *my* father!'

His face darkened with anger and his eyes bulged, glaring at them all.

'Too bad, isn't it?' nodded Sweyn in sympathy. 'Mine choked on a bit o' cake and never got over it. Had a stroke, he did.'

'At least that were an accident – mine wasn't. One day I'll get my revenge. My father didn't deserve to die.'

'I thought he'd killed your mother?' said Swift mildly. Jay turned on him, looking for someone on whom to vent his aggression.

'He didn't mean to! My Granny Vetchling said it were my mother's own fault. She went on and on at him, nagging and whining all the time until one night he snapped and tried to shut her up. Remember she was that cow Marigold's daughter and we all know how *she* goes on. That's why the old Magus brought him back, Old Violet said, 'cos he knew my father were innocent. Alright?'

'Yeah, of course,' said Swift. 'I'm sure you're right.'

'Too right I'm right. So don't say anything against my father again!'

'I wasn't.'

'Yes you—'

'Enough!' said Kestrel. 'For goddess' sake, let's talk about something else. The Maiden, for instance – have they picked her yet? Anyone know who it's going to be?'

They all shook their heads. Every year a girl was chosen for the Imbolc ceremony as it was the festival of the Maiden, celebrating new growth, purity and femininity. The girl had to be under sixteen and would partner the Archer in the ceremonies. All the little girls of Stonewylde took part too, and each one dreamed of one day being chosen to be Bright Maiden.

'I reckon it'll be Tansy,' said Sweyn.

'Or Honey.'

'No,' said Kestrel. 'Not Honey – it's her Rite of Adulthood at the ceremony. She told me herself and we all know why.'

'Maybe Bryony?' suggested Jay. 'She's fifteen.'

'What about Leveret?' said Swift.

'*Her?*' laughed Sweyn.

'She'll be fifteen too, won't she? It could be her.'

'They wouldn't choose a scrawny little bitch like her,' sneered Gefrin. 'No, I think Bryony too.'

'It could be Leveret,' said Kestrel speculatively. 'I wouldn't be surprised.'

'Goddess, can you imagine it?' groaned Sweyn. 'She'd embarrass us so much, the stupid little cow. I don't think it'll be her – it's always someone really pretty.'

'She is really pretty,' said Swift. 'I got the shock of my life at the Outsiders' Dance when I saw her.'

'She's not pretty!' scoffed Jay. 'She were just tarted up, that's all. It made me want to slap her, showing off to everyone like that. I was itching to bring her back down to earth with a thump. But I hear you were interested, Kes?'

He nodded and shrugged. 'Yeah, I was surprised at the difference. She's pretty in a different way to all the others. But no big deal – she's just another unripe apple at the moment. This time next year and I'll consider her of course.'

'Eugh!' cried Gefrin. 'Not even you would have *her*, surely? That's horrible!'

Kestrel laughed at this reaction and Swift smiled at her brother's naivety. He was sure they'd choose Leveret as the Maiden – she'd be perfect.

While the boys and men down at the Village Green competed to be named the Archer, Maizie and Miranda went together to see Sylvie to discuss the forthcoming ceremony and choose the Bright Maiden. They found her sitting all alone in the huge room in the window seat staring out over the trees, a piece of embroidery for the quota untouched on her lap. She regarded the two women with weary eyes, her face pale and drawn. She'd had a bad night with Bluebell who'd woken screaming that someone was standing by her bed watching her. Terrified, Sylvie had turned on the lights to banish the shadows, which had then woken Celandine. They'd all three moved into the great four-poster for the rest of the night but sleep had eluded Sylvie. She was too frightened to relax and then she'd started worrying about the business with Buzz. By morning she was thoroughly exhausted and irritable.

Now, with the girls out of the way in the Nursery, she was trying to do some work but failing miserably as she just couldn't concentrate. She hadn't seen Yul at all since dinner the night before when they'd barely spoken, and he rarely ate breakfast with them anymore. When her mother and mother-in-law turned together up her heart sank – the last thing she wanted today was to face these two. But it had to be done so the three women sat around the table in the grand apartments and began to discuss suitable girls. There were several of the right age to choose from and Maizie was pleased when Sylvie mentioned Leveret. Miranda, however, frowned at this.

'But she's been dreadful recently, hasn't she?'

'No, 'tis all sorted out,' said Maizie comfortably. 'She's as good as a gosling now.'

'But Yul was furious with her.'

What Miranda was really remembering was the rude flick gesture Leveret had made at her.

'Well 'tis all fine now.'

Maizie was hoping desperately that her daughter would be chosen but couldn't be seen to favour her – it would've been an abuse of her position.

'I think Leveret would be a good choice,' said Sylvie warmly, remembering the poor girl's sadness and the way her daughters had discovered a sweet side to her. This may be just what was needed to boost her self-esteem.

'But what about ... you know ... about the mushrooms at Quarrycleave?' asked Maizie.

'That's all in the past now, gone and forgotten,' said Sylvie.

'But surely it sends the wrong message if we pick her. Do something silly like that and you'll get chosen as Maiden,' said Miranda, frowning. She was anxious not to offend Maizie and this was a delicate matter, but she had genuine concerns about choosing Leveret.

'I think the fact she was so unhappy as to even contemplate taking her own life, along with that strange boy Magpie, is all the more reason to choose her,' said Sylvie. Maizie glanced at her gratefully, surprised at her support.

'I still think it's giving other girls the wrong idea – bad behaviour rewarded.'

'Hardly bad – more like desperate,' said Sylvie. 'Poor Leveret has been through a terrible experience and this would be a good way to make her feel valued in the community. I choose Leveret.'

Miranda sighed and looked at Maizie questioningly.

'Well, o' course I'd love her to be Maiden but I can't favour her.'

'Fair enough – we'll have Leveret then, if you both think she's the best choice. You know Kestrel's the Archer again?'

'He's a fine young man, Edward's son,' said Maizie, beaming with joy. 'He'll be a good partner for Leveret. The ceremony will be lovely.'

'And Celandine has a special solo part in the dance,' said Sylvie, smiling at the memory of her daughter's excitement and dedication to making her performance perfect. 'Apparently all the women in the Nursery were so impressed by her dancing that Rowan arranged it specially, which was kind of her.'

'Goddess bless her, dear little soul! 'Twill be a very special Imbolc for us mothers, won't it? Just a shame Rufus isn't quite old enough to be Archer yet. Well, I'd better get sewing then,' said Maizie. 'My girl must look beautiful. I'll go down to the stores now and get some o' the best white linen. She were going to wear last year's Imbolc dress with a little alteration but if she's to be Maiden I need to make her a new outfit altogether. Harold's blooming quotas will have to wait.'

Sweyn, Gefrin and Jay were not impressed that Leveret had been chosen as the Maiden. They discussed it one evening in the pub when Jay had returned from college, Gefrin had come back from the fields and Sweyn had finished his work in the tannery.

'I'm on my way to visit the three biddies,' said Jay. 'I'm dying for a smoke. Now that bastard cousin of mine has moved out I have to chop firewood for them every night and get the water too. It's no bloody joke, I can tell you.'

'We still do it for our mother,' said Sweyn.

'Yeah, well there are two of you. And anyway, Magpie's always done all the heavy work – it's all the thick git's capable of. Why should I have to start doing it? Come and give me a hand, would you? I'll get 'em to give you a pipe too.'

The brothers agreed and they left the pub and walked along the lane towards the dirty cottage down at the end.

'What about your sister being the Maiden then?'

'Stupid bloody choice!' muttered Sweyn. 'Goddess knew why they chose *her* – she's going to be so cocky about it.'

'Then we need to put her in her place,' said Jay. 'We'll have to plan something good and we never did follow through after Yule, did we? She must think she got away with it.'

'What shall we do?' asked Gefrin excitedly. 'Something terrible – something that'll really show her up.'

'But no one must guess it's us,' said Sweyn, ever mindful of Maizie.

'Let's ask the crones,' suggested Jay. 'They'll think of something awful.'

The two old women cackled with glee at being asked to help and put their evil minds to the task of finding something nasty for Maizie's daughter. Having finished their supper they were sitting smoking their pipes when the boys arrived, whilst Starling finished off the day's bread with a big bowl of gravy. Everyone was entitled to fresh bread daily and she liked to finish the loaves every evening, along with the milk and anything else left over. Food wasn't rationed in any way and she could collect as much as she wanted from the stores each day. She sat like a great hog bent over the bowl on her lap, a huge hunk of bread clutched in her fat hand, the gravy greasing her lips and chin as she dunked and ate, dunked and ate. Sweyn and Gefrin watched her in fascination for a while, finding the sight of such compulsive eating quite compelling. Finally it was all gone and she sat back replete. She sighed with contentment and let out a long and loud burp. Gefrin in particular found this very amusing.

'Tis Imbolc – the wells and springs are sacred to the Maiden. There's something there,' said Old Violet.

'Aye, sister, something there alright,' piped Vetchling with her reedy voice. 'Put her down the well! That'd be a fine to-do – Maiden in the well!'

'It's a bit public,' said Sweyn. 'It has to be secret so nobody knows we did it.'

'Don't see why! Meddling girl – 'twas her fault they took the boy away.'

'Aye, all her fault. She took him up Quarrycleave to poison him and now they're making her Maiden! 'Tis all her fault and we're going to set her straight. Meddling, that's what she is.'

'Why don't you poison her then?' suggested Starling, reaching for her pipe now that her belly was finally full. She shifted her huge bulk to pass wind, like a low rumble of thunder. 'She wanted poison so let's give her poison.'

'We can't kill her!' said Gefrin, balking at going that far. 'We just want to hurt her or do something nasty to upset her.'

'Poison don't have to kill,' mused Old Violet. 'Poison can just make you feel like your guts are turning inside out, or make your mind wander and stray. 'Tis a good idea, Starling. I'll think on it, lads. Who wants a pipe now?'

They sat in cosy companionship, the three women in their rocking chairs and the boys on pieces of log that served as stools. Jay drew on his pipe with expertise, savouring the heady experience that he thought of with longing most afternoons. It was worth keeping in with the crones just for this – nobody else at Stonewylde mixed a pipe like they did. Sweyn and Gefrin coughed and spluttered on the strange mixture of dried herbs and plant material that Vetchling had tamped into the bowls of the clay pipes, but then it started to take effect and they relaxed into a haze of gratification. Starling sent Jay to get the cider from the kitchen and they all indulged in this pleasure too, their tankards being topped up at regular intervals.

'I remember your father,' mused Vetchling, looking at the two visitors in their midst.

'Aye, I remember Alwyn,' added Violet. 'A fine figure of a man he were.'

'A real man – you're like him,' said Starling, regarding Sweyn's heavy, flushed face.

'Terrible what happened to him,' said Violet, sucking on her pipe. 'He were cut down in his prime like corn not ready for the harvesting.'

'Aye, sister, cut off afore his time and we know who's doing that was.'

'Aye, we know. We know 'twere dark work afoot there.'

'What do you mean?' asked Gefrin, his head reeling with the smoke and alcohol.

'He choked,' added Sweyn, equally addled. 'Our father choked and had some sort of stroke, Mother said. He held on for months but he never got his health back and he were a Death Dancer at Samhain that year.'

The crones cackled at this.

'Aye, my good lads, he choked alright. But there were dark work afoot.'

'Aye, meddling and dark work and poor Alwyn were cut down before his time.'

'Are you saying it weren't an accident? Someone killed him?'

The old women looked at each other, their toothless mouths puckered in their attempts at a smile.

'Aye – someone hexed him. And apart from us there were only one other it could've been,' said Starling, regarding them over the mound of her stomach spread hugely before her as she relaxed back in her chair.

'Who?' cried Gefrin. 'Who hexed him?'

'Old Mother Heggy!' said Jay. 'Who else?'

'And we know why, don't we, sister?'

'Aye, we know why. Alwyn did a good job on the bastard in his midst. Kept him in his place, kept him down where he belonged.'

'You mean Yul?'

The crones spat into the fire in unison.

'Aye, we mean him. Alwyn treated the boy hard, as he deserved. Whipped him and beat him regular. What man wouldn't, forced like a cuckold to raise another's as his own?'

'But then that bitch Heggy had to meddle, her and her scrying and her prophecies. She were the one who hexed your father.'

'Aye, sister, and she didn't work alone. She got the dark-haired one to aid her, do her bidding. He were the one who carried out her hex.'

'I don't understand! You mean Yul did it? Yul killed our father?'

'Yul didn't kill him,' said Starling. 'But he did Heggy's bidding and made it happen. 'Twas down to him the hex worked.'

Sweyn jumped up and almost toppled into the fire. He stood there swaying, huge and sweating, his fists clenching and unclenching. Starling regarded him admiringly. He was as fine a figure as his father had been – pity he was so young.

'I'll kill him!' the boy cried. 'I'll avenge my father!'

'And me!' said Gefrin, his rat face twisted with bitterness. 'All these years we thought it were an accident!'

''Twas no accident, be assured,' muttered Old Violet. 'But steady, lads – not so hasty.'

'No, not so hasty. It must be done right. There's other things to be thought of.'

'You won't succeed if you rush in,' said Starling. 'You must listen to the old ones, lads. Bide your time and be patient.'

''Tis not yet time,' crooned Old Violet. 'But it will be soon, and then we'll be ready. The dark-haired one will be cut down and the silver one put in his rightful place.'

'Aye, sister. The Magus is silver, not dark. We know the ways, we know how it should be.'

'Why can't you just hex him now?' asked Jay. 'Why have you let him rule us for so long?'

Old Violet spat into the fire again, the hiss making Gefrin jump.

'He's shielded. There's protection, with his love binding him safe and making a ring around him. Him and that Outsider girl – pah! She may be Clip's daughter but she don't belong here. We know.'

'Aye, we know. The darkness and the brightness were strong together but there's trouble brewing, dark trouble enough to break the shield.'

The crones cackled in unholy unison.

'You lads be ready, and we'll help you with that sister o' yours.'

'Aye, we'll help for she too must be broken. We know of her, we been watching as she's grown. Another cuckoo in the nest but we're ready for her. She'll be no match for us.'

'Nay, no match for us. We're the old ones, the wise ones, and we know the ways. She knows nothing yet nor ever will.'

They cackled again and offered the boys another pipe.

'I'm not happy about the choice of Maiden,' said Yul, watching his wife across the table. They were eating dinner, candles and silver on the white cloth, food on the plates. Their daughters slept further down the wing and they were alone. This had become the only time of the day when they had any real contact and even this was fraught with uneasiness. Sylvie looked up at him, the candlelight flickering on his honed face and casting shadows under his cheekbones and brow. His deep grey eyes gleamed as they regarded her. He lifted his wine glass and drank the ruby liquid.

'The choice of Bright Maiden is for the women to decide,' she said neutrally, trying to keep annoyance from her voice. 'Maizie, my mother and I chose Leveret together. It's not something the magus gets involved with – you know that, Yul.'

'Nevertheless, you should've consulted me. She's my sister and you know the trouble she's been in recently. It's not right that she should be given this honour when she doesn't deserve it.'

'That's what my mother said.'

'Ah, so it wasn't unanimous then? Of course Mother would push for Leveret – she's running around after that girl as if nothing's happened, desperate to keep her happy and it makes me angry to see it. I might've known my mother would drag you along with what she wanted. You need to learn to stand up to people and stop being so soft all the time.'

'How dare you!' cried Sylvie, feeling cold fury rising inside her. 'I make my own decisions, as you well know! Actually it was *my* idea to choose Leveret.'

The twitch of his mouth showed his disbelief.

'And don't you get any ideas about changing our choice! We've announced it now and it can't be altered. Leveret will be a lovely Maiden.'

'It was very ill-considered, if it really was your choice and not something you'd been manipulated into. You need to think these things through carefully, Sylvie, and not make poor decisions that only reflect badly on you.'

She glared at him, unable to belief his arrogance. He stared back coldly, watching the emotions playing on her face. He was pleased to have finally penetrated the shell she now wore, keeping him at bay from her inner as well as her outer self. Maybe if he could break it down altogether they could start again, with no secrets or hidden agenda. He knew she was keeping something from him but had no idea what it was.

Yul poured himself some more wine which he savoured as he sat watching her across the table. He'd finished his dinner but she'd barely touched hers. She was getting thinner again and he didn't like it; another reason to get this sorted out.

'And one more thing, Sylvie. I know you're sleeping badly, you look exhausted and you're losing weight – I'm not sure you're actually up to this Imbolc ceremony at all.'

'*What?* Of course I'm up to the ceremony! It's the only one I lead and you're not muscling in on this as well!'

'No, not me of course – it must be led by a woman. I thought maybe Miranda could lead it this year as you're looking so weak. We can't have you overdoing it – you know where that might lead.'

'*I am not ill!* How many times do I have to tell you that? Yes, I've been sleeping badly, having nightmares, and so has Bluebell which makes it worse. But I'm perfectly well. And if I'm losing weight it's because you put me off my food. I was quite enjoying this meal until you started having a go at me. That's your fault!'

'Are you saying you don't want me to eat dinner with you any more? Finally cut off the last contact we have? Is that what you're saying, Sylvie?'

'No! Yes . . . no, I do want to have dinner with you but only if you get off my back and stop haranguing me!'

To her utter dismay Sylvie burst into tears which wasn't how she felt at all – she was furious. She rose swiftly and turned away from the table, going to stand by the fire where she sobbed quietly into her hands. Yul watched her from the table then drained his glass and poured out the last of the wine, knowing there was another bottle waiting in his study downstairs. He too stood and quickly tipped back the last of the rich contents, then crossed to the fireplace and took her in his arms. She stayed hunched up and resisting, not wanting his comfort. Not when he'd upset her in the first place with his arrogance and bullying. But he firmly unclenched her arms and put them by her sides, enfolding her in a large, safe embrace, gently stroking her hair until eventually she started to relax.

'Come and sit on the sofa,' he said softly. 'Come on, Sylvie, stop fighting me. There really is no need.'

He led her to the sofa and pulled her down next to him with her head on his chest. He felt her resistance but continued stroking her hair, tracing the contours of her face with coaxing fingers until gradually she let go and began to unwind. Yul had a sure and compelling touch and knew her of old. He found her proximity difficult to bear as it had now been quite a while since they'd made love properly. He couldn't count the failed attempt after her return from Bournemouth which he'd brought to an end, much as he'd regretted it later as he lay alone in the darkness of his study. But Yul knew he mustn't rush this tonight; he must take it slowly and carefully until she was completely ready. She was vulnerable and must be handled very delicately.

'You know I love you, Sylvie,' he murmured, running her silky hair through his fingers. 'I don't know what's wrong between us but never forget how much I love you. You're my whole life, you know.'

She snuggled into him, the worries and fears receding a little. This was what mattered; this was how it should be. He continued his caresses and she started to loosen under his touch, letting go of the anxieties that kept her tied in knots. He knew how to make her feel so good. In the soft lamplight and the flickering firelight Sylvie could see him clearly, his beloved face so handsome and full of want. His eyes gazed down at her lovingly as slowly his fingers smoothed and admired every curve and angle of her, until neither of them could hold back any longer. As one they rolled onto the soft rug in front of the fire and forgot their recent troubles, forgot their differences, and remembered only the joy and passion of each other's bodies.

Later as they lay in each other's arms on the sofa once more, both feeling infinitely more content than they'd done for a long time, he risked broaching the subject of their estrangement.

'Is it something to do with the bedroom itself?'

She gazed into the fire, and nodded.

'You've been having nightmares, you said? Is it all linked to that?'

'Yes, I suppose so – kind of.'

'But in here you feel better?'

'It's not . . . that's too simplistic, but partly, yes.'

He smiled above her head – that was easily sorted out then, and it explained her passionate kiss downstairs in the entrance hall too when she was leaving for the ballet.

'Shall I still sleep downstairs tonight? I will if you prefer it –

I just want to make you happy, Sylvie, to get back to how we used to be. This rift between us is killing me. I love you, my angel, you know that, don't you?'

She nodded again, feeling relaxed and at peace now. Maybe it would be alright after all.

'And this business about Imbolc . . .' he began, feeling her tense up again ready to fight him. 'Do whatever you think best, Sylvie. If you want to lead the whole ceremony, that's fine – I don't want to upset you. It's just that I love you so much and I'm worried you're over-doing it. I only want what's best for you.'

'What's best for me is not being bossed about or controlled by you,' she said quietly. 'I don't think you realise how much you dominate. You exhaust me, trying to stand up to you all the time. Just give me space and don't crowd me, don't try to control me.'

'Alright, I'll try harder not to. I really don't know I'm doing it.'

'I think you do, Yul. You know I've never taken it from you and you're using my past illness as a way to bully me into doing what you want. We're equal – we're a partnership.'

'Of course – the darkness and the brightness.'

'Exactly! In balance, not one overpowering the other.'

They were silent then, both thinking how they could make it work and neither wanting a return to the bleakness of the past couple of months. As Yul stared dreamily into the flames he felt a great rush of love for the woman lying against him, her silver hair spilling over his chest. She was the only one, the only woman he'd ever wanted, and he knew in his heart that part of it, part of his desire and need for her was her refusal to let him take over. The balance must be right if there was to be harmony between them. He sighed, tracing the bones in her shoulder, and knew he must rein himself in and let her come to the fore. Stonewylde needed them both working together, not against each other. Together they were strong and powerful, able to hold the centre together and keep the whole community in harmony and accord.

Neither of them saw the shadows thickening behind the sofa

nor felt the presence of another in the room. Neither had any idea of quite what they were up against. They were both thinking things would start to get better now – they didn't realise their troubles had only just begun.

21

F aun let herself into the cottage and made straight for the kitchen – she was starving. Her grandmother was at the range putting chopped vegetables into the cooking pot. It smelled like beef stew and Faun's mouth watered. Her grandmother looked up and smiled.

'Blessings, Faun my dear. Hungry? Go and sit by the fire and I'll bring you some tea and cake. Did you have a good day at school?'

Faun nodded and went into the sitting room, throwing herself down in the armchair and tugging off her winter boots. Soon her grandmother brought in a tray and Faun tucked in ravenously. She was almost thirteen, growing fast and putting on weight too. But her mother had assured her it was only calf fat and would rearrange itself into beautiful womanly curves as she got older. Her grandfather brought in a basket of logs and settled himself down too, asking about her day in Senior School up at the Hall. Faun had only started there in September but she seemed to be doing very well. Her mother and grandparents, who all lived together in the cottage, doted on her; she was the apple of their eyes and given a great deal of attention.

By the time Rowan arrived home from the Nursery, Faun had almost dozed off by the warm fire. Rowan pulled off her cloak and boots and sat down in another chair watching her daughter. Rowan was immensely proud of her. Faun was beautiful, she thought, perfect in every way. She was tall for her age as Rowan had been, and becoming as statuesque as her mother. Her body was well developed for a girl and she was becoming a stunning young woman. The girl's skin was creamy and flawless, her hair blond and wavy and halfway down her back. She had her father's dark velvet eyes which made Rowan feel very strange at times – it was almost like looking into the eyes of Magus himself.

Rowan sighed deeply. It had been a long day at the Nursery, especially with the coughs and colds plaguing so many of the little ones at the moment. She'd been trying to get the girls to practise for Imbolc but without much success. She knew they'd be fine on the day – they always were and, anyway, nobody minded if a tiny girl made a mistake. It was a different matter with the older ones of course – they were expected to do all the rituals properly. The only one in her Nursery who came anywhere near perfection was Celandine. Rowan had to admit she was a wonderful dancer. The girl was so very light on her feet, seeming to skim the floor, and held her body with the controlled tautness of a true dancer. She remembered steps faultlessly and could create dances to order whether there was music or not. Celandine was so excited about Imbolc now that she was doing a little solo, and Sylvie had been delighted and grateful when Rowan had suggested it.

Rowan's mouth twisted bitterly at the thought of Sylvie, feeling free to do so in the privacy of her own home. Sylvie was just over a year younger than her, for Rowan had reached her sixteenth birthday at Beltane in the year that Sylvie and Miranda had moved to Stonewylde. That Beltane was the zenith of Rowan's life, the high spot which she relived constantly to the point where every other part of her life seemed meaningless and pale in comparison.

Rowan, like all the other girls, both Villager and Hallfolk, had always been in Magus' thrall. Every girl dreamed he might partner her in the Rite of Adulthood, which in those days had involved sexual initiation up at the Stone Circle when all the other festivities were over. Rowan had always hoped desperately that she'd be chosen for her special night. She wasn't the only girl reaching sixteen at Beltane and Magus could've chosen another. Then she'd have had to make do with a Villager and there hadn't been a single boy she found in the least attractive – not compared to Magus.

She'd almost fainted with ecstasy when he'd found her out one day in the Hall laundry where she worked, and told her solemnly that not only would he be happy to partner her for her Rite if she wished, but had also chosen her to be his May Queen. Rowan had replayed that moment so often in her mind, remembering how she'd been hanging out sheets on the great drying racks at the time in one of the hot basements of the Hall where fires and a boiler roared. She'd been sweating in the heat, her sleeves rolled up and her uniform unbuttoned a little. She'd looked a mess, she thought, her long brown hair tied back in a glossy ponytail with stray curly tendrils stuck to her perspiring cheeks and forehead. She was flushed and damp and the sight of Magus striding through the maze of hanging white sheets calling her name had made her cheeks even rosier. He'd looked down at her, towering over her despite her own height, his dark eyes gleaming and flushed himself from the heat of the place. He'd been wearing his riding clothes and smelt of horse and fresh air.

Rowan closed her eyes and relaxed further back in her chair as she relived the memory for the ten thousandth time. Magus had smiled at her, that enigmatic smile that made the lines around his mouth deepen and showed his white teeth. Then he'd asked her so eloquently if she'd partner him, as if there may be a question of her having to think about her reply. He always did this apparently, never wanting to force a girl who wasn't eager. She'd gasped with joy and beamed at him, wiping her damp forehead with the back of her hand and stammering her delighted acceptance of the great honour. He'd bowed slightly, told her the honour would be his, and that she'd be taught the rituals she needed to know for the part of May Queen as well as being measured up for her costume, headdress and robes.

'As for the other side of it, Rowan – we can make that up as we go along. I can promise you it'll be a memorable experience.

It's slightly more involved as you'll be the May Queen and I'll be the Green Man so it won't just be the simple initiation rites in the Stone Circle. We'll need to go into the woods for most of the night, for this is a fecundity ritual as well as being your initiation. Can you cope with that, do you think? It can be quite an ordeal and you'll be exhausted in the morning. I know I always am.'

She'd assured him it would be fine, completely melting inside at the thought of spending the whole night with him in the woods. She'd heard tales from other girls – that he was gentle at first and very skilful, making the experience so pleasurable and unforgettable. How lucky was she? Not only to be initiated by Magus for her Rite of Adulthood but to be his May Queen too! She'd have him all to herself for the night of Beltane Eve in the woods and be by his side all day during Beltane itself, with perhaps that night as well if she proved herself worthy of it. She couldn't wait to tell her parents – how proud they'd be that their daughter had been chosen for the honour. And as for all her friends . . .

Magus had smiled at her eagerness, stooping to kiss her lightly on the lips. But Rowan had swayed slightly, her lips apart with longing, and before she knew it he was kissing her long and hard, one strong arm holding her upright as her knees went weak whilst the other hand found her full breast and caressed her with a perfect, knowing touch. On and on it went, his masculinity and passion overwhelming until she was breathless with desire. She was more than ready to lie down on the stone floor of the hot basement, with the white sheets billowing around them, and give herself to him there and then. Fortunately he had more control and reluctantly pulled away. She knew he was very aroused and his dark eyes had practically set her alight the way they burned with that black fire.

'Well, Rowan,' he'd chuckled a little shakily, 'it promises to be a Beltane I'll never forget. Save yourself for me, won't you? No sneaking off before then with a Village boy.'

'Oh no, sir!' she'd breathed, her chest still rising and falling fast and a flush spreading up over the creamy skin of her throat. 'It's only you I want, nor ever will.'

He'd laughed at this.

'I doubt that very much. Once I've given you a taste for it you'll be favouring the whole Village I'm sure, a beautiful goddess like you. You were made for love with curves like those.'

He'd watched her with admiration as she straightened her clothing and did up a few of the buttons that had burst open under his eager hands. He'd tenderly smoothed the damp wispy curls off her face and kissed her once more, gently this time.

'Tonight I'll dream of you lying amongst the bluebells,' he murmured.

Then he was gone and she was alone amongst the white sheets and the drying racks.

Rowan roused herself from her reverie, not wanting to start Beltane right now. She'd save that memory for later. As always when reliving her perfect moments with Magus, she came out of it feeling depressed and bitter. It had been so short-lived – Beltane itself and a few more times after that during the month of May when she'd managed to be in the right place at the right time. But by the end of May it was over for Magus had moved on to another for the Blue Moon at the end of the month – Miranda.

Rowan felt the familiar tide of jealousy flood through her. Why would he prefer a woman in her thirties, and an Outsider at that, to a ripe young girl like her? She knew she'd pleased him – she'd worn herself out pleasing him and she knew it had been good because he'd come back for more, which he rarely did. But then he'd passed her over for Miranda whom he'd continued to favour that summer, although Rowan knew that he'd been with others too including the young doctor up at the Hall. A man like her Magus needed many women and there was no shortage of offers. Rowan's rapture at discovering she was carrying Magus' baby – his first child, or so everyone had thought then, since Buzz – had been marred by the fact that a month later, Miranda had also fallen pregnant. The news had only added fuel to her resentment of the red-haired Outsider.

And then of course by the autumn he was sniffing around that skinny girl Sylvie. The gossip was that he was totally obsessed with her in a way he'd never, ever been with a Stonewylde girl, except perhaps Maizie, some said, several years before. He'd practically locked Sylvie up with him in his rooms throughout December and Rowan, heavily pregnant at the time, had wanted to die. She could've accepted him acting normally and having a different woman every Moon Fullness and every festival. But she couldn't bear to think of him constantly with one girl and besotted with her. It twisted Rowan's heart and made her baby leap inside her ... and then at the Solstice, her beloved Magus had died. Yul and Sylvie – they were the ones to blame. Rowan had never forgiven them and she never would.

When her baby was born just after Imbolc she'd hoped desperately for a boy just like his father. But the tiny girl was beautiful and had Magus' eyes. Rowan had named her Faun in memory of the night of Beltane Eve spent in the green woods with her very own Green Man, when they'd stumbled on a faun lying camouflaged amongst the undergrowth. Magus had talked to it softly and it had stayed there, mesmerised by his deep voice, and she'd stroked its woolly hide and looked into its velvet eyes. So the baby was named Faun, but even that had been spoiled by the early birth a week later of Miranda's baby, Rufus. Once again Rowan was hideously jealous, especially as Miranda had a son who also had Magus' dark eyes. But Rowan had been remarkably adept at hiding her bitter jealousy of Sylvie, Miranda and Rufus, and her hatred of Yul. She was a proud girl and kept her feelings to herself, which was just as well. To this day she'd never shown anyone truly how she felt. But her feelings of adoration for Magus were as strong today as they'd been that Beltane almost fourteen years ago; nobody else could ever compare to him.

Faun opened her eyes and gazed sleepily at her mother, her cheeks flushed from the heat of the fire. Rowan was struck again by her daughter's beauty and ached with love for her.

'Hello, sleepy-head. Did you have a good day at school?'

'No!' said Faun petulantly, frowning at her mother. 'It was horrible.'

'Why? I thought you loved Hall School.'

'It's Leveret – she makes me sick!'

'Ah yes, the Maiden.'

'*Why* was she chosen, Mother? I thought I was to be Bright Maiden this year? You said—'

'No, my darling girl, I never said you'd be Maiden. I said 'twas possible but you're still too young really. It's usually an older girl, fourteen or fifteen, so maybe next year.'

'But it's not fair! I'm much, much prettier than her – everyone says so. She's ugly and skinny with that horrible wild black hair and that nasty pointed little face. Her teeth are like a rat's and her eyes like a cat's. She'll be an awful Maiden.'

'I know. I can't understand why they chose her either.'

Rowan had a very good idea why but she kept it to herself. She was fed up with Yul and Sylvie's family being chosen for all the honours whilst her lovely girl – Magus' daughter – was overlooked. Everyone seemed to forget that Faun was a Hallchild but that seemed to count for nothing any more, not like in the old days when she'd have had special privileges.

Rowan's mother called in for the table to be laid ready for supper and Rowan automatically stood up to do the task. Faun was never expected to do any of the work and the three adults were happy to run around after her and spoil her. Faun watched her mother spreading out the tablecloth and fetching a jug of water and glasses.

'Can't you say something to Yul about it, Mother?'

'No, darling, it wouldn't do any good.'

'But it's not fair! I'd be the best Bright Maiden and I was so hoping they'd choose me. Wouldn't I be the best?'

'Of course you would. Nobody's as beautiful as you, Faun – nobody. Don't be upset, please. I can't bear for you to be upset. Just think of how lovely you'll look in your Imbolc dress, joining in the Dance of the Maidens. And you can choose a fine young partner to dance with and be your escort now you're at Hall School.'

'Yes, but I want Kestrel and he's the Archer of Imbolc again. So Leveret will have him as well as being the Maiden, and even if I am Maiden next year then I won't have him because he'll be too old to be the Archer. I can't stand it!'

'Think of your new dress, darling. Granny's spent hours making it beautiful for you. Have you seen all the special embroidery she's done? You'll look so lovely and I'll curl your hair if you like.'

'Will you? Really curly so it falls in ringlets?'

'If that's what you want, my darling. We'll be up half the night putting in the rags but it'll be worth it.'

'Do you think Kestrel will notice me even though he's partnering Leveret?'

'Of course he will! All the boys'll notice you but especially Kestrel. You'll be the most beautiful girl there and everyone'll say what a terrible mistake they made choosing Leveret.'

Faun giggled at this and sat down at the table so her grandmother could serve her a generous helping of beef stew, making sure she had all the tastiest pieces of meat and the softest end of the bread. Nothing was too good for their Faun.

It was just over a week until Imbolc and preparations were well under way. This festival was held largely in the Village itself, using the Green and the Barn. With so many young girls taking part in the ceremonies it was just too cold up in the Stone Circle. The beginning of February could be bitter, or worse, very wet. So the archery was done on the Green and all the dancing, singing and poetry in the Barn, as well as the usual feast and dance in the evening. Only a few hardy Stonewylders went up to the Stone Circle to welcome in the dawn of Imbolc, but the stones were decorated nevertheless with the symbols of the festival.

The snowdrop was the first flower to push through the frozen soil and show that spring was on its way and the earth was reawakening after its winter sleep. The bulb was the symbol of new life growing in the earth full of the promise of fertility. The flame of a white candle symbolised the spark of feminine intuition and creativity burning brightly within the breast of the Maiden. But the most important symbol of all was the silver crescent moon, which was also the bow of the Maiden Huntress. For although Imbolc celebrated purity and virginity, hence the young girls all dressed in white, it was also about the potential of later fecundity stored deep within. Imbolc celebrated too the young female as the harbinger of intelligence and wisdom, and powerful sexuality and fertility.

The cart full of painting materials went up to the Stone Circle to begin the task of decorating the stones with these motifs. First they must be scrubbed clean of the faded Yule symbols, so the mistletoe, holly, ivy, deer and golden suns were erased until the next year and briefly the great stones faced the Circle in their unadorned and natural state. Then the Imbolc designs could be charcoaled on by the artists whilst Greenbough, now in his seventies and feeling every one of his hard-working years, supervised the cleaning of the site and the laying of a small bonfire.

The new art teacher had requested that his young protégé Magpie be allowed to help with painting the stones for this festival. David had never seen such raw talent and was convinced he'd something very special on his hands. Magpie wasn't cluttered with formal education and established ways of thinking; he was a true natural and his gift came from the soul, not from studying or art history. Miranda had agreed to Magpie helping Merewen and the team, but only on the condition that David looked out for the boy himself.

David and Magpie strolled up the Long Walk, the avenue of smaller stones overhung with bare branches which in warmer months made a long green tunnel. Magpie was very excited and understood about decorating the stones. Every year of his life during the eight festivals he'd gazed in simple wonder at the beautiful paintings on the stones. The symbols were ingrained in his soul and were a major factor in the way he made sense of the world. He knew what Imbolc represented at a deeper level than those who understood it intellectually. Magpie's mind operated at the subconscious level, not analysing but absorbing, not interpreting the symbols of life but echoing them. The symbols resonated within him and now he longed to let images flow from his fingers with paint and brushes, those magic wands that enabled him finally to unlock the treasure trove that was his creative psyche.

'Now Magpie, you know what pictures we use at Imbolc, don't you? Delicate white snowdrops with a sheath of green, great rich brown bulbs with the kernel of creation within them. Flames with layers leading in to a central core, like the bulbs. And the silver bow – with an arrow crossing it and just pointing up slightly, aiming for higher things than an animal target. You understand, don't you?'

The boy nodded happily, his turquoise eyes shining with excitement. He wore a warm cloak against the harsh January chill and his cheeks were rosy from the cold air. His bright butterscotch-coloured hair was covered by a thick felt hat such as the men wore in winter. He was unrecognisable from the filthy, half-starved cur who'd skulked around Stonewylde only a couple of months ago; he'd even learned how to use a handkerchief.

'Magpie, today you *must* listen to what you're told. The others will show you the pattern they've adopted and you must follow it carefully so the whole Circle is linked through the images. If you do it wrong it'll be scrubbed off. Please, Magpie, do this right! I want them to be pleased with you just as I am, so you won't take it in your head to do your own thing, will you?'

David was a little worried about this for Magpie could be stubbornly independent at times. Often when David was teaching him an idea or new technique, the boy would ignore him and do what he felt was right. David had to admit that whatever Magpie created was usually far superior. But that wouldn't do today, not when it was the first time he was allowed to join the established painters.

They reached the Circle where the people were already well

into cleaning the stones. Old Greenbough looked up at the new arrivals and raised a gnarled hand.

'Blessings! And young Magpie come to help us – there's a turn up. Looks a deal cleaner now hisself. Right then, lad, here's a brush and a bucket o' water – get to it then.'

Magpie had been peering into the cart examining the pots of pigment waiting to be mixed with water and the special binding agent, a blend of organic material that held the paint to the stones for the six or seven weeks required. He looked up and beamed at Greenbough, then took the proffered tools and set to work a little clumsily, sloshing water onto the stone and scrubbing in great sweeps. Greenbough shook his head, the dewdrop on the end of his nose flying off as he muttered in David's direction.

'I don't know – how can that lad paint the stones good enough when he's so ham-fisted? We don't want the Circle looking messy or daft. I hope you're right about the boy.'

Greenbough had little faith in any Outsider recruited to teach in the Hall School. They didn't have Stonewylde in their bones so how could they do a good job here? But orders were orders and he'd give the boy a chance. Not that he was in charge of the painting – that was for the artists. It was Merewen, the Stonewylde potter, who supervised it for every ceremony. She lived and worked in the Pottery further down the river from the Village where the great clay beds lay. She was grizzled and gruff, striding around the Circle in her coarse linen tunic splattered with old paint, her cloak flung back over her square shoulders, hob-nailed boots clumping in the soft earth floor.

She glared at Magpie, as doubtful as Greenbough about the outcome of this daft venture. She too knew the boy of old – everyone did – and she couldn't equate her memory of a gormless and dirty outcast with someone who could possibly decorate the stones to her satisfaction. Merewen had worked with the clay all her life, like her father and grandfather before her. She'd inherited the role of potter of Stonewylde as in the old days children usually followed in their family's traditional occupation. So she now lived alone in the cottage by the Pottery, in charge of all those who worked there to produce ceramics for Stonewylde's needs.

Although Merewen loved the medium of clay and was a gifted potter, her real talents were artistic. She decorated her wares beautifully with patterns and motifs, so the role of supervising the stone decorations was an obvious one for her and she'd been doing it for many years. She knew Greenbough well as she must liaise with him about charcoal for firing her kilns. She caught his rheumy eye now and they grimaced together at the spectacle of Magpie with his bucket of water. Cleaning wasn't something he'd had much experience of in the cottage where he'd grown up.

But later in the day when they began to charcoal the designs onto the stones, Merewen was pleasantly surprised. First the group had discussed the overall pattern which was different each time, giving the Circle a feeling of innovation and excitement as well as tradition and beauty. Magpie couldn't join in with the talk but had listened carefully and during the discussion, began to sketch rapidly onto the rough paper laid out ready for the first drafts. Merewen was grudgingly impressed with his deft hand and instinctive interpretations. His ideas were incorporated into the overall design and Magpie glowed with pride when he realised this. The rough outlines completed, the painters packed up their cart of materials and covered it carefully with canvas for the night. They'd return each day until the stones were finished.

The women were working together in the Barn; the Dark Moon closest to Imbolc was traditionally spent sewing baby clothes. The tiny white garments were carefully cut from soft linen and stitched into the long nightdresses worn by all Stonewylde babies for their first three months or so. The outfits were embroidered on the chest with white and green snowdrops and a small silver crescent, so whatever time of year the babies were born they'd bear a reminder of the promise of Imbolc, the potential of new life to grow into maturity and fulfilment. Most women completed a nightdress during the first day and would then knit vests, caps, jackets and long booties from the finest wool the next day.

The Barn buzzed with enthusiasm as this was one of the favourite Dark Moon tasks. Groups of women sat around together on the log stools and benches or at the trestle tables, some of the younger girls with aching wombs making big nests of cushions and sitting on the floor. Everyone worked diligently on their nightdress, warm and contented in the haven of the Barn – everyone except Sylvie who sat to one side with her mother. She surveyed the women sadly, not sewing the tiny pieces of linen with their enthusiasm.

'It's such a shame, Mum,' she said quietly. 'Look at them all sewing and putting their best efforts into making such beautiful tiny things. They don't realise, do they?'

Miranda glanced at her daughter who'd seemed a lot happier today and had been so for the last couple of days. Her face wore a whisper of that dreamy contentment which Miranda had always envied, knowing its source. She'd been so worried about Sylvie but perhaps things between her and Yul were now on the mend.

'Don't realise what, darling?'

'They're still making all these lovely baby clothes just as they've always done and by the end of this Dark Moon there'll be a great wicker hamper of beautiful new baby things. But where are the babies to wear them? The birth rate at Stonewylde is so low now, and once this batch of teenagers has grown up it'll be even lower. We just don't need baskets and baskets of new baby clothes made every year, especially not when everyone uses old things until they fall apart. There're probably enough baby outfits at Stonewylde already to last for the next fifty years, and yet every Imbolc it's the same, more and more being produced.'

'I see what you mean – I'd never thought of it like that. But it's nice for young mothers to have new things for their babies, isn't it? I always longed for lovely pure white clothes to put you in.'

'But Stonewylde isn't about using new things, is it? Everyone makes things last and that's how it should be. Do you know what actually happens to all these little outfits? And has happened for a while now?'

'Well, I imagine ... oh! You mean they're sold on Stone-wylde.com?'

Sylvie nodded sadly.

'They keep some in the clothes store but the rest go to the warehouse and are advertised on the website. Stonewylde baby-clothes sell for a fortune, I believe, because they're of the highest quality and so beautifully made. Hand woven fine linen, home-grown organic wool, and all that hand stitching and exquisite embroidery, all that loving care put into them. And then sold to strangers with too much money to burn – it isn't right.'

Miranda put down her sewing, which had suddenly lost its charm. She'd imagined a tiny Stonewylde baby wearing the nightdress, not a rich woman's offspring. She sighed.

'I see what you mean. But ultimately everyone benefits, don't they? I mean the money made from Stonewylde.com is ploughed back into the community so everyone gains in the end, don't you think?'

'I suppose so, but ... it seems immoral to me, almost exploit-ation. At least the women should be told what's happening.'

'But then they wouldn't look forward to it – or put in so much effort,' said Miranda. 'It's bad enough now with Harold's quotas. Maizie was telling me again the other day about the growing ill-feeling in the Village over those quotas and how people aren't taking such care any more.'

'Exactly – they feel exploited. And what happens to all the money? I've never really got involved with the accounts – Yul and Harold deal with that and use an accountancy firm from Outside. But the profits must be enormous – the materials are home grown, labour's free, even our electricity comes from the wind farms, so profits must be almost a hundred per cent. But where's all the money going?'

'Yul's always said money's needed to maintain the status quo and how much we must buy in, as we aren't truly self-sufficient. Things like toothbrushes and glasses and school books, and

Outside clothes and shoes for the students at college too. Fuel for the coach, the vehicles and the tractors, and the telephone bill. The computers in the Hall – you know all the senior students over fourteen have their own. And university fees! That's where money's needed.'

'Yes but not the thousands and thousands that must be made every year from selling our things. Stonewylde.com has grown into a really big enterprise, you know. I worry about it and I think after Imbolc I'm going to find out a bit more.'

'Be careful, Sylvie – don't fight with Yul again. You seem happier at the moment and I assume things are better between the two of you?'

'Yes,' smiled Sylvie, a look of contentment creeping across her face. 'Things seem to be on the mend. But this is something different, Mum – I won't have people exploited.'

'Alright, darling – just don't go upsetting the applecart. You know what Yul's like.'

'I do, and he'll have to accept what I'm like too.'

Over on the other side of the Barn, Leveret sat with her mother trying to keep her stitches small and neat, but too aware of the dull ache deep inside her to concentrate well. She'd started off sitting with a group of her contemporaries, but their excited chatter about Imbolc in just a few days' time had filled her with burgeoning dread and she'd moved over to be with Maizie. She was terrified of the forthcoming ceremonies and not as ecstatic about being chosen as Bright Maiden as everyone assumed her to be. The other girls were very envious and many had wondered why a strange-looking, quiet girl like Leveret had been chosen. Traditionally, the role went to someone very pretty and bubbly. Some who'd seen her at the Outsiders' Dance understood that Leveret was beautiful, in a slightly outlandish way, but generally it was thought she'd only been chosen because she was Yul's sister.

Leveret felt hostility amongst some of the girls; Faun in particular gave her antagonistic looks from across the floor. Faun was one of the younger girls there and enjoyed sitting with older girls and feeling special. Leveret had never liked her – Faun was spoilt and indulged and seemed to think she was something above everyone else. Leveret had always found her bland face and long, plump limbs unattractive and her petulance irritating.

Leveret hunched on the stool hugging herself and wishing the cramps would ease off. She'd feel a lot better by the evening but that didn't help her now. She had to speak to Maizie about the evening ahead, hoping to catch her mother in a good mood. Leveret had asked Clip's advice about the Dark Moon. It was special to her and she wasn't sure if she should cast another circle again and raise the energy, hoping to contact Mother Heggy, or whether that was best left alone for a while. Clip had been tentative in his advice.

'I'm not a Dark Moon person,' he'd said, 'so I don't really know. I've always felt an affinity with the Moon Fullness, like my mother Raven and my daughter Sylvie, and it's when I journey best. The Dark Moon's a mystery to me – it's a different sort of magic and not what I'm in tune with. You must have an affinity with the Moon Fullness too, Leveret. I'm still amazed how successful our Wolf Moon journey was. It can take months, if not years, to make contact with your spirit guide, let alone make a full journey. You have the gift, you truly do. I felt it that day up at the stone on the hill when you passed out but I hadn't appreciated just what potential you have.'

Clip had promised to speak discreetly to Maizie about their working together, and had also agreed not to bring up the incident about the apple barrel again. Clip knew he must handle this carefully as Maizie wouldn't approve of anything that whiffed of magic, not after the trouble with Yul and Mother Heggy's prophecies. And there was always the risk of her telling Yul too, which Clip knew would be a disaster. So he'd told Maizie that Leveret had a fine intellect and he intended to leave his books with her when he departed from Stonewylde later that year, as she was the only person he'd encountered at Stonewylde who'd truly appreciate them.

Clip had explained that he was trying to broaden Leveret's mind, taking her for long walks and showing her plants and rocks that would help with the book studying. Maizie had confided her wish that Leveret become a doctor one day and he'd agreed that she had the potential to be a great healer. He said her studies with him would help as every healer needed a broad and deep knowledge. Clip felt a little guilty misleading Maizie but knew the end would justify the means; Leveret would be a great Wise Woman and shaman for Stonewylde.

But he was unsure about the Dark Moon, worried about her casting and scared that with so little experience she might conjure something unwanted. Clip felt Leveret was on the cusp of something and when the time was right, all would be made clear. In the meantime she shouldn't do anything to put herself in danger.

'What do you feel at Dark Moon?' he'd asked her.

'A great excitement inside me,' she'd replied. 'A thrill, a sort of rush of power and magic. I tingle with it as the skies darken and the stars come out. I feel as if I could do anything and it's growing more powerful as I get older.'

'I think you should walk in the night,' he'd advised. 'Go somewhere you feel the Earth Magic and let the Dark Moon flow through you. But don't try to channel anything yet, not until you've learnt more.'

So now she must broach the subject with her mother. Maizie had been fine about the Wolf Moon because Clip had said they were working in his tower for the evening. How far could she bend the truth now without actually deceiving her mother?

'I saw Clip yesterday at school, Mother,' she began nonchalantly, stitching with sudden diligence.

'Oh yes? Was he pleased you were chosen as Bright Maiden?'

He'd been delighted, saying it was highly symbolic.

'Yes, he was thrilled and wants to help me prepare spiritually.'

'Ah, the spiritual side. We've been thinking of your outfit and making sure you know the rituals, but the spiritual side is important too, o' course.'

'I must go out this evening and Clip's keen for me to do so. Is that alright?'

'Yes, if Clip wants you to. I know he'll look after you.'

Maizie had followed her trail of implication without her having to actually lie. Leveret smiled, her green eyes lighting up.

'Thanks, Mother – I won't be late.'

'I'll keep your supper under a plate on the range. I'm at the Hall with Miranda and Sylvie tonight, running through things for Imbolc so I'll probably be late back. Oh Leveret, I'm so excited!'

'Mmn, me too.'

In fact Leveret was dreading being the centre of attention. Despite evidence to the contrary at Yuletide, she was convinced of her ugliness and worried sick she'd forget the complex dance steps and words she must chant. And despite her crush on him, Leveret was nervous about Kes being her partner. She was scared of making a fool of herself, terrified of dancing with him and sure that he'd hoped for one of the pretty, amusing girls to be his Bright Maiden, not a boring, plain one like her. He must be feeling disappointed.

But she hid her fear and self-doubt for her mother's sake, putting on a brave face and letting the chatter wash over her – at least she'd be out tonight celebrating the Dark Moon. Leveret felt a sudden tingle of excitement and forgot all about menstruation pains and the proximity of Imbolc. All she thought of was the night ahead and the dark joy of being out, wild and free, in the magic of the Dark Moon.

22

Yul strode into the Stone Circle, his long legs covering the distance quickly; he wanted to be here for the sunset and it was almost time. He took a great leap onto the Altar Stone and stood there, tall and powerful, both hands raking his dark hair back from his face as he turned towards the golden pool of light that was the setting sun. It was already a month since the Solstice but as yet there was little noticeable difference in the days' length. As he stood waiting, Yul noticed the charcoaled designs on the stones and frowned at the thought of Imbolc. He was still angry that Leveret had been chosen, and that he'd had to give in and agree to let Sylvie lead the forthcoming ceremonies when she wasn't completely well.

But at least things were finally improving between them. For three nights now they'd eaten dinner together, actually talking to each other and then moving to the fiery hearth to make love. It wasn't maybe quite as spontaneous and passionate as in the past, but was a big improvement on the situation in recent months. As they started to relax in each other's company again hopefully they'd return to their former happiness. He grinned suddenly, thinking that whatever happened he felt a damn sight better now than he'd done for ages. It was a shame it was now Dark Moon.

A great cloud of black starlings flew overhead blocking the light, and as the shadow passed over Yul he shuddered involuntarily. He felt a tremor of green magic below his boots, a glimmer of the energy that had once doused him completely.

Why wasn't it coming back to him? Surely now he and Sylvie were united again, the equilibrium had been restored and the magic could once again seek him out? Yul was convinced that his role as magus and his ability to channel the earth energy was somehow linked to his relationship with Sylvie. None of it had started until she'd come to Stonewylde and he'd fallen in love with her, and it hadn't stopped until recently when things became so bad between them.

He thought suddenly of her moondancing – perhaps that held the key to his problems too. Maybe he'd been wrong to stop her going last month. He'd encourage her to go to Hare Stone next Moon Fullness and see if that helped. But he was sure that at the heart of it all was their passion for each other, and when that was fully restored the Earth Magic would return as well. He'd just have to work at it a bit harder.

The sun had now disappeared completely and the clouds were darkening. Then Yul felt a thrill of a different nature – the Dark Moon. He breathed deeply, filling his chest, and tipped back his head to the skies. A sinuous thread of power stirred within him; it had always been like this at the Dark Moon. His fingertips tingled with this dark energy, the delicious sensation of power and control over everything around him. He smiled to himself and leapt off the Altar Stone, his boots landing with a thud in the soft earth. But as he strode back across the great Circle towards the Long Walk he sensed a movement, something stirring behind him. He spun around, seeing nothing.

'Who's there?' he called, his deep voice bouncing off the stones in faint echoes. There was no reply so he continued to walk, but the hairs on the back of his neck had risen, and try as he might he couldn't rid himself of the notion that he hadn't been alone in the Stone Circle. He jumped at the sound of a sudden mew and looked up to see a great buzzard with barred wings circling overhead.

Leveret stood with her back to the Hare Stone, also watching the sun set. She'd spent a long time thinking about where to go and decided that this was the special place for her. There was also symmetry in the fact that this was where Sylvie used to dance at the Moon Fullness. Leveret had no Dark Moon dance but she felt sensations coursing through her. She closed her eyes and concentrated hard.

'Mother Heggy, are you here with me? Or are you out there in the night?'

She sensed no answering reply but still the magic tingled in her fingertips. Her stomach knotted with excitement – should she cast a circle after all? Clip had admitted that he didn't really know what to do for the best and maybe he'd been wrong to advise against it. The spell of protection she'd cast for Magpie seemed to be working, for nobody had harmed him yet, so perhaps calling Mother Heggy tonight would work too, especially now she had her own spirit guide. Leveret looked up into the skies where the light was fading fast now the sun had gone, hoping to see a raven or crow as a sign. But there was none – only the call of a jay from the distant woods at the bottom of the hill, and a jay was no good at all.

Sighing, Leveret realised she didn't have the tools for circle casting with her anyway – the salt for protection and the objects to represent the elements she'd summon. So that was that. She began to walk slowly down the hill but then thought better of it. Retracing her steps, she started to move anti-clockwise, moon-wise, widdershins around the stone at the summit. It was growing dark and of course there was no moon, but the stars were emerging now, twinkling and flickering, and she sensed the great stone to her left emanating some sort of energy of its own.

It was an ancient energy, very powerful, and Leveret wondered why this huge monolith was here on top of this particular hill. Had it been some kind of marker stone to guide people? If so, what was it marking? As she walked, her feet sure on the stiff, cold grass, her breath pluming out into the January night air, she began to feel a rising, a creation. It was similar to the sensation she'd experienced when walking around her circle on the Green at the last Dark Moon. She was raising something without even trying to. Round and round she walked, gazing up at the brilliant stars, thinking of the dark magic that surrounded her. Then suddenly she stopped dead. Something had joined her in the darkness.

'Mother Heggy?' she cried hopefully. 'Are you here?'

But again there was no answer and she felt the fine hairs on her arms start to rise.

'Is it you, Mother Heggy?'

There was a whispering in the still air, a stirring of very slight movement like leaves sighing in the trees. Except that there were no leaves in the trees.

Leveret started to go back down the hill, still tingling all over and not sure if she were terrified or exhilarated. What had she raised? Who or what had joined her by the Hare Stone? She refused to panic and run, for the grass further down was too long and tussocky and she could fall. She made herself stop when she reached the rocks, just to prove she wasn't frightened. Leveret sat on a boulder and looked up at the stars sparkling in the blackness. She felt a little strange, not just with the dark magic but something else. She started to get the prickling sensation that she knew preceded her absences, the funny turns her mother so dreaded. She felt the world start to spin too fast but for the first time she was aware of it and fought the feelings, struggling to remain conscious. Her tongue felt too big in her mouth but she swallowed hard, staring at the stars and concentrating on staying there and not letting her mind disappear.

Suddenly her head was filled with the image of a serpent, a great viper with slashing zigzags black on his silver skin. He writhed slightly, his flickering tongue tasting the air, and she saw the vertical slits of the black pupils in his eyes, which gleamed like jewels. He was all around her and as he moved, she could see other vipers beneath him, a writhing mass of snakes, hundreds and hundreds of snakes. Snakes of destruction, of venom, of attack, writhing and hissing and ...

'Raven!' she shouted. 'RAVEN!'

Her raven shimmered into her head, banishing the image of

the snakes. Its bright eye regarded her steadily, then it blinked and cocked its head.

'Raven, why am I seeing snakes? What's happening?'

But the raven only cawed loudly and flapping its massive wings, it flew off.

'Beware of walking blind into the vipers' nest. Beware the snake that sheds one skin to return in another.'

And then the starry night was back in focus and Leveret felt very cold. How long had she been sitting on the boulder? She rose stiffly, finding her feet numb, and walked briskly down the hill and into the woods. She wasn't scared in the darkness for she knew these woods so well; Yul had brought her here almost daily as a child, teaching her the names of the trees, birds, flowers and creatures, and she felt safe here away from any threat that the hill had posed. Leveret was feeling elated – that was the first time she'd ever gone into a trance and remembered what happened. Maybe she was learning to control her strange absences after all. And she remembered the message clearly – but what on earth did it mean?

As she approached the fork in the path near the Village, Leveret decided to take the right-hand route and make a detour up around the other side of the river to Mother Heggy's cottage. Her mother had given her permission to go out tonight and would be late back herself, so Leveret knew she wouldn't be waiting impatiently at home getting worried. Leveret felt a little guilty that she'd allowed her mother to assume she was with Clip, but pushed that qualm aside – she hadn't actually lied. Her stomach gurgled with hunger and it almost prompted her to change her mind and go the other way, the way straight back home where her supper was waiting warm on the range.

But it was the Dark Moon, the special night, and this might be her last chance for a whole month. If she called into the tumbledown cottage and just sat there for a while maybe she'd feel the crone with her. Leveret was sure someone had been there on the hill with her but wasn't convinced it was Mother Heggy.

There'd been nothing since the last Dark Moon and the unexpected return of the gathering knife. She so longed for contact with her and the answer she'd been given during her journey with Clip had filled her with hope.

But as Leveret skirted around the back of the Village close to the river she began to feel uneasy. She had the strangest feeling that someone was behind her, and plucked up the courage to look around. She could see nobody but the feeling persisted, and then she started to lose her nerve. She began to hurry, her boots clattering on the cobbles as she walked faster and faster, breaking into a run. Something was closing in on her. She heard voices and laughter up ahead and almost sobbed with relief, quickening her pace still further. And then the voices were clearer and she saw torchlight swinging, and just as she stopped being scared, stopped panicking about the shadow in the darkness behind her, she realised with terrible clarity whose voices they were. But too late.

Leveret actually ran straight into the bulk of Sweyn, who caught her with a shout of laughter.

'Here she is! She's found us!'

'That's amazing!' cried Gefrin. 'We called into the cottage looking for you, Hare-brain, but you weren't there! Fancy your coming looking for us – how did you know?'

She struggled in Sweyn's grip but of course it was useless for he was adept at holding her when she wriggled. Then she heard the third voice that made her heart sink even further; there'd been the slight glimmer of hope that it was only her brothers out in the darkness.

'She enjoys all the fuss we make of her, don't you, Leveret? We make you feel special and you are so special to us – the Maiden of Imbolc!'

They roared with laughter at this.

'You are so going to wish you'd never been picked!' cried Gefrin. 'Just you wait!'

'I didn't want to be picked,' she said desperately. 'I don't want to be the Maiden.'

'Oh yeah!' said Jay in disbelief. 'Of course you do – all the girls do. You can't wait to stand there showing off to everyone, all tarted up again and thinking you look pretty when really you just look like some ugly little weasel in a party dress.'

Leveret hung her head; that was exactly what she'd been thinking.

'Your friends are really pissed off with you, Leveret.'

'I haven't got any friends.'

Gefrin laughed. 'I'm not surprised.'

'Except my half-wit cousin,' sneered Jay. 'He's all you can manage.'

Leveret bit off her retort, not wanting them to dwell on Magpie. She stood silently and hoped that once they'd finished laughing at her they'd let her go home. In the darkness she heard the glug-glug of a bottle.

'Pass it over,' growled Sweyn, 'and hold on to her while I have some more.'

She felt Jay's hands on her arms and shrank under his touch. She could smell him – a mixture of cider, sweat and smoke – and it made her recoil further.

'I have to get back,' she said. 'Mother'll be wondering where I am. She's waiting for me.'

'No she ain't – she's up at the Hall till late. She told us and that's why we went back to the cottage to find you,' said Gefrin.

'And how come you're out on your own?' asked Sweyn suddenly. 'You're not allowed out at night on your own.'

'I've been up at the Hall too.'

'No you haven't. You're lying again!'

She felt Jay's grip tighten on her arms and realised she'd tensed up.

'Clip was with me,' she said desperately.

'No he weren't! We saw him as we left.'

Sweyn's face loomed into hers and she caught a blast of his foul breath.

'Back to your old tricks, eh, Lev? Lying to Mother, deceiving

364

her? You won't get away with it – I'll tell her and she'll be so upset with you.'

'No!' she cried. 'It's none of your business what I do and I'm sick of you and your bullying, you stupid, thick oaf!'

He punched her in the stomach just as he'd seen Jay do at the dance, but harder. She felt as if her guts were exploding and bent over double with the pain, retching into the grass. Jay had let her go, knowing she couldn't run, and she slowly straightened, wiping her mouth with her sleeve and relieved now that she hadn't yet eaten. She clutched her stomach and groaned with pain.

'Nice one!' said Jay, taking a swig of the cider and passing it round.

'Mother's going to see that,' whispered Leveret when she could speak again. 'She's fitting me for my Imbolc dress and she'll see what you did to me.'

'Shit!' muttered Sweyn.

'I'm going home now,' she said quietly, turning away from them and starting to walk.

'Not so fast!' barked Jay, grabbing her arm and swinging her round. 'Did we say you could go? We ain't finished with you yet.'

'What are we going to do with her?' cried Gefrin, capering about excitedly. 'Make her drunk again?'

'Nah, done that,' said Sweyn. 'I wish we could put her in the well like your granny said.'

'Yeah!' laughed Jay. 'But it's still early and people are about in the Village. Pity, though, 'cos that would've been a laugh.'

'The river!' yelled Gefrin, beside himself with glee. 'Let's dunk her in the river like we used to!'

Leveret stood there whilst they discussed her fate, sharing the cider around as they egged each other on. She didn't dare argue in case one of them punched her again and she couldn't run; her stomach was agony. She started to curse them silently, calling on the Dark Moon magic, calling on Mother Heggy to help her. It didn't seem to work because they dragged her towards the bridge.

'We'll grab her ankles and dip her head in,' said Jay. 'The river's very high.'

'Yeah, and hold her under like we used to! See if we can beat our record.'

'If we let her go she'll drown, so hold on tight,' said Sweyn, and from the way he staggered she realised they'd had a lot to drink. They'd probably been kicked out of the pub as George was very strict about young lads not having too much, but had taken more cider from home when they called in to look for her. Leveret was really frightened now; she could hear the river and it was indeed high. In the winter months the spring flowed fast and was joined by many tributaries until the river was swollen into a torrent, very different to the peaceful, lazy meander of the warmer months. They might well drop her in and she knew how swift the currents were. She began to cry, hating herself for showing her fear but unable to control it.

They reached the low-sided stone bridge which was just wide enough for a cart to cross. The river was really loud now and Leveret sobbed frantically, begging them to let her go, begging them to do anything they liked but not this. The memories of past torture in the water came crowding in; it had always been a favourite because it left no evidence. Many times her brothers had held her under until she thought her lungs would explode and she'd die. And they'd been sober then and not had Jay with them to add his cruelty.

'She's shit scared!' laughed Jay, holding her easily as she struggled in his grip. 'She's really trembling.'

He shoved her down onto her knees and made her bend over the low wall so her head hung over the edge. She resisted all the way, struggling desperately to kneel up. Jay pushed his knee onto her back and pressed her down hard onto the stone, which dug into her sore stomach and hurt badly.

'You two take an ankle each and for goddess' sake hold on tight. I don't want to kill her – that'd spoil all our fun. Have you got her?'

She felt her brothers both gripping tightly onto her ankles

whilst Jay held her down. She saw glimmers of the dark water not far below, swirling and raging, moving very fast. Jay had to shout to make himself heard over the noise of the water.

'When I say "go", lower her down and stop when I tell you!'

Leveret started to thrash about at this, trying to kick their faces, trying to raise her body off the wall. Jay just thrust down even harder making her ribs crunch, and he shouted again.

'Ready boys?'

She felt the stone scrape her stomach as Jay began to slide her over the edge towards the racing water.

And then it was all gone: the river, the darkness, the three thugs. She was in the bright place before the other realms and the raven was there. It hopped towards her and spoke softly.

'Be brave, Little Hare, for this will come to an end. They'll suffer as they make you suffer now. You have a friend who looks out for you and soon she'll show herself, when the time's right.'

'But why must I put up with this?' she asked. 'I've never hurt them – why do they do this to me?'

'They envy you. They're scared of you because you're different and not like them. They see something in you that's strange and they try to destroy what they don't understand. It is ever thus.'

'Bloody hell! What's happening?'

Jay felt her go limp, which was odd as she'd been rigid with terror the second before, and then her whole body started to jerk. He hauled her back up and turned her over to see her face.

'Shine the light on her!' he yelled and Gefrin fumbled about with the torch and managed to switch it on. He screamed as the harsh beam found her face. It shone from below her chin, so the shadows cast by her sharp bones made the face look like a skull. But more frightening than this was her eyes – they'd rolled up in their sockets and gleamed whitely as she shook.

'She's having a fit!' screamed Jay, who'd seen a boy like this once at college. 'Quick, let's get out of here!'

'We can't leave her here,' said Sweyn, scared by the sight of his sister. 'Look, it's stopping now.'

Jay felt her go completely floppy in his arms and they saw her eyes return to normal. She screwed them up in the bright light, unable to see a thing. She was utterly confused and thought she was still in the bright place.

'Where are you?' she called feebly. 'I can't see you anymore. When will she come to me?'

'Leveret!' said Sweyn sharply. 'Snap out of it!'

'I don't like it,' moaned Gefrin. 'She's weird.'

'She's always bloody weird. Leveret!'

Jay shook her then, not caring that her head bounced back and forth.

'You're putting it on now!' he said harshly, more shaken by her behaviour than he liked to show. 'Stop it, Leveret! Get that bloody light out of her eyes, Gef!'

The torch moved slightly and she blinked, focusing on the three faces hovering over her.

'This will come to an end and you'll suffer as you've made me suffer.'

They'd finally reached the cottage and Jay let her go, having half-carried, half-dragged her back. His fear had receded and he was just angry with her now.

'You've messed us about tonight, girl,' he said, shaking her slightly again but careful not to overdo it just in case. 'You think you've fooled us with your party tricks but you haven't. You wait, Leveret – just you wait!'

'If you say a *word* to Mother about this we'll tell her you were out on your own again,' growled Sweyn, jabbing her hard in the chest. 'Do you understand?'

She nodded, utterly exhausted and wanting to get inside the safety of the cottage.

'How am I going to explain the marks on me?'

She was sure her stomach would be bruised from the punch. It was also scraped sore from where Jay had held her down so hard on the rough stone bridge and then dragged her almost over the edge and back again. Her back felt bruised too from the weight of his knee.

'You'll think of something,' said Jay. 'Or you'll make sure she don't see. Now you'd better get some beauty sleep ready for Imbolc – you need it.'

'Yeah, and think about the lovely surprise we got for you!' said Gefrin.

'Shh! Shut up, Gef,' warned Sweyn.

'You'll regret it,' she said wearily. 'I know you will, whatever it is.'

'Are you trying to threaten us?' asked Jay quietly.

'No, I'm warning you. I know.'

'Well stuff your bloody warnings, you mad bitch! You'll regret being the Maiden, that's for sure – you'll regret that alright. Come on, lads, the three old girls should be finished their Dark Moon stuff now. Let's go and have a pipe with them and see what they've come up with.'

They shoved her in through the garden gate and went on up the lane, laughing.

As Imbolc approached, Leveret became more and more nervous. She somehow managed to conceal the livid bruising and her scraped skin, and Maizie teased her about becoming so modest all of a sudden. She tried not to flinch as her mother fiddled about with the bodice of the dress, pinning and tucking the white material tight so it fitted her snugly over the fine camisole, clucking and tutting and loving every minute of it. Leveret, meanwhile, stood like a stone statue hoping for a miracle to make them choose somebody else at the last minute.

She had to practise the chants and steps endlessly, with the other girls giggling and chattering around her and enjoying themselves no end. Little Celandine beamed at her constantly, desperate for Leveret to notice her special dance and make some comment. But Leveret was so wrapped up in her own despair that she didn't realise. There were even a couple of practices with

369

Kestrel which she found a terrible ordeal. He was as charming as ever, making all the girls laugh with his jokes, and couldn't understand why Leveret wasn't bowled over too.

'What's wrong?' he whispered once, as they stood in the sidelines waiting for their cue. 'Didn't you want me for the Archer?'

'No, no, it's not that,' she whispered back. 'I just wish I wasn't the Maiden. I hate it.'

He stared at her in complete astonishment.

'But all the girls want to be the Bright Maiden!'

'Not me.'

The afternoon before Imbolc just as they'd all returned from the woods after picking snowdrops for the head-dresses, Marigold came bustling in, rosy-cheeked from the bitter wind and searching for Leveret.

'Ah, there you are, my dear!' she gasped, relieved at having found the girl. 'I just had a message from one o' the painters in the Circle. Can you go up there quick? There's some trouble with our Magpie and he's upset. They can't get through to him and they want you to try and make him understand. They said he's done the painting all wrong but he won't let 'em wash it off.'

Afraid for Magpie and glad of the excuse to get away from the stifling excitement and high-pitched anticipation in the Barn, Leveret pulled on her cloak and ran as fast as she could up to the Stone Circle. Poor Magpie – she'd not seen him all week as she'd been so busy, but she'd meant to go and see his paintings and tell him how proud she was of him. She felt terrible for neglecting him and now worried that he'd messed up his chance to be useful in the community. She met Merewen halfway up the Long Walk, puffed out from running most of the way and trying to ignore her stomach and back which hurt badly with every lungful of air she took. Merewen was stomping towards her, cloak billowing out behind her.

'Ah, Leveret – good! They say you're the only one he listens to. Come and see if you can talk some sense into the boy.'

'Has he really messed it up?' she gasped, in agony now from

the great breaths she gulped in. It had been a mistake to run so fast with her injuries.

'No, no, the boy's brilliant – perhaps the best artist Stonewylde's had. Love his style – completely natural. 'Tis not that. He's got confused and thinks it's the Equinox and he's painted the wrong symbol, right behind the bloody Altar Stone too so everyone'll see it. He won't let us clean it off, though, and he's yowling and guarding it with his body. We don't want to manhandle the boy – see if you can talk some sense into him, will you?'

When they entered the Circle, Leveret saw a whole group of people gathered around the great stone. As she drew closer she saw Magpie in his painter's smock facing them all, arms outstretched to shield his painting and screeching in panic.

'Come on, lad,' growled Greenbough. 'Stop making that noise and let us clean it off. Nobody's angry with you, 'tis just the wrong picture for Imbolc.'

Leveret pushed her way through the people crowding around him. When Magpie saw her his face crumpled with relief and he flung his arms around her, sobbing into her cloak. She patted his back gently and made soothing noises.

'Stand back, folk!' called Merewen. 'Let Leveret talk to him. You're all making it worse crowding in on him like this.'

Leveret pulled Magpie gently off her shoulder and wiped his tears with her sleeve.

'It's alright, Maggie,' she said softly. 'Levvy's here now and it's alright. Show me this painting then. Did you get muddled up with the Spring Equinox? Show me.'

He pulled away from the stone and let her see his painting. There was the pattern of snowdrops along the top, interwoven in the design they'd all agreed on. Under this there was an enormous flame outlined in gold and blue and taking up most of the stone, and within that a great bulb of rich brown. The scale was huge as this stone was the largest one in the Circle, and the ladder and paint pots stood nearby. Inside the bulb Magpie had painted a great silver crescent moon, the symbol of Imbolc.

This much was perfect and all as it should be; exquisitely done and entirely right for Imbolc.

But instead of the usual single arrow pointing slightly upwards, he'd painted a golden-brown hare leaping across the crescent. It was beautiful, a perfect hare, lithe and long. On its head it wore a tiny silver crescent and it had bright green eyes. Magpie looked at her face anxiously and then beamed when he saw the understanding light up her eyes. Leveret turned to the watching crowd all staring in consternation, and smiled at them.

'He wasn't muddled at all!' she cried. 'It's not the Equinox hare. Magpie's painted the Maiden of Imbolc. The hare is me!'

For a moment there was a stunned silence and then Merewen roared with laughter and began to clap.

'Well done, Magpie! What a splendid idea! A hare to represent Leveret the Maiden. Why didn't I see it? 'Tis obvious now.'

Everyone started talking at once and in the buzz of excitement, Leveret turned back to Magpie and hugged him.

'You're a dear friend to me,' she said quietly, 'and I love you, Maggie. What a lovely thing to paint for me. Thank you!'

He hugged her back and then took her hand, looking into her eyes. She felt his joy and exhilaration and images started to flow. He was painting the snowdrops. He'd seen snowdrops in the woods all around. He was thinking of the flame and how he'd looked carefully at a candle flame to see the exact shape and the right colours. He'd examined a bulb and peeled it apart. He'd remembered the crescent moon of only a couple of nights ago, and she could see it through him, the bright silver bow glowing in the night sky.

And then the hare. She saw his images of hares in the field, the leaping and dancing they loved to do, the joyous way they stretched their long hind legs and laid back their ears. She saw the image of Magpie sketching rapidly onto the stone with charcoal, saw the hare growing on the stone, turning from a few black strokes into a creature so real and precise. She saw the paint going on quickly before anybody could notice and stop him because he knew they wouldn't understand. She saw the tiny silver crescent being painted on its brow, and the eyes – not amber as they should be, but green. She saw an image, a memory of herself smiling, her green eyes glowing brightly. She saw all the inspiration and imagery that had built up his painting.

And then Leveret saw something else, his final message to her. He squeezed her hand hard now so she knew this was really important. She saw the face of a very old woman; an ancient face, whiskery and toothless, the nose hooked and a shapeless old hat on the almost bald head. She saw a pair of eyes, sunken and rheumy but peering out intently. She went cold and a shiver chased down her backbone.

'That's Mother Heggy?' she whispered. 'You saw Mother Heggy?'

He nodded frantically, almost crying with relief that she understood. Then he opened his mouth and said clearly, *'Heggy.'*

23

On the morning of Imbolc Leveret awoke long before dawn. She lay silently in her bed and felt calm, accepting the role she'd been given and the honour she hadn't sought. She was to be the Bright Maiden of Imbolc and had Mother Heggy's blessing; by making contact through Magpie, the Wise Woman's message was clear. At Old Heggy's bidding, channelled through Magpie, Leveret's image was depicted up in the Stone Circle for all to see. So now it was Leveret's duty to accept the role of Maiden Huntress whether she wished it or not.

Deep inside she was terrified about the day ahead; the ordeal of standing up in front of the entire community, dancing and chanting, being the focus of everyone's attention. It went against her nature but Leveret knew she must face it. She felt that Mother Heggy would be watching over her today and ensuring she did the whole thing properly. She wanted so much to make her mother proud and to prove wrong everyone who thought she was a bad choice. Kestrel would be delighted with her – and maybe she'd even manage to please her grim brother Yul.

She lay warm in bed and tried to contact Mother Heggy and her raven, but saw nothing apart from a brief flash of blue-black quills. So instead she imagined all the people who'd be up already in the darkness. The baker and his assistants would be making the special Imbolc bread, the sweet rolls in the shape of a crescent moon that everyone loved so much. Sylvie would probably be awake as she must be in the Circle for the dawn too and had her own robes to don and words to run through. Yul would be there also, as the magus, but his role was minimal today. Imbolc was a female ceremony, the only one where the women led and the men took a back seat.

In the Barn, women would soon be arriving to check all the maidens' head-dresses and make sure the decorations were properly in place. The Barn had looked lovely yesterday when she finally left, with white candles everywhere and silver crescent moons and arrows hanging from the rafters. Edward and his helpers would be setting up the straw targets ready for the archery display on the Green, and the little dais where the Bright Maiden would sit and hand out trophies to the winners. Kestrel would be waking soon to don his costume as the Green Archer. He'd look gorgeous in the traditional green jerkin and leggings, brown boots and jaunty hat.

Leveret heard Maizie moving around in the room next to hers and knew this was the last peace and quiet she'd have today; once her mother was up and about the busy day would begin in earnest. Then she remembered her brothers and Jay and a black doubt crept into her heart. She knew they were plotting something; they'd hinted at it enough times. It was bad enough knowing they'd be laughing and jeering in the crowd as she performed the dances and sang the songs, without worrying about what else they had in store for her. They'd ridiculed her ever since she was tiny and taking part in her first ceremonies. They were why she now dreaded being the Maiden. They'd always spoiled everything and she felt a sudden rush of anger at the way they'd blighted her life. What a different person she'd be today if they'd treated her kindly, or at least as most brothers treat their little sisters. Leveret wondered yet again what they'd planned for her today that filled them with such glee, and shuddered at the thought.

Last night they'd called round to 'wish her luck'. Fortunately Jay hadn't been with them, although Maizie probably wouldn't have let him in the house anyway. They'd sat in the armchairs by the fire sniggering to each other while Maizie bustled in the kitchen, a delicious smell of baking wafting into the sitting room.

'Come and sit down, Mother!' called Sweyn. 'You work too hard.'

'I will in a minute, Sweyn love,' Maizie had replied. 'I'm just doing Leveret's breakfast for the morning. She'll have such a long day and she'll need to keep her strength up.'

Their mother had always done this on festival days – knowing it would be a rush and there'd be no time to cook a normal breakfast she laid out their breakfast the night before. She usually baked little cakes and left two on each person's plate under a cloth, with a mug ready for milk. It was one of the kind things she always did, one of the many things that made her a special mother and earned their love, even from boys like Sweyn and Gefrin.

Finally she'd come to sit down, bringing a big plate of extra cakes with her. She still baked enough for seven children even though there was only one left at home. The boys loved their mother's baking and had tucked in ravenously, devouring the delicious little cakes in no time. When Sweyn had gone through the kitchen to use the privy in the back garden, Maizie had called out jokingly to keep his hands off Leveret's breakfast lying under the cloth on the dresser. On more than one occasion in the past he'd eaten her cakes as well as his own, before she got the chance.

'I wish you boys were taking part in the archery display,' she'd said as they sat round the fire together.

'Don't like archery, Mother,' mumbled Gefrin through a mouthful of cake.

'I know, your father didn't neither, nor Geoffrey and Gregory,' she'd said. 'Yul's always loved it though.'

There was a silence at this. The fact that Yul had a different father had always been a sore point. Sweyn and Gefrin couldn't stand the idea of a young and pretty Maizie catching Magus' eye and being pregnant before she married their father. The mood in the cottage darkened and eventually Maizie had shooed them out, saying she and Leveret must be awake very early in the morning and needed their sleep. They'd stood up, grinning at their sister as Maizie went into the kitchen to stoke up the range for the night.

'We're so looking forward to your big day tomorrow,' said Gefrin, his narrow face alive with mirth. 'We'll be there looking out for you as always.'

Sweyn had come over to her chair and she'd shrunk up trying to avoid any contact with him, scared he'd hurt her again. But he'd bent and ruffled her hair in a travesty of affection.

'How's the stomach, Hare-brain?' he asked softly. 'Still painful?'

She'd glared at him, despising him with all her heart.

'Don't look at me like that, Lev – it just makes me want to punch you again. Oh, I have a message for you from Jay. He said to remind you what an ugly little bitch you are and how he'll laugh when he sees you dolled up in your stupid clothes tomorrow. And so will we – everyone will laugh, especially when you make a fool of yourself, as we know you will.'

'Why are you always like this? Why can't you ...'

Maizie had come back in then.

'Haven't you boys gone yet?'

'Just wishing Leveret good luck for tomorrow, Mother. We can't wait to see her all dressed up.'

'Oh, you'll be amazed!' beamed Maizie happily, kissing both boys soundly on their cheeks. 'She looks so lovely in the Imbolc clothes and you'll be really proud of her.'

'We can't wait, Mother.'

Then they'd gone, Sweyn making a flick gesture at Leveret behind their mother's back. And that, Leveret had thought with a flash of insight, was the real problem. Maizie saw what she wanted to see and no more; it was no reflection on her kindness and love, it was just how she dealt with life. She'd eliminated all the bad things that had made her so unhappy in the past by focusing resolutely on the good things, such as family unity. Leveret couldn't be the one to make her face the reality of Alwyn's legacy to his two youngest sons. She couldn't and wouldn't break her mother's heart by revealing their predisposition to cruelty and bullying that bolstered itself up by victimising the weak.

Leveret got out of bed as Maizie came in with a jug of hot water.

'Ah, you're awake my little Maiden. Bright blessings for Imbolc! Come here and let me kiss you.'

She hugged her mother, grimacing at the embrace as her stomach was still so sore. Maizie poured hot water into her earthenware bowl and started fiddling with the flannel and soap.

'Mother, I can wash myself!' Leveret smiled. 'Stop fussing over me.'

Maizie left her bedroom whilst she quickly washed and pulled on the camisole and petticoat, but insisted on returning to help put on the special dress. When Leveret was laced up at the back she stood aside to admire her daughter.

''Tis perfect and fits a treat. You look so lovely in white.'

The dress was similar in style to the green one she'd worn at Yuletide, tight around the bodice and waist, with long pointed sleeves. The full skirts reached almost to the ground and ended in points, each one tipped with a green glass bead. Snowdrops were embroidered around the neck line, their green foliage making a pretty pattern that linked together to form a chain. She wore dainty green leather boots with heels, and later on in the Barn she would change them for silver dancing shoes.

When Maizie had admired her and tweaked at the lacing to her satisfaction, she sat Leveret down straight-backed in front of the small mirror and brushed her hair vigorously before sweeping the mass of long curls up and pinning them in a loose knot on her crown. Once again the transformation was startling – from wild-haired girl to an exquisite young woman. Then Maizie carefully lifted the head-dress and placed it on her head. It was a fine wicker wreath painted silver and interlaced with a whole drift of snowdrops, and it had sat outside in the cold all night so as not to wilt. On the front was an ancient crescent moon made from real silver that glimmered in the candle-light. It sat perfectly on Leveret's head giving her added stature and making her green eyes seem enormous. Maizie sighed with pleasure.

'Leveret, my little one, you're the most beautiful Maiden there's ever been,' she breathed. 'Even more beautiful than Sylvie was all those years gone by.'

Leveret smiled and thought wryly how blind a mother's love could be. They went downstairs then and Maizie placed the special, heavy robes around her shoulders. The myriad silver moons embroidered on the snowy white material glinted and sparkled in the candlelight, and Leveret began to feel a little more confident. The Bright Maiden's robes were a delight and wearing them, as countless other young girls had done over the years, made her feel magical.

'Right, the carriage will be here any minute to collect us so there's just time for your breakfast.'

Maizie rushed off into the kitchen and Leveret groaned at the thought of food. Her stomach was churning; cakes were the last things she wanted now. But ever anxious not to hurt her mother's feelings, she nibbled a cake and sipped at the milk.

'Come on, girl, get it down you! I know you're nervous but you'll feel better for having something in your belly. And it'll be so cold up in that Circle. No, not just one – eat 'em both.'

Leveret forced the second cake down – they seemed heavier than usual with an after-taste too, though maybe that was just her nerves. She felt the crumbs sticking in her throat and hastily swallowed some milk, not wanting a choking fit now.

'Aren't you having any, Mother?'

'No, I only left these two out for you. Those boys were so hungry last night that I brought in the lot apart from yours. I'll have breakfast later in the Barn. Right, quickly brush your teeth and nip down to the privy. Mind your dress and boots!'

When Leveret returned from the earth closet outside she found her sister Rosie in the cottage talking with their mother. Rosie was all bundled up against the early morning chill and she carried a lantern.

'I just popped in to wish you well today, Leveret,' she said, kissing her little sister's cheek. She stood back and surveyed her.

'Don't she look beautiful?' said Maizie, pulling on her own cloak and woollen hat. 'My special little Imbolc Maiden.'

'Aye,' said Rosie, staring at Leveret. ''Tis amazing how she's transformed – a green caterpillar into a white butterfly. Leveret, I'm proud o' you being chosen but make sure you do your best today, won't you? You know all the words and the steps?'

Leveret nodded, her stomach somersaulting queasily.

'My little Snowdrop's so excited that her auntie's the Bright Maiden, and so are Celandine and Bluebell,' said Rosie. 'Celandine has worked really hard so do make sure you say something kind to her, won't you? 'Tis her dearest wish that you're pleased with her special dance.'

Leveret nodded again, still tasting the grease from the cakes and wishing she'd never eaten them.

'I'm very nervous but I'll do my best today,' she said quietly.

'That were kind o' you to come specially to wish her well,' said Maizie, looking for her mittens.

'Aye, well . . .'

As Maizie went into the kitchen looking for the mittens, Rosie grabbed Leveret's arm and whispered to her urgently.

'*Don't* let Mother down again, will you? She's so very, very proud o' you and it'll break her heart if you spoil today. That's what I really came to say.'

'No, Rosie, of course I won't,' said Leveret, hurt that her sister had no faith in her.

'Don't sound so surprised!' hissed Rosie sharply. 'We both know that—'

She stopped as Maizie came back in the room and then the carriage arrived and they were off, with old Tom at the reins, up to the Stone Circle.

It was still dark up there and very wintry indeed. Leveret trembled with cold and nerves and was relieved that so few people attended this ceremony. Flickering lanterns had been placed under each stone making the darkness even deeper somehow. Yul was dressed in green robes decorated with crescents and stood behind the Altar Stone scowling at everyone. He'd been furious to discover the painting of the hare with green eyes on the biggest stone, not wishing his sister to be honoured any more than was strictly necessary. Sylvie looked beautiful in her silver and white ceremonial robes and smiled warmly at Leveret when she arrived.

'You look lovely,' she whispered. 'I know how you feel – I was terrified at my Imbolc ceremony too. And happy birthday, Leveret! You're fifteen today, aren't you?'

Leveret had completely forgotten that, as had Maizie. Then Kestrel arrived with his father, looking strikingly handsome in the green outfit with a great cloak swirling round him. He looked at her admiringly and put a comforting arm around her shoulders.

'They made the right choice, Leveret – you're gorgeous. Pity it's not your sixteenth birthday today.'

She blushed at this and looked at the ground as her insides gave another queasy leap.

The ceremony started well, the intimate atmosphere making it feel all the more magical. Leveret remembered what she had to do, which wasn't much at this ceremony beyond making some sweeping gestures with the traditional besom, stepping forward at the right moment to take the ceremonial silver bow from the Green Archer and chanting a few lines. Sylvie did most of the work, delivering her words faultlessly, her lovely clear voice rising out of the Circle. The sky gradually lightened to the south-east, becoming brighter and paler in the chill air and finally the sun rose, golden and bright. The bonfire was lit and crackled into life as Yul chanted on the Altar Stone, receiving the Earth Magic from its source and standing with his arms outstretched, his head tipped back.

He felt a mere flicker of energy pass through him and was bitterly disappointed. He'd really hoped that at this festival the Earth Magic would return to him but once more his hopes were dashed. He thought back to the night before with Sylvie. They were going through the motions and Sylvie was doing her best but clearly not feeling anything of her former passion or abandonment with him. He felt a surge of anger that completely doused the faint tingle of Earth Magic. What was the matter with her? It wasn't *all* his fault.

When the people came to receive the energy from him, their obvious disappointment made him feel impotent. What he'd dreaded had come to pass and he glanced angrily at Sylvie, standing stony-faced and watching him with sadness in her eyes. He didn't need her damn sympathy either. Leveret came forward then in her glimmering robes and despite his anger with her, he had to admit she was a perfect Maiden, tiny and delicate and so very pretty. She smiled tentatively up at him but he glared back at her, his face hard, and her smile faltered and died. She bowed her head as he took her hands in his, and withdrew them quickly when she realised that once again there was no jolt of magic flooding from him.

It wasn't until the cakes and mead were passed around that Leveret started to feel really strange. She swallowed her cake and felt sick, still full from her breakfast. She quickly gulped down the mead and then regretted it, thinking she actually might be sick. She swayed slightly and Kestrel, standing next to her, put out a steadying hand. After that he held her hand and she was grateful for the warmth and comfort of it, and stunned that she was holding hands with the boy of her dreams.

Then the ceremony was over and Yul climbed down from the Altar Stone and went over to the bonfire to warm his hands. He felt humiliated about the lack of energy he'd passed on, and deeply concerned about where this was leading. He'd been magus for thirteen years – why was this happening now? The only consolation was that there weren't many here today to witness it; hopefully he could rely on people's loyalty not to tell the whole community. By the Spring Equinox he had to have the problem sorted and he glanced over to Sylvie who was talking with Greenbough. She must start moondancing at Hare Stone again – maybe that'd do the trick.

As he dwelled on his problems Leveret, standing near Sylvie and her mother, started to hallucinate. The ground was rising and falling in great waves which made her feel dizzy. She looked across the great Circle; Greenbough had moved away to speak to Martin and Edward near the entrance to the Long Walk, and Yul still stood by the bonfire.

'Who's that man with Yul?' she asked, her voice sounding faraway in her ears. Maizie and Sylvie looked up.

'What man?' asked Maizie. 'There's no man with Yul.'

'Yes there is – a tall man. Look, standing right by him.'

They both frowned at her.

'Really there's no one there, Leveret,' said Maizie. ''Tis just Yul on his own, warming his hands. It must be the firelight playing tricks with your eyes.'

Leveret stared again.

'There! He's moved around the fire and now he's facing us.'

Sylvie had turned very pale all of a sudden and she closed her eyes in despair. The man looked up then, staring straight across the Circle at Leveret. His silvery hair gleamed in the firelight as he smiled at her, bowing his head in a gracious gesture of deference to the Bright Maiden. Leveret smiled back and then blinked in surprise as he seemed to dissolve before her eyes, leaving Yul standing alone by the flickering flames of the Imbolc fire.

Two carriages were waiting at the end of the Long Walk as Sylvie had arrived in one too; it was important that the women's lovely white and silver robes and dresses remained unmuddied. Sylvie climbed into the same one as Leveret, so Maizie and Miranda shared the other one and everyone else walked as usual. As they drove back to the Village Sylvie looked sideways at her sister-in-law, who sat bolt upright staring ahead.

'Are you feeling alright, Leveret?'

She was feeling far from alright. The tiny carriage seemed to be breathing around her, closing in on her and then receding again. She felt very strange indeed and wished that Clip were here, but he'd told her that today he must celebrate privately in the Dolmen.

'Yes.'

Sylvie swallowed and clasped her hands to stop them trembling.

'That man you saw in the Circle near Yul – can you tell me what he looked like?'

'I don't know,' mumbled Leveret, trying to focus her eyes.

'Please, Leveret, it's really important,' said Sylvie urgently, her heart beating wildly. 'Please try and describe him. I have to know what you saw.'

'He was big and tall and he had blond hair like Martin's and Clip's. But ... it was strange ... apart from his hair and his age he looked *exactly* like Yul.'

Sylvie sat back in her seat abruptly and took a ragged breath, relief flooding through her.

'Thank you, Leveret,' she said quietly, her voice shaking. 'At least I know now I'm not going mad.'

Breakfast was laid out in the Barn – sweet crescent-shaped rolls and a warming brew of milk, honey and malt. Leveret could face none of it and sat silently in her own world as people gradually started to arrive for the day's festivities. After breakfast there was a brief opening ceremony led by Sylvie, who passed another beribboned besom to the Bright Maiden who must ceremonially sweep away the winter debris ready for the shoots of spring.

Then the Green Archer had to perform his first duty of the day. A tall ladder was brought in, also decorated with white ribbons, and placed upright against a rafter. After bowing to his Bright Maiden, Kestrel began to ascend steadily, the crowd chanting as each rung was climbed, until he reached the rafter. There lay the great Corn Spirit dolly on a nest of woven straw. Carefully Kestrel lifted the huge spiralling neck of woven and plaited stalks, its wheat ears still fanned out at one end, though spilling a few kernels, the red, gold and green ribbons dusty and a little cobwebbed. He placed the huge dolly, as long as his arm but even thicker, into a wicker pannier strapped to his belt. He descended to excited cheers and solemnly handed the dolly to Leveret with a sweeping bow. She took the huge dusty neck in her arms and stared blankly at him.

'Put it on the table, Leveret!' he whispered helpfully, worried that she was becoming overcome with nerves. 'Remember? *"The Corn Spirit has survived the winter and is with us at Imbolc – soon she will return to the land."* Say the words!'

She managed to repeat this, with a little more prompting from Kestrel, then everyone donned their cloaks and went out onto the Village Green for the archery displays. It passed in a blur for Leveret. The trees appeared to be moving around the Green, engaged in their own Imbolc dance. She sat on a special carved chair that had been set up on the little dais, pale-faced and impassive in her white and silver robes, the great head-dress giving her a regal aura. She attracted a great deal of attention for she looked so lovely and many people hadn't seen her transformation at the Outsiders' Dance. Celandine came up shyly and told her she was the most beautiful Maiden she'd ever seen, but Leveret could only gaze down at the little girl with unfocused eyes and Celandine crept away, disappointed.

As the morning wore on she felt more and more surreal. People were moving strangely, their voices coming as if from the end of a long tunnel. Faces loomed suddenly in front of her, mouths stretched in odd grimaces, and then disappeared again. She looked at the arrows arching through the sky and saw rainbows trailing from the fletchings, each arrow briefly silhouetted against the cold, grey winter's sky. Finally the competitions came to an end and she must present the winners with their silver trophies – a miniature bow and arrow mounted on a piece of yew. She stood and the world swam sharply around her, faces and trees and lots of green grass. Silently she handed out the trophies, feeling as if she were balancing on stilts and scared she might topple over.

Rufus won in his age-category and came up to the dais to collect his trophy. Like Celandine, he smiled shyly at Leveret remembering their conversation that day in the Dining Hall.

'Thank you, Bright Maiden,' he said, lowering himself to one knee before her as was the custom. Prompted by Kestrel, she handed the boy his trophy but didn't say a word, looking straight through him with no recognition at all. His face fell.

'Excellent bowmanship!' said Kestrel kindly, trying to compensate for his partner's increasingly worrying behaviour. 'I shall have to watch out for you, Rufus – you'll be challenging me soon.'

Everyone then moved indoors for the lunch laid out on long trestle tables up and down the Barn. Leveret, whose outer robes had now been removed, sat at the centre of the top table with Kestrel by her side. She looked down at the plate in front of her in surprise; it appeared to be spinning around very fast. People were putting bizarre objects in their mouths and making a lot of noise. Maizie, frantically busy helping organise the food, appeared at her shoulder.

'What's the matter, love? Have something to eat, for goddess' sake – you look so pale. You got all the dancing and chants to do this afternoon, Leveret. 'Tis your busy time so keep your strength up, my girl.'

Kestrel tried to make conversation but she merely stared at him. Her pupils were enormous, like a cat's eyes in the dark. Her brothers had always said she was weird and they were right – she was making him feel uncomfortable and he couldn't understand how the shy but competent girl he'd rehearsed with had turned into this silent automaton. He spoke to Faun instead, on his other side, Rowan having somehow secured her daughter a place right next to him at the top table. Faun was in her element, tossing back her blond ringlets and flashing her dark eyes at him, loving every minute of his attention. She flirted quite outrageously in a way an older girl couldn't have done, but at the same time played on the fact that it was her thirteenth birthday which she said made her feel very grown up all of a sudden. She also made much of the fact that she was Magus' daughter and had true Hallfolk blood in her veins. Then she began to make funny comments about the unresponsive Maiden seated next to him, who stared around her slowly in unnatural wonder. Before long Faun and Kestrel were roaring with laughter at their oblivious victim.

The feast was well underway when the Barn doors were thrown open to the cold and in came three unexpected visitors, cloaked against the wintry weather outside. There was a ripple of shock – it was a long time since Violet, Vetchling and Starling had attended any ceremonies or festivals. They kept to themselves in their cottage at the end of the lane and conducted their own private rituals to mark the turning wheel of the year. But they were perfectly entitled to join in if they wished and, with a bit of disruption, space was found for them at the end of long table. The two crones hobbled towards their seats, muttering and casting malignant glances all around as people stared at them. Starling waddled along in their wake, more used to contact with the community as she was a frequent visitor to the food stores in the Village.

They established themselves around the end of the table with much fussing and grumbling. Starling began to eat steadily while the crones sucked and smacked their gums on whatever soft morsels they could manage. Everyone was speculating about their unforeseen attendance but kept their glances surreptitious, not wanting to be caught by the crones. Marigold hovered protectively by Magpie whom she'd seated near the kitchen entrance where she could keep an eye on him. She was so proud of him, sitting up at the table using his cutlery with reasonable accuracy for the very first time at a public festival. He looked clean and smart, his face glowing and hair glossy, and she wasn't going to let those evil witches spoil his day. He'd jumped up in fear when they'd entered but Cherry and Marigold had pulled him back down in his seat, soothing him and promising that nobody would let the three women take him back to the hovel at the end of the lane.

Leveret had stared in horror as the three black birds hopped down the Barn to sit at the far end. She could see them pecking at their food, gobbling and squawking. Then she noticed her brothers and Jay sitting further down another table but constantly looking her way and laughing. Jay caught her glance and raised a hand in greeting, grinning from ear to ear. She saw his face splitting open like an over-ripe peach, all red inside, and she gasped in horror and made the sign of the pentangle on her chest for protection. Several people nearby watched her in fascination for she was acting very oddly indeed.

Kestrel was feeling increasingly uncomfortable about her behaviour and looked around for somebody he could voice his concerns to. She'd not eaten or drunk anything and barely said a word to him, and what had started out as funny behaviour was now becoming serious. He could see Maizie but she was very busy, as were many of the older women, bustling about with large plates of food and jugs of drink and making sure the tables were well stocked. Sylvie was sitting far away with all the little maidens in their white dresses and Yul was over by the bar. The whole Barn was alive with movement and merriment but there nobody he could confide his misgivings to. He even looked about for Hazel but she was nowhere to be seen. The afternoon was going to be long and arduous and he couldn't see how Leveret would cope. He wished that the bubbly and vivacious Faun could take Leveret's place. They should never have chosen her as Maiden.

Finally the feast ended. The tables were cleared and stacked away and the floor prepared for the afternoon's events. Many people went outside onto the Green for a stroll and some fresh air and some even went home to their cottages for a rest. Kestrel rose and looked down at Leveret, who still sat bolt upright staring blankly ahead as if she were in another world. He shook his head in despair – he had a horrible feeling she was going to make him look like a fool this afternoon.

'Up you get, Leveret,' he said, putting a hand on her arm and encouraging her to rise. She gazed up at him and he was shocked at the vacancy in her eyes. She stood, swaying like a sapling in a gale, and he grabbed her to stop her falling.

'The birds are coming in to roost,' she mumbled. 'All the birds are gathering.'

Faun caught his eye and burst into peals of laughter.

'It's not funny, Faun,' he said desperately. 'I've got to dance with her. What the hell am I going to do?'

'I should've been the maiden,' she murmured, rubbing against his arm. 'I wouldn't let you down.'

Maizie was still occupied organising the clearing up. Sylvie had gathered some of the little girls at one end of the barn and was going through their lines with them. People were milling around everywhere moving furniture and benches, all busy and engrossed in what had to be done and looking forward to the afternoon's events. Kestrel glanced around frantically for someone to help. Yul leant against the wall watching the scene with a dark scowl and Kestrel managed to catch his eye, signalling his urgency. Yul strode over to where Kestrel stood holding Leveret upright.

'Yul, I don't know what to do! Look at her – she's on another planet.'

Yul frowned at his sister, tipping her chin so he could look into her face. He saw her deathly-white demeanour and glassy eyes, the pupils huge and black, and his face darkened.

'Sacred Mother! What the hell's the matter with her?'

Kestrel shook his head hopelessly.

'She's been like this ever since we got here. She hasn't eaten or drunk anything and she keeps saying strange things.'

'This is bloody *typical*!' Yul spat. 'Leveret up to her dramatics again, letting people down and ruining her mother's day. She looks like she's taken drugs.'

'Where's Hazel?' asked Kestrel, scanning the crowds.

'Not here today – she stayed on duty at the Hall with some of the sicker folk in the ward. She's really needed up there as one of them isn't expected to last the day.'

He grasped his sister's slight shoulders and shook her.

'LEVERET! Pull yourself together, girl! You're the Bright Maiden, remember? You're letting everyone down!'

She stared at him.

'The darkness within you is too dark now – it's a black evil and staining everything.'

'DON'T TALK RUBBISH, GIRL!' he shouted in her face. He turned to Kestrel. 'Goddess but I'd like to shake her! How *dare* she do this today of all days?'

Just then Sweyn and Gefrin came up, having spotted the huddle around Leveret. They'd left Jay with his trio of women in the corner where they'd firmly ensconced themselves, marking out their territory.

'Is something the matter, Yul?' asked Sweyn.

'Leveret's looking a bit odd,' remarked Gefrin.

'Too bloody right she's a bit odd!' snapped Yul. 'She's out of her bloody head and I don't know what to do with her! She must've taken something – her damn mushrooms again, I shouldn't wonder.'

'Shall we take her outside for some fresh air?' suggested Sweyn. 'We could walk her round the Green a couple of times – maybe that'd clear her head.'

Yul glanced at him gratefully. Sweyn reminded him forcibly of his brutish step father but the lad couldn't help that and maybe Maizie was right – these two gormless half-brothers of his seemed to have improved with age.

'Excellent idea! Thanks. March her around and try to sort her out, would you? And keep her well away from Mother – I don't want her upset today.'

'No – Mother was so excited about Leveret being the Maiden.'

'I know,' said Yul gloomily. 'I said this damn girl should never've been picked. Look at the state of her!'

'Don't worry, Yul, we'll deal with her,' said Gefrin.

'Try to get her to eat or drink something if you can. Kestrel says she's had nothing at all.'

'We've got just the thing,' said Sweyn, smiling slightly.

'And take the head-dress off – she's too conspicuous like that. Find something plain to cover her up with so nobody realises it's her. I'll get Rosie to keep Mother out of the way.'

Gefrin nodded eagerly and Sweyn took his sister's arm.

'Come on, Levvy – let's go and sober you up.'

Wanting only to be shot of the embarrassment, Kestrel was more than happy to let them lead her away, one on each side holding her up. He turned to find someone a little more amenable to his charms than this awful partner who'd been foisted on him. He saw the delightful Faun now standing amongst a group of giggling girls and made his way over to them. Faun was much too young for now, but what promise for later!

Leveret was hustled into a small side room where the boys quickly snatched off the snowdrop and silver wicker head-dress, flinging a plain black cloak over her beautiful white dress and pulling the hood up. They had to get her out quickly before Maizie could come looking, and hoped Rosie would keep her away. They managed to get Leveret outside unnoticed and bundled her onto the Green, through the throngs of people milling around and towards the denser trees at the far end. Before they'd got half way Jay had run up behind them laughing in triumph.

'Got her out, then?'

'Piece o' cake!' cried Gefrin, nearly wetting himself at his own joke.

'And better still, that murdering bastard is pleased with us for doing it!' said Sweyn, tugging at Leveret's arm beneath the black cloak as she stumbled along beside him. 'He actually thinks we're doing him a favour.'

They all laughed at this.

'Let's have a look at her, then,' said Jay, trying to peer under her hood.

'Wait till we're under the trees,' said Sweyn. 'We got plenty of time. After all, they can't start the festival without her, can they?'

They went quite deep into the wood where they wouldn't be seen by anyone on the Green.

'What do we do now?' asked Gefrin.

'Not much we can do except give her the potion. Those cakes worked a treat, didn't they?' said Jay gleefully. 'She is so out of it. Leveret! Can you hear me, Leveret?'

He passed a hand close to her eyes but she didn't blink. Slowly she turned her face towards him and stared intently into his eyes.

'This will come to an end,' she said tonelessly. 'You'll suffer. I know – I've been told.'

'Bloody crazy bitch!' he hissed, hating the way she looked right through him with her wild, glassy eyes. 'You're the one who's going to suffer, believe me. STOP STARING AT ME!'

'Let's sit her down and get that stuff inside her,' suggested Sweyn.

They pulled her onto the ground, thick with leaf-mould, and propped her up against the trunk of an elm tree. She sat impassively, her legs straight out in front of her, gazing up at the rooks flapping about in the bare branches overhead.

''Tis a pity we can't do anything else to her today,' said Gefrin.

'Where's the potion then?' asked Sweyn looking at Jay, who produced a small bottle from his pocket. He pulled out the cork stopper and sniffed the murky liquid, grimacing with disgust.

'Right, you dozy cow – time for a little top-up. Just what the doctor ordered – or do I mean Old Violet? Open wide!'

He cradled her head roughly and tried to push the mouth of the bottle between her lips. He tipped her head back and pulled her chin down, pouring the contents into her mouth. She swallowed a little but began to choke, the liquid running down her chin.

'Watch out! You'll mess up the dress and somebody'll notice,' said Sweyn.

But Jay was determined to make her drink it all and kept going until the little bottle was empty.

'There, taken your medicine like a good girl,' he laughed, wiping her mouth with his sleeve. 'Now all we have to do is sit back and watch – should be fun!'

Gefrin giggled wildly.

'Is it the same stuff that were in the cakes?'

'No, completely different. Violet said it'd mix well with some great effects. It'll wear off some time tonight, but that's okay –

the festival will be over by then and she'll be in such trouble. Did you put the mushrooms by her bed?'

The brothers nodded, grinning slyly.

'I suppose we better get her back then,' said Sweyn.

They stood up and Jay yanked Leveret roughly to her feet. She fell into him like a rag doll and he caught her under her arms, making her sway around. There was no resistance at all.

'You're right, Gef,' he murmured. 'Pity we can't have more fun with her while she's like this. Maybe another time.'

Yul was waiting for them outside the Barn, glowering across the Green. He watched them approaching slowly with Leveret supported between them. Jay had already slipped off to the side of the Barn not wanting any connection made to his family.

'Any luck?' Yul barked. 'Is she back with us now or still orbiting the moon?'

'I'm not sure,' said Sweyn. 'She's still very floppy but she's starting to speak more.'

'Well done and thanks for trying. We've made a contingency plan in case the dance goes wrong. And all her chants – Harold's just brought photocopies down. The other girls will have to read it all out instead of her. I can't believe she's done this – just wait till I get my hands on her tomorrow!'

'Did you say you thought she'd been at the mushrooms?' asked Sweyn nonchalantly.

'Yes I did. It's possible, isn't it? We'll find out tomorrow. Come on, let's get her inside now and put the headdress back on her.'

Leveret stood passively while her three brothers whipped the cloak off and tried to reposition the head-dress. Sylvie came into the side-room, quickly shutting the door behind her.

'Thank goddess she's alright and hasn't fainted. You shouldn't have taken her outside in the cold – why didn't you come and find me? Leveret, what's wrong?'

She looked anxiously at the pale girl.

'You won't get any sense out of her!' snapped Yul. 'Give us a hand with this thing, would you?'

'We've got to be quick,' said Sylvie, hurriedly arranging the head-dress onto Leveret's mass of curls. The top-knot had fallen down when Jay shook her and there was no time to re-pin it. 'Everyone's waiting out there. She's in no fit state to dance, is she? Let's leave the green boots on and forget about the silver shoes. We'll just sit her on the Maiden's chair in the middle, as we agreed, and Celandine will do Leveret's dance with Kestrel. The others have got the lines and we've had a very quick practice. It'll be alright.'

'It's a bloody disaster!' growled Yul, pulling Leveret roughly towards the door. 'Look at the state of her! Poor Mother – she's going to be devastated.'

Sylvie peered into Leveret's glassy eyes – her green irises were almost swallowed up by her dilated pupils. Then Yul opened the door and led her out to the waiting crowd who all turned, eager to see the arrival of the Bright Maiden. As Sylvie followed Leveret into the huge room a distant memory stirred in her mind. She remembered a Dark Moon thirteen years ago, when she'd entered this very Barn wearing a scarlet cloak, floating in to a sea of faces on a cloud of hallucinogen.

24

As Yul had predicted, it was a disaster. When the Dance of the Maidens began and the girls started to move in a white cloud around her, Leveret gripped her chair and shut her eyes. Somehow the performance went ahead, mostly thanks to Celandine dancing like a dream in her new white satin ballet shoes. The little girl managed to give the impression that Leveret was part of the ceremony, constantly dancing up to her and acting as if she were merely doing the Bright Maiden's bidding. She wove Leveret's dance moves with the Green Archer together with the special solo that she'd worked on so hard, whilst Leveret sat like a carved figure gazing out at the crowd, her dilated eyes eerily vacant.

The chants and songs, poetry and drama took place without her and everyone coped using the photocopied sheets and stumbling through Leveret's major part. It was obvious to all that something was terribly wrong; these rituals were very old and everyone knew how they were supposed to be performed. The Bright Maiden should've been the central figure leading the whole performance, and instead she sat there like a statue, silent and unmoving. Kestrel was furious; rather than having a manful role as the Green Archer to a beautiful and nubile Maiden, he had to dance with a six year-old. She may've been lovely in the white dress with her white-blond curls cascading from beneath her snowdrop head-dress, but he felt a complete fool. Several times he caught Faun's eye and she smiled in sympathy.

All the other girls of Leveret's age who could've been chosen as the Maiden were up in arms, angry that not only had Leveret messed it up but also that Celandine had been chosen to step in. They didn't realise she was the only one capable of improvising a complicated dance at short notice with no practice. They only saw the apparent unfairness of the situation – Yul's family being favoured yet again.

Sweyn and Gefrin stood near the back and smirked throughout. Leveret was like an automaton and Yul's dark face was a picture. Jay stood with the three women who muttered and cackled amongst themselves the whole way through. At one point, much to everyone's bemusement, Violet and Vetchling lit their pipes and glared and cursed at anyone who dared to comment. Starling managed to find a great dish of sausages which she enthusiastically worked her way through with belches of satisfaction. Jay watched the whole scene with a twisted smile on his face, enjoying every moment of Leveret's disgrace. He didn't know why he hated her so much – it wasn't a logical thing and he wasn't one for self-analysis. But he knew that there was something about the girl that he wanted to crush; a magical spark he longed to douse. Poor Maizie had taken refuge in the kitchen with Rosie and was crying her eyes out. She'd never felt so humiliated or furious in her life.

Finally the dancing and chants came to an end. Sylvie stood to close the ceremonies and send everyone home for a few hours so the Barn could be cleared for the food and dancing tonight. She was relieved the whole terrible day was over but still dreaded having to deal with Yul. He was enraged, his face like thunder, and she knew he'd blame her. Leveret should've been such a lovely Maiden and it was such a shame; instead of boosting the girl's self-esteem as she'd hoped, there'd now be even more censure and punishment. She could see how angry he was and he'd make very sure that Leveret suffered the consequences.

Just as Sylvie rose and raised her hands for quiet, Leveret stood up. Unsure what she intended Sylvie sat down again, thinking that maybe the poor girl felt a little better now and wanted to say a few words of apology. Leveret stood on the small stage in the centre of the Barn straight-backed, her clinging white dress beautiful and her dark curls wild and free beneath the silver head-dress. There was absolute silence and stillness, everyone eager to hear what she was going to say.

Leveret slowly surveyed the vast area, scanning the faces with wide-open eyes, turning to make a complete sweep of everyone present. Then she raised her arms almost in a gesture of supplication, her palms spread to the people, and started to speak in a strange and slow voice.

'Folk of Stonewylde, there is darkness ahead! There are shadows at Stonewylde, shadows that will engulf us all. We must be strong. We must fight the darkness and evil that is coming. The birds are gathering, the dark birds who smother the brightness. The viper is among us! The raven has spoken—'

In one fluid motion, Yul strode across the empty space to her side.

'That's enough, Leveret!' he said clearly. 'Stonewylders, please forgive my sister. She isn't well. I want—'

'You will be overshadowed!' she cried. 'The darkness is already blackening your soul. The shadows are—'

'*Enough!*'

He picked Leveret up bodily and flung her over his shoulder. Her head-dress fell to the stage and bounced off, rolling right across the floor in the shocked silence. She struggled and kicked but Yul held her tightly and moved towards the great doors, desperate to get her out of the building before she humiliated him any further. The Stonewylders stared in absolute astonishment at the spectacle of their magus carrying their Bright Maiden out in disgrace. Then the voice of Old Violet rang out, audible to all.

'Eh, sister, that were the worst Imbolc I ever seen! 'Tweren't like that in our Magus' day – *he* always ran things properly!'

'Come on, lad – have your wash and get up to bed,' said Marigold, busy laying the breakfast table for the morning. Magpie hovered near the door staring at her pleadingly.

'No, Magpie. 'Tis past your bedtime and it's been a long day, a terrible day. That poor little maid.'

Still he hovered, his hand now on the latch.

'No, I said bedtime. You must be tired and you can't go dancing in the Barn. 'Tis not for you this year, Magpie. Jay's down there and we don't want him doing nothing nasty, do we? You're safe here with me, safe and warm. Be a good boy now and get washed.'

He loped over and took her hand in his, staring into her eyes desperately.

'That don't work with me, boy, you know that. 'Tis only Leveret as can understand you like that.'

She saw the light appear in his eyes and he nodded eagerly.

'Leveret? Oh I see – you want to find Leveret?'

He was almost comical in his affirmation, running back to the door again. Marigold sighed and came over, taking his arm and leading him gently back into the sitting room.

'No, Magpie, you can't go to Leveret. I know you love her, but now 'tis not the right time. There was something badly wrong today and she's not well. You remember Yul telling us he took her back to her cottage, don't you? She's been put to bed and she'll be sleeping now. We can't go and disturb her.'

Magpie held her hand against his cheek and pleaded with his eyes.

'No, Magpie! You be a good boy and in the morning when I done the breakfasts at the Hall we'll go down to the Village, you and me, and call on Leveret. How's that? 'Tis my final word, Magpie – you're not going there tonight.'

He stared sadly into the fire, his shoulders drooping. Then he stroked Marigold's plump arm briefly, his way of showing affection, and slowly climbed the wooden stairs to his bedroom.

The gang of boys stood in corner of the Great Barn steadily drinking cider. For Sweyn, Gefrin and Jay it had been a very good day indeed and they toasted each other and grinned with delight. Everything had gone perfectly, even better than they'd planned, culminating in their wonderful triumph when Leveret had stood up and spouted all that rubbish before being carried out in disgrace by Yul. The only blight on the day, for the brothers at least, was that their mother was so very upset.

Maizie was sitting at a small table with Rosie and Robin. She'd been persuaded to stay and have a few drinks as there was no point in her going home feeling lonely and unhappy, with Leveret asleep upstairs. As Rosie had wisely pointed out, it was better not to hide away tonight but to brave it out now and show the world she could cope. Maizie had reluctantly agreed and was beginning to care less about it as the rhubarb wine kicked in. Sweyn looked across at his mother, her cheeks flushed and eyes a little too bright. With a complete lack of guilt for the part he'd played in today's fiasco, he vowed to get Leveret back for what she'd done today.

Kestrel had joined them and was rapidly becoming roaring drunk. He'd fulfilled his assignation with Honey earlier on in the hayloft, although he'd been too angry to do the lovely girl justice and would have to make it up to her another time. Now he just wanted to blot out the whole ghastly day and have a serious drinking session with his mates. They were full of sympathy for him, agreeing with his every complaint about the mad girl who'd been mistakenly chosen as Maiden. Sweyn and Gefrin tried to cheer him up with tales of the tricks they'd played on her over the years. They'd decided with Jay not to enlighten Kestrel as to the cause of Leveret's bizarre behaviour all day. They didn't think he'd see the funny side of it at all.

Jay was as drunk as Kestrel and on a high, feeling victorious and omnipotent. He thrilled with pleasure and power remembering how Yul had carried Leveret off screaming and kicking. That was his doing, putting her in her place like that – him and his great-aunt, Old Violet. They made good allies he decided; she had the knowledge and the potions, he had the muscle and cunning. Swift stood drinking with them too, sober compared to the other four but drinking more than he usually permitted himself. He too thought it had been a brilliant day; Yul had been totally humiliated.

'And what about Old Violet then, when she said how Magus had always run things properly?'

They shouted with laughter.

'Did you see his face when she said that? I thought he were going to explode!'

'He looked such a bloody idiot, didn't he? Black-haired bastard!'

'Did you hear what people was saying? They agreed with Old Violet – I heard 'em all muttering.'

'Well, boys,' said Kestrel, swaying alarmingly and trying to drag them all into a huddle, 'today has shown us that he ain't the king he thinks he is. He makes stupid mistakes like allowing his whacky sister to be chosen as Maiden. What a bloody idiotic choice! I tell you, when his time comes I'll be ready. I'd like to see him fall, I really would – especially after what he put me through today.'

Swift nodded at this.

'Me too! He's an arrogant bastard and he shouldn't be in power here. We're ready! Father said ... well, never mind what Father said ... anyway, the sooner Yul's brought down, the better!'

'He killed our dear father, you know,' said Sweyn mawkishly. 'Hexed him. I'll see him finished, I will!'

'Made a widow of our mother, he did,' added Gefrin. 'All those years we thought 'twas an accident.'

'And my father too! 'Tis all Yul's fault,' said Jay.

They chorused their intense desire to see him get his come-uppance.

'We'll have to get together and make plans,' said Swift. 'Form a sort of alliance to bring him down and make it happen, not just sit around talking about it.'

'Brilliant!' slurred Kestrel. 'I like it – we'll do all sorts of things behind the lines like agents who sabotage their enemies under-cover.'

'Yeah – smash it up! Destroy it!'

'When our gang's done, Yul will be history!' cried Swift and they all drank to that.

Clip sat alone in his tower in his white and silver robes and stared despondently into the fire burning in the hearth. He thought sadly of Leveret, his little protégée, who must now be asleep at home. This should've been her big day, the day she'd remember for the rest of her life. She'd certainly do that, he thought wryly, but for entirely the wrong reasons. If only he'd gone down to the Village earlier maybe he could've helped. It was obvious she'd been drugged and he was sure it was no coincidence that the three hags had chosen this event to mark their return to Village life, wanting to see the effects of their handiwork.

Clip had arrived just as the afternoon's performances were about to start, slipping in to the Great Barn and standing quietly at the back of the crowds. He'd wanted to see Leveret starring in her role, overcoming her fears as he knew she would and fulfilling her promise as Maiden. She had no idea of the true significance of the role but Sylvie must've known it instinctively when she chose Leveret for the part. The spiritual aspects of the role – the celestial spark of intuition, feminine creativity, divine inspiration – were Leveret's by destiny and right.

But it was all in ruins, sabotaged by the dark forces at work in Stonewylde, and poor Leveret was now in deep trouble. He'd wanted to intervene but hadn't really appreciated what was happening until it was too late to do anything. If only he'd come earlier and realised. Clip shuddered at the memory of Yul's face, so very like Magus' in his dangerous anger. Yul was not sadistic like his father had been – there'd be no torture in the stone byre – but his anger was almost more frightening for that. Leveret would pay a steep price for the fiasco today for Yul had been humiliated in front of the whole community and was far too proud to let that pass unpunished. Clip had heard the mutterings and complaints as folk wondered why Yul's sister had been allowed to ruin the whole afternoon ceremony with her crazy behaviour. He also heard some whispering about the lack of Earth Magic at the sunrise ritual and guessed that this would be the real source of Yul's humiliation, though doubtless he'd take it all out on

Leveret. Clip would have to step in and intervene if he didn't want to see the girl crushed.

Clip sighed deeply. Leveret had been right when she'd stood and made her prophecy – he didn't know whose voice she was echoing but it was one of truth. There were shadows at Stonewylde and the darkness was gathering. He'd sensed a collective chime of affirmation amongst the community as she spoke. They'd all felt it – their instincts told them something was wrong in the heart of Stonewylde and troubles were building like dark storm clouds towering higher and higher in inky blackness until eventually – soon – they must erupt into a torrent of destruction.

Poor Leveret – she was so young and fragile to be bearing this enormous responsibility. More than ever Clip was convinced that she'd been given a gift. She was the one who must channel the forces of creativity and light to counteract the shadows and destruction that were looming. He'd help her in every way he could but he shuddered to think what lay ahead. He couldn't be part of it; staying at Stonewylde was no longer an option for him. It was as if by announcing his intended departure Clip had made it an irrefutable fact. He had to leave Stonewylde. Now, more than ever, Yul would make sure he did – and as he thought that the serpent in his belly twisted, making him writhe again in agony.

Martin stood silently on the wide staircase, the entrance hall in near darkness below him and the upstairs landing only dimly lit. The shadowy staircase was a space between worlds and Martin was a part of the shadows, only his silvery Hallfolk hair glinting slightly as it caught the faint light. Most people who lived in the Hall were still drinking and dancing down in the Great Barn, trying to make the most of a bad day. What a shambles it had been, Martin thought bitterly. His mother, Old Violet, had been absolutely right although her outburst had been a little embarrassing. Things *had* been done properly in Magus' time – everything ran like clockwork, everyone knew their place and they were content with it. There was none of this grumbling and moaning that he encountered now in the Village, none of the rudeness and disrespect amongst the young. Magus would never have stood for it; a public whipping or two to make an example and everyone would've knuckled down again and been grateful for what they had. But times had changed and they'd changed for the worse, with only more problems to look forward to if things continued as they were.

He heard something from upstairs and silently climbed the rest of the steps up to the landing. The noise was coming from Yul and Sylvie's rooms – Magus' apartments as he still thought of them. They were arguing again. There'd been a lot of that in recent months and tonight's row sounded like a heated one. Martin knew what was going on; they made so much noise it was impossible not to. Yul was too weak. The magus shouldn't stand for that sort of behaviour in his wife. Martin smiled slightly at the very thought of Magus letting any woman argue back or try to run things her way. He would never, ever have permitted it! Martin wouldn't either – neither his first late wife nor his younger second wife, Swift's mother, would've *dared* to speak to him the way Sylvie spoke to Yul, as if she were his equal. The magus was the leader of Stonewylde – always had been, always should be, but not anymore. Things were falling apart and it was time to call a halt to it. Stonewylde deserved better than this.

Martin winced as he heard Sylvie's voice rising. How could Yul permit such lack of respect? He shook his head and moved away without a sound, unable to bear any further eavesdropping. They deserved each other, the pair of them. They deserved everything that was coming to them too. It'd be a while before the rowdy youngsters returned and Martin must make the most of this peace and quiet, this lull before the storm. He silently padded back downstairs towards his office. Others might be out there enjoying themselves or arguing with recalcitrant wives but Martin was dedicated and loyal. Stonewylde was his life. There was very important work to be done and it must happen tonight, if everything were to be set in motion. Martin rubbed the scar on his temple and smiled.

Sylvie glared at Yul. He stood with his back to the fire silhouetted against the flickering flames that licked the logs in the hearth. The large sitting room was shadowy, for they'd only switched on a small table lamp before their conversation had grown heated. The girls were in the crèche at the Nursery along with all the other young children, worn out from the long day. Sylvie wished that she were asleep too. She had a pounding headache as the stress of this disastrous Imbolc finally caught up with her.

They should by rights still be down in the Barn as the party was far from over, but neither of them could face any more. Yul was in such a black mood he knew he might do something he'd regret if he stayed. Sylvie was simply exhausted and the thought of any more time spent jigging around the heated and noisy Barn trying to pretend all was well was simply too much. They'd both left early and walked back home accompanied, to their dismay, by Magpie and Marigold. They'd had to keep up a pretence of normality, making conversation and concealing their irritation as Marigold chattered on endlessly about what a good boy Magpie was. But now finally they were alone.

'It *was* deliberate, Sylvie! She'd been eating mushrooms. When I took her home I saw them lying there on her bedside table – she didn't even have the wits to hide them!'

'Why would they be lying there if she'd taken them? It doesn't make sense.'

'She's obviously got a supply. We know she's been messing about with the things – she looked drugged up at Samhain and we had that incident at Quarrycleave too. Leveret's been experimenting with mushrooms for a while now.'

'I just don't believe she'd do that, not at Imbolc. Not when she had such a key role to play.'

'Well she damn well did! Anyway, why are you defending her when she's clearly in the wrong? What's she ever done to deserve your taking her side?'

Sylvie sighed wearily, wishing he'd go down to his office and leave her in peace. If he thought she was up to any love-making tonight he was mistaken, especially when he was seething with unspent anger like this.

'I feel very sorry for her. You're always on her back and I don't think it's warranted. I think there's something else going on here but you won't even consider the possibility. You've really got it in for poor Leveret.'

'That's not true and you damn well know it! I only got involved in the first place because Mother asked me to help sort out her bad behaviour, and I've tried to. Leveret was a lovely little girl but not anymore – she needs discipline. She's been running circles round poor Mother and all I've tried to do is provide that discipline. She's as out of control as some Outside World teenager and you know we don't allow that sort of behaviour at Stone-wylde.'

Sylvie sat silently, too tired to argue back. He looked down at her noticing how pale and strained she looked, wraith-like in this shadowy light in her white Imbolc dress. She may seem weak, he thought bitterly, yet she was always arguing with him, challenging everything he said or did, never accepting his judge-ment or good sense. She was making his life hell. He felt the anger, always bubbling inside him lately, well up again. All he'd ever done was love her, try to look after her and care for her. Why had life become a constant battle with her? What had happened to their peace and harmony?

'I'll speak to Mother in the morning and we'll decide what to do with her,' he continued. 'Leveret may have to move in here with us or perhaps into a dormitory with some of the older girls as I don't think I want her influencing our daughters. Or better still, I could send her to boarding school in the Outside World – that'd sort her out. She won't get away with what she did today, bloody little nuisance.'

'Have you heard yourself, Yul? What's the matter with you?' Sylvie felt her voice rising but was beyond caring. 'Leveret's a young girl – your own little sister – it's her birthday today, she was terrified of the ceremonies and she made a silly mistake. It's not the end of the world, no great crime, and yet the way you go on anyone would think she'd done something awful.'

'She has! She completely ruined everything today! One of our eight festivals of the year was spoiled for everyone because of *her* behaviour. That's something awful in my books. She'll be punished for today – she deserves it.'

'You're a bully!'

'I'm the magus! It's part of my role to mete out justice.'

'You sound like an arrogant pig-headed brute to me!'

'So now you're resorting to cheap insults? This is all your fault anyway!'

She glared at him, her head pounding with pain.

'I wondered when you'd bring this up!' she yelled. 'I knew from the minute I saw Leveret falling apart that I'd get the blame. You couldn't wait to say "I told you so", could you?'

'Not at all! I went along with your decision even though I didn't agree with it. I let you have your own way yet again. But now we both know how wrong you were. You made a serious error of judgement and clearly you should've consulted me about it first.'

'Why should I? You never consult *me* about anything! You never, *ever* ask my opinion. You're as arrogant as your father was.'

'No I'm not!'

'Yes you are, Yul! You're like him in almost every way. There are days when it could be him here and not you, dominating and pushing everyone around. Sometimes I wonder just how like him you're going to become. Will you bring back whipping for anyone who stands up to you? Will you start taking girls up to the Stone Circle on their sixteenth birthdays?'

He'd stepped forward at her tirade, towering over her as she sat on the sofa. She leapt up to stand face to face with him, refusing to give him any advantage. Now they glared at each other, anger in their eyes and their hearts. Yul took a deep breath to calm himself; rage was making his hands shake.

'Well, Sylvie,' he said bitterly, 'if I ever did resort to that we'd both know why. Being married to someone so cold and unresponsive who doesn't want you is enough to drive anyone to desperate measures.'

'What rubbish! The only reason I don't want you is—'

She stopped abruptly, aware too late of the crevasse that loomed suddenly at her feet. Yul smiled slightly and his voice became silky.

'Yes, Sylvie? You were about to tell me why you've become so frigid – why the thought of me leaves you cold when it used to set you on fire. I think we've reached the heart of the matter, haven't we?'

But she shook her head and sat down again, refusing to be drawn.

'I'm very tired, Yul, and it's been a long day. I'm exhausted – all I want to do is sleep.'

'I knew today would be too much for you and I was right,' he said firmly. 'You should've let Miranda lead the ceremonies as I suggested.'

'Oh for goodness' sake, shut up! I'm fine.'

'You just said you were exhausted! Getting confused again, are you, Sylvie? You need a day in bed tomorrow to get your strength back. I won't let you become ill again.'

'I'm NOT falling ill again! Stop using that as an excuse to keep me in my place! I've had just about enough of you, Yul – you're bullying Leveret and bullying me. You're turning into a hard, arrogant bastard! You're not the boy I fell in love with.'

'No, Sylvie, I'm not,' he said quietly, an edge to his voice. 'I'm the magus now and things are different.'

'Too right they're different!' she cried. 'You wonder why I don't want you anymore but look at what you've become. You don't even feel the Earth Magic now, do you? It's abandoned you, just as it did your father.'

This was finally too much for Yul. His eyes were hard and cold as he grasped her chin in his hand so she had to look him in the face. The shadows and firelight danced around him, hollowing his cheeks and making his grey eyes gleam.

'And you don't feel the moon magic any more either, do you Sylvie?' he said softly. 'You're not the girl I fell in love with and all your magic has gone. You're over-tired and not well and tomorrow you're to spend the day resting quietly in bed. If you argue I'll send Hazel to deal with you. I'm sick to death of this never-ending battle between us and things are going to change, because as from tonight I've had enough. It's time you remembered what your duties are here. I'll deal with my sister tomorrow, I'll do it as I see fit, and I don't expect any interference from you. Is that understood?'

She gazed into his eyes and felt her will to fight him drain away. It was too much effort right now and she just wanted to be rid of him. She nodded, hoping he'd disappear into his office and she'd be free of him until tomorrow.

'That's more like it.'

He stood up and went to pour himself a large glass of wine. Savouring it, he watched her narrowly as her eyelids drooped with fatigue, her face almost as white as her dress.

'Go and get ready for bed, Sylvie, and when I've had my wine I'll join you. From now on I'm sleeping in our bed in my rightful place.'

25

In the filthy cottage at the end of the lane the three women sat toasting themselves and smoking their pipes in peaceful contentment. The two old crones' faces were creased and lined, the dirt accentuating every wrinkle. Their toothless gums sucked at the stems of their pipes and they rocked gently in the warmth, slurping occasionally at their mead. Starling had eased out her rolls of flesh comfortably and propped her enormous legs on a stool; her feet were aching after such an active day. She was happily contemplating a further snack when she'd finished her pipe as she'd managed to cram a large bag full of left-overs from the feast. She belched loudly and patted the mass of her stomach in contentment.

'Eh, but that were a good day's work!' mused Old Violet.

'Aye, sister, a good day's work. That set the weasel amongst the rabbits and got things a-going nicely.'

'Made 'em look fools, didn't we? Heh heh! That black-locked one – he were so angry! Shouldn't wonder there'll be trouble up at the Hall tonight, the state he's in now.'

'Aye, he'll be spoiling for a fight. That skinny wife of his – she'll be in for it tonight, no doubt. Stupid Outsider – she ain't got no right to be here. She'll get her come-uppance that one.'

'And that hare-girl, his sister!' chuckled Starling. 'Didn't she ever look a fool? Sitting like a carving when she should've been dancing and chanting. She were just a mommet with no life in her. You did well, Auntie – your cakes and potion were just the thing.'

'Aye, just the thing. Old Violet knows how to mix a good potion and bake a good cake. Just like in Magus' time when he used to come calling for his tins o' cakes. Heh heh! Soon be like old times again only better this time around! We know, don't we?'

'Aye, sister, we know, we've seen. We know what's a-coming – what's come already, waiting in the shadows.'

The flames died lower to a red hot glow and still the three sat, reluctant to leave the heat of the fire and climb upstairs to their cold and foetid beds.

'But what o' the hare-girl? She were talking from beyond, weren't she?' whined Vetchling.

'Aye, sister, from beyond. She has the gift, that one, and we must watch her with a sharp eye.'

'Do you think she knows?' asked Starling. 'Does she know what she's saying?'

'Nay, shouldn't think so. That were prophesying and she weren't in this world, was she? Not with what we'd put inside her! That were another's voice speaking through her mouth.'

'Is she a danger to us?'

'I've not seen it. But we'll scry tomorrow and see what's what. Shouldn't be surprised if that old sow Heggy were trying to get through, but we can put a stop to that. She's only a young maid, the Hare, with no wisdom and no knowledge o' the old ways. We are three and we are strong and powerful. She ain't no match for us three.'

'Aye, you speak the truth, sister. We are on the wax and that dark-haired brat is on the wane. No sister can help him now – 'tis all set.'

'But nought is fixed,' mumbled Starling through a thick mouthful. 'You always told me that, Mother. All can be set but nought can be fixed.'

'Wise words, Starling, wise words. But we can try to fix, can't we? We can cast and we can summon, we can hex and we can blight. We have the wisdom, and the Hare does not – nor ever will.'

In the soft candlelight, Rowan gazed adoringly at her daughter. Faun was still flushed and her eyes bright from the dancing and heady wine. She lay now with her head on the snowy pillow, tattered ringlets spread about her. Rowan tenderly stroked her smooth skin.

'I've brought you some milk, my little one. Try to drink it – it's good for your complexion, especially after the wine.'

Faun sat up and dutifully drank from the cup her mother held to her lips.

'Was I beautiful tonight, Mother?'

'Oh yes, yes you were! You shone like a star,' said Rowan, helping the girl to lie down again and plumping the pillow for her.

'They should've chosen me. I was right all along.'

'Yes, they should've. Leveret was a disgrace.'

'Kestrel said it should've been me. He was all over me, Mother.'

'I know, I was watching you. You played it just right – you made him aware of you, showed him your promise, but you held yourself back too. You've got age on your side, my darling Faun. He knows you're too young now but there's nothing wrong with tempting him a bit with what's to come.'

Faun giggled.

'It was such fun! And I reminded him that I'm a Hallchild.'

'Good – he'd like that. He wants quality and you're the best at Stonewylde – Magus' beautiful, perfect daughter. 'Tis a pity more people don't remember you're a Hallchild and so special, like your father.'

Rowan sighed and a dreamy look came into her eyes.

'Was he really wonderful?' asked Faun wistfully.

Rowan shook her head, glossy brown hair rippling over her shoulders and shadowing her face.

'I can't describe him to you, Faun – he was more than wonderful. I *wish* you could've known him.'

'Why did he have to die? It's not fair – he'd have loved me, I know it.'

'He'd have adored you and you'd have been his special girl – his only daughter. You're right, it's not fair! And we know who's to blame.'

'Yul! I hate him so much, Mother. I'm his half-sister but he never takes any notice of me. I enjoyed it today when that ugly little sister of his made him look stupid. He looked such a fool when she started going on about the darkness coming and vipers and things. He couldn't get her out of the Barn fast enough, could he?'

'It were perfect! And Old Violet spoke the truth – things were run properly when Magus was here. We need to get back to how things were and after what's happened today, things'll start to change I'm sure. We'll be ready, you and I, ready for whatever comes and whatever the future brings. Now you must go to sleep, my beautiful girl. I want you to sleep in tomorrow and Granny will bring you breakfast in bed.'

Faun smiled and closed her eyes contentedly as her mother stroked her forehead soothingly, just how she liked it. What a successful day it had been.

Leveret woke gradually and opened her eyes in the darkness. She couldn't think where she was or what day it was. Imbolc? The ceremony up in the Stone Circle would be starting soon ... but then the memories started to flood in and she closed her eyes in despair. No, no, she'd done that. She'd sat with Sylvie in the carriage going back to the Village. She remembered the breathing walls and Sylvie asking her about the strange man in the Circle. She vaguely remembered the archery display and the rainbow-trailing arrows. After that there was little more other than vio-lently-coloured images and strange, illogical incidents. The whole day was a snaking nightmare of disjointed, jumbled up events.

There'd been a long table that stretched away into eternity and someone by her side, someone she felt good with but couldn't talk to because there was a glass cage around her. Three black birds had pecked up crumbs and a great white cloud of snowdrops had swirled around her in a snow-storm as she sat in the glass coffin, dead but not dead. So many things had confused her. But then her raven had flown in through the purple skies and bright blue clouds and had sat at her feet. It had spoken wisely of the darkness and the vipers, the shadows and the danger.

Then – she cringed at the thought of it – Yul had smashed the glass coffin and hauled her away, the darkness that hovered around him trying to stain his soul. She remembered a ring of snowdrops with the silver crescent moon rolling across the floor like a wheel and coming to lie at the feet of a man who stood among the crowd of gaping onlookers. She'd seen him clearly as she hung over Yul's shoulder. It was the same man she'd seen in the Stone Circle at dawn, and once again he'd made that little bow of greeting. He wore the same lazy smile and his eyes danced with mirth.

Leveret lay in her bed and tried to piece it all together. What on earth had happened? She vaguely remembered the jolting journey home down the lane, Yul's shoulder driving into her sore stomach and him kicking the door open as the stream of invective poured from his mouth like a spilled jar of dark honey. He'd almost thrown her on her bed, shouting at her and berating her, and then he'd started waving mushrooms about and had shouted even louder right in her face. She'd been terrified of his venom and had closed her eyes. But he'd yanked her upright on the bed and shaken her violently, more angry than she'd ever seen him before. She didn't remember anything after that; great black clouds had rolled in and obscured everything.

Alone in the darkness Leveret began to cry. She sobbed and sobbed until her throat hurt, her eyes stung and there were no more tears to shed. What had gone wrong? Gradually, for her mind was still not functioning normally and lucidity came only in short bursts, she worked out the sequence of events and realised what must've happened. It could only be the cakes ... it had to have been Sweyn last night when he went out to the privy – there was no other explanation. She knew nothing of the potion they'd forced down her throat under the elm tree. She only knew that Imbolc had been a complete disaster. She'd failed as the Bright Maiden and let her mother down, along with her sister, Kestrel, Celandine, Clip, Magpie, Mother Heggy's spirit, the folk of Stonewylde – everyone. They must all be so disappointed in her, so sad that she'd failed them once again, betrayed their love and their pride in her. And as for Yul – he'd really punish her now. Her life would be a misery if he could make it so.

Slowly the soft desperation and sadness within her began to harden into anger and bitterness. She'd had enough of being abused by her brothers and Jay. This was too much – the whole community had been affected by this terrible trick today. If her memory of Yul shaking her and shouting in her face was accurate, she was probably in more trouble now than she'd ever been before. The mushrooms he'd found in her room must've been planted there by her brothers but whatever she said, she wouldn't be believed – not with her apparent track record of subterfuge and deceit.

As ever Maizie would have to choose between believing her or believing her brothers, and she knew which way that would go. Her mother couldn't bear the possibility that she'd raised two sadistic bullies who'd tormented their little sister throughout her life. If she believed her sons capable of such a cruel deed today it would make a lie of the past fifteen years. Her lovely vision of a happy, loving family would be destroyed. It was much easier to dismiss her youngest child as a difficult trouble-maker going though an awkward adolescence.

Leveret came to understand all this with complete clarity and felt a sense of detached relief. It wasn't that Maizie didn't love her or favoured her brothers over her – it was more that she needed to love the whole family and believe in its unity to make sense of her own difficult life. Leveret would have to take the full brunt of blame for what had happened today and the inevitable punishment that must follow. She decided she wouldn't fight it.

She'd take the blame willingly for Maizie's sake, so her mother's view of her two youngest sons wouldn't be sullied forever. But she'd never let this happen again.

Leveret took a deep, shuddering breath, her tears now dried. No more tears. She needed to be strong, strong enough to fight Sweyn, Gefrin and Jay, strong enough to stand up to Yul and strong enough to withstand any threat from the three old biddies at the end of the lane. For who else could've baked the poisoned cakes? She must learn the old ways quickly – learn the folklore of the plants, herbs and fungi so she could counteract any further poisoning attempts. Learn the magic so she could protect herself and cast spells when she chose. She must learn to bind and to banish, to cast and to summon.

She had to do it quickly. The darkness was gathering ever closer. The image of the viper flashed through her mind again, coiled and hissing and preparing to strike. She must call those who'd help her and ask for their aid now – she must take control of her life and cease to be the victim. In that moment, in the darkness, the Bright Maiden of Imbolc left her childhood behind and became a young woman.

Leveret carefully climbed off her bed. Her legs were wobbly as she groped her way to the door and opened it, finding the whole cottage in darkness. She called for her mother but there was no reply, which was an indication of her mother's anger. She would never normally leave one of her children alone and unwell in the house in the pitch blackness. Leveret felt the tears prickle again but she squashed them down. She had no idea of the time but when she opened the front door, she heard the sounds of music coming from the centre of the Village. The party must still be going strong in the Barn and the ongoing merriment made her feel bitter. There was she, sobbing her heart out alone in the darkness, forgotten while the rest of the community were feasting, drinking and dancing.

Leveret located her dark woollen cloak on the back door peg, pulled on her brown leather boots and stepped outside. The night was cold and raw and stars shone through the broken cloud as she silently walked up the muddy lane towards the Village. She still wore the beautiful white dress and knew it must be getting ruined but she didn't care anymore – Imbolc was ruined anyway. The sounds grew louder as she approached the heart of the Village, and she saw light spilling from the Barn and the pub, where some of the older men would be taking refuge. Reaching the cobbled area outside the Barn, Leveret paused, imagining the heat and excitement inside. She pictured the community in there, some sitting at the tables around the edges or standing by the bar, others galloping round to the lively music, everyone talking, laughing and having a good time. Whilst here she was outside in the cold night with fury in her heart. She turned away, thankful that the night was so wintry for there'd be no couples strolling around the Green or dallying under the trees.

Leveret stepped onto the grass of the ancient clearing and walked across to the first in the great ring of trees that clustered around the open arena. Her head was completely clear now. She strode straight-backed around the circumference of the Green under the branches of the many trees. Her dark cloak billowed around her, the white dress clothing her in its symbolic purity. She called the name of each tree as she passed beneath its boughs – lime, ash, hornbeam, oak, chestnut, beech – summoning the tree spirits that were sleeping now but would soon awaken. Leveret called the trees from their slumber and bid them add their strength and energy to hers. When she'd completed the circuit she proceeded into the centre of the Village Green and stood there, her breath clouding around her in the cold night.

Leveret tipped her head back to the skies and saw the setting moon behind the dark branches. It was still a waxing crescent, grown from the new moon of earlier in the week, and shone huge and golden as it dipped in the sky in a great bow. Leveret raised her arms to the heavens, the cloak falling back to reveal her Bright Maiden costume. Her silver crescent birth charm hung round her neck. With outstretched hands she gathered in the energy of the crescent, calling upon the elemental forces to come to her and fill her with their magic. Leveret summoned the spirit of the Huntress, the goddess in her aspect of the Maiden. She chanted her many known names: Isis, Artemis, Selene, Diana, Bride, Brighid, Freya – the names given over thousands of years by such different people and cultures, but all addressing the same energy source. She called on the powerful spirit of the emergent female huntress, reborn every year at Imbolc and every month with the new moon.

'I summon you, Huntress! Fill me with your energy and magic! Come to my body and make me as strong and powerful as you. Give me the strength of your bow and the sharpness of your arrows so I may fight my enemies. Take my softness and weakness and tears and fill me with your force, purpose and steel. If I falter in my intent, stiffen my resolve. Make me hard and pitiless towards those who try to hurt me. I summon you, Maiden, and I ask for your powerful magic!'

The darkness thickened around her as she dropped her arms and turned away. No casting a circle or the protection of salt tonight – Leveret had made contact with the power source directly like lightning finding its earth. Walking back in her bedraggled white dress with the dark cloak flying around her, she tingled with a spiky new energy. Tomorrow, when they all trooped up to the Lammas Field to burn the dolly harbouring the Corn Spirit and return it to the earth amongst the ashes, Leveret would go to the springhead instead, sacred to the Maiden, and make her own personal offering. She made her way back across the Green towards the cottage, her sharp teeth glinting in a small smile, the light of battle in her green eyes.

She was watched by a figure standing in the shadows, a figure which melted into the darkness as she passed by, not wishing to be seen by her again this night.

Alone in his office, Harold stared at the screen intently, his quick brain analysing the projected figures. He'd visited the Barn briefly earlier on as a token gesture of community participation, but had quickly sensed the hostility amongst many of the people present.

His quotas were becoming an increasing bone of contention and after a drink at the bar Harold had left to come back to the Hall. It didn't matter as he wasn't one for socialising, far preferring the solitude of his office. This was where it all happened; this was the little kernel that kept Stonewylde going.

He was expecting an important e-mail tonight, something so big that the mere thought of it sent a shiver shimmying down his backbone. He'd have to let Yul in on this soon, he knew, but had yet to find a way of broaching the news about his contact and the potentially profitable connections. Harold knew it could make all the difference to Stonewylde's economic future and was desperate to get the go-ahead from Yul. But Harold also knew Yul's history, and in his heart he doubted that his dark-haired boss would ever accept this exciting proposal from Outside. And he might even be livid with Harold for all the undercover ground work he'd been engaged in for so long, trying to set this up.

Harold glanced at the connecting door to Yul's office. He knew Yul and Sylvie had already returned, having heard them as they crossed the entrance hall. By the sound of their angry voices he guessed Yul would be back downstairs soon, sleeping alone on his sofa bed yet again. What had started last year as an occasional habit, necessitated by long and late hours, had increasingly become the norm. Harold had seen the empty bottles being removed from the office in the mornings and knew the marital situation wasn't good.

But at least Yul's increased alcohol consumption had meant less interference. As late night working had turned into late night drinking, Yul was allowing Harold more responsibility, giving him a free hand to set up new ideas and schemes. At least Yul understood that Stonewylde needed to move out of the dark ages and join the modern world, become a profit-making organisation and not just a turnip-producing country estate – which is how old die-hards like Clip and Martin would keep it, given the chance.

Harold smiled faintly as he tapped a key and a whole temple of columns appeared on the screen. He loved figures, loved profit analysis, loved the thrill of watching money grow. There was so much untapped potential at Stonewylde. Food and clothing were selling faster than they could be produced. The whole agricultural set-up of Stonewylde needed to be restructured this year; certain goods were so hot they sold out before even reaching the warehouse. And there was so much else to be developed. The stone at Quarrycleave was of beautiful quality. The water from the springhead was equal to any English spring water on the supermarket shelves, and Harold was looking into setting up a bottling plant above the Village to exploit this natural resource. And the Wildwood! The thought of it made Harold's heart thump a little faster in his chest. This was virgin forest, utterly untouched, and covering vast acres. The wood in there must be worth a fortune, either in its lumber state or, better still, transformed by craftsmen into the highest quality furniture and goods.

Harold was still amazed at how much money was to be made in the luxury market, both at home and especially abroad. The Wildwood was a project he was intending to start soon, convinced he was on to a huge money-spinner. Free resources, free labour – almost pure profit. Yul could be persuaded he was sure, and now there was this other opportunity for partnership as well ...

Harold pushed his chair back and stretched. Time for bed. It was late and the youngsters would soon be arriving home, noisy and drunk. He glanced around his office, smiling to himself a little. Several monitors lit the darkened room and the network hummed busily. Harold felt like the queen bee in a hive, sitting at the heart of the community and creating the wealth that fed everyone. All the students had computers linked to the network and at this very moment, thought Harold with uncharacteristic whimsy, they'd all be displaying the Stonewylde.com logo he'd designed – that curly, snake-like S. He felt a thrill of power.

Stonewylde was so huge, had such immense potential for development and so many resources that could be exploited. With Yul on board he could create vast wealth from the natural materials just lying around, like the stone, water and wood. And with the

Villagers knuckling down and producing goods to order, he could make vast profits from the fruits of the earth – food, drink, leather, linen, wool. He let his imagination run free for a moment and saw himself at the head of a vast business enterprise utilising hundreds of people, all creating wealth from the natural resources of Stonewylde. And it wasn't just a dream – it was fast becoming reality. All down to him, a simple Villager who'd risen from his humble origins and grasped every opportunity offered him, including this latest one.

Anxious to see if the e-mail had come through, Harold decided to save his work and close the files he'd been working on. He clicked on save and blinked when nothing happened, no obedient little bars racing to complete the task. The network was bang up to date, all the very latest technology, and always responded instantly. He clicked save again, and the screen turned red. Harold went cold, alarm coursing through his veins and making his fingertips tingle.

'What the hell?'

Harold pushed his glasses up his nose and once more tried to save his files. His mouth tightened in horror as the figures slowly began to disintegrate before his eyes, melting into the red. The screen scrolled down slowly of its own accord, showing him pages and pages of reports and figures melting away. Files began to open of their own accord and their contents dissolved. Harold sat in the shadowy room staring in disbelief at the dark red screen. A virus! It had to be – despite all the protection in place. He glanced frantically at the other monitors in the room and saw that they too were red. The whole network must be affected – all those computers upstairs, in the school-rooms, in Yul's office and Martin's too – everything must be blighted.

Harold shook his head slowly, devastated at losing all his data, all his work. Totally destroyed – hours, days, weeks of work, all those figures and contacts, projections and accounts, so much invaluable data that could never be replaced. Much was backed up but not all. There was a chance it might be retrievable, of course, but he'd heard about the latest viruses – they infected and destroyed everything, even backed-up files.

And then the message began as Harold gaped in absolute horror at the screen, his vision for Stonewylde's future in ruins. Slowly growing out of the dark red, one huge black word appeared. It flashed on and off, on and off, almost mesmeric in its intensity, followed by another word and a message:

MAGUS
MALUS
MAGUS
MALUS

I am here

amongst

you

Acknowledgements

My thanks go to:

My son George (for persuading me that Stonewylde couldn't end at the third book), my other sons Oliver and William and my foster daughter Kirsty – I'm the luckiest mother to have you four behind me.

My fabulous literary agent Piers Russell-Cobb of MediaFund.

Gillian Redfearn, my talented editor at Gollancz.

Jen, Nina, Charlie and all the team at Gollancz and Orion.

My sister Kim for your fantastic help with publicity.

My sister Claire of Helixtree and Rob Walster of Big Blu Design for the beautiful Stonewylde logo.

All my lovely family, close and extended, for your support and enthusiasm.

My friends and ex-colleagues in Dorset – for your encouragement right from the very beginning.

The Stonewylde readers, and especially those in my online community – I can't thank you all enough. You've bought my books, spread the word, travelled to meet me, rooted for me, praised and encouraged me. You've made Stonewylde successful and I really hope you all enjoy this fourth book – you've waited long enough!

Mr B, my wonderful husband. I saw the crescent but you saw the whole of the moon; I'd have faltered long ago without your faith in me. Thank you xxx